Praise for
of Ron Sarti's epic fantasy adventure

THE CHRONICLES OF SCAR

"Thought provoking . . . An absolute pleasure to read . . . Should move to the top of everybody's to-be-read pile."
Michael A. Stackpole, *New York Times* bestselling author of *Star Wars® X-Wing: Rogue Squadron*

"Shines with intrigue, humor, and well-crafted, believable characters."
Lynn Flewelling, author of *Stalking Darkness*

"Ron Sarti single-handedly revitalizes the post-apocalypse subgenre."
Robert J. Sawyer, Nebula Award-winning author of *The Terminal Experiment* and *Frameshift*

"[Sarti] gives us real people, throws them into hard circumstances, then threads them through a story that compels our attention."
William Barton, co-author of *White Light*

"Ron Sarti handles his story with the skill of a writer who's been at it for years."
J.R. Dunn, author of *Full Tide of Night*

ARMCHAIR "FAMILY" BOOKSTORE
USED PAPERBACKS • COMICS • MAGS.
WEEKDAYS 10-7 SAT 10-6 SUN CLOSED
3205 S.E. MILWAUKIE AVE PORTLAND
OREGON 97202 (503) 238-6680

Other Avon Books by
Ron Sarti

THE CHRONICLES OF SCAR

LEGACY OF THE ANCIENTS: BOOK TWO
OF THE CHRONICLES OF SCAR

Avon Books are available at special quantity discounts for bulk
purchases for sales promotions, premiums, fund raising or educa-
tional use. Special books, or book excerpts, can also be created to
fit specific needs.

For details write or telephone the office of the Director of Special
Markets, Avon Books, Inc., Dept. FP, 1350 Avenue of the Americas, New York, New York 10019, 1-800-238-0658.

THE LANTERNS OF GOD

Book Three of
The Chronicles of Scar

R O N   S A R T I

AVON · EOS

This is a work of fiction. Names, characters, places, and incidents either are the product of the author's imagination or are used fictitiously. Any resemblance to actual events, locales, organizations, or persons, living or dead, is entirely coincidental and beyond the intent of either the author or the publisher.

AVON BOOKS, INC.
1350 Avenue of the Americas
New York, New York 10019

Copyright © 1998 by Ron Sarti
Published by arrangement with the author
Visit our website at **http://www.AvonBooks.com/Eos**
Library of Congress Catalog Card Number: 98-92624
ISBN: 0-380-73026-X

All rights reserved, which includes the right to reproduce this book or portions thereof in any form whatsoever except as provided by the U.S. Copyright Law. For information address Avon Books, Inc.

First Avon Eos Printing: September 1998

AVON EOS TRADEMARK REG. U.S. PAT. OFF. AND IN OTHER COUNTRIES, MARCA REGISTRADA, HECHO EN U.S.A.

Printed in the U.S.A.

WCD   10 9 8 7 6 5 4 3 2 1

If you purchased this book without a cover, you should be aware that this book is stolen property. It was reported as "unsold and destroyed" to the publisher, and neither the author nor the publisher has received any payment for this "stripped book."

For Odile

Contents

Foreword
1

PART ONE
ACROSS THE PLAINS

Chapter 1
The Letter
9

Chapter 2
Robert
19

Chapter 3
Dangers and Decisions
31

Chapter 4
Many Partings
50

Chapter 5
On Our Way
62

Chapter 6
Struggle at the Ruins
78

Chapter 7
The Vigilant
94

Chapter 8
The Plains
112

Chapter 9
Beasts of the Prairie
125

Chapter 10
The Outpost
135

PART TWO
ACROSS THE MOUNTAINS

Chapter 1
Into the Mountains
159

Chapter 2
The Colorado Clan
171

Chapter 3
The Tunnel
191

Chapter 4
The Witch Woman
204

CONTENTS

Chapter 5
Loyalties
221

Chapter 6
Arrival
237

Chapter 7
Debate and Decision
254

Chapter 8
Means and Ends
265

Chapter 9
Home Again
285

Epilog
301

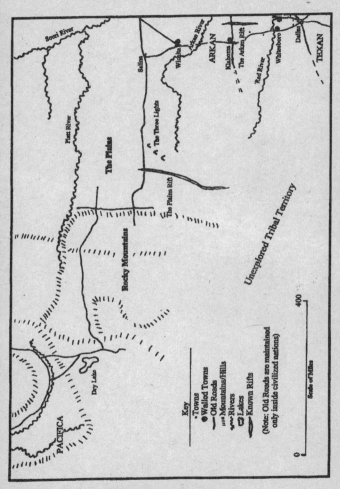

CROSSING THE CONTINENT. 2654 A.D.

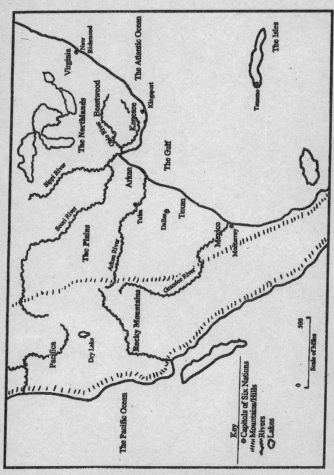

The Isles

Tomamo

The Atlantic Ocean

New Richmond

Virginia

Beanwood

The Northlands

Kingsport

Kanesee

Ohyo River

Sippi River

The Gulf

Arkan

The Plains

Tulsa

Dallas

Texan

Bonni River

Mexico

Monterrey

Adza River

Grande River

Rocky Mountains

Pacifica

Dry Lake

Scale of Miles

0   500

Key

⊙ Capitols of Six Nations
⌠⌠⌠⌠ Mountains/Hills
〜〜 Rivers
⌒ Lakes

The Pacific Ocean

AMERICAN CONTINENT, 2654 A.D.

Foreword

Early in the twenty-first century, the world was torn by a geologic cataclysm that ended the golden age of civilization and changed the maps of the globe. In North America, gone was the advanced culture that had brought back the dinosaur and the mammoth for its zoos and parks. Gone was the organized society that had maintained a space station orbiting above and a colony on the moon. Gone were the power plants and electricity. Gone were the fabulous communication systems.

The survivors—technical specialists in a world that now needed basic skills—faced lives of hardship and danger, and their offspring struggled on amidst the ruins. With each generation, a very few were born with powers of the mind—psychic powers—and were prized by their rulers. More often seen were those born with hair on much of their bodies, which earned them the feared name of beastmen. Most of the beastchildren were killed at birth, but many were spirited away by parents and left in the Beastwood, to be raised by others of their own kind.

For four centuries, human society consisted of wild clans and nomadic tribes amid the western mountains and central plains and northern forests of America, while in the varied east hundreds of tiny communities struggled to survive under a succession of petty, despotic, and violent rulers, who warred on each other with appalling frequency. During those years of darkness, the tools and weapons of the golden age—or the Old World, as it came to be called—were gradually used up or worn out, and armaments became unstable and dangerous to handle. Eventually, the sword and the horse-drawn plow became the common tools of war and peace. Most worrisome during those four centuries, the human population gradually declined on the continent, people becoming dangerously few and scattered.

One fortunate area along the new western coast survived the dark centuries better than most and formed a new nation, Pacifica. The Pacificans were concerned mankind might slide even further into darkness, or actually become extinct on the continent outside Pacifican borders. While offering help to all, Pacifica noted that there was still a density of population in the southeast to offer some hope of developing a civilization. Pacifica sent out its ambassadors—and its agents—to every tiny community in the southeast, and through patient effort united and built those communities into six nations: Kenesee, Arkan, Texan, Mexico, Virginia, and the Isles. A special advisor called a "representative" assigned to each leader of the six nations bestowed lost knowledge to help the new countries—medical techniques, pharmaceuticals, agricultural procedures, and high-yield grains. The six nations endured, while the famine, mindless tyranny, and endless conflict abated.

Pacifica also gave the Codes of Progress to the six nations. The Codes were a series of rules and guidelines to regulate technological progress in machinery and weaponry in order to prevent horrors such as gunpowder weapons. The Codes were taken to heart, and functioned successfully for two hundred years while the population of the continent slowly rose.

In *The Chronicles of Scar*, the first book in the Scar series, six hundred years have passed since the Cataclysm. Arn Brant narrates his early years. He tells of his childhood in the streets as a homeless gutter rat, and revealed is the emotional price he has paid for survival: all his feelings are walled-up or buried, leaving Arn numb. He relates being discovered as the son of King Reuel Brant, and his education as a prince of the kingdom of Kenesee alongside his older brother, Prince Robert. As prince, Arn meets the formidable High Wizard Graven, and becomes friends with Megan Sims, daughter of Sir Meredith Sims of Lexington.

Barely into his manhood, Arn's story covers the events leading up to and including the great war of that era. Duty takes him far from the warm smile of his Angela, the only person who is able to dispel his sober demeanor and lighten his heart. Just before the beginning of the conflict, he chronicles his mission into the Beastwood, where reside those men covered with hair. In the Beastwood he takes a wound, and thereafter is given the name Prince Scar.

It is on this mission to the Beastwood that Arn becomes acquainted with Wizard Murdock and meets the beastman Major Kren, both of whom become his companions in future adventures. Other people of influence during these early days are Sergeant John Black; the Pacifican Paul Kendall, who is advisor to King Reuel; and Paul's father, Jason the Healer, who years before had retired from the position of king's advisor. The feisty Sergeant Jenkins and the hunchbacked Apprentice Wizard Lorich also play significant roles in Arn's adventures.

A handful of scheming leaders defy the Codes by creating an Alliance that would unite the six nations and serve the leaders' hunger for power. Only one nation, Kenesee, stands in the way of their plans. Thus begins the War Against the Alliance, in which Kenesee fights not only for its own survival, but also for the survival of the Codes. As a young man during the War Against the Alliance, Arn is unwillingly thrust into command of the forces of Kenesee. By a desperate and costly ploy in which he must use Angela and Megan and the women of Lexington as bait, he manages to destroy the Army of the Alliance and gain Kenesee the victory.

Angela, Megan, and many townswomen have been brutally used, but they survive. Angela forgives him, though Megan is another matter. Casualties have been heavy, and Arn has lost many friends. Amidst the mass graves of a battlefield, he finally breaks through the walls of numbness to grief and feels the emotions that have so long been denied him.

The second volume of Prince Scar's narration, *Legacy of the Ancients: Book Two of the Chronicles of Scar*, begins only a few months after the conclusion of *The Chronicles of Scar*. A visit to the Royal Museum of Kenesee is interrupted by the arrival in Kingsport of a Texan delegation beseeching Arn's brother, King Robert, for help in overthrowing General Jack Murphy, the President of Texan. General Murphy lives in Castle Corral in Dallas, and has been one of the ruthless leaders of the Alliance. Now he is violating the very heart of the Codes, building gunpowder muskets for his army.

While King Robert warily guards Kenesee against Governor Rodes of Virginia, who is forming a new army, Prince Scar is to go with a few companions to Texan to foment the rebellion. Arn provides a guarantee of Kenesee assistance in the struggle. His friend Angela wants to go too, but Arn fears for her safety, and pretends he no longer loves her in order to prevent her following. The Lady Megan, still unable to forgive Arn, shows him what she thinks of his treatment of Angela.

To cover their departure, Arn's party pretends they are going on a dinosaur hunt. In a battle with dinosaurs it is discovered that Apprentice Wizard Lorich has a great and unique power.

Using a clever disguise to travel, Arn's party makes its way to Arkan, only to find Angela, Megan, and their friend Beth awaiting the party's arrival. The High Wizard of Kenesee has foretold that the women are necessary to the success of the mission, dangerous as it may be for them. Bowing to the inevitable, Arn allows the three women to come along. On the journey, young Wizard Lorich meets an Arkan woman and discovers that it is not easy to find love.

Arn and his companions reach Dallas and set the rebellion in motion. Arn also meets his dying mother,

Nancy Brown, after which he and Angela are captured by General Murphy's men and taken to the infamous Castle Corral.

Forced to leave Angela a prisoner, Arn escapes and is given command of the Army of Rebellion and the Kenesee regiments sent by King Robert. Robert has been very bold, for Arn learns that Virginia is marching against Kenesee. Robert destroys the Virginian Army and captures Governor Rodes in his capital.

Matching his brother's accomplishments, Arn defeats General Murphy's loyalist Texan army in spite of facing an elite guardos regiment equipped with the forbidden powder weapons. Anxious to free Angela, Arn hurries back to Dallas, which is still under the control of Murphy's trusted henchman, the formidable Matthew Bartholomew. Arn retakes Dallas and Castle Corral, but Bartholomew's malice and distrust deny Arn his goal, and Prince Scar learns the tragic personal cost of all great adventures.

The Lanterns of God: Book Three of the Chronicles of Scar begins a few weeks after the events concluded in *Legacy of the Ancients*.

PART • ONE

ACROSS THE PLAINS

1

The Letter

The day wasn't really hot. Not like it can get when the Texan sun shines down upon the flat countryside around Dallas in August. It was just uncomfortably warm and muggy, so that sweat appeared even when one was at rest. A perfect day to take off from work, get outside the town walls, and enjoy time with friends and companions. And so we had.

Beneath a spacious awning I sat on one of the simple wooden chairs arranged around a table and sipped from a mug of cool water, watching the activity around the corrals with lazy interest. I was alone in the shade, royal guards carefully watching over me from a distance to allow both privacy and protection to their honored and revered Prince Scar. With them about I could relax and watch my companions have a good time. I could not partake in their gaiety. Not yet. But I could feel satisfaction that they were enjoying themselves, and take comfort in the change of scene from the castle, with all its bitter memories. I would let nothing bother me today. Or so I thought.

Sergeant Jenkins stood in the black uniform and service cap of the Kenesee Royal Guards, erect and confident in the center of the training ring, watching the horse and rider trotting around him. Bouncing awkwardly upon the saddle of the small mare, an eight-year-old girl stared forward with intense concentration, grasping the reins too tightly. She and the horse were both sweating.

Jenkins noted their condition. "All right, Sabrena,

let's break for a few minutes. Go to a walk. Good. Give her a loose rein, and relax. You're doing fine, girl.'' His field voice was loud enough that I could hear him without difficulty. Anyone could have. He gestured to a stable hand who entered the corral with water bucket and canteen.

"Sabrena, bring your horse over here for a drink, but watch how much she takes. You take that canteen and have a drink too.'' Jenkins waited until she had dismounted and both child and horse were enjoying the water before he ambled over to the fence where a half dozen men and women watched.

"Not bad for only her second lesson,'' said Jenkins. "I think she'll be a good rider.''

His voice had returned to normal volume, but I could still hear him though he was thirty yards away. Acute hearing, to say the least. Actually, it was my lone wizardly ''talent'' as Murdock had identified it for me. Maybe someday it would actually prove useful.

The beastman Major Kren leaned on the top rail of the fence and nodded appreciatively beneath his large, round hat—a sombrero, as the Texans called it. He was at ease, his sturdy chest covered only by an open, sleeveless leather vest that revealed the hair of his pelt, damp with a light sweat. The rest of the party lounging along the rail wore wide-brimmed hats or the large sombreros that Texans used to keep off the summer sun.

"You see, Murdock,'' the beastman told the dark-skinned man beside him, ''it's as I told you. Riding is innate. True ability can't be acquired, only enhanced. Some—like me—are excellent riders. Others are like you.''

Wizard Murdock fluttered his loose white cotton shirt to cool himself and looked sideways at the beastman. ''Is that so? The Great Murdock hasn't had any trouble keeping up with you on the road, now has he? Anyway, I'm older. You get to my age and see how a day in the saddle feels.''

"Excuses. Nothing but excuses," Kren scoffed good-naturedly.

Murdock folded his hands on the fence rail. "And nowhere was that ability of our hairy friend more obvious than in the Great Swamp. Truly, only a natural rider could have controlled the dinosaur with such grace and style."

"That was different," Kren objected. "I didn't have any reins."

"Bah," Murdock retorted. "A natural rider doesn't need reins. Brains, but not reins."

The two continued their banter while the others listened with open smiles. Beside Murdock stood the two Pacificans. The first was the gray-headed, bespectacled Jason Kendall, or Jason the Healer, as he was more commonly known. Next to him was his son, Paul Kendall (or Mr. Kendall, as Megan still liked to call her betrothed), advisor to King Robert. Paul Kendall's left sleeve was pinned up to the elbow so it would not hang empty. He had lost his arm in service to the Codes and Kenesee the previous year during the War Against the Alliance. Just beyond Paul Kendall was the young, hunchbacked apprentice to Murdock, Wizard Lorich.

Further down the fence stood the Lady Megan Sims and her friend Beth in long, loose cotton dresses, the women chatting happily while watching Sabrena with motherly approval. The third woman, who should have been standing with Megan and Beth, was gone forever.

My only consolation was that Angela was in a better place, and need never fear again.

The ring was one of several corrals outside the west gates of Dallas and next to a row of large stables that had once held horses for the elite Presidential *Guardos* of General Jack Murphy. The guardos were disbanded now, but the stables came in handy for the horses of the Kenesee Tenth Cavalry Regiment, which still awaited orders from King Robert to return home. Some members of the Tenth loitered and watched us from various points around the ring or from the doors of the stables.

I eavesdropped shamelessly on the conversations occurring amongst my friends and companions. Beyond Kren and Murdock's chatter, I could hear Mr. Kendall speaking with Lorich. Kendall leaned toward the young wizard so that their heads were close together. "You know, Lorich, I've heard about that incident with the dinosaur. Megan told me."

Lorich gave a quick glance at the beautiful Megan. "She did?"

"Yes. She heard the story, but figured out what really happened. She concluded that you killed the dinosaur. By magic."

For once, Lorich considered his answer. "Oh."

Was the lad finally learning discretion?

"Your secret is safe with me. And I've warned her to tell no one else. That's a very great power you have, Wizard Lorich. But very dangerous."

"Yes, Mr. Kendall."

I'll admit it. I felt uneasy after hearing the exchange. Kendall had been a loyal and true friend, one of those few people with whom I could feel truly comfortable. Yet Kendall had other loyalties besides Kenesee. The Codes of Progress, and his homeland of Pacifica, meant at least as much to him. He had devoted his life to enforcing the Codes, and had killed in their defense. If Kenesee were seriously to violate the Codes, where would Kendall stand? And what would he do? Would Kendall consider the good-hearted and malleable young wizard a tool that might be used to his purpose?

He'd be a fool not to.

I moved my leg, stretching the muscles. The wound I'd taken in the attack upon Castle Corral had healed and my limp was almost gone, except after periods of inactivity when the muscle stiffened. I wasn't going to complain, because the wound just missed severing a tendon. Instead, an opened vein almost bled me to death.

Other wounds were not so easily healed. The woman I loved was gone, taken from me and from this life even as I watched, helpless. So many that I knew had been lost, so many close to me torn away by death. Perhaps the emotional numbness I had so long known—perhaps that void, that lack of feeling—was the easier condition, after all. To feel the joy and pain of life is well and good. But why was it my lot that joy came by the tiny cup, and pain by the bucket?

Too often, my head was troubled and my heart tormented. The days were not pleasant, and the nights worse. But at least beer and wine were not forbidden, and helped me to sleep.

As if aware of my mood, Murdock and Kren headed toward me.

"How is it today?" Murdock asked.

"My leg?"

He frowned impatiently. "No, not your leg. Stop playing games."

I forced a smile. "One of my better days."

He seemed pleased. "Really? Good. It's still hard, but you'll have more good days. And the bad days won't be as bad. You know that."

"I know. It will get better." Or so I told myself.

"We've kept busy," Murdock continued, "and that has helped, hasn't it? But it's good to have time off too. We all needed it. So just enjoy the day, and the fact that so many of us are still here together."

"Yes, Murdock. Thank you."

"Such demure agreement. Not a single disparaging comment have I heard from you today."

"Later. I'll insult you later."

Kren poured two mugs of water. "Why wait? Now is *always* a good time to insult Wizard Murdock."

Sergeant Jenkins helped Sabrena back onto her mount, the horse shying away just as her bottom made contact with the saddle. The girl recovered, but admitted, "The horse scared me."

"Maturity is learning to hide your fear," Jenkins replied, resuming his position in the center of the ring

"Let's get to work, Sabrena. Put your horse back together."

The girl looked at the animal front and back, puzzled. "But Mr. Jenkins, sir, I can't put her back together. She ain't come apart yet."

My companions developed a fit of coughing.

Jenkins tried to keep a straight face. "It means to balance your horse. And yourself. I told you about balancing a horse."

"Oh, that. Yes, sir. I can do that." And she did.

At that moment a rider trotted up, reined to a halt, and saluted. He wore the uniform of an official Kenesee courier, and carried a mail pouch on his saddle. "The guards at the castle told me I could find you here, Prince Arn. Official messages from the king."

Murdock's eyes met mine. He could guess what was in the pouch, or at least, what one of the topics of discussion might be. And so could I. My brother Robert had directed via an earlier letter that the guardos' gunpowder muskets taken after the Battle of Tyler should be sent back to Kenesee. Instead, I'd had them destroyed—a willful act of disobedience to the King of Kenesee. Robert would not be pleased. I'd found myself delaying a response to Robert's letter, and not till a fortnight after the act—with Murdock's nagging to spur me on—had I finally sent off a letter. It informed Robert of the progress we'd made in Texan, and casually made comment to the effect that I'd disregarded his instruction and had the muskets destroyed.

And now, his response had arrived.

The courier gave Murdock the pouch. Inside was a flat leather envelope embossed with the royal seal of Kenesee and wrapped with a security ribbon. The wizard looked at me again for approval before unsealing the ribbon on the leather envelope and taking out two letters, each glued shut at the flap. One letter was secured with a wax seal denoting official diplomatic messages; the other was secured with another ribbon. Not an official document, but a private letter.

Murdock scanned the addresses. "One is addressed to Prince Arn." He handed me the private letter, and I noted the envelope was in Robert's own hand. The wizard held up the other. "This is addressed to Mr. Scott Chalmers, President of Texan." That envelope was in the hand of a scribe. Robert had sent it through the Kenesee mail service to ensure I knew the Texan president had received official correspondence from him.

Pretending to ignore me, Murdock and Kren watched Sabrena's riding lesson. Though their curiosity must have been rife, they allowed me to read in peace. I unsealed the letter with Robert's message. Like the address on the outer flap, it was in his script.

The King's Castle
Kingsport, Kenesee
August 7, 2654

Dear Arn,

Many matters deserve comment, several of great import.
First, I am relieved to hear that you are recovering from your wound. I know well the pain and distraction such wounds can cause, and am confident that you will enjoy a complete recovery. Guard your health. One of us must be whole for the great task before us.
Though you mention her only most briefly, I know the loss of Angela Kauffman must weigh heavily upon you. She was an extraordinary young woman, and well matched for your needs. Father knew you loved her even before you knew it yourself. I pray for her, and I pray for you. Do not despair. Eventually you will remember her with more fondness than grief, and her memory will warm your heart in the days ahead; for it is true that time heals all wounds.

I stopped reading for a moment. Yes, time healed wounds. Most of them.

The loss of Colonel Daniels is deeply regretted. I have seen firsthand that General Black's opinion of him was well deserved, and that he had a greater role to play in the future. Daniels is one more whose counsel and ability will be missed.

It is good that Scott Chalmers has recovered and is able to assume the duties of Texan president. Your assessment of his potential was very helpful. Do his detractors still call him "Clerk Chalmers"? It would not be the first time an unlikely hero has reluctantly accepted the mantle of leadership. We shall measure him by what he does.

Which brings us to the letter I have sent to President Chalmers. It is an invitation. I have invited Texan to join our Confederation of Nations. Chalmers is not the only one to receive such a note. All the other countries in the six nations have been invited to join the Confederation. And the Beastwood as well. The new Governor of Virginia has already agreed to join (he saw the light very quickly), and I would hope Texan could agree as readily.

You will note that joining the Confederation is voluntary. I think the others will see the benefit of a truly benign unity. If not, some astute diplomacy may help them understand. For this purpose, I will tour the nations, and visit with each leader to convince them of my sincerity and the benefits of membership. My first destination will be Texan, for I need to see you about matters that cannot wait. There is a task I must ask of you. I will arrive at Tyler on August 25th, if all goes well. Time is of the essence.

As for the muskets, I think it better we discuss
that matter face-to-face.
Keep yourself well.

Your brother,
Robert

Face-to-face. So, the reckoning with Robert would
have to wait until he arrived. I wondered how unpleasant
an encounter that would be, though it couldn't be helped.
I had opposed his will, and would have to endure his
displeasure.

I folded the sheets of paper, and my two companions
immediately paid me attention. The rest of the party was
still at the fence rail, though it appeared as if Sabrena's
lesson might be ending.

The wizard took a gulp from his mug. "Well, what
did Robert have to say?"

I stated the information about his plans to visit all the
nations, starting with his coming visit to Texan, and
noted that August 25th was only four days away. I
added, trying to sound casual, that Robert had sent in-
vitations to the six nations and the Beastwood, asking
them to join the Confederation of Nations.

Both Murdock and Kren sat up.

Robert and I had talked about such a possibility
months ago. But it had been mere speculation, wistful
plans built upon vague possibilities, the dreams of a new
king with enemies still facing him. Now, with the defeat
of Governor Rodes of Virginia and Jack Murphy of
Texan, the dream suddenly became a practical course of
action. And Robert, never one to tarry when he saw the
rightness of a thing, had gone forward without counsel.
Or at least, without *my* counsel.

"So he's actually going to do it," said Murdock. "A
bold move."

"Yes, it is." Bolder than Murdock could know. The
Pacificans wouldn't like the idea of confederation. They

might take action against Robert. Deadly action.

"We'll have to discuss this later," Murdock continued, watching the others at the fence look our way. "Did he say anything about the muskets?"

I shrugged. "The muskets he'll discuss when he gets here."

"Hmmm," was the wizard's only comment.

"And there's something urgent he has to talk to me about. A task."

"Aha."

"You know what he might be talking about?" I asked.

It was Murdock's turn to shrug. "I have an idea or two, but best we wait to see what Robert says. He'll be here soon enough."

2

Robert

We left for Tyler the next day. Joining our party for the short journey were Texan President Scott Chalmers and his trusted friend Colonel Metaxis, as well as a hundred Texan cavalry as escort, nicely balancing my squadrons of royal guards.

President Chalmers was a short, stocky man in his thirties with a balding pate, who still moved gingerly from the musket ball he'd taken in the chest at the Battle of Tyler. He was the former senior aide to the late General Jack Murphy, and the chief instigator of the rebellion. Colonel Metaxis was younger but taller, and distinguished by a large mustache and a noticeable limp. The ex–guardos officer was newly promoted, and dressed now in the tan uniform of the Texan Army. His limp was the courtesy of a guardos lance point taken while helping me escape from the dungeon of Castle Corral.

We were certainly good at making cripples, if nothing else.

The party arrived at Tyler to find the town in a flurry of activity as it prepared for the royal visitor, festooning walls and buildings with banners and flowers, the main ways swept and washed, the people adorning themselves in their best go-to-church outfits. When the church bells announced that the expected ships had been sighted, hundreds rushed to line the walls of the town while thousands crowded the dock area where we waited. The citizens were held back by a cordon of Texan infantry so that the Kenesee Sixth Infantry Regiment and royal guards could deploy in ceremonial order. The Kenesee fleet of six ships pulled into harbor. Five ships dropped anchor, while the sixth edged into the waiting dock.

Robert strode down the gangplank, using his cane much less than the last time I'd seen him. Following him came two of his royal advisors, Bishop Thomas, the head of the church in Kenesee, and Sergeant Major Nakasone, commander of the royal guards, who looked about with a critical eye to confirm the effectiveness of the security arrangements. High Wizard O'Dowd was still in Virginia monitoring the organization of the new Virginian government, and Sir Meredith Sims was in Kingsport managing Kenesee and serving as the center point for the far-flung deployment of force that we now experienced.

Behind Robert's two advisors came Dr. Amani, Professor Wagner, a dozen aides and courtiers, and a contingent of royal guards. The usual entourage for traveling kings.

I must admit that I had mixed feelings about his arrival. It was good to see Robert again, for the melancholy that had afflicted him since the Battle of Yellow Fields was dispelled, and Robert was his old self, proud and confident as he stepped off the gangplank. Yet there was a reckoning between us still to come, and my stomach signaled its dislike of that encounter with a rumble. Robert greeted me effusively with a bear hug reminiscent of King Reuel. His affection was, for the moment, reassuring. The hug roused a spontaneous cheer from the Sixth Regiment and royal guards. Working his way down the waiting host, he greeted old friends and acquaintances with obvious pleasure, and the assembled officials of Texan with dignity and charm.

At the town hall there was a reception, with Robert meeting yet more Tyler and Texan notables and their spouses. Megan and Beth entertained the wives who did so want a chance to talk to the handsome King of Kenesee and tell him of their eligible daughters, and steered them away from him, so Robert could conduct the social business of state. Amid the flow of wine and beer, Robert found himself in innumerable discussions with various groups of Texans, all wanting his opinion on one matter or another. He did find time to get into a corner alone with President Chalmers for a quarter hour, but that was all.

I participated in a few of these encounters, but for the most part left Robert to meet the Texans alone. They would speak more freely were I not present, since a goodly number were unhappy with some of my decisions. Many held me largely responsible for promulgating unpopular rulings, and thereafter "influencing" the judgment of President Chalmers. I would quite happily plead guilty on the first count. I had not been timorous in my rulings before Chalmers's recovery. But I gave little or no advice to Chalmers that he did not seek out, and he followed his own mind, in any case.

I did pull Sergeant Major Nakasone aside during the reception. The muscular little commander of the royal guards looked fit and hard, his baldpate shiny. He smiled and shook my hand. "Good to see you again, Prince Arn."

"And good to see you too, Sergeant Major. Unfortunately, there is a security concern for King Robert."

He became all business. "Yes, sir?"

"The Pacificans."

The warning startled him. "The Pacificans? Mr. Kendall and his father? Are you sure, Prince Arn?"

"No, I'm not sure. But Robert is taking a dangerous course, and Pacifica may not like what he's doing. The Pacificans do not hesitate to do what is necessary to preserve the Codes. *Whatever* is necessary. We should be watchful."

He became grim. "I'll let the men know to be alert when they're around the king." A note of sorrow crept into his voice. "The Pacificans. Who would have thought it? Lord help us."

A welcoming banquet was held that evening, with

speeches of congratulation by Chalmers, Mayor Dobson of Tyler, and Great Landholder Mason. After these, Robert rose to enthusiastic applause (the Texans were not complete fools) and gave his own speech. He congratulated the Texans on all they had accomplished, their courage in ridding themselves of a tyrant, and their wisdom in choosing a man of Scott Chalmers's stature for their new president. More hearty applause. Robert then explained that President Chalmers and he would be discussing the new Confederation of Nations, which they had all doubtless heard about in the last few days.

This brought a stir among the audience. Robert added that Chalmers had not yet made a decision about the confederation, and would doubtless be seeking their opinion in the days ahead. Robert asked that they all keep an open mind as they were presented with facts and discussed the merits of confederation. He sat, and the applause this time was merely polite. Too much to digest at one meal.

Robert was indeed back in his old form.

There was entertainment, including jugglers, acrobats, a circus of trained animals, and the poet laureate of Texan rendering an ode to King Robert. The poet had done one for me weeks ago, a miserable effort in rhyming verse lauding my courage on the battlefield and the heaps of dead I'd made with my "flashing blade, there in the glade." He served Robert little better.

At last the ceremonies were over, farewells exchanged, and the guests departed. Robert and I, Chalmers, and our parties were all put up in the large inn next to the town hall. Robert's room was next to mine, with royal guards posted at each of our doors and at the stairwells. Outside, the guards shared duties with Chalmers's soldiers. Just normal security for the leaders of Kenesee and Texan.

A goodly number of our companions went down to the common room to catch up on news and share stories, while others retired to their rooms for more private conversations. Robert beckoned me to join him in his room, where a pitcher of beer and mugs awaited our pleasure. The inevitable meeting had come at last.

The room was the best in the town. A single large bed stood out from one wall, with a washstand on one side, and a bureau on the other. On the opposite wall was a generous window, its shutters open to the evening air. Between was a square table with chairs. Craftsmanship had gone into the sturdy furniture that was, while not ornate, smooth and polished in form and finish. A carpet fan hung from the ceiling, the pull-cord strung along to the wall and disappearing into a hole in the floor. Only months ago, the fans in the inn might have been in constant motion, powered by some poor slave tugging on a master cord below. Now, the fan hung still.

And where was the unfortunate soul who had served that task? Enjoying his freedom, or wandering jobless, or—the fan started to move. Well, maybe the poor devil wasn't so far away after all. Proclamations of freedom from Dallas were well and good, but freeing thousands of slaves was not accomplished with just the stroke of a pen. I would have to check on the matter in the morning. The room had been warm, but the fan and the cooling breeze from the bay made it comfortable within minutes.

Robert took off his crown and tossed it casually upon the bed, positioned himself in a chair while carefully favoring his bad side, and stretched a leg out in front of him with a sigh. There were flecks of gray in his hair. Gray at twenty-two. "The damn hip still plagues me, Arn. The pain is sometimes faint, sometimes intense, but always there. How is your leg?"

"Still sore, but that should pass."

"Good. Good. I wouldn't wish such an infirmity like mine on anyone. Now, tell me how things went since you departed Kingsport last November." And so I did. He had received written reports from Wizard Murdock and me, but not all events could be included on those pages. I told him of our voyage across the gulf, the attack by pirates, and our arrival at Arkan. I related our success as a traveling theater. Most surprising had been when Megan, Angela, and Beth had arrived to join our theater troupe.

He stopped me with a wave of his hand. "Yes, I can imagine. Our decision to send the women was not easily reached, Arn. We knew they were planning on sneaking away to join you, and I had no intention of letting them go—until Wizard O'Dowd came to me most reluctantly with his premonition. The dreams were very clear, he said. He saw them with you, and felt they *must* be with you. We searched for an alternative, but there was none." He paused, looked into his mug solemnly, and then locked his eyes onto mine. "Being responsible for Angela's death is not an easy thing. But I was the one who approved their going. So if there is any blame for Angela's fate, it is mine."

"There is none left to blame," I said truthfully, though I had indeed sought to blame at first, searching for victims of my wrath. My tormented heart had tried to attach the responsibility to Murdock, to Robert, to Lorich, and even to myself. But the blame would not stick, for there was no purpose in blaming. I might as well blame Angela's mother for giving birth to a daughter foolish enough to love me.

The only one to blame had died with Angela.

Robert poured more beer into my mug. "In spite of our losses, it was well-done, Arn. Well-done by you and all your party. Wizard Murdock is an exceptional man, and an exceptional wizard. You are fortunate to have him at your side."

"I know that."

"And Scott Chalmers. Tell me more of him."

I told him what I could. "Chalmers recovered from his wound and took over as President of Texan only a few weeks ago. His support comes from men who thought he could be molded to their designs. He is proving to be his own man, though that doesn't surprise me. He was responsible for my escape from the dungeon of Castle Corral, and has shown himself to be honorable, brave, and decisive. A clever man, though too soft when dealing with scoundrels. In a way, he reminds me of Murdock.''

Robert looked up from his mug. "That's helpful. Will Chalmers go along with our Confederation?''

Our Confederation? Well, perhaps it *was* mine as much as Robert's, whether I wanted it or not. At least, the world would see it as such. King Robert and his brother Prince Arn—would one do anything without the complicity of the other? In the eyes of the world, hardly.

But would President Chalmers, new to his position and still consolidating his power, go along with the idea of a confederation? Would he give up autonomy for membership in a nebulous effort at unity? Would he be so selfless?

"Yes, Robert. I think he will.''

"Why?''

I had talked to Chalmers much over the weeks, and could answer without a qualm. "Because he has vision. He always sees the possibilities. And because his personal ambition is the good of Texan.''

Robert seemed pleased. "You think highly of him, don't you?''

"He saved my life. I learned the make of the man.''

"Well, let's hope you're correct. I think you are. But only Chalmers can give us the final answer to that question, though I suspect he will have a bit of convincing to do among his followers. Still, he is the key to Texan support, and if he agrees, Texan will follow.''

"Let's hope so,'' I mumbled.

"Time will tell.'' He took another swig of beer and savored the flavor. "Not bad, though certainly with a different tang than Kenesee brew.''

"It's easy to get used to,'' I agreed.

He finished off the mug, set it upon the table, and considered the empty container in silence. The fan swished slowly back and forth above our heads.

"Now, to a different topic.'' He took his cane and slowly walked to the window, which looked out upon the town plaza. "Arn, you know how much I've appreciated your help and support. You've been tireless in your efforts, and all the successes we've enjoyed, ultimately, are due to your efforts. I owe you more than I can ever repay."

"I only did my duty, Robert." Which was absolutely true. And even duty was done quite reluctantly, most times.

He leaned forward, his hands on the sill. He didn't move, but I could see the muscles of his shoulders tighten, and stand out against his shirt. I'd seen that tension before. It occurred rarely, but it occurred. And only when he was angry.

"Yet, there is this matter of the muskets," he said.

So, we came to it at last. "Yes. The muskets."

"They are destroyed?"

"Yes, Robert," I admitted reluctantly. "A thousand of them. And the gunpowder for them thrown into the sea."

His voice had a hard edge to it. "And you had already received my letter indicating they should be sent to Kingsport?"

"Yes, Robert."

"So you willfully disobeyed my order."

"It wasn't actually an order," I haggled. "More of a directive."

"Granted. It was a directive. And you ignored it."

"Well . . . yes." He had me.

He turned, and the frown on his face was not a pleasant sight. "Why did you ignore it?"

"I wasn't trying to challenge you, Robert. I wasn't trying . . . to question your authority." Drat. The old hesitation had returned to my voice.

His tone was sharp now. "But it *was* a challenge, Arn. You *were* questioning my authority."

I met his hard stare. "That wasn't . . . my intent."

"Your intent does not matter," he retorted. "There can be only one king. Only one source of authority. Only one person to give orders for the good of the kingdom.

You did not want that job. I offered it to you, and you spurned it. Well and good. But if you don't take the responsibility of kingship, then you lose the privilege of ruling. I have it now, and as long as I do, orders must be obeyed. Directives must be followed. It is a matter of principle. And I will not be gainsaid.''

"I'm sorry," I said contritely. "I'll try to obey your orders. I'll try to follow your directives." I hesitated, then almost of their own bidding the words came blurting out. "But I can't promise."

He let out an oath and turned away, limping back and forth across the room, the tip of his cane thumping the wooden floor with each harsh step. All the while, he held forth on the logic and need of central direction and obedience. It went on for over a minute, and for my even-tempered and calm brother, that was a very long time.

It was a long time for me, too.

At last Robert stopped at the window, staring out again into the darkness of the plaza. The stiffness slowly went out of his shoulders, and he sighed. He returned to the table, tossed the cane onto his bed, and lowered himself into the chair. His features softened, and his voice lost its sharp edge.

"Arn, as much as I may rant about obeying orders, the cause of my anger is not your disobedience. I mean—it is an issue, but not the reason for my anger. I am upset because of the result of your action. Don't you realize what you've done?"

"No, Robert. Tell me. What have I done?"

"Before I answer that, let me ask one more question. Why did you destroy the muskets?"

Why indeed? I said what came to mind. "Too many widows. Too many children without fathers."

He raised an eyebrow. "As simple as that?"

I shrugged. Perhaps it was that simple, in the end.

Robert considered me, and something flitted across his face. A painful memory? Or sadness, perhaps? "Yes, some of us are very good at getting men killed, aren't we? The muskets, are they so horrible?"

That was easy. "Murphy's guardos shot down almost two hundred men from the Sixth Regiment in a single volley. The weapons are deadly. Facing equal numbers, an army equipped with muskets will slaughter troops without. Spear, sword, even bow, can't prevail against powder weapons. And muskets don't require months and years of training to use properly. Give any commoner a few weeks' practice with the musket, and he becomes a capable musketeer. There is little skill involved."

Robert listened without visible reaction, but when I was done he leaned forward across the table and placed a hand upon my arm. "And after explaining this to me, you don't realize what you've done? Arn, think of what you're saying. Think of the challenges that Kenesee faces. Think of an enemy marching upon us equipped with such weapons. Isn't that reason enough to have preserved the weapons for our use?"

"*If* there were an army with such weapons," I qualified his argument. "But there is none. Or am I wrong?"

"No, there is none. Not now. Not yet. Arn, if I could eliminate these weapons from existence, I would. But we must face the fact. The genie is out of the bottle. We still have the unused Virginian cannon and gunpowder, after all. And the usefulness of the muskets has been seen by thousands of men. We cannot go back to where we were. Things have changed. It wasn't our doing, but it has been done. With cannons and muskets, Kenesee would have nothing to fear. The Confederation would have nothing to fear."

"Are these weapons so important?" I asked. "Is this all we've gained from the War Against the Alliance? Powder weapons?"

Robert rubbed his forehead. "No, Arn. The weapons are not the goal. My first thought when we discovered the cannons was to destroy them, but then I thought better of it. These weapons are tools, Arn. Just tools, to be used for good or ill by the wielder. They are not the reason for what we do. But they may allow us to succeed in what we do, or attempt to do."

I pondered his words. I was tired, and I wanted to believe Robert, to go along with him, to make him happy and secure in my agreement. The words were seductive. Robert's logic sounded so reasonable. And yet . . .

"Robert, just what are you trying to do?" I asked, unable to suppress the exasperation in my voice. "What do you hope to accomplish with the weapons, these plans, this Confederation? Don't you realize how dangerous this is?"

He beckoned to me, and I followed him to the window. "Look out there, Arn. What do you see?"

Actually, I didn't see much. Except for streetlamps, and the oil lanterns of sentries, the town was dark.

And then I understood.

Robert's voice was filled with hope and conviction. "Arn, the world has lived in darkness for hundreds of years. I want to do away with the ignorance and strife and hardship that afflict the people—the people of Kenesee, the people of the nations, and all the people of our world. I want to bring us to a new golden age of knowledge and health and prosperity. I want to lift the darkness from the land: the real darkness out there, and the darkness that besets our minds."

I waited.

He gestured at the night. "I want to light the world. I want to illuminate men's minds. I want a world in which we need have no more deadly wars, no more bloody battles, no more starving gutter rats, no more chained slaves. To do this, I need unity. I need stability. I need military security and civil peace. I need a free hand to guide progress and development."

"Uhh, isn't that rather a tall order for us? The human race doesn't have a very good record for peace and benevolence."

He smiled. "No, our record isn't very good, is it? But that doesn't mean we can't try."

"And you think a new government and central control will accomplish all this?"

"That—and one more thing. Electricity."

Well, Robert always had been fascinated with the topic.

"Robert, there are other considerations. I think you should talk to Kendall about these matters. There is more you should know. There is much to discuss."

"Yes, I should talk to Kendall. You see, Arn, as I mentioned in my letter, I have a mission for you. As emissary."

I grimaced. "Where this time?"

"Across the continent," he admitted unhappily.

Across the continent. And that told me all I needed. I knew where I was going. West across plains and mountains to a far-off land that had, to that moment, seemed as distant to me as the moon.

"Pacifica," I said with painful surety, and Robert confirmed my guess.

"Yes. Pacifica."

3

Dangers and Decisions

Another mission. In the past, I might have considered turning the offer down. I would have groped for excuses not to go, mitigating factors to preclude the need for the mission, or at least, for my participation. And I might have done so again, except for the knowledge that this mission might be essential not only for my continued survival, but for the safety of Robert as well. For Robert in particular. I was not happy.

"All right, I'll go."

Robert looked surprised. "What, no objections? Am I dreaming?"

It was time he knew about the Pacificans.

I did not hesitate. "Someone does need to go to Pacifica. Robert, there are some things you have to know. Things I haven't told you yet. I've spoken to Gregor Pi-Ling."

"Pi-Ling? Wasn't he the Pacifican representative to Texan?"

"Yes. I met him in the dungeon of Castle Corral. And then I spoke to Mr. Kendall. The Pacifican representatives are more than just advisors. They're enforcers."

"Enforcers?" Robert asked calmly.

"Assassins. Executioners. Or, as they see themselves, soldiers devoted to their cause. Remember Professor Jameson? That was Kendall's work." I waited for some reaction, but there was none. "You're not surprised?"

Robert unbuttoned his shirt collar and leaned back against the window frame. "No, I'm not surprised. Disappointed to find my suspicions confirmed, but not surprised. So High Wizard Graven's mistrust of the Pacificans was not wholly misplaced. I've long suspected such was the case, though I think King Reuel did not believe it was so—or did not want to believe. The Pacificans are valuable advisors, and have given much to the six nations. Yet, they always had their own ends, and the preservation of the Codes came even before the good of Kenesee."

"Yes. The Codes come first. And that's why I must go to Pacifica."

Robert grinned. "Am I in that much danger?"

"More than you can know," I said.

The grin faded slowly as he watched my grim face. "Are you saying we should put Mr. Kendall in chains?"

"Mr. Kendall may be a danger. I can't rule that out. But there's another threat to you. And to me. Perhaps you should hear it from Kendall himself."

I had Sergeant Jenkins call for the Pacifican. Kendall soon joined us, along with his father, Jason the Healer. Certainly, it was not improper to have the senior Kendall accompany his son. I considered having Jenkins join us in the room, since Robert and I would be leaving ourselves alone with the Pacificans. Yet we were trained fighters against an old man and a man with one arm. I decided Jenkins wasn't needed, but felt sadness that I had to worry about such matters at all. We were subdued, but polite. Robert gestured towards the chairs, and I filled mugs as they sat. Then, we faced each other around the table, brothers facing father and son.

The old, familiar smile of Kendall found its way onto his features. "I'm glad you called for me, King Robert. There are matters to discuss."

"So Arn has been telling me. Was the death of Professor Jameson so many years ago really necessary?"

Well, there it was. Robert did know how to cut through the niceties.

Kendall's glance fell as he considered his answer. He lifted his head and looked at each of us in turn before

THE LANTERNS OF GOD   33

returning Robert's gaze. "King Robert, as protector of Kenesee, would you hesitate to condemn a citizen who betrayed the kingdom to the enemy?"

"Not for a minute, once guilt was proven," Robert responded. "You're making a point?"

Kendall nodded. There was sadness and regret in his voice, as well as resolve, all at the same time. "I too am a protector. I protect the good of Kenesee, and all the nations. And I do it by guarding the Codes. In Professor Jameson's case, I condemned a man who was betraying the Codes. It was necessary. Unfortunate, but necessary. He had warnings and ignored them. I spoke to him one last time before the end. He could not be swayed from his purpose."

"For the tiny steam engine he built? It was a mere toy."

"The toy was only a precursor. A working model would have followed. And that could not be allowed. The gates would have been opened, and technology developed without controls."

"And so you killed him."

Kendall did not flinch. "And so I killed him."

Jason sighed. "May God forgive us."

Robert regarded the healer. "You were involved in Jameson's death?"

Jason shook his head. "Not with Jameson. I left King Reuel's court years before Jameson joined the faculty. But there were others. Perhaps as many as a dozen over two decades. And their blood is upon my hands. It was the reason I resigned as Pacifican advisor to ply my calling in medicine. Too much guilt. Too many bad dreams. But I still believe in the ideals of the Codes. And for all the guilt, perhaps what we did was necessary. I hope so. Otherwise . . ."

Kendall studied his father, and the look upon his face was not unsympathetic. "There is no 'otherwise,' Father. Our goals were valid, our efforts necessary. And they still are, in spite of all that has happened."

Robert tapped a finger on the tabletop as he pondered

their words. "If that is so, then how will you deal with me, Mr. Kendall? Is not my call for confederation a change that threatens the independence of the six nations? Am I not a threat to the Codes?"

The Pacifican rubbed his armless shoulder. "You may be, Robert. We fought the War Against the Alliance to prevent the upheaval of the six nations. Your ideas for a confederation are akin to those of the Alliance—"

"Except," I interrupted, the words spilling out, "that Governor Rodes and General Murphy were interested in power for their own gain. Robert seeks the betterment of the nations."

Kendall gave me a sad nod. "That is so, I think. And that does count for much. Yet it goes against the plan we Pacificans have been following for so long. The organization of the nations into six countries is not a thing of chance, but of design. Alter the arrangement, and the plan is altered."

"The plan has already been altered," I argued. "Your colleagues Pi-Ling and Raashi and Hashimoto altered it when they sought to circumvent the Codes."

"Arn has the truth of it," Kendall admitted. "I have spoken long with Jason about this matter, and our discussion has been difficult. I don't know anymore what to do—or I don't want to do what I think I should do. We need resolution, and so I'm ready to make a proposal."

"A proposal?" Robert inquired.

"Yes. I'm going to journey back to Pacifica and seek guidance from our leaders. They need to be informed of the truth about what has happened, and what is happening. Perhaps a solution can be reached in this matter, a compromise which will prevent further tragedy."

"Well," said Robert, not mentioning our own discussion of a similar journey. "That sounds promising, Mr. Kendall. Yes, a trip to Pacifica might be in order. You would go alone?"

"Arn should go too," Jason responded for his son. "As with the mission to the Beastwood, his presence will pledge your sincerity and allow our leaders to judge your case in its best light.''

Well, this meeting was certainly working out well. I had been prepared to warn Robert about the danger Mr. Kendall posed. If Kendall went with me to Pacifica, then that was one threat removed. However, there was the other danger that Kendall had informed me about. Would he tell Robert?

"So we are agreed," Robert confirmed. "Mr. Kendall and Arn and a few trustworthy companions will travel to Pacifica. By ship or by land?"

Jason took out his pipe, the large one with the porous stone bowl. I handed across my tobacco pouch, and he packed the bowl while answering Robert's question. "Overland, I think. From the expression on Prince Arn's face, he is not amenable to another sea voyage. I've heard about his seasickness, and wonder if such a long trip might not prove a real danger to his health. There are some who never adjust to the open sea, and every so often a new sailor ends up dying from it. This might be such a case. The resurgence of the pirates among the treacherous passages of the Isles also warns against such an approach. No, I think overland is to be preferred, in spite of the time it will take."

Robert considered. "If you think it best. It is a long overland journey, but we have months before winter, so there will be no hurry."

"On the contrary," the younger Kendall stated. "Winters come early in the Rockies, and we have only eight or ten weeks before snow closes the passes. But that's not the reason that spurs us to go now and race the winter. Robert, you are at risk—grave risk—until we can get to Pacifica."

Robert's tone was casual. "And the nature of this threat to me?"

Jason sent a huge puff of smoke toward the ceiling. "Our leaders—our Board of Administrators—sent out a special enforcement team to remove Governor Rodes and General Murphy and Pi-Ling and the other advisors who challenged the Codes.''

"But we've just taken care of those villains," I said. "We've done the job for these enforcers."

"That is so," Kendall agreed. "Except the enforcers have the discretion to redirect their efforts against new threats. Robert became such a threat when he announced the Confederation. And by association, so have you, Arn.''

Robert realized he was tapping the table with his finger, and folded his hands together. "Can't you contact these enforcers and call them off?''

Kendall leaned forward. "No, we can't. Jason and I don't know who or where they are. They'll enter—or perhaps already have entered—the six nations through the chinks, just as you did entering Texan. They'll close upon their targets slowly but surely. Nor can we contact Pacifica directly. We could have at one time, but Pi-Ling and his cohorts damaged our communication system with Pacifica. We might get a message through, but would they call off the enforcers just on our word? I doubt it. Not after all of us have been made suspect by the treachery of Pi-Ling and the others. No, we have to go to Pacifica ourselves, and make our case in person. That's our only alternative.''

"And what of Robert during that time?" I asked.

"Robert must go into seclusion," Kendall stated firmly. "No public travel. No ceremonies. He must go back to the King's Castle and stay within it until we return. Only those known and trusted should be permitted entry, and he should stay off the battlements.''

Robert frowned, and waved a hand in dismissal of the idea. "I can't do that.''

"King Robert, my son is right," Jason affirmed. "These enforcers are skilled assassins. They have weapons that are not permitted under the Codes—''

Robert put up a hand. "You mean Pacifica does not follow the Codes?''

Jason gestured back with his pipe. "The Codes were

promulgated for the six nations. They weren't made for Pacifica."

"So," Robert stated gravely, "while Pacifica is allowed unbridled development and progress, the six nations are shackled to stagnation."

Kendall responded with patience. "Aiding the six nations has been done at great cost to Pacifica, Robert. The substantial population increase all the nations are experiencing is at least partially due to Pacifica, and the knowledge and techniques we've shared."

Robert was impassive. "So I grant. Still, you enforce the Codes with forbidden weapons."

"Yes," admitted Jason. "And the enforcers will not hesitate to use them, and it will not be difficult to accomplish their mission if you give them opportunity. Deny them that opportunity. Please."

The sincerity of the older man's words seemed to have their effect upon Robert. He laid a hand upon the table and drummed his fingers upon the wood once, twice, thrice. "I must travel to the other nations. But I'll vary my schedule and routes, and finish my travels as soon as possible. After that, I'll return to the castle and seclude myself there, as you request."

Jason was reassured. "Heed my words, and you may be all right. Let Sergeant Major Nakasone know of the threat, and that they have silent missile weapons which can reach out accurately from many yards away."

"Like a crossbow?" Robert asked. "I see. Thank you, Jason, for your concern. I'll do as you say."

Kendall was thoughtful. "I'm not saying I go along with your idea of a confederation, Robert. You've charted a dangerous course, and that decision may yet be your undoing. We'll let the Board of Administrators in Pacifica decide that. However, to lose you now would cause uncertainty and turmoil among the six nations."

Robert accepted the compliment without comment. "Then, we are left only with the planning for Mr. Kendall's and Arn's journey. When should they leave?"

Jason left no doubt. "Soon," he said. "Very soon."

* * *

Kendall and I picked our travel companions with little debate. Wizard Murdock would go, of course. His magical talents would be helpful in avoiding encounters with tribes in the plains and the mountains. Equally valuable, his abilities as statesman and emissary would give us our best chance of persuading the Pacifican Board of Administrators.

Wizard Lorich, Murdock's apprentice and a powerful magician in his own right, would also go. He had already saved my life at least once, and I wanted him around to do so again, if need be. Likewise, Sergeant Jenkins.

And so we were five. I thought that was the end of it, but the beastman Kren found me the next morning. He gave me that look that said "you-wouldn't-leave-me-behind-would-you?"

"Let me guess," I groaned. "Someone told you about our mission."

"I think it's about time a representative of the Beastwood met the Pacificans too, don't you think? I'm sure Ambassador Sokol would want me to go, though there's no time to ask. Besides, who else is there to keep Wizard Murdock under control? You need me, Arn. I just wanted to spare you the embarrassment of having to ask."

And thus we were six.

Orders for goods went out to various merchants and craftsmen in Tyler by noon. Our journey would be long and hard, and the winter might be colder than anything we had faced. Woolens of all sorts were obtained, as well as warm sheepskin hats, long coats, boots, and sleeping blankets. We were also fitted for soft leather shirts and pants. Whatever couldn't be found in Tyler was ordered to be ready at Dallas.

Maps were collected for study. Kendall's and Jason's experience and insights were particularly helpful, for they had made the overland journey, though two decades had gone by since Jason had seen Pacifica, while Kendall had not traveled the overland route for six years.

They would try to get a message to Pacifica asking that a guide meet us somewhere east of the mountains, but there was no guarantee the message would get through.

The two Pacificans each had a surprise announcement as well.

Kendall made his during a break in the planning. "It is my pleasure to announce to you all that Lady Megan Sims and I will be married tomorrow by Bishop Thomas in the town cathedral. And it's my privilege to invite you all to the wedding."

So, they had decided to formalize their relationship. Well, I couldn't blame them. We'd expected a large, formal wedding in Kingsport or Lexington once we'd all returned to Kenesee. It would have been the formal event of the year, without doubt. But Megan had waited long beyond the year and a day required, and now that Kendall was to suddenly leave her side for more months, she had probably put her foot down. And then a thought struck me worthy of the gossips. Could there be another reason for this hurried wedding? Could Megan be in a delicate way? Not that it mattered, of course. We wouldn't have been ready to travel the next day, in any case.

Jason the Healer followed this with his own announcement. "Guess this is as good a time to ask, as any. I'd like to go along, Prince Arn."

I hadn't expected this. "You want to come, Jason?"

"Yes, I do. I'm not getting any younger, and truth be told, I'd like to see Pacifica again before I—that is, it would be nice to spend time there and renew acquaintance with my homeland."

"I see," was the answer he received while I pondered his request. Lord knew, Jason had a right to go. He'd earned it thrice over, and deserved my approval of his request.

And yet, I hesitated. The journey would not be an easy one. He would not be able to ride comfortably on the driver's bench of his healer's wagon. We would all be mounted. Days in the saddle could be difficult even for young riders accustomed to long hours on horseback. Jason had to be at least sixty.

Murdock, fortunately, recognized my difficulty, and took the problem upon himself. "Jason, my friend, you haven't made the overland journey for many years. It will be a difficult trip for all of us. Do you think you can keep up?"

Jason snorted. "I'm not saying it will be easy for me. But I was a good rider, and I'm no stranger to long days. I won't slow you down. I think I'm worth taking along. If you run into trouble, you'll have a physician with you. And I'm not without stature in Pacifica. I can explain your case, just as I did when I escorted you to the Beastwood."

I would not have approved for gratitude alone. After all, my life would be at risk on this journey, and I wanted companions who would help us arrive safely, not put us in peril during the trip by delay. However, the last two arguments weighed considerably. A physician would be handy, and we'd need every card we could play in Pacifica. I looked about me. Nods from all around.

And so we were seven.

The next day, the wedding was held in the Tyler Cathedral. It was an impressive edifice, vaulted stone and crete with stained-glass windows set high on either side so that rainbows of light illuminated the interior. It was pleasantly cool inside even in the heat of the day, and absolutely still except for the echoing footsteps as Robert escorted Megan up the aisle. Her hair shimmered golden in the rainbow, her face aglow, her eyes locked on her betrothed. They arrived at the altar where Mr. Kendall stood, a ridiculously innocent grin of happiness on his homely face.

Robert stood in for Megan's father, Sir Meredith. He gave away the bride and retired to his seat in the front pew, leaving Megan and Kendall standing before Bishop Thomas. Murdock took his place next to Kendall as best man, while Beth took position beside Megan as maid of honor. At one time, I might have been Kendall's best man. However, recent events had strained that relationship, as we both recognized. It's hard to trust a man who might be planning your death.

The wedding was quite a small affair, as such things go. Only the first two pews were occupied, holding the royal party and followers such as the three Kenesee regimental commanders. Among the rare Texans were President Scott Chalmers and Colonel Metaxis. The only others in the cathedral were the twoscore of royal guards standing at rest around the walls.

Bishop Thomas went through the brief ceremony with all due dignity, the rings were exchanged, and the deed was done. Though, if truth were told, the deed had been done many months ago in the King's Castle. Megan had made clear her love for the Pacifican, and Kendall had slipped a ring on her finger before taking her to his room. Some relationships are never sanctified, no matter how many marriage ceremonies are conducted. Some are sacred from the first kiss. And others . . . others drift into sanctity without the couple even knowing it.

There was no formal reception, though a simple noon meal was served at the town hall to all that had attended. The tables had been arranged into a large U-shape, with Megan and Kendall at the center and the rest of us ranged all around. Platters of chicken and potatoes and greens were brought, and the celebration began. The bride and groom ate little, listened to dubious advice from the married guests on a successful life together, and smiled at each other. Kendall raised an eyebrow to his bride, Megan nodded, and the two rose. They waved and left us still finishing dessert while they retired for the evening—though it was barely past midday.

"Now where could they be going?" Jenkins asked in a loud voice, and the hall dissolved into laughter. The sergeant was attending as a guest with Beth, rather than on duty with the other royal guards.

Jason watched the newlyweds go with a satisfied look

and took the opportunity to wipe his spectacles, the kerchief then dabbed quickly at each eye and put away in embarrassment. "My son has done well for himself. He was so shy around women. I never thought he'd win such a beauty for himself."

Kren nudged Lorich, speaking softly to the young wizard so others couldn't hear. "You see? Anything is possible."

Lorich finished his mouthful before answering. "Not for me."

"See what the future brings, lad," the beastman encouraged him. "Patience is a virtue."

"The loneliness is hard," Lorich said softly, so that perhaps even Kren could not hear. "Like water on a stone. It's wearing me away."

I would have given Lorich an encouraging word, but I didn't have much encouragement for anyone at the moment. Reality weighed too heavily upon me.

The newlyweds deserved their one night together as man and wife. It would be months before they would have another, for my party (including Kendall) was leaving for Dallas on the morrow. Megan and Beth were departing Texan with King Robert the day after to ensure their safe return. Given Jason and Kendall's warning, Robert had decided not to visit Dallas, but to go directly from Tyler to his next destination. He had effectively accomplished his purpose by meeting President Chalmers, and if he did not get to meet every important personage in Texan, he had by now made acquaintance with a goodly number. He could proceed to Mexico and then the Isles for his visits there. Robert would take all the royal guards with him, while the three Kenesee regiments would gradually ship back to their homeland over the next month or two. With the royal guards and escorting ships of Robert's fleet, it was the safest way for Megan and Beth to get home.

It was a time of happiness, but for me everything was tainted by a cloud of restraint, a memory of those gone, a realization that yet more partings would be taken on the morrow. To gain, and lose. To come, and go. To say hello, and then farewell. The same for us as it had been for the ancients, enduring the silent hours before dawn when one lay awake and asked *why*, and never received an answer.

Beside me should have sat a young woman with brown hair, flashing a smile that could outdo the sun. I looked at my plate and the cup, and for a moment my vision blurred and I had to blink before I could look up and see Murdock giving me a gentle smile from across the table.

"That Texan dust does irritate the eyes," the wizard said. "But it will pass. Be happy for them, Arn."

"I am, Murdock. I am."

That afternoon, President Chalmers and Colonel Metaxis stopped by the inn and asked for me. I immediately had them shown up to my room, where I had been discussing the journey with Robert and Murdock.

Extra chairs were brought in, and all seated. Chalmers put on his official business face. "Prince Arn, I'm sorry to bother you, but it seems we've had a complaint about your royal guards. One of the most respected citizens in Tyler is missing, taken by a detachment of your guards. In a separate incident, another important citizen has been seriously injured."

I made sure my face showed that I was taken aback by the nature of the problem. The guards were most proper in their behavior with the Texans. No less was expected, and they knew what would happen if they weren't. Even the Kenesee regiments had been instructed in the importance of good behavior in Texan, and so far had conducted themselves with admirable control.

"Are you sure royal guards were involved?" Murdock asked.

Metaxis nodded. "Witnesses were clear about the black uniforms, and even identified the King's brand on the horses. The perpetrators didn't take any steps to hide who they were."

"Well, then, they must be punished," Robert stated with vigor. "Have any individual guardsmen been identified?"

"Yes," Metaxis confirmed. "I'm afraid from the description we received, their leader was your Sergeant Jenkins."

Murdock's eyebrows raised. "Jenkins, of all people? This isn't like him. Not like him at all. I've never known him to act improperly. Unless—" Murdock cut off his words and stared at me suspiciously.

I avoided his gaze.

A guard went to summon the sergeant while Metaxis related the story of witnesses. "Sergeant Jenkins—assuming it was he—and more than a dozen royal guards. left town through the south gate yesterday afternoon and appeared at the villa of Landholder Hardiman. His holding is about five miles south of Tyler near the Coast Road. Hardiman is not one of the Great Landholders, but his property is extensive, and he is a very prominent man in the community."

"Hardiman. Hardiman," Murdock intoned. "Why does that name sound familiar?"

"Sergeant Jenkins stormed into the villa, confronted the young landholder as he was having dinner with his family, and dragged him out into the courtyard. There, Sergeant Jenkins and other guardsmen beat the landholder and broke his arms."

"What?" I asked. "They actually broke his arms?"

"Both of them, according to reports," confirmed Metaxis. "The guardsmen left the landholder moaning on the ground, after which they marched through the slave quarters, had all the ankle irons removed from the slaves, and took one of the slave women with them when they left."

Robert frowned. "I thought the slaves had been freed."

Chalmers responded. "They have been, by writ and

decree. But the owners still have a month before they must free the last slave. The idea was to allow a gradual processing of the slaves for their own safety and well-being. Doubtless, some owners will wait until the last day before granting any of them their freedom.''

"And turning them out of their quarters," Robert added astutely.

"Exactly," said Chalmers. "After which the owners will hire them back at miserable wages and charge rent for the quarters the slaves lived in before. We've been reading old books. It's happened before.''

"Nothing is easy," Metaxis explained. "We tried to come up with a better way. There seemed none. At least, the former slaves can move on if they dislike their employers. There will doubtless be hardship involved. But they are free. That is the important thing. The few slaves seized from other countries can return to their homelands. Most have been born into bondage, and know nothing else.''

Murdock was thoughtful. "Quite right. But about the other incident . . . ?"

Metaxis shrugged. "Sergeant Jenkins and his cohort again. Later that same day. They came in through the south gate on horseback, reportedly with a young woman who may have been the slave they took from Landholder Hardiman's villa. They left her at the command post of the Kenesee Sixth Infantry Regiment.''

"I see. But what of Sergeant Jenkins?''

"Jenkins and his men went to the house of Señor Domingo Cantrell, a wealthy trader who is well connected to important families in Tyler and Dallas. They entered the house, dragged him out into the street and onto a horse, and rode back out through the south gate. Less than an hour later, about dusk, the guardsmen returned to town—but without Señor Cantrell.''

There was a knock upon the door and Sergeant Jenkins entered, coming stiffly to attention before us. "Sergeant Jenkins reporting as ordered, sir,'' he said, and slipped into parade rest.

No snappy salute or cocky greeting this time. Jenkins was being formally correct before his king, as was proper. But he was my man, and I had to be the one to confront him.

"Sergeant Jenkins!" I addressed him in a severe voice. "President Chalmers and Colonel Metaxis have brought us disturbing reports of assault and kidnapping against citizens of Texan. Do you have any knowledge of these incidents?"

He looked at us resolutely. "Aye, sir. That I do."

"Could you expand upon that, Sergeant?"

"Certainly, sir. What would you like to know?"

"Landholder Hardiman was assaulted at his villa, his arms broken, and one of his slaves stolen. Was that your doing?"

"Aye, sir. And a good afternoon's work it was."

Murdock and I exchanged a glance. Chalmers and Metaxis looked startled. Robert almost spoke, but cut off the words. This was more properly my affair, and he would let me handle it—unless I tried his patience.

I folded my hands together on the table. "Sergeant Jenkins, please elaborate on your reasons for this action."

"Yes, sir." So sure of himself, the little rooster. At least he wasn't grinning. "Landholder Hardiman purchased a Kenesee woman taken captive by Texan troops during the war. We saw him buy her from the auction block when we came through Tyler as a traveling theater. We couldn't do anything for her then, but we could now. We freed her. Hardiman put up some resistance, and we were forced to subdue him."

"By breaking his arms?" Metaxis asked.

"Well, sir, perhaps the men were a bit too enthusiastic. But I told them how slaveholders use these women, and they didn't take kindly to that."

"I must express my sympathy for Sergeant Jenkins's actions," Murdock stated. "I remember seeing this Kenesee woman on the block, and the intentions of Landholder Hardiman were clear."

Chalmers nodded. "I can understand his anger. Well, perhaps this case is not so important. But what of Señor Cantrell?"

I cleared my throat. "Perhaps I should mention that Cantrell is the gentleman who tried to purchase Sabrena at the same slave auction."

Metaxis spoke. "Ahh. So he's the one."

Jenkins hesitated a moment. "You see, sir, we didn't plan to do much more to him than we had to Hardiman. But when we entered his house by surprise, we found him with another little girl, couldn't have been more than six or seven." Jenkins had worked himself up as he spoke, and his face had turned a bright red with indignation. "What he was doing—well, we took Mr. Cantrell out to a pier in the bay and had a little talk with him. Somehow, a piece of anchor rope got tangled around his neck, and when the anchor fell into the water, he went with it."

"Good Lord!" exclaimed Metaxis. "Sergeant Jenkins, you murdered one of our citizens for no reason?"

"We don't know for sure he's dead, sir—though he didn't come back up. But it wasn't murder. Just an accident."

I looked at the ceiling. "Too bad about losing a perfectly good anchor that way."

The room was quiet for a long moment. I had conveyed my message quite clearly with those words. President Chalmers looked at Metaxis expectantly. The colonel shrugged.

Chalmers made up his mind. "Prince Arn, we have been allowing the men of your regiments to come under Kenesee justice for violations of Texan law. So far, we have not been dissatisfied with that procedure. Though this case is more serious than any others which have arisen, I believe it will be in the best interests of all concerned to allow you to determine what is just in regard to Sergeant Jenkins and his men."

So. Chalmers had sidestepped the responsibility. Astute.

I harrumphed. "Since the President of Texan wishes me to administer justice in this instance, I will do so. Sergeant Jenkins, you and your men are fined one month's pay each. I will also think about appropriate additional punishment for you. Dismissed."

Jenkins fought the smile that tugged at the corners of his mouth. "Aye, sir. One month's pay. And additional punishment for me. I'll tell the men. Thank you, sir." He came to attention, faced about smartly, and marched off.

I looked at the Texans. "Is that satisfactory, gentlemen?"

"A month's pay for murder?" Colonel Metaxis looked doubtful.

Murdock put a hand on the soldier's arm. "Are you a family man, Colonel? Ever had a daughter?"

"Hmm? Oh. I see."

"Extenuating circumstances," the wizard explained.

Extenuating circumstances, indeed. I would make up the month's pay out of my own pocket, and Jenkins's additional punishment would be to meet with me for a beer and describe how our kindly gentleman with the penchant for little girls had looked when Jenkins threw him into the water. I had little sympathy for slave owners, especially when the slaves were Kenesee citizens. I had none for men who molested children.

I would have to ask Jenkins if he wanted a medal.

Chalmers smiled grimly. "An unfortunate incident, but understandable. Prince Arn, thank you for making clear to us the circumstances surrounding these matters, and for taking action. It will allow me to placate those who have raised concerns. I will let them know that the perpetrators have been dealt with justly."

When the Texans had taken their leave, Robert eyed me with an appraising look. "I come to see how you accomplish what you do, Arn. This was not the way I would have handled the matter. And yet, I think I would have been wrong. There is law, and there is justice. The one serves the other. I must remember that." He grinned. "If I forget, I trust you and Murdock will remind me of the truth."

"Oh, we will," Murdock assured him in all innocence. "We will."

4

Many Partings

The next morning we breakfasted in the common room of the inn, taking a last meal together before my companions and I departed for Dallas. The seven of us would be leaving today. Except for Colonel Metaxis, the rest were remaining in Tyler for the day. President Chalmers and King Robert would spend the time in discussion and planning, with Robert scheduled for departure on the morrow.

Chalmers found me and shook my hand after the meal. "I wanted to thank you for all you've done for Texan, Arn. None of this would have been possible without you. Colonel Metaxis will accompany you while you're in Texan and assist you in every way possible. If you have any needs, just ask."

"That will be helpful," I admitted.

"I also wanted to express my continued sorrow for your personal loss. I knew her only briefly, just those few minutes in the dungeon, and yet her conduct gained my admiration." He gave me a smile and clasped me on the shoulder. "May you find happiness in her memory."

Well, that was one farewell out of the way.

Others were taking their leave as well. Sergeant Jenkins was giving Beth the benefit of his advice. "Stay with the Lady Megan, and don't go off alone when the fleet stops at ports. When you get to Kingsport, check with the lenders and make sure they're investing our money properly. Insist on seeing the ledgers."

She smiled tolerantly. "Yes, my love. Just as I've done for years before I met you."

"Well, a reminder doesn't hurt."

"That's true. And let me remind *you*. Do your duty, but don't take chances. You don't have to right every wrong in the world. And try not to let Prince Arn get you killed."

"The lad hasn't yet, though he has tried hard a few times . . ."

She smiled and stroked his cheek. "You'll find me in Kingsport, waiting for you."

"Aye, and it'll be past a year and a day. We'll get married, then."

Her smile was replaced by a pensive stare. "Are you sure about that? You'll have to resign from the guards. I know how you love being a guardsman. Are you sure you're willing to give up your first love?"

Jenkins laughed. "You *are* my first love," he told Beth, which was quite the right thing to say, judging from her reaction. "We'll be married as soon as I return, if you can avoid finding another lover before then."

"Another lover? Only one?" she asked innocently, and then the two were laughing together as she buried herself in his arms.

I looked away. I was happy for them, and yet . . . I wondered when I'd be able to look at a man and woman together and not feel a sense of loss.

The newlyweds said little this morning, though Megan clung to Kendall's arm through much of the meal, which made it difficult for him to eat. He looked tired, though I could not for the world imagine what might have worn him out so. Megan looked tired too; but more, she looked worried.

In a rare moment she left Kendall and came to my side. I watched with surprise as she approached.

She stood stiffly before me, her hands clenched. "Arn, I will try to think better of you. For Paul's sake. He asked it of me. And for Angela's too, since she asked it also months ago."

This certainly was unexpected. "Thank you, Megan. Your feelings were understandable. But I appreciate your thinking well of me. Or trying to." And I was surprised she was even willing to try again.

"I will do my best. But I have a request, too."

I was suddenly cautious, as I was when anyone indicated they had a request for their prince. "Yes, Megan? What is it?"

"My Kendall. Bring him back to me. Safe and sound."

"Yes, Megan. I'll try."

"We are going to have a child. I want the child to have a father. And I—I could not bear to lose him."

"Megan, I can't know that he will come back. I can't promise that any of us will return. But I will do what I can to ensure the safety of the party. We all will."

I had the feeling she wanted more. But what more could I have offered? My promise? How can any man promise the future of another?

Still, she seemed to accept my words at last. "Then all is said. I wish you and all your companions safety and success." And with that she returned to the side of her husband.

A second farewell done, such as it was.

We went to our rooms to fetch the last few items before departure. Robert accompanied me. I tucked my pipe and pouch in a pocket and a good-sized bag of Kenesee tobacco into a saddlebag, collected my sword, and put on my hat.

"How do I look?"

Robert forced a smile. "As disreputable as ever. Are you growing a beard again?"

"Started yesterday. Have to cover the scar."

"Ah, yes. Wise."

"Murdock reminded me. And it'll be hard to shave every day where we're going."

"I see. Quite." He paused. "Arn. Don't let anything happen to you. You and Murdock must reach Pacifica and make our case. There is too much at stake. Not just what happens to you and me, but what happens to our society, possibly to all of mankind. I think—I almost know—that we're at a critical, a decisive, point in history. I dream at night, and see a dozen roads stretching out to a dozen futures, a dozen worlds. Worlds that might be. And in most of those worlds I see Man falling into the same dismal errors of the past, helpless to prevent famine, and plague, and war, mired in the ignorance and stupidity of his own nature. But there are one or two worlds—just one or two—where things are better. Not perfect, but better. And those are the worlds I want.''

Poor Robert. So sincere. So well intentioned. Should I tell him his hopes were but pipe dreams? Should I tell him how the visionaries of the past, those who would devise a system to better man, had failed time after time, often begetting greater evils than those they tried to eradicate? But he knew that already. Or he should. Well, there was time when I returned—if I returned—to bring him back to reality and dispel the delusion under which he labored, to make him see the world through a different facet of the gem of truth.

"We'll try, Robert. Murdock will convince the Pacificans, if anyone can.''

"Yes." Robert took a breath. "Yes, he will. And you *will* all come back, well and whole." And then he took me in that bear hug of his and squeezed.

"Robert," I gasped, "if you want me to go, it would be better if my ribs aren't cracked.''

He let go and stepped back. "Yes, I suppose so. Come, it's time to see you off.''

Three farewells done.

My party was assembled in front of the inn with our mounts, and filling the plaza were the ordered rows of five companies from the Kenesee Tenth Cavalry Regiment escorting us back to Dallas. Standing at attention, ranks of black-uniformed royal guards waited to either side of the inn. After months of duty in Virginia and Texan, the royal guards were finally reassembled. But where five hundred guards had once stood, not more than two out of five were still in ranks, their comrades dead on a half dozen battlefields, or retired from wounds. Except for Jenkins, they would all be going with Robert.

And that was unfortunate. I slept much better with a squadron of guards around me.

There was no one else in the plaza. It had been cordoned off from the populace. Many good-byes had already been given by the time we stepped into the open, but not all. Murdock was contending with little Sabrena, who clutched his thumb in an unyielding grip.

Murdock went to one knee beside her. "Lorich and I have to go now, my girl."

"I know."

"Lady Megan and Beth will take good care of you while I'm gone. You'll be safe with them, and no one will hurt you. You'll see Kenesee, where I live. And that's where I'll find you when I come back."

"Yes, you will," she said. "But how long will that be?"

"Oh, six or seven months. Certainly less than a year. Not long, really. And when I come back, you'll be dressed in fine clothes and learning your numbers and letters. And you'll ride like a true horsewoman. I'll be very proud of you. Now give me one more hug. That's it. Good girl. Now, go say good-bye to Prince Arn."

Reluctantly, she released his thumb and, with a glance back, came over to me. Murdock took the opportunity to mount quickly before she could change her mind.

This would be the fourth farewell, and hopefully the last.

She took a position that left a clear space between her and Robert. Sabrena had attached herself to Murdock and Beth. She had determined the rest of us who had rescued her from the auction block posed no threat. But all other people—especially men—were not to be trusted.

She put out her hand. "Good-bye, Prince Arn."

I took it and we shook hands soberly. "Good-bye, Sabrena."

Robert could not repress a smile. She looked up at him and studied his face. "You don't want him to go. You're worried he won't come back. You'll be all alone then. That frightens you."

Robert's smile faded. "I—perhaps you're right."

"He'll come back." She said it calmly, with utter assurance.

Robert glanced at me, and then at Murdock "Is she . . ."

Murdock nodded. "King Robert, make sure you allow High Wizard O'Dowd adequate time from his duties to work with Sabrena. Given her—experiences—it wouldn't be appropriate to send her to the School of Magic. All boys, and her the only girl. But she needs guidance in the talents. He'll know what to do, none better."

So, I had another soothsayer. But for once, I liked what I had heard. I would, apparently, make it back to Kenesee alive.

Then again, even the best seer made mistakes. And could she tell what condition I'd be in?

I shook hands with Dr. Amani and Bishop Thomas and Professor Wagner and Sergeant Major Nakasone and a dozen other notables before retreating between the horses, where I checked the saddle girth of my mount. And there, Beth found me. I'd already said a brief good-bye after breakfast, but I could guess what she wanted to say.

"Beth, don't worry. With Murdock's talents, we'll be avoiding anyone who might cause us trouble. Jenkins will come back. We all will."

"That's up to God," she said. "I know you'll take care of your companions, and they'll take care of you. But that's not what I wanted to talk to you about."

Lord, what now?

"Prince Arn, when you paid me to help King Robert, I did it for the money, and thought that one more time would not really matter. But it did. I fulfilled my part of the bargain, but it didn't feel right, then or after. Jenkins and I had given our oath, and that made all the difference. I could not go back to the old trade.''

Ahh. She was feeling regret over that little arrangement, and was blaming me. Well, if it made her feel better, she was welcome to think me the villain.

To my surprise, she took my hand and held it between hers. ''I still weep for Angela too. I know your sorrow. I've seen how hard it's been for you, and it hurts me to see a friend in such distress. I wanted to comfort you, as a woman can comfort a man. I wanted to come to you in the night and comfort you. Out of friendship. But I couldn't do that, neither for money nor friendship. Now that Jenkins is in my heart, I can't do such things anymore. I wanted you to know. For friendship's sake.''

So that was it. Truly, Beth was a woman to admire. She had been a gutter rat like me, and while escaping the worst fates of the rats, had found one way of securing her livelihood. There had been none to rescue her, as I had been rescued, no one to save her from the harsh necessity of making her way in a world which gave her few or no choices. That she had avoided the human leeches that lived off such women, that she had cared for the health of her customers and herself and guarded against the pox, that she had used her earnings to provide for her future rather than spending them upon material comforts, all spoke to her credit as a survivor, as a woman, and as a human being.

Beth put her arms around me and held me chastely— or as chastely as any woman with her looks and form could hold a healthy male.

I blinked. Comfort. I hadn't had a woman's comfort since Angela was killed. Each day my mind thought of passion, but my body seemed dead from the waist down. Yet now in Beth's arms, even her chaste hold produced a stirring that I had not felt during the long weeks of grief. And for that, I was most exceedingly grateful.

Life *does* go on.

She released me. "Arn, are you going to visit the graves before you depart Dallas?"

That gave me pause. I hadn't been able to bring myself to visit Angela and Nancy's graves. "I wasn't planning to."

"You have to say good-bye to Angela. And to Nancy Brown too."

"Perhaps I will," I agreed to placate her.

"It will help. Believe me." And then she stepped away, ducked beneath the neck of my horse, and found her way back to Jenkins's side for a last moment with her lover. He had a woman to come back to. Lucky man.

I mounted, and those few who weren't in saddle hurried to their horses. Jason made it up in one, smooth motion. Maybe he wouldn't slow us up too much after all.

There were many hail-and-farewells called, and much hand-waving from all we left behind. I gave the escort leader a signal, and two companies of his command trotted toward a wide street heading south. My party fell in behind them, and the other companies took station behind us. Out through the south gate, around to the east road, and then on our way. The lead company broke into a canter, riding forward to scout the way and examine any potential positions of ambush. They were doing their job well, and that was all that could be asked. Hopefully, Robert would be as cautious.

Two days later we arrived at Dallas without incident, though Jason was sore from the ride. We stayed at the castle that evening through the next day, trying on the new clothing we'd ordered, checking equipment, and packing everything for the trip. Besides our own mounts, we'd each be leading a good packhorse carrying the winter gear and rations we were hauling along. There was a lot. The list had been long, even after paring it to the bone. For example, we carried hammer, nails, and an extra set of fitted shoes for each horse. Farriers would be few or none when we left the civilized nations.

Besides our swords and knives, Jenkins, Kren, Lorich, and I each added a good horse bow and a full quiver of arrows to our weaponry. In the open plains, the bow would be an important weapon. Jenkins thought it would be nice to have lances too, but we would succeed not by meeting danger, but by fleeing from it. The bow would be handy, the lance an encumbrance.

Besides, being armed like soldiers didn't quite fit in with our roles. While journeying through Texan and Arkan, we would be surveyors on our way to the northern plains to map river courses and determine what resources those lands might hide. Our party's cover was not as thorough as the traveling theater ruse we had used to penetrate Texan, but was adequate now that we faced no worse than the relatively benevolent security of Arkan before striking the plains frontier.

The day passed quickly, but the bitter reminders of past events in Castle Corral became too strong, and I needed to get away from the walls, away from the battlements. Inspecting the horses for our trip provided a good excuse to head for the stables outside town the next afternoon. Jenkins and a half squadron from the Tenth Regiment hurriedly saddled and went with me.

I looked over my two animals, and Jenkins looked them over too. Then we went down the stalls of the other horses going with the party, and checked them as well. All were good, spirited creatures, bred for sturdiness and speed, and able to serve as mount or packhorse while subsisting on the grasses of the plains.

It was at the back of the barn that I saw the familiar yellow-scrolled wagon of Jason the Healer parked against a wall, and Jason's team of grays resting in stalls nearby. He emerged from the wagon carrying a half-filled sack, moving stiffly, still feeling the two days in the saddle. He looked surprised to see us.

"Prince Arn. Sergeant Jenkins. Are you looking for me?"

"No, sir," Jenkins replied. "Just checking the mounts. They all look fine. And yourself, sir?"

Jason looked back at the dusty old wagon. "Taking a last few items that might be handy. You know, I've lived in that wagon for almost twenty years. It's been my home. And now, I'm leaving it behind. Strange feeling."

"It's not the things you leave behind that matter," said Jenkins. "It's the people."

"Quite right, Sergeant Jenkins. Quite right." Jason turned away from the wagon to join us, hesitated, and stopped at the stalls of his grays. He put out a hand and patted the neck of each. The horses nuzzled him, and examined his hand for treats. "No, no carrots today. Getting enough feed, old girls? Yes, they're taking good care of you, aren't they? You don't have to worry. I've arranged it with these nice Texans, and it'll be the pasture and barn for you both until the end of your days. And maybe for me, too."

He gave each horse a last gentle pat, pushed up the spectacles that had slid forward on his nose, and turned away from the animals. "Well, I'm ready to go."

The next morning we ate in the dining hall of the castle, all the members of my party dressed in common traveling clothes, not that we really needed to take up our disguise so soon. We collected the last items from our rooms and met in the courtyard of the castle. The horses were waiting together in one corner, attended by several stable hands. It reminded me of the night in which Chalmers and Metaxis had rescued me from the dungeon of the castle. The horses for our escape had waited in exactly the same spot.

How long ago it seemed.

President Chalmers, who'd arrived late yesterday after seeing Robert set sail, was the only official to see us off. He reviewed the security precautions taken while each of us checked our mounts and equipment for one last time. "A squadron of the Texan Fourteenth Cavalry left yesterday," he said, "and will check out anything suspicious along the route north. And before dawn a second squadron left to scout the road as well. Colonel Metaxis will accompany your party to the border as well, and make sure you have no interference from any Texan official. Still, guard yourself well, Arn. You, and all your companions. We can ill afford to lose you.''

And with that, we mounted, waved adios to Chalmers, and trotted across the courtyard, under the portcullis, through the tunnel, and out into the streets of Dallas, eight riders and fifteen horses. Metaxis led us through a side street to the familiar eastern gate, and then around the outer town wall to the north gate and onto the road that led from it. The road near town was made of assembled crete slabs, and thus was not an old road, but would lead to one within a few miles.

We had proceeded up the way no more than a few hundred yards when Murdock raised a hand and brought our little column to a halt where a dusty cart path led off to the west. He looked at me a moment, considering, before he spoke. He pointed in the direction of the cart path. ''Over there is the town cemetery.''

''Oh.''

''Beth made me promise to remind you.''

''Wasn't that nice of her,'' I said glumly.

''Come. I'll go up with you,'' said Murdock, but I put out a hand and he stopped. ''What's wrong, Arn?''

The rest of the party waited patiently, studying the trees and the grass and the flowers and the road, pretending not to know what our wizard and I were discussing.

A slight rise could be faintly seen behind a line of trees and brush, dotted with tombstones. I shuddered and looked away. ''I—I can't, Murdock. I can't. I can't go there.''

''Arn . . .''

I tried to swallow the wad of dry cotton that choked me. ''No, I won't. You can't make me.''

We sat staring at each other for a long minute before he shook his head. ''Well, perhaps it is too soon. All right, Arn. We'll go on.''

I avoiding looking at the cemetery until it was out of sight behind us and felt myself able to breathe easier.

"You'll have to do it someday," Murdock warned me as we rode away.

Someday. Perhaps someday I would. Perhaps someday I could.

If I survived.

5

On Our Way

The road divided a mile beyond the cemetery, one fork angling westward before swinging north on its way to Whitesboro, while the other fork, an old road, went directly northward to Denison. The party followed the left fork, a way paved with chunks of crete which soon merged into the smooth crete surface marking an old road.

The squadrons riding before us did their job well, for we encountered no delays or threats, though in truth there was little likelihood of assassins on the route. We made good time under clear skies on the ride, the horses fresh, the countryside flat, the road in decent repair, and easy crossings—if not always bridges—established at the watercourses.

We were able to put over forty miles behind us, and could have done more, but Murdock insisted we stop at villages where hay and grain were readily available for the horses. "We want to keep the horses as fit as possible while we're in Texan and Arkan," Murdock stated during one rest, Jenkins nodding agreement to the wisdom of that philosophy. After all, everything we did was based on the well-being of our animals. Thus, whenever possible we actually stayed just to the edge of the exposed crete, where grassy sod covered the hard surface below and made it easier on the hooves of our mounts.

"But also, it's Jason," the wizard explained, making sure the healer was nowhere near. "He doesn't complain, but I know the hours in the saddle must be hard on him. They're hard on me, and I'm ten years younger and used to riding."

We stopped at dusk in a small town and took rooms at the largest inn. The party ate in the common room but spent little time there afterwards, retreating to our rooms quickly and leaving Metaxis to answer any questions that might arise about the strange group of travelers staying at their inn. We turned in early, which Jason seemed to appreciate.

The next day Jason did better, with hardly a grimace through the day. The improvement was largely due to the padding he'd stuffed into the legs and seat of his pants that morning to ease the chafed spots. We were able to cover another forty miles, so that dusk brought us to the walled town of Whitesboro, where we noted the horses for two squadrons of Texan cavalry in corrals just outside of town.

We took rooms while Colonel Metaxis went to have a talk with the mayor of Whitesboro. The mayor talked to the town's chief inspector of the border guards, and the next morning the chief inspector waited to escort us across the bridge and into Arkan.

Colonel Metaxis stood beside the inspector at the approach to the bridge and solemnly shook hands with each of us. "I'll be going back to Dallas, now. It's been a pleasure being with you all." He came to me last, and clasped my arm while we shook hands. "Thank you, Prince Arn. For everything."

More thanks. And for once, I deserved such words. And Metaxis deserved them too. "Thank *you*, Colonel. For saving *me*."

He stepped back as the party mounted, saluting as we followed the chief inspector across the bridge. And then he mounted his own horse and passed through the gates into town. Strange. I hadn't ever thought I would count Texans among my friends.

The Texan inspector stopped at the northern end of the bridge when his Arkan counterpart stepped out in front of us. The Arkan wore an embossed metal plate hanging from a chain around his neck, his badge of office. Our inspector hailed the other. "Hello, John. How are you?"

"Well enough, Jose. Who do you have with you?" The Arkan inspector looked at us suspiciously. Some of General Murphy's scum had escaped across the river in the wake of his overthrow, and the Arkan inspector looked like he thought we might be more of the same, fleeing the wrath of the new government.

"A party of explorers. They're headed for the northern plains." The Texan inspector approached the Arkan, and the two conversed in low tones. The Arkan eyed us again, though with less of a frown on his face, and finally nodded. "All right, Jose, I'll take your word." He and Jose entered a little shack that stood next to the bridge approach, and a few minutes later they reappeared with an entry paper duly made out to our "traveling" names, with an official seal in the corner. The Arkan handed it to Murdock. "Well, you're free to travel north to Klahoma, Wichita, and beyond, which is how the entry certificate reads. But I wouldn't advise you linger anywhere or make any trouble."

"Any raiding by the plains tribes to worry about?" Jose asked the Arkan.

"We captured one from a scouting party yesterday," the Arkan responded. "His horse went lame, or we'd never have caught him. Those warrior ponies are fast. Some people worry the tribes might be planning raids. That'd be unusual for this time of year. But with the war last year, they might figure we've taken losses and are weaker. Or maybe one of their chiefs just has his dander up. We'll never know. Our cavalry regiment's been called up, and our companies are north at Klahoma."

The Texan Jose explained for our benefit. "The tribes usually cause trouble in the spring, when they're short of food after winter." It was not unheard of for the tribes to send raiding parties eastward along the banks of the Red River. There wasn't much worry about the raiders occupying a town, unless they caught the defenders by surprise. Then, it was loot, rape, and burn for a day or two before scuttling back west to their tribal grounds with prisoners and spoils.

"But no attacks reported so far," the Arkan added. "Anyway, we got this one in the stocks."

"I'll have to come take a look at him later," Jose responded.

"Do that," the Arkan responded with a smile, which faded away when he looked at my party. "And *you* travelers be careful."

The old familiar warning and threat.

Murdock thanked them, and we departed, leaving the Texan to handle the doubts of the Arkan inspector as we rode away. Well, I'd be suspicious of us, too. The small town of Cleburne sat upon the northern bank of the river among open fields, without palisade or walls, though the outer streets had great wooden gates at their ends that could be closed at night or in times of danger.

We followed a cart path around the town's edge to avoid attention, but instead of avoiding people, we ran into them. Fortunately, their interest lay elsewhere. More than a score of townsfolk were clustered around the fence rail of a small corral. We reined in behind the people to take a brief look at the central attraction. In the middle of the enclosure was the upper portion of a great stone, the rest long buried in the well-trampled earth. A heavy, metal ring was fixed to the stone, and to the ring were attached chains.

The chains shackled a slight man of whipcord hardness dressed in nothing except buckskin pants and wrist irons. He didn't look far different from any of us. He was of medium height, his blond hair long and greasy and tied in a ponytail, his beard short, his skin tanned and wrinkled by the sun—where it wasn't bloodied by scrapes and scratches, or swollen with bruises. Over skin and hair and beard and blood was a coating of dust that made even an onlooker feel dry and thirsty. He might have been any age between twenty and thirty.

So this was one of the vaunted warriors of the plains tribes.

Occasionally a child—or even a brave adult—would toss a clod of earth at the man. Sitting cross-legged next to the stone, the warrior remained immobile, ignoring the missiles even when they bounced off his chest or face. The man must have been hurting, and yet displayed not a hint of distress. He endured it all with stoic calm, though the hard cast to his mouth and the squint of his eyes left little doubt what he would do to his tormentors should any come within his reach. In spite of his shackles, the man was indeed daunting. He was formidable not for his physical stature, but because of the unremittingly watchful stolidity he exhibited in the midst of his enemies. I would not want to face him in an even fight.

Of course, I didn't want to face *anyone* in an even fight.

"Is that all they normally wear?" our beastman asked. Kren had learned to be clothes-conscious, given the repeated need to hide his real appearance over the last year. Our beastman wore a tightly woven long-sleeved shirt to cover his pelt. His cap was adorned with a cloth skirt around the back and sides that hung to his neck, and a dust flap went across his chin, mouth, and nose. We'd seen others wear such summer caps for riding in the dusty lanes, and it served Kren's purpose quite well. He was just another dusty traveler unless he removed his cap.

"No," Jason replied to Kren's question. "They wear cloth and buckskin according to the season, hats and shoes and coats as the weather demands—except they do like to uncover their chests in the summer."

"Like the Plains Indians of the Old World," Murdock ventured.

"I suppose," Jason agreed, a note of doubt creeping into his voice. "Certainly, the tribesmen share the nomadic lifestyle of the Plains Indians. The teepee they use is the direct descendant of the Indian teepee. And each warrior marks a personal victory over an enemy by adding an eagle feather to his hat. But that's about all. Everything else is different, based on what little I've read and seen.''

"Except that they like to burn their captives at the stake," Kendall added.

"Well, yes. There is that," Jason admitted.

There was motion amidst my comrades. Lorich slipped to the ground and undid the waterskin from his saddle.

Murdock watched him and shook his head. "Lorich."

The young wizard looked up and met Murdock's gaze. "Yes, Master?" The words were spoken with perfect respect. And complete faith.

The older magician paused, and sighed. "Nothing."

"Thank you, Master," Lorich said, and made his way through the watchers. He bent over, stepped between the rails of the corral fence, and straightened. At this, the townspeople fell silent.

The warrior rose from the ground in a single, smooth motion without even using his hands for balance. He stood silently, arms relaxed at his sides, all his attention focused upon the ungainly creature that had joined him in the corral.

Sergeant Jenkins looked back and forth between the two magicians. "Murdock, is this wise?"

The wizard never took his eyes from the apprentice. "Probably not."

Lorich stepped forward slowly. One pace, a second, and a third. He stopped an arm's length from the warrior, and held out the waterskin.

All was well and good if Lorich had judged the length of the chains correctly. If he had misjudged and placed himself near enough for attack, then he'd be in trouble. Yes, the warrior was unarmed, and we were but a few steps away to rush to his rescue. But any trained fighter knows a finger can put out an eye, and a knuckle can crush a larynx. No, it's not as easy as it sounds. Yet driven by despair and hatred, the strength could be found to deliver a fatal blow so quickly that Lorich would not have time to use his own powers.

The warrior extended his arms.

Sergeant Jenkins's hands tightened on the reins, while Murdock drew in a breath through clenched teeth.

The man took the waterskin, held it, then uncorked the end and drank deeply, never taking his eyes from the young wizard. Lorich remained in place, unmoving.

The way the man was drinking, I wondered whether one waterskin would be enough. At last he had his fill, plugged the skin, and handed it back, his eyes still locked on Lorich. The young wizard took a step backward, and then another. Safely out of reach, he turned and stepped through the fence rails, the townspeople parting before him. They might not have been happy with what Lorich had done, but they were not about to challenge one who had shown such courage. Not with a half dozen of his mounted friends right behind. He tied the waterskin back on his saddle and mounted.

Kren shook his head. "That was dangerous, lad. One more step, and he would have attacked you. Without hesitation, and without mercy."

Lorich smiled at him. "I know. I was very careful. The chains were too short for him to reach me. I wouldn't risk myself otherwise. I'm too valuable to lose."

Too valuable to lose. He made the statement with only a hint of pride.

Well, he was right, after all. And that didn't make it any easier watching him put himself at risk. We could have criticized our companion's act of mercy, but why bother?

It seemed young Wizard Lorich was growing up.

Murdock breathed easier now that Lorich was safely back with the party. "Who knows, maybe this tribesman is the son of a great chief. Maybe he'll escape and return to his tribe. Maybe we'll be captured, and he'll step forward to speak to his father of our kindness. And in gratitude, maybe the chief . . ."

Our silent stares brought Murdock to a stop.

He shrugged. "Then again, maybe not."

We left the corral, finished our circle around the town, and regained the old road heading north. The road was in good condition, a strip of crete varying from six to eight feet wide kept clear of all except a thin, inevitable layer of dust that the wind deposited upon random stretches. There were rough spots, certainly, where the land had twisted and the crete buckled, but those had been smoothed out and repaired. The benefits of following the easy course carved out by the ancients could not be denied. With the terrain varying from flat to gently rolling, we needed to take advantage of these easy miles, for harder ones lay ahead. Time was going by, and winter was coming. I kept remembering what Kendall had said about the mountain passes. Four feet of snow in October. Incredible.

Murdock's horse found its way next to mine, and for several minutes we marched together in silence.

I broke down first. "Well? What is it?"

Murdock scanned the horizon. "You know, Arn, this is going to be a long journey, and we all have to put up with each other over that time."

"A brilliant deduction," I complimented him.

"In spite of the easy comradeship you have with our companions, they still look to you for constancy and confidence. Especially Lorich. If your morale is low, it will lower theirs."

I mulled over his words. "Have I been bad?"

"You're normally serious. That's fine. And even a bit of melancholy is not unusual for you."

"Have I been melancholy?"

"No, not melancholy. Gloomy, depressed, ill-humored, irritable, and moody. But not melancholy."

"That bad. I hadn't realized."

"You're making progress. But for the sake of the others, hide your feelings. Don't try to be cheery and bright. Just hide the gloom and doom. After all, it's a beautiful day."

I looked around. The sun was shining, the sky was blue and clear. "Perhaps it is a beautiful day," I admitted. "But I can't see it, Murdock. I can't feel it. All I feel is—is sadness."

Murdock cast a glance my way. "Still, for the sake of the others. Try."

I worked at my cheeks. A smile formed. "Is that better, Wizard Murdock?"

"A smile on you isn't natural. But a tight-lipped smirk would do, I think."

We went on, and after a while I put a hand on his arm. "Murdock?"

"Yes, Arn?"

"Thank you for telling me. I'll try."

"That's all we can ask, my boy. That's all we can ask."

That evening we approached Ardmore, a village of three or four hundred people set between two gentle hills. Camped just outside the village proper was a squadron of Arkan cavalry. More than twoscore of men were standing at muster in precise ranks before a neat row of two-man tents, being reviewed by a young officer. Across from the tents, tether lines secured their mounts, saddles and bridles laid by. Clustered at either end of the row of tents, children watched the soldiers, fascinated by the entertainment. Two sentries paced the edges of the encampment, keeping an eye on the children but also watching us approach. We were different enough from the local inhabitants for them to inform their leaders, who came out to the road to meet us.

One Arkan was taller and well built, a handsome man wearing sergeant's stripes on his sleeves. The other, a shorter man with a large nose, wore the insignia of a major on his shoulders. Neither had put on a helmet. Murdock and I looked at each other. We recognized them. And soon it became eminently clear that they recognized us.

"Well, well, well," said the officer. "Now don't these fine travelers look familiar. And what might they be this time? Merchants, perhaps? Or pilgrims on their way to the cathedral at Klahoma?''

Murdock put on his best face. "Major Miller! Sergeant Nordstrom! How good to see you again." We had met the two on our journey through Arkan during the winter and spring, and Major Miller had allowed us to continue on our way, though he suspected who Murdock, at least, might be. Good men, but not to be trifled with.

Major Miller stepped close, and looked at each of us in turn, identifying us by our former traveling names. "Papa Thomas, of Thomas's Traveling Theater. Your son, James. Luke. Klod the beastman . . ." He stepped close to my horse, and peered at my face. My new beard did not yet hide the scar completely. He shook his head, as if in disbelief. "And here, we have Andrew."

"Good evening, Major Miller."

He looked beyond me. "Who are these last two travelers?"

Murdock answered the question. "They are Paul Kent, and his father, Jason Kent. Our new companions."

The major studied their faces for a moment, and then turned back to the wizard. "And your purpose in traveling through Arkan?"

"We have given up the theater for a season, and are commissioned by the new government of Texan to explore the northern wilds of the plains tribes for potential trade and knowledge."

"Ah. Thus the reason for the extra mounts and supplies. I see . . ." He thought a moment. "You'll be staying at the village inn? Good. We'll join you shortly for dinner. There is much to discuss."

Ardmore boasted a large, thick-walled inn, with attached stables enclosing a brick-paved courtyard. The edifice probably doubled as the village's refuge in times of danger. We had the horses stabled, took rooms, washed off the grit that coated us, and went down for evening meal. At our request, the innkeeper, a short-haired, dignified, no-nonsense man of moderate build, put us into an alcove that could be separated from the common room by sliding doors.

We ordered pitchers of beer and food, the beer arriving first, the food held until Miller and Nordstrom arrived. They joined us at the single, long table that filled the alcove. With mugs and full plates of stew before us, and the sliding doors closing us off from the chatter of the common room, a silence fell upon the table as we ate. Subtle glances were exchanged by members of our party, while Miller and Nordstrom stared openly at each of us in turn, as if we were subjects worthy of study. Who knows, perhaps we were.

After a moment, Miller dipped a chunk of bread into his gravy, but paused with it suspended above his plate. "I am only a simple king's constable in civilian life, and such matters as we are dealing with may be far beyond my norm. Still, some matters must be clarified. Perhaps now would be a good time for proper introductions. Don't you think so . . . Wizard Murdock?''

The wizard swallowed a mouthful of stew, unperturbed. "Perhaps it is time. Well, let me start on my left." And with that, Murdock introduced each of us in turn by our true names. Miller was impassive, while Nordstrom gave a slight nod as each name was spoken. Only when the Pacificans were introduced did the major raise an eyebrow. "Pacificans. Is there a clue to be found in their membership within your party? But let's leave that for the moment. Instead, could you share a bit more about your previous journey through Arkan and Texan?''

Our wizard shrugged. "I could—and will—but first would like to hear what you think the tale will be. How much have you figured out?''

Miller's answer was impressive. The major had been suspicious of us from the start, but had no specific facts he could cite. There were only inferences, and speculation based upon those inferences. Once he'd made the possible connection between Papa Thomas in Arkan and the wizard he had seen once from a distance in Kenesee, he knew our purpose must be significant, but possibly to the detriment of Arkan. He put out word to local sheriffs and officials along our route in Arkan to watch the theater troupe closely, but not to interfere with us except in extreme circumstances. He had guessed Kren might really be a beastman, and that I might actually be Prince Scar.

Major Miller had no particular love for Kenesee, nor any particular dislike, other than the galling humiliation of the disaster endured as General John Black defeated and checkmated their army, segment by segment. The generous surrender terms we'd offered had prevented the humiliation from turning into bitter hatred. But it was only as our theater troupe neared the southern border of Arkan that Miller began to realize our purpose had to do with Texan, and not with Arkan. Given the low esteem he and many Arkans had for the Texan regime of General Jack Murphy, he was not displeased with that realization. He would be rid of us, and he could concentrate again on the bandits whose depredations he had prevented, even if they had so far eluded him.

The addition of women to the troupe had been a change that he had to check out, and he had caught up with us only as we'd readied ourselves to enter Texan at the Arkan town of Monterey on the Red River. He interrupted his narrative for a question. "By the way, Sergeant Jenkins, how is Beth?"

Jenkins squinted at the inquiry, but kept his voice civil. "She's fine, sir. She should soon be back in Kenesee, if all goes well."

Miller nodded. "Good. I'm glad to hear that. I was impressed by her demeanor. She's quite a woman."

Jenkins met the man's eye, and nodded. "Thank you for the compliment, sir. I think so, too. Are you married?"

Miller looked at his plate. "I am," he admitted in a reluctant tone, and there was no further need to inquire about his marital happiness. He looked up. "Prince Arn, I have been remiss in not extending my sympathy and condolences for your loss. I have heard the tale. Angela was a woman to be proud of.''

I took a gulp of beer. "Yes . . . Yes, she was.''

He considered me a moment, and then looked around. "That, I'm afraid, is the extent of my knowledge. Now the tale is for you to tell. We did hear that Prince Arn took on six guardos, killing four and driving the other two off.''

"That he did,'' Jenkins confirmed. "Saw it myself. He's always doing that kind of thing, and I've got to watch him every moment, or he goes off trying to defeat the enemy single-handed.''

Jenkins was exaggerating. I'd only killed two guardos. Two, I wounded.

Murdock related to the two Arkans the significant events during our journey through Texan and leading up to the Gathering of the Great Landholders, and then the tense weeks following which culminated in the Battle of Tyler, the capture of General Murphy, and the taking of Dallas and Castle Corral.

"And you've been busy since,'' Nordstrom offered in his gravelly voice, his first comment of the evening. "Those poor wretches. Is slavery really going to be abolished?''

"Yes,'' Kren answered. "Really and truly.''

"And so, now we know everything,'' Miller stated with an astute smile.

Murdock smiled right back. "Yes. Everything.''

Well, quite a lot, at least.

"So. A theater troupe. Who would have thought it? It was a grave risk, and yet it worked.'' Miller leaned back in his chair. "Then we may move on to the present, and explore what your current journey involves.''

We told him, leaving out some details such as our concerns about Pacifican assassins. We talked more about the possibilities of confederation, bits of strategy in the War Against the Alliance, and Kren asked about the vicious bandit gang that Miller and his men had been pursuing when last we were in Arkan. Sergeant Nordstrom answered that question with a great smile. "We kept them pressed, so they decided to move inland to continue their banditry. We followed. Major Miller figured out where they'd most likely be, and there they were. Caught them with the evidence. Those that surrendered we hauled back to Tulsa. They had their trial, all fair and proper. And then they hung, all fair and proper."

That was nice to hear.

Miller asked about our travel plans, and had a quick response to our itinerary. "I'll bring the squadron and we'll escort you to Wichita. There have been reports of war bands from the plains tribes on the border. If so, they'll need to be protected from you."

We caught his joke, and laughed accordingly.

"And," he continued with an ironic grin that was growing familiar, "it might be appropriate to keep an eye on you while you are in Arkan. Who knows what government you might decide to bring down next."

The morning dawned dry and clear, with every promise of being yet another hot day. We started an hour after sunrise, my party tucked into the middle of the Arkan column. It was nice to have a full squadron escorting us north. After all, how many war bands were greater than our numbers?

We watched some ruins to the northeast get steadily larger as we marched, several shards of ancient buildings thrusting out of the prairie. None was more than forty or fifty feet high, and all were surrounded by hillocks—mounds of debris now covered with prairie grass. The column stopped for lunch beside a small streambed that still had a goodly trickle of water running down its center. We ate our bread and cheese, and had a chance to chat with Miller and Nordstrom's men. We recognized only half of the men, the detachment that had been with them the previous winter. Now, the full squadron was present, under the command of a bright and eager young lieutenant.

Those men that we knew introduced us to their comrades, and were quick to fill us in with the gritty details of their capture of the bandits, as well as many complaints about the length of time they'd been on active duty. "Wouldn't you know it," said one, "just when we wrap up the bandit problem and expect to go home, they tell us to patrol the roads out west in case the tribes attack. I don't think they'll attack. Do you?" he asked Murdock.

The wizard was staring off at the western horizon, and beckoned to Major Miller. "Major, are there any Arkan squadrons west of us?"

Miller looked at the horizon. "Shouldn't be. That's why we're here. The cavalry regiments have been mobilized and sent north to Wichita—where we heard the tribes were massing. Didn't have any problems down this way."

Murdock stroked the new whiskers on his chin, then pointed to the northwest. "That situation may be changing. There's something out there. But my eyes aren't what they used to be. See anything?"

We all squinted at the horizon, so flat that it seemed to go on forever. The lieutenant had sharp eyes. He spotted a light wisp of dust rising. Once pointed out, I saw it too.

"How many?" I asked.

Murdock closed his eyes for a moment. "Fifty? No, more than that. A hundred or more is more accurate."

Major Miller nodded. "From the cloud, I'd say the latter number is more likely. Lieutenant, get your men mounted."

We took to our horses, but did not move, instead watching the cloudy wisp growing larger. "They're coming our way," I observed. "Bad luck."

"Bad luck nothing," Miller corrected. "They saw our dust before we stopped to eat. Well, it won't do any good just waiting."

We started out at a trot, and held to that pace only a short time before going to a canter. The cloud was getting larger and larger. I looked behind us, and saw our own dust billow up, rising upon the hot air. No doubt about it now. They knew we were here. I spurred up next to Miller and asked what he planned.

"They're too many for us out in the open," the major stated loudly over the clatter of our hooves. "Light cavalry to our medium. If we charge with lances, they fall back, pepper us with bow fire, and send out flankers. If we hold, they skirmish us to death with horse bows. We've got to get into cover of some kind."

I looked around. Where in this open prairie could there possibly be—.

"The ruins?"

"Prince Arn, you are much smarter than your companions seem to believe."

Ahead the old road divided, a spur of paved surface curving off to the east, toward the ruins. A hundred yards more and we would be upon it. As far to the west, scores of mounted figures topped a rise in an irregular mass, and descended towards us with a whoop of delight.

Tricky air currents. They'd been nearer than we'd thought. And the race for the ruins was on.

6

Struggle at the Ruins

The faces of the charging warriors were a mixture of anticipation and bloodlust, which they expressed with yells as they waved their weapons over their heads. Many carried lances, while others brandished hand axes or saberlike blades, all of them complementing their weapon with a light shield. A quarter of the tribesmen wielded bows as their main weapon, and had full quivers across their backs.

Half the warriors were bare chested, while the other half wore a colorful variety of shirts or vests. They all had wide-brimmed hats, a number of which bounced around on their backs, each securely attached by a long rawhide string around the neck. Sewn into the headbands of many hats were an eagle feather or two, while a few hats boasted a goodly cluster of feathers.

Not that I noticed all this wonderful detail at the time. I was too busy spurring my horse forward and trying to hide my terror. This ancient road to nowhere was not maintained for use as the main route was, but still could be made out by the even ribbon of tall grass that marked its course. There were places where the grass seemed taller or shorter, and that indicated danger. Our column lost its coherence as individual riders swerved left or right around such spots. The taller grass might hide a jagged corner of crete thrust up from the roadway. Shorter grass bespoke a hole carved into the broken pavement by erosion. Bad as the road was, to head off it into the fields and hillocks on either side would have been even more dangerous. Ruins and a galloping horse were sure ingredients for disaster. So it was with concern that I saw Miller lead us off the road and through the grass.

Where was this idiot taking us now?

The tribesmen apparently didn't like this area any better than I did, for their yells died out as they concentrated on their course through the fields. Sergeant Jenkins spurred forward beside my mount, waving and shouting, "Follow me!" If the good sergeant saw his duty as leading the way for me through the dangerous terrain, who was I to argue? Besides, he was just doing his job, no matter how heroically. Dutifully, I kept my mount a horse length behind the sergeant's.

Seeing us turn, a number of the bolder warriors had cut across the grass rather than follow our path, and they were now almost parallel to us as we galloped on. These foolish—or courageous, if you will—men let their ponies find the safe way while they let fly with arrows at our group. Most of the arrows passed over or between men and horse, but an Arkan took one in the side, while a horse had one stuck in his hindquarters. Wounded man and wounded horse each continued flight as if unscathed, though blood was flowing in both cases. Another man was not so lucky. Hit in the neck, he slid from his horse and bounced along the ground, other riders swerving to avoid his body. But the casualties were not just on our side. One warrior galloping along to our left swerved near, his spear tip coming uncomfortably close. Suddenly the bold warrior disappeared into the ground, horse and all. There was a yell of surprise and despair, abruptly cut off as the tribesman met his fate in an ancient cellar of the Old World.

Still, the encounter was not going well at all.

Though low mounds surrounded us, the tallest ruins of the city were still several miles off. Would we have to ride all the way there to find safety? If so, most of us were not going to make it. Miller led us around several grassed hillocks that channeled the warriors behind us, then through an eight-foot-wide gap between two steep mounds. We entered a flat cul-de-sac perhaps thirty meters in diameter. Surrounding the cul-de-sac was a circle of mounds, hillocks, eight or nine feet high that formed a quite respectable defensive position, given the circumstances. Apparently Miller had investigated the ruins earlier, and remembered the value of this spot for defensive action. The only weakness to the bastion was the gap we had ridden through.

The warriors would soon be riding through that gap.

Major Miller shouted instructions to the lieutenant and Sergeant Nordstrom. The air rang with commands as men dismounted and detachments scrambled to take positions upon the hillocks. There were only moments left before the tribesmen would be upon us. Two detachments deployed around three sides of the cul-de-sac. Two more detachments took position on the mounds, one to either side of the gap. The last detachment formed two ranks of four in the gap, using their lances as infantry spears, though their shields were too small to actually form a shield wall.

With a "Stay down here, sir," Jenkins grabbed his bow and quiver, leaped off his horse, and scrambled up the mound to the left side of the gap. Almost as quickly, Kren had his own bow and quiver and clambered to a position on the right of the gap. Lorich followed soon after, taking a position beside Jenkins. The sergeant yelped when he saw Lorich standing there, erect. He pulled the young wizard into a crouch that took advantage of the cover provided by the slope of the mound.

"Shouldn't Lorich be staying down here with us?" I asked Murdock.

He had unsheathed his sword and was preparing to follow the others onto the mounds. "Perhaps. Then again, he has to see to be effective, with bow *or* magic. I'll go up to watch him. Remain here, Arn. I can't guard you both against arrows."

Only Kendall, Jason, and I were still on horseback. The rest of the mounts were behind us, nostrils flaring as they neighed and snorted and nervously pranced about the cul-de-sac with nowhere to go. From beyond the hillocks we could hear the whoops of the warriors and the sounds of hooves as they came on.

"The gap?" Kendall asked his father.

Jason glanced all around. "The gap," he concurred, and both dismounted. They took station near Major Miller behind the double line of Arkans, Jason with his sword in one hand. Kendall's sword was still in its scabbard, his lone hand tucked into his pocket as if he were going for a Sunday stroll.

All this had taken but a few seconds, and I was the last man still on horseback. In reserve, so to speak. There was little I could do from horseback, and in spite of Murdock's admonition, I knew where I should be. Our party had the only archery support among our force. And I had one of the bows. We needed bow fire too badly for me to hang back.

I knew I should have left that weapon behind in Dallas.

Grumbling to myself, I took the bow and quiver and made my way up to crouch near the beastman Kren. He grinned when he saw me. "Just in time, Arn. Here they come."

And true enough, they were almost upon us. The warriors had followed hard after us and decided—correctly, given their numbers—that a direct assault might be the best tactic. Or perhaps there was no real military decision involved, other than a warrior's desire to close with an enemy. They were no more than twenty-five yards off as I crested the mound and started firing into the oncoming mass of horses and men. One horse to the side went down, and a man desperately clung to his mount with an arrow in his ribs. The rest came on.

"Steady!" said Miller. The Arkans in the gap—frightened as any sane men on foot would be facing charging horses—took heart at his calm firmness and set the butts of their lances firmly in the earth. The ponies had better things to do than spit themselves on the fence of spearpoints. The front horses slid to a halt, forcing those behind to do the same, though there was a terrible jumble of unhappy riders. Those following spread out, some firing arrows from the saddle, some riding left or right to seek other ways into the cul-de-sac on horseback, some with hand weapons dismounting and coming forward to challenge our possession of the gap and the hillocks to either side.

The tribesmen struggled up the sides of the hillocks, trying to fend off with their small shields the jabbing spearpoints aimed by the men of our thin line. This made it hard for the archers on horseback to fire, since fellow warriors were climbing into their line of fire. And that was all to the good, for against our four bows the plains tribe had at least thirty.

Ax in hand, a young warrior with an unadorned hat crabbed up the side of the hillock, angling directly for me, a greedy look on his face as he anticipated earning his first feather of honor. I aimed at him. Realizing at the last moment that I might do unto him before he could do unto me, he brought up his shield just in time. The arrow penetrated the shield, the point continuing into and through his upper arm. With an "Aaiiieee" of pain and surprise, the enlightened warrior turned and bounded down the hillock, anxious to find a safer place to examine the new addition to his arm.

The feather must not have been so important after all.

I would have given him another arrow in the back, but several horse archers fired at me, and I ducked low behind the top of the hillock as the arrows whizzed through the air where I had recently been. Pretty good shooting, especially from horseback. I fired back at one archer and missed, though his pony reared up with an arrow in its hindquarter. I never was a very good shot.

While I was using up arrows, a good score of warriors were wending a way through their jumble of horses and throwing themselves at the Arkans in the gap. Some of the warriors bravely dived under the spearpoints, rolling on the ground till they reached sword range. The gap became a tangle of struggling bodies and yelling men, axes swung with abandon, spears jabbing fiercely, swords cutting and thrusting with passion. The air was filled with *clangs* and *thunks* and grunts and yells and screams. It all added up to the absolutely terrifying reality of battle—a reality of which I had far too much acquaintance.

Miller threw himself into the melee. Kendall and Jason did not hang back either. The two stepped into the mass of struggling men. In a matter of seconds a half dozen plains warriors went down in the gap and the rest broke back, retreating to their ponies and leading the mounts away.

Seeing their fellows falling back, the warriors on the hillocks gave way too and retreated to a safe distance, where their archers began to snipe at us with arrows. We took covered positions and waited, watching while their force fanned out around us, surrounding the cul-de-sac.

The attack had been poorly coordinated. If all the warriors had dismounted and simply rushed us in one mass, they probably would have carried the hillocks and then overwhelmed the rest of us. But such was not their way. Cavalry maneuver on the open plains was their strength. Close combat in rough terrain against trained soldiers went against their experience. Thank goodness.

We took advantage of the respite to count casualties and adjust our own deployment. Several Arkans went among the horses, calming them and moving them back from the gap and the danger of a stray arrow. Other men tended the wounded. The rest improved their positions and crouched behind any cover they could find. My comrades were all alive and well, I saw with relief.

Kren was beaming. "Not quite the Rift Gates, but good for a bit of entertainment."

I didn't bother replying.

Murdock stared at me from the next hillock, and even from that distance I could see the sweat beading his brow. "Stay low, Arn," he called out.

"Guess I didn't need your help this time," I called

back with bravura based largely upon relief, and ignoring the gurgling in my stomach.

Murdock pointed at my feet. On the ground nearby was an arrow of the tribes. So Murdock had been watching over me as well as Lorich, and had turned an arrow that I'd never seen coming. I mouthed a silent thank-you to the wizard.

Major Miller was not finished with strengthening our position. "I want that gap blocked," he told Sergeant Nordstrom. Bodies were moved, and soon a dozen men were pulling pieces of crete from the hillocks and piling them in the gap until a three-foot-high barrier blocked access to the cul-de-sac. A half dozen men with spears could crouch behind the barrier, secure from archery fire, and turn back any mounted attack. It would help against warriors on foot, as well. Only when the gap was secure did Major Miller seem satisfied with our situation.

The bodies of three or four warriors were left on the hillocks, and from the gap another seven warriors had been dragged inside the cul-de-sac. The tribe's wounded had fled or been carried away by their friends when they retreated. Three of the Arkans were dead, including the eager—but unlucky—lieutenant. Another half dozen were wounded. It had not been any major affair, as combat goes. In the scheme of things, it barely ranked as a battle at all; more a skirmish. Yet the lieutenant was just as dead and the Arkan soldiers were just as dead, and the tribesmen were just as dead. For these men, it had been a great struggle, a supreme effort—and a supreme sacrifice.

And great battle or small skirmish, I had escaped death once again.

Kendall was talking to Major Miller and pointing at several of the warrior bodies in the gap. "Four of them are not dead. You'll have to tie them. They'll be coming around in a few minutes." Miller gave those indicated a quick look, then beckoned for Kendall and Jason to follow him away from the others. Curious, I crept down the hillock and joined them. Murdock added his presence within a moment.

Miller arched an eyebrow at Murdock and me, then turned his attention back to the Pacificans. "You say those four are unconscious, but will be awake within the hour."

Jason nodded. "That's right. You'll need to tie them."

Miller considered the words, tapped his chin thoughtfully, and gave the order. Sergeant Nordstrom listened dutifully, gave a shrug, and said, "Yes, sir." The unconscious captives were bound hand and foot. One had the idea that if the respected Major Miller had not issued the order, the sergeant would have had other things done with the warriors left alive.

Miller sheathed his sword and crossed his arms. "We're not used to taking tribesmen prisoners—unless we need entertainment. But my concern now is that they don't have a mark on them," he stated to the Pacificans.

Jason and Kendall exchanged glances.

Miller grew stern. "I want to know how you did that. How did a one-armed diplomat and an old healer strike down four plains warriors in as many seconds? Hmmm? What were you holding in your hands? Come, I'll keep the knowledge to myself, but I want to know. I insist on knowing."

An Arkan detachment leader approached. "Major Miller, Private Delarose has found something. Maybe you'd better take a look, sir."

Miller nodded. "I'll be there in a moment, Corporal. Let Sergeant Nordstrom know."

The Arkan left in search of Nordstrom.

Jason gave his son one more glance, and took a small slab of wood from his pocket. No, it wasn't just a slab, whatever it was, though it was certainly made of wood. It was only a few inches long and shaped almost like a bar of soap. Jason held it in his open palm. "Major Miller, this is a dart gun, as we call it. It fires tiny hollow darts containing a drug which will quickly knock out a man.''

Murdock's face lit up. "So that's how you did it. John Black always wondered how you took out those two bandits when they attacked your wagon on the way to the Beastwood. He couldn't find any wounds on the bandits.''

Jason turned the gun over. "It's a simple weapon, really. Holds two darts with a powerful spring behind each. These two buttons are the triggers. The drug inside the dart is a nerve agent—that is, it works on the nervous system. Not much good beyond ten feet or so, but it's handy for rendering dangerous situations manageable without fatal consequences."

I could think of occasions in which a dart gun might be used for more lethal purposes.

Miller put out his hand, and Jason reluctantly gave it to him. "It doesn't violate the Codes," the major stated thoughtfully.

"No, it doesn't," Jason agreed, "though I doubt any of the nations could match the tensile quality of the metal for the spring.''

"And the nerve agent?" I asked, trying to remember all the subparagraphs that made up the Codes of Progress.

"Such things aren't covered by the Codes," Miller answered for the Pacificans. "But I know of no substance available to the six nations which could have such an immediate effect upon a man."

"There is none—within the six nations," Jason confirmed, pushing his spectacles back up his nose. It was his turn to put out his hand, and Miller reluctantly handed back the dart gun.

The Arkan gave his familiar sardonic grin. "Well, it certainly made a difference this time. I'm afraid their charge might have broken through the gap if you hadn't helped out. My thanks for your courage and effectiveness."

"My father really was quite formidable in his day."
Kendall grinned.

"In his day?" Miller asked, appraising the elder Pacifican. "I think his day is not yet past."

"You know," said Jason, "I like this Arkan."

Sergeant Nordstrom joined us, his raspy voice loud
over the horses. "Major, you may want to take a look
at what Private Delarose found."

"What are we talking about here? Just what did Delarose find?"

"A cave or tunnel in the ruins. Looks like it goes
down a ways, sir." Nordstrom led Miller around the
horses and across the cul-de-sac, with the rest of us trailing along behind in idle curiosity. There wasn't much
else to do while waiting for the plains tribes to attack
again, though clustering so much of the leadership together might not have been the wisest move. Then again,
as a mobile reserve, one part of the cul-de-sac was as
good as another until we knew which way they'd attack
from.

Murdock walked next to the elder Pacifican. "Well,
Jason, what else do you have in your saddlebags to
amaze us? A radio, perhaps?"

Jason glanced at the wizard slyly. "Of course not.
They're much too bulky. I had one in my wagon, but it
failed just after I sent a message that we'd be journeying
to Pacifica—assuming the weak signal it could produce
actually was received."

"Oh." Murdock had little else to say.

And I could not figure out whether Jason was joking
or not.

Nordstrom arrived at a hillock just opposite the gap
in the cul-de-sac. An Arkan private saluted. "Delarose
found it, sir," Nordstrom said, gesturing at the side of
the hillock.

"It shifted under me," Delarose explained. "I was
changing position, and the ground just moved and
opened up that hole."

In the side of the mound a large, grass-covered slab

of crete had slid down under the Arkan's weight, opening a triangular hole less than a yard on a side. The
afternoon sun lit a crete wall and floor inside the hole,
but beyond the light dimmed.

"I've looked in," Nordstrom said. "Couldn't see
much, though it looks like maybe there are crete steps
leading down. Tossed in a few stones, but didn't seem
to disturb anything. Guess we don't have to worry about
rattlesnakes."

Wizard Lorich came limping up to us excitedly, bow
in hand. "I heard there's a cave. Can we explore it?"

Miller passed an order to Nordstrom. The sergeant
bellowed out a question. "Troop leaders. Report on your
fronts. Any enemy activity?" The five troop leaders
scanned their fronts, and yelled back. The tribesmen
seemed to have dismounted and gone to ground. Other
than the occasional arrow, there was no immediate
threat.

Miller made up his mind. "All right, there might be
some value in finding out where this thing leads. But
I'll only allow three men at a time to go in. You, Jason.
And Wizard Lorich, since he's so anxious. And who
else?"

Lorich looked at me expectantly. "Don't you want to
go too, Prince Arn?"

Miller had heard the remark. "All right, Prince Arn,
since he wants to go."

I hadn't said I wanted to go.

Murdock brought a small oil lamp he had in his supplies and lowered the light through the entrance to the
cave to the length of his arm. "Yes, there are steps leading down, starting just a few feet below the entrance.
And this slab seems stable now. It should be all right.
So, who wants to go first?"

"I'll go, Master," Lorich volunteered.

Murdock ignored him. "I'll hold the lamp until you
get your footing, Arn."

I studied the entrance a moment, braced my hands,
and lowered my legs into the gloom. Yes, there was

footing about four feet down, so that my head and shoulders were still out in the open. Murdock handed me the lamp.

"Are you sure it's full?" I asked the wizard.

He gave me a look. "No. I emptied it out to make sure you'd be lost forever."

"Just asking."

I crouched down, sword in one hand and lamp in the other, waiting for my eyes to adjust to the dim light of the flame I held. There were rusted metal handrails along each wall, so I had to be at the top of a stairway. Each step had a layer of rubble and dust over it, though the cracked walls showed water stains from past rains. There was a musty smell. The cave had been closed, but not sealed from the elements. The way was about four feet wide, and headroom increased with each step downward. I carefully tested my weight on each step as I descended. There was a small landing, and the steps turned back and continued down. I waited at the landing. Lorich came through the opening, his bow exchanged for a sword. And last came Jason, lowering himself slowly through, then bending over with a grunt.

I waited till their eyes adjusted and they came forward before I continued down the steps.

"See anything, Arn?" Jason asked from just behind me.

"It's another landing. There's a rusted metal door, half-open. Looks like the quake popped off its bottom hinge. Don't know what's on the other side of the door." I held the lamp before me, made sure I would be safe, and only then stepped through. It was a room of some sort, a large room with a crete floor. The wall extended straight left and right beyond the circle of light provided by the lamp. The scattered droppings of mice and other small creatures crunched beneath my boots.

Lorich and Jason came up beside me, the young wizard's face reflecting his awe and enjoyment of our exploration. Jason was more thoughtful. "This was an underground level in the Old World. Air still seems

good. Must be cracks to the surface somewhere. Let's
go on a bit more.''

We moved slowly forward, Jason at my right shoulder
and Lorich at my left, scanning up, down, and to both
sides with each step. We passed what looked like a crete
support column. And then another. I looked back. The
faintest glow of light showed where the doorway might
be, and the opening to the surface above it. That was
reassuring. Even if the lamp went out, we might be able
to find our way back.

At last, Jason pointed. ''That's what I've been expecting.''

Lorich drew in a breath. ''I've never seen anything
like it.''

Before us were lined up several rows of rusted shapes.
I recognized them. Horseless wagons—or automobiles,
as the ancients called them.

Jason poked at one with a sword. The point went
through the metal, which crumbled further as he twisted
the blade. ''We're in a place they used to keep their
automobiles. I believe it was called a parking garage.
Come, let's go on a bit more, though I don't think we'll
find anything helpful to our situation.''

We continued on past the automobiles and approached
another wall with a large crack running down it. Lorich
spotted them first, spread out beneath the wall. Skeletons. Perhaps a score, some fairly complete, others
spread across the floor as animals had left them. The
intact skeletons—those where the separate bones were
all in one place—had the ragged remains of clothing still
wrapped around them.

Lorich shook his head and said a prayer. ''What happened to them?''

Jason grunted. ''A common enough fate. When the
Cataclysm hit, most buildings collapsed. Some underground levels remained fairly intact, but the exits were
blocked with rubble. Those inside were trapped.''

Lorich looked around, trying to imagine the horror of
that time. ''But these were Ancients. With all their won-

derful devices—couldn't they have tunneled out?''

"How?" Jason asked. "What would they use to dig? And we're not talking about digging through soft earth. The walls are twenty inches of solid crete. And there are tons of rubble blocking the entrances, massive blocks of crete. Even the slab that had covered the opening we came through must weigh close to a ton. The tragedy is that they might have moved that slab with a combined effort, had they known it was the only thing between them and salvation. They must have assumed there was a mound of rubble on top of it. So instead, they clustered here, near this crack in the wall. They probably felt fresh air coming in from above, and stayed close, and waited for someone to rescue them. Until their food and water gave out.''

"So their machines couldn't save them.''

"No," Jason said. "Their machines couldn't save them. They should have kept seeking an exit. They should have depended on their own strength and courage and intelligence. Instead they waited for rescue, but there was no one to rescue them.''

Lorich took a step forward, walking among the skeletons. "It's all so sad. They had so much. And then they died. I—what's this?'' He put out thumb and forefinger to lift a rusted piece of metal into the air. "Is this a weapon?''

Even I knew the answer to that one. "Yes, Lorich. An ancient powder weapon. A handgun, or pistol.''

He stirred the rags, so that they disintegrated into dust. "There's another! And another.'' He wandered among the skeletons, counting weapons, and when he had a total, he was puzzled. "Eight. Eight handguns for twenty people. Why did they carry these, Jason? This was one of their cities. What did people fear in their own cities?''

What did they fear? I knew the answer again. "Lorich, they feared each other.''

He tried to decide whether I was joking or not.

Jason poked his sword through the scraps of dry leather and cloth that were all that remained on one skeleton, revealing coins and various pieces of crumbling plastic. "Sad to say, Lorich, but Arn speaks the truth. Amid all the splendor of their cities, crime and poverty and hatred were common. Barbarians with weapons were loose within their society. In response, the common citizens armed themselves."

Lorich shook his head in disbelief and sadness. "No wonder God struck them down with a quake." And then he grew thoughtful. "Can we make use of these weapons against the tribesmen?"

Jason coughed. "Well, the circumstances of our tactical situation do provide a temptation, I must admit. However, other factors prevent the issue from arising. The guns are not in operable condition, and even if they were, the ammunition would not work. There's no hope to be found down here."

We continued our exploration of the underground, but the one large chamber was all that we could reach. Other potential exits and passageways were blocked by rubble. We finished our circuit of the chamber, climbed the stairs, and emerged from the "cave" into the afternoon light.

It was good to be above ground again.

Our beastman winked at us as he helped Lorich emerge from the hole. "Don't suppose you found some ancient weapon to dispatch the enemy? Or maybe a secret passage that will allow a surprise sally upon the rear of the tribesmen? That's what happens in all the adventure tales."

"No, Major Kren," Lorich answered. "Nothing like that. It was very sad. There were bones of people trapped during the Cataclysm. We did find some old guns, but they were all rusted. And it's just a big underground room that's sealed off. Nowhere else to go."

"That's how it is in life," said Kren. "Never an easy way out of a mess."

Lorich responded seriously to the beastman's jest. "Yes, sir. We'll just have to use our own strength and courage and intelligence."

The young wizard retrieved his bow and quiver while Murdock and Kren watched him with appraising eyes. "You know," said Murdock, "I think our Mr. Lorich is, at long last, learning wisdom."

"You may be right," Kren agreed. He was silent a moment. "Still, wouldn't it have been something if they *had* found a secret passage?"

7

The Vigilant

Except for the occasional arrow that was launched at one or another of the Arkans guarding us on the hillocks, the afternoon passed into evening without incident. Apparently, the tribesmen hesitated over the cost of another direct assault—especially since they had already lost a tenth of their number in the first attempt. We did everything to discourage them. An Arkan detachment watched each quadrant of the compass, while a fifth detachment and my party remained as reserves in the center of the cul-de-sac.

The afternoon faded into evening, and though we could have managed a small fire with the brush available, we avoided that luxury. There was no moon, and we wanted to preserve our night vision. The tribesmen seemed to have the same idea, for we saw no glow of campfires anywhere.

The total darkness did provide its own problems and potentials. Such blackness made an organized attack difficult. But it was the ideal condition for individual warriors or small parties to infiltrate our position and take us out one by one. To avoid such calamity, the Arkans were organized into teams of two atop the mounds surrounding us, and their sergeants checked on each team every quarter hour. Other than that, the men on the perimeter of the cul-de-sac remained silent, listening for sound to betray the movement of any warrior sneaking up upon them.

Of particular value were the talents of our wizards.

Accompanying the sergeants each quarter hour, Murdock and Lorich took opposite sides of the cul-de-sac and in the blackness slowly felt their way along the top of the mounds, using their skills to detect the proximity of warriors.

Major Miller was pleased at this addition to his security arrangements. "Thank you for reminding me of your magical talent. I had forgotten, and it could be critical tonight."

After the two wizards came back from the first such round of the perimeter, my party sat cross-legged, in a tight circle, on the ground. Heads close together, we munched on bread and conversed in whispers.

The horses had all been hobbled and tethered in lines, and the hindquarters of one line were only a few yards from where we sat. The horses had almost no forage, and of water they would get none. If there'd been light, they'd have been turning accusing eyes on us as we took miserly sips from our waterskins. No one could tell how long we'd be stuck here, and the water might have to last for days.

I could hear Kren, only a dark form, chewing his bread and swallowing dryly. "Will we be staying at any more inns on this adventure?" he asked in a quiet voice that barely carried to the members of the party around him.

"Why?" Murdock responded, his voice as faint as the beastman's. "Missing a soft bed?"

"It's not the bed, so much," Kren answered. "It's the food. I thought we'd have opportunities to pack some hot meals away before starting across the plains. Turns out the adventuring started sooner than I expected."

"Sooner than anyone expected," Paul Kendall said.

The beastman took a sip of water. "If we can't even get through civilized Arkan without being attacked by tribesmen, what's it going to be like when we get out on the plains?"

"Easier, perhaps?" Murdock ventured.

Kendall shifted his legs. "Our good wizard may be

right. The plains tribes perceive the six nations as vulnerable to raiding owing to war casualties. If this is a major assault upon Arkan, a goodly portion of the plains warriors must be in or near Arkan. If we can get around them, they'll be behind us as we head west.''

"How many warriors are there?'' Lorich asked.

Jason snorted. "From all the plains tribes? That's a good question. More each generation—just like in the six nations—but less than the number of men Arkan has.''

"Arkan took relatively few casualties during the war,'' Kren stated. "The tribes would be better advised to attack the Texans.''

"The plains tribes have many admirable qualities,'' Kendall responded. "But strategic flexibility is not one of them.''

"Admirable qualities?'' the beastman asked.

"Their culture is a unique mixture of Old World influence and the reality of the plains. They are stoic, fiercely loyal, admire courage, and will not break their word. The tribes live a hard nomadic life, dependent upon game and gathering.''

"That's it?'' Kren responded. "That's their great culture?''

Kendall. "There's a bit more to it than just that.''

Kren. "But their lofty culture doesn't prevent them from raiding. Nor, I've heard, from burning prisoners at the stake.''

Kendall. "It's their way of making war.''

Jenkins spoke up. "I don't like any culture that includes roasting me to death as one of its rituals.''

"Do they obey the Codes?'' Lorich asked.

"No, not formally, at least,'' said Jason. "But the nomadic life is not conducive to developing mechanical technology. And until now, their population has been too small to allow the specialization required to reach even the technology level of the six nations.''

"Until now?'' I ventured, curious.

We could hear Lorich yawn.

Jason. "Like the six nations, the plains tribes and the mountain clans have been given medical advice and medicines. The result has been an increase in their population."

Lorich. "There are *mountain* tribes too?"

"Clans," replied Jason. "And they're no longer nomadic."

It was a long night. Three times our wizards detected the presence of tribesmen nearing our perimeter, and each time they informed the sergeants, who sang out instructions to their men to watch out, that the enemy was coming their way. Invariably, the warriors would fade away into the night when they heard this warning, and probably wondered how the devilish Arkans could see them in the dark. And a half dozen times one Arkan or another thought he'd heard something, and would shout out the alarm. I suspect most of the time the Arkan reports were just the result of raw nerves. The tribesmen could move with uncanny stealth. Regardless of the cause of alarm, those of us in reserve would rush to the threatened side of the cul-de-sac as we heard the alert called out for one reason or another.

Just at dawn, as the faintest light became available to see by, Murdock reported that the tribesmen were assembling opposite the gap. We prepared for their mass charge until the wizard reported again, this time that the tribesmen were drawing off to the west. This was our sole clue to their movements. From around our cul-de-sac there was only silence. Major Miller pondered a moment, and decided we would stay in place till daylight. It would just be too hazardous to leave our position until there was more light.

We waited an hour. Assured by Murdock that the warriors had departed, the debris forming the barrier was removed from the gap, and mounted scouts were sent out. In a few minutes they reported back that the warriors had indeed gone. The Arkan wounded were placed near the gap with as much water and food as could be spared, under the care of a man who had taken only a minor cut to his head. Sergeant Nordstrom lent them encouraging words. "We'll send someone back for you soon as we can. Anticipate two days, maybe three."

Major Miller whispered something to the sergeant, and he in turn gave instruction to four of his men. The four men mounted, and with their lances prodded the four warrior prisoners, who marched ahead of the horses, hands bound behind them and a rope linking them all by the neck. The warriors were impassive. They knew where they were going.

Murdock put up a hand to stop the little procession and approached the Arkan leader. "Major Miller, I presume you're going to deal with the prisoners?"

Miller pulled on a riding glove. "We'll take them off a ways, first. Don't want to attract predators to our wounded."

"I see," Murdock said. "May I ask a favor?"

"Depends. You want to kill the prisoners yourself?"

"No, just the opposite," said the wizard.

About to pull on his other glove, Miller stopped. "Are you asking me to spare them?"

Murdock nodded. "Yes, I am."

Miller gestured around him with a sweep of the hand. "And just what do you expect me to do with them? We'll be riding hard. We can't take them along. If I leave them here, they'll be a threat to the wounded, and need to be watched. Plains warriors are notorious for their escapes. It creates a dangerous situation."

"I understand that. Still, I would ask that you spare them."

The major gave the magician a long stare. "What do Kenesee troops do when they capture prisoners from the tribes of the Northern Forests?"

"They are supposed to keep the prisoners safe for later exchange or negotiation."

"I see. And do they? Keep them safe, that is."

Murdock glanced at me, then answered the question. "No."

I knew what happened to the tribesmen of the north-lands when we captured them. They were interrogated for information—though *tortured* might be more descriptive of the process—and disposed of as quickly as possible. Given the brutality of the northern people, there was little sympathy for any of them taken alive.

The familiar sardonic smile appeared on Miller's face. "So you want an Arkan to show mercy to barbarians when your own troops show none."

Murdock stared back. "That's right."

A long pause. Finally, Miller laughed. "No, I'm not laughing at you, but at myself. You are a remarkable man, Wizard Murdock. I don't think anything can stop you."

"I hope not," the wizard replied.

"Sergeant Nordstrom, I've changed my mind. The prisoners are to be spared. Make sure the men we leave behind know that. Bind the warriors securely hand and foot, and secure them apart from each other."

Nordstrom kept his voice even. "Yes, sir." Not a hint of disrespect, and yet it was clear the man did not agree with his superior. I couldn't blame him.

A column was formed. The troops waved good-bye to the wounded and started out of the cul-de-sac at a walk, retracing our path through the grass and onto the unused old road, moving cautiously all the way. We followed it back to the old road that we had been traveling the day before, and there the column halted.

Major Miller looked up and down the road, north and south, and looked carefully at the ground with Sergeant Nordstrom. "Wizard Murdock, you're sure the tribesmen went south?"

Murdock answered quickly. "Without a doubt. I can't guarantee that further south they did not turn off into some gully where I can't detect them, and then change direction. But when they left us, they headed south initially."

"Then Ardmore is at risk," Miller said. "The tribesmen have decided to go after easier game. They'll fall upon the village in a rush, and the people will need help.'' He looked at Murdock and me. ''I'd thought to provide you escort throughout Arkan. But I need to take the squadron south where it's needed. Will you come? Your assistance would be a great boon in a fight.''

Murdock considered. ''I hate to sound ungrateful for all the help you've given us, but we're working against time. I'm afraid we've got to head north.''

Miller nodded. ''That's probably wise, from what you've told me. When you get to Klahoma, tell the authorities what happened down here. Have them send help to the wounded, and let them know I request another squadron or two to join me. The tribes' incursion is much larger than expected, and extends further south.''

We'll do that,'' Murdock assured him. ''Go with our wishes for the safety and success of you and your men.''

''And our best wishes for you,'' Miller replied. ''Though as a follower of the Codes, I have my doubts about the goal of your mission, as I have imagined it. Yet, nothing stands still, and change comes whether we will it or not.''

The Arkan turned his column southward at a good trot and, with many of his men lifting their spears in a wave of farewell, went in pursuit of the tribesmen.

Our party continued north on the old road, everyone watching for potential enemies, Murdock and Lorich using their magical talents to detect trouble and provide early warning. We went on for a good hour before Murdock lifted his hand and brought us to a halt.

''Trouble?'' Kren asked.

''Could be,'' the wizard responded thoughtfully. ''There's people ahead, possibly a score of them. All are agitated, and some feel fear. It could be another war band, or—'' Murdock seemed distressed. ''Well, whatever it is, we'd be pushing our luck to get involved. Let's swing west off the road and go around them.''

We took to the fields, the terrain open except along

watercourses, the ground gently rolling beneath the knee-high grass. Murdock kept to the low ground as we worked our way west and then north again, which helped prevent our being sighted either visually or by magical talents, but limited our sight in the same way.

However, the high ground could not prevent us from seeing the black column of smoke that rose into the sky, drifting away to the east with the breeze. Murdock brought us to another halt.

He estimated the distance. "A mile?"

"About that," Kren confirmed. "Could be a farmstead burning, I'd guess. Is that where you detected the people?"

Murdock nodded. "But there are fewer people now. What happened to the others, I wonder?"

"So what do we do? Ignore it?"

The wizard's features formed into a little-used expression. Indecision. "We should just go on—"

Of course we should just go on. I could have told him that. No use getting into further trouble.

"—But I can't. I felt fear. And now—" Suddenly he spurred his horse forward, and there was nothing to do but follow him.

Now we didn't stick to the low ground, but rode at a canter over rise and dip in a beeline for the column of smoke that grew thicker and taller before us. Ahead, two or three bumps at the source of the smoke became small buildings, and then grew clearly identifiable as a farm cabin and barn made of wood planks and sod, the barn revealing itself as the source of the smoke as it was consumed by fire. Well back from the barn and cabin were a dozen ponies tethered to bush or post. They were made skittish by the flames of the conflagration. And scurrying about near the buildings were plains warriors, some searching for loot, others with clothing and dishes and sacks of food and metal tools in their hands and tucked under their arms.

We released the leads of our packhorses, drew swords, and descended upon the tribesmen. They were surprised to see us. All interest in looting gone, they dropped their treasures and bolted for the ponies. A good half dozen made it to one mount or another, jerked the animals' heads around and galloped off into the fields. Two were unable to reach a horse in time. Kren cut down one from behind as he ran for his horse. The other saw he could not make it, turned, and drew a club from his belt. Jenkins went straight in on him. The warrior leaped nimbly aside as the horse went by, but he could not avoid Jenkins's sword, and went down without his head.

Three more popped out of the farm cabin, one of them trying to tie his pants up as he ran. They saw their demise and bounded for the remaining horses. We intercepted them. My man turned, a sword in hand, and slashed out. The blade caught my horse across the neck, and blood began to gush from the deep cut. A fatal wound. At the same time I drove the point of my sword into the warrior's chest, and then pulled it loose. He staggered back, fell to his knees, and went facedown in the dust. In the open, a horseman always has the advantage over a man on foot.

All of the warriors were dead, five of them in all, while we suffered no casualties. They had been surprised in the middle of looting and raping, and caught in the open by mounted opponents. If ready and on horseback, the outcome would have been much different.

Watchful for the warriors who had escaped, we collected the roaming packhorses and began searching the farmstead for bodies. We soon found the family who lived on the farm. The tribesmen had caught the father and two older boys in the plowed fields. They'd been run down and killed, just as we'd run down the warriors. The two younger children—girls perhaps seven and nine years old—had been finished cleanly with swords and left in the main room of the cabin.

In the bedroom we found the mother, who had been suffering the usual fate of a female captive. The warriors' fun had been interrupted when we'd charged into the farmyard. The warriors had hurriedly slit her throat, and she was spurting the last of her blood in tiny pulses when we found her. Jason took one look at her and shrugged. There was nothing he could do.

Within a minute it was all over.

We carried the bodies of the family outside, and then found shovels in a shed next to the house. Jenkins looked askance. "Sir, we're going to bury them? Won't that take a while? With this smoke signal going up, we should—"

Murdock cut him off. "Yes, we're going to bury them. You have some objection?"

Jenkins saw the look on Murdock's face, and then shook his head. "No, sir. No objection. Where do you want the graves?"

A pile of rocks culled by the farmer from the plowed fields was nearby, so we carried the bodies there. We took turns shoveling, two at a time, and those not shoveling watched for trouble. Murdock took the first turn with Kren, the wizard digging fiercely into the brown soil until Jason put a gentle hand on the wizard's shoulder.

"That's enough for now. You aren't a spring chicken anymore. I can bandage wounds. I can't do much for a heart attack."

Murdock blinked at him through the sweat trickling into his eyes, then straightened with a groan and set the shovel aside. "Jenkins was right. We shouldn't take time for this."

"Possibly. But the soil is soft, and you've made a good beginning. Here, let Lorich take your place for a while. We'll be done in a half hour or so, and can move on."

"Yes, Master. You rest." Lorich set to with determination.

We took our turns, and soon a shallow grave had been hollowed out of the ground. The six bodies were placed next to each other in the grave, dirt shoveled in and mounded, and then rocks from the pile arranged over all so that varmints couldn't dig up the grave.

There was never any doubt who would give the service. We stood around the grave with bowed heads while Murdock intoned a few lines of verse, and then added his own words. "Lord, to your judgment come these souls. Four innocent children and two adults whose lives were cut short by the short-sightedness of others. Judge them mercifully, and let your goodness find a place for them with you. And forgive us all our faults and errors. Amen."

We watered the horses from the well while Murdock wandered out of sight around the farm cabin. Normally, I would have left him to his privacy, but something in his face stirred me to follow. He was leaning his chest against a wooden fence, staring at the horizon. The wizard raised a tight fist and brought it down fiercely. At the last moment, he checked its descent, and lowered the fist gently to the top of the fence post.

I stood next to him.

His gaze never wavered from the horizon. My footsteps had given me away. "Six innocent people dead, Arn. Four children who will never grow up. And I could have saved them. There was time."

I tried to find words. How does one comfort another in such a case?

"Murdock, you couldn't know."

"I couldn't know." The fist lifted an inch above the post, and dropped onto it like a fleshly gavel, rendering judgment. "But I suspected. Their fear—I felt it. That was the clue. And I turned us away."

I searched futilely for words. I was unable to console the man who had provided consolation at every crisis. Poor Murdock, to be cursed with such a friend.

But I was not his only friend. "Well, Murdock, another crisis of conscience?" asked Jason the Healer. The Pacifican's gray hair was windblown, and his spectacles had slipped halfway down his nose. He removed them, took a kerchief from his pocket, and began to wipe a fine coating of trail dust from the lenses, waiting patiently for an answer.

Murdock straightened. "No. I'm fine."

Jason snorted. "No, you're not. You've taken responsibility for the fate of these people."

"They *are* my responsibility."

"You think that if we'd ridden up earlier, we'd have made a difference. And perhaps we would have saved their lives. Perhaps we would have distracted the tribesmen before they cut down the father and sons in the field. Perhaps we'd have distracted the others before they broke into the cabin and slaughtered the little girls. And instead of surprising a dozen looting tribesmen on foot, we'd have found a dozen warriors mounted and ready. And then what would we have done? How many of us would have survived that encounter? What good would our mission be if you and Arn were killed?"

"I know," the wizard admitted. "I know. I know. But it doesn't do any good. The choice was mine. The responsibility is still mine. The guilt is still there."

"So you're letting a little guilt bother you?"

"You don't know what it's like."

"I don't know, you say?" The Pacifican grabbed Murdock's arm and gave it a fierce shake. "How can you say that to me? I've told you the story, you know what I've done. I killed a dozen men face-to-face, men I knew, men I liked, men I respected, men who were loved by wives and children. And I made widows and orphans of them. I watched their husbands die before my eyes, their eyes full of disbelief and sadness as they saw me betray their trust and friendship. Who has done worse? Who has greater cause to feel guilty?"

I could think of someone.

The wizard regarded him carefully, and gradually the pain on his face was replaced by sympathy for the old healer. "You were only following orders. It was your duty as you saw it."

"Orders. Yes, I was following orders. Orders to kill. Orders to betray. Orders to still the best and bravest minds on the continent. And not a word of my doubt did I voice. Duty stole my youth, and my peace, and my self-respect. Duty left me with nothing. Nothing but atonement.''

Murdock reached out and placed a hand on each of Jason's shoulders, and from his lips poured goodwill and common sense. ''Jason, Jason. Don't you see? Your feelings define the kind of man you are. The extent of your doubt, the depth of your emotion, the responsibility that you torment yourself with—these are the indicators of your goodness. Don't you see that?''

The Pacifican arched an eyebrow, and a sly smile played across his lips. ''Well, perhaps I should. Do you? Don't you see that it applies to Murdock the Magnificent?''

The wizard was taken aback. ''You—you turned it all around. You did that on purpose.''

''Well, yes I did,'' Jason admitted with satisfaction. ''You're not the only one who can turn an argument inside out. But you made me do it. I couldn't stand that sickening display of guilt-riddled self-pity. Such indulgence does not become you, Wizard Murdock.''

''No, I guess it doesn't,'' Murdock said. ''I am out of my mood. I'm still accountable for my error, but I won't make that mistake again. For I don't think I could bear it.''

''Oh, you'd be surprised at what you can bear,'' I commented, and the two looked at me. ''You'd be surprised.''

Having lost my mount to the warrior's blade, I saddled my packhorse and took one of the tribe ponies for a new packhorse. We traveled more cautiously after the events of the last two days, and made fewer miles per day than hoped because of stops at various settlements along the way. The first village we came to was warned of the events at the farmstead. They had seen the smoke on the horizon, and had taken appropriate security measures already. The main street was partially barricaded, and all the menfolk carried weapons. We continued on, leaving word at each habitation that the tribes were raiding. Still, we managed to come into the walled town of Klahoma by noon on our fourth day in Arkan, and sought out the local regimental commander.

He was not much interested in us, but was very interested in our news. "We didn't think they'd be raiding that far south. How many warriors were there? You're sure there were more than a hundred? All right, then, I'll see what I can do about Major Miller's request. The Wichita cavalry is assembled too, so I think we can send one or two squadrons back south without weakening ourselves dangerously up here. Thank you for bringing me this information, Mr.—what did you say your name was? Mr. Thomas. Thank you, Mr. Thomas. But before you go, can you describe once more about where the wounded can be found in the ruins? Perhaps if you made a map . . ."

We continued north that afternoon, seeking to make up lost time, and found that here they had been warned of the raiding parties. The towns and villages were all watchful and had taken precautions, with a variety of defensive preparations put into place according to the geographic and structural characteristics of each community. Usually, it meant barricading a street, or restocking their village redoubt. Local infantry units were prepared to defend their communities, though they would prove useless for pursuit of the mobile tribesmen on the open plain. Cavalry patrols were also on the road, and each approached our group with caution. Upon hearing of our adventures with Major Miller, they allowed us to proceed with good wishes and advice for our safety.

Four days later we came to Wichita, the last major town, the last walled town, before we left Arkan behind us. Wichita was tucked against the bank of the narrow Arkan River. Cultivated fields and pastures surrounded the town, its thousands of inhabitants protected by a wall consisting of a steep earthwork that also served to keep out the river during spring floods. A sturdy palisade studded with wooden towers every hundred yards topped the earthwork. The gates were open, though an alert sentry was posted in each tower, and a detachment of guards challenged any strangers.

With the benefit of Murdock's narration, our story got us into town without incident. We went in through the south gate, and found an inn that Kendall remembered as being respectable. It was still respectable, and conveniently located next to a private bathhouse with two wooden tubs. Despite my noble rank and position, my companions still made me cut cards to see which two would get to have a bath first. Murdock drew an ace. And I drew an ace.

"You sure you didn't teach him any card tricks?" Jason asked Murdock.

"I did not," objected Murdock. "His ace was luck."

"And your ace?" our beastman asked the wizard.

"I have no comment," Murdock said solemnly.

So with a clean set of clothes under one arm, Murdock and I went into the bath while Jenkins and Kren, who drew the next highest cards, waited outside on the street. Kren drew no attention, for he was still attired in his traveling cap, and well-covered.

The manager of the bath was named Wallace, a thin-faced, wiry-muscled man wearing an oilskin apron and carrying, strangely enough, what looked like a riding crop. He was polite enough, though a note of insincerity could be detected in his voice, as if he really wanted to say you're-scum-but-I-need-your-money.

"Yes, sir, the bath is hot. The water and towels are fresh for each bather. And each bather gets a full quarter hour. I time it on the hourglass there."

He excused himself and departed for a moment.

Giving him his due, the bath was clean and neat. The baths were simply two wooden tubs set in the middle of a room, privacy for each provided by a draw curtain. The water was heated on a stove in a small room adjacent. The attendant, a boy perhaps ten years of age, staggered out with a last heavy bucket. There was a bruise on his face, and another nasty welt on his arm. On his leg was a large spot of wrinkled scar tissue that indicated a burn. The boy averted his eyes as he emptied the hot water into my tub and returned to the stove room.

I followed him with my eyes, watching as he went about his duties.

"Does it bring back memories, Arn?" asked Murdock.

"One or two," I said quietly. It had been a long time ago.

We each retired behind the curtains to our tubs, set clean clothes upon a stool provided, and made a pile of our dirty clothes on the floor. The water was pleasantly warm, and I enjoyed scrubbing off the accumulated sweat and dust of a week's travel. I preferred bathing daily, but traveling didn't always allow such luxuries. I did not pass up such opportunities willingly.

I could hear Murdock singing a lusty song about the miller's daughter, his baritone rich but slightly off-key. I heard a second voice lifting hesitantly, and then more confidently as it harmonized with Murdock's. It was the young attendant. The boy really was a fine soprano.

As they were finishing the last stanza, there were hurried footsteps across the floor, the sound of a whack, and another, and another. I tried to identify what could be making the sound. A riding crop, perhaps?

"Don't have enough to do, is that it?" the manager whispered fiercely, probably directly into the boy's ear, and there was another whack. "Bothering the customers with your wailing." Whack. "I'll give you something to sing about." A final whack. "Now get out there and do your work."

I took my leisure in the tub for the remaining minutes allowed, toweled dry, and dressed. Murdock had not yet emerged from behind his curtain. The boy was waiting, and immediately drew the curtain back from around my tub and pulled the plug so that the dirty water could spill into the drain. I took a step forward as he picked up my discarded towel, and he drew back, immediately cautious.

"What's your name, lad?"

"Mr. Wallace don't allow nothing improper to go on here, sir," he warned me.

"Good. That's one thing in his favor, at least. But what's your name."

"Patrick. Patrick Norton."

I held out my hand. "Here, Patrick Norton. For your service."

His palm came out, and I dropped two Arkan coins into it.

The boy's eyes widened and his mouth fell open. "Sir? You've made a mistake. These are five-dollar pieces."

"No mistake, lad."

"You don't expect anything else from me?" the boy asked, suspicious.

"No. The coins are yours. No strings."

He was still in disbelief. "But—but why?"

"Let's just say you remind me of someone I used to know. Have anywhere safe to keep the coins? No? That's what I thought. Is there a moneylender in town? Good. When you need money, you go to him and tell him your name. He'll be keeping them safe for you."

"Yes, sir. Thank you, sir."

"You don't have to work here anymore, if you don't want to," I hinted.

"Oh, I can't leave, sir. I have another year on my service."

Indenture. Well, we had it in Kenesee too. Not a good system, perhaps, but it had its purposes.

Murdock came out, and the attendant went back to work. "I'm finished. Are you?"

"Not quite. You can let Kren and Jenkins know it's their turn."

I found Wallace in the stove room, lifting an impressively heavy kettle from the stove and pouring its contents into a bucket. In spite of his thin frame, the man was strong. His riding crop was stuck into the apron strings wrapped about his waist.

"Yes, sir?" he asked. "Everything satisfactory?"

"The bath was fine."

"Good. Worth the price, isn't it."

"But the boy, Patrick. Has a lot of bruises, doesn't he."

Wallace grew wary. "The boy doesn't obey. Sometimes, he needs a lesson."

"I'm sure he does. Most boys do. But I think maybe you enjoy giving him lessons a bit too much."

"The boy is my worker, signed over to me proper according to the law. I have the paper. I'll do with him as I please."

"I'm sure you will. But I'll be coming back to Wichita in a few months. And I think I'll want another bath. And I'll ask the boy what kind of lessons you've been giving him."

The man recognized the challenge, looked me up and down, and gave a mocking smirk. "So, you think you're man enough to give me a lesson?"

With exquisite timing, I heard my companions coming in. I beckoned Wallace to the door of the room and pointed to them. Murdock regarded me pensively, while Kren and Jenkins looked on questioningly. "If I can't," I said, "they will."

Wallace wasn't frightened of our numbers—though he might have been if Kren had been uncovered, and he would certainly have a surprise in a few minutes when the beastman disrobed. But Wallace wasn't a fool, either, and realized my threat was not idle. "I'll keep your words in mind," he said evenly. "And now, sir, if you'll excuse me, I have work to do." He went back to the stove while I joined Murdock and left Kren and Jenkins to enjoy their baths.

Outside, the wizard clapped me on the shoulder.

"You know, Arn, if you keep this up, you may someday turn into a decent human being."

8

The Plains

Early the next morning Jenkins purchased two horses from a reputable seller in a cash and trade deal. One replaced a packhorse that was wheezing, and another took the place of a mare Jenkins rode that was developing a bad hoof. My other companions acquired extra supplies we had decided upon, with emphasis upon as many rations as could be carried, so that our packhorses were loaded with sacks and bundles and odd implements.

We rode out of Wichita less than two hours after dawn, and followed the old road north all day without incident, making good time upon the old highway. Only Jenkins had any concerns that day. When we stopped for noon meal, he remained on his horse as we dismounted, scanning the rolling grasses and the tree line following a nearby stream.

We watched the sergeant in silence until Kendall asked the inevitable question. "Trouble?"

Jenkins frowned. "Don't know. Murdock, is there anyone around?"

Murdock conferred with his apprentice before answering. "I don't detect any presence, nor does Lorich. Why?"

As flat as the ground was, how could someone hide from the wizards?

Jenkins readjusted his hat. "Must be nothing. Just a feeling that we were being watched. But I can't see anything, and if you don't detect anyone, then that settles it. Enough false alarms. Let's eat and be on our way.''

That night we camped, then rode most of the next day to reach the village of Salina on the Kansas River before dusk. It was a typical farming community with many wheat fields and cornfields, though they also raised a goodly number of cattle that seemed to thrive on the tall grass. Three squadrons of Arkan cavalry were temporarily garrisoned at Salina and, after showing our papers and explaining our purpose, we provided them with as much information about events further south as we knew.

The major in command was an easygoing fellow named Osborne, who listened with interest. ''So things are heating up down south. And here we thought the tribes might be going after Salina and Wichita. Being stuck out here so far north and west, Salina is usually one of their favorite targets. The beef, you know. There aren't any settlements after this—you're out of Arkan, and into the open plains. Well, if it stays quiet around here, that's all right with me.''

The village had two taverns, but was so remote that it had no regular inn. A widow with a large house in town did provide room and board to occasional visitors, and was recommended. This might be our last chance to sleep under a roof and in comfortable beds, and I at least was looking forward to the amenities. But the flinty-faced widow did not hesitate to charge outrageous rates, and even Murdock's charm had little effect.

His objection to the cost elicited a single response from the woman.

''Pay the price, or go elsewhere.''

A most convincing argument. We paid.

The party did eat well and sleep comfortably, and the horses had a barn to stay in, so maybe it was not such a bad bargain after all. After a commendable breakfast served by the widow herself, we saddled our mounts, loaded the packhorses, and readied ourselves.

And then we paused and looked around us at the rustic little community. Jason confirmed the feeling. ''This is where we leave it all behind. There's not another civilized town or village west of Salina. If we've forgotten anything, we'll have to do without."

"Is everyone ready?" Murdock asked, and was greeted with silence. "Then we'll be on our way."

From now on it was to be the campfire, and the bedroll, and the darkness of the night. I was surprised how well I accepted this step in our journey. Perhaps I was growing accustomed to hardship and danger.

Or more likely, the reality just hadn't sunk in yet.

Under Murdock's leadership, Kendall and Jason were our guides from that point on. Jason had not trod this path for twenty years, but still remembered its general course. More recent was Kendall's experience, as he had last taken the route six years before. Aiding them were several maps we had taken showing the old roads westward.

We proceeded north for a few miles before picking up the ancient highway that we would follow eastward. The road was not maintained in any way, and most of it had been overgrown with grass, except where it intersected or followed wooded river valleys—and there the old road was similar to Kenesee, overgrown not only with grass but with trees. Yet the smoothness of its course and the cut of the earth around it betrayed the path, and we followed it walking and trotting at a pace that ate up the miles. At infrequent spots the old pavement had been shattered by the Cataclysm so that shards thrust up through the grass, and at other places the ground had been eroded beneath the crete so that it tilted or collapsed into holes or gullies. Neither of these features hindered our progress, and we made between thirty and forty miles each day, though it required mounting at dawn and not making camp until dusk. We weren't in the saddle all that time. During the day we would stop at regular intervals or when opportunity offered to let the horses forage.

A potentially serious problem was the occasional downed overpass or collapsed bridge. We wended our way around the shattered crete of the former, and for the latter made our way down to the watercourse that the rusted skeleton had once spanned. Most of the streams were only a foot or two deep, and we could wade our horses across. If the water rated the title of river, a ford was usually found up- or downstream, and we could continue our progress with little delay. If the fall rains came upon us, it might not be so easy. Until then, we would take advantage of conditions and put as many miles behind us as possible while ensuring the well-being of our horses.

There was little to disturb the tranquillity of our journey during these first days on the Great Plains. Hawks and an eagle or two would fly overhead, and at night we'd listen to coyotes howling to each other. We saw a herd of a dozen wild horses roaming to our north one day, and on another we passed a few hundred buffalo peacefully grazing a half mile to the south. But of the plains tribes we saw nothing, though we did come across one or two old campsites near streams.

After a few days we noted that the flatlands and gentle rises were giving way to rougher terrain, that the nights were a bit cooler, and we seemed to be gradually rising in elevation. The grass grew shorter here, and the land itself seemed dryer, with little significant vegetation growing away from watercourses. Five days out from Salina the land had became positively hilly, and Lorich was enthused.

"Are these the Rockies?" the young wizard asked hopefully.

Jason scoffed. "These little hills? They flatten out on the other side, if I remember correctly. Don't worry. You'll know the Rockies when we get there. They rise straight out of the plain, and you can see them fifty miles off."

Someone really would have to work with the boy on his geography.

Jenkins turned in his saddle and scanned the horizon. "Not a thing," he stated in frustration.

"What is it?" I asked.

"That feeling of being watched. I felt it once yesterday, and the day before too. Yet there's not a thing. Anything, Mr. Murdock?"

"No, Sergeant Jenkins. If anyone were watching, I'd be able to detect him. If humans were located behind a hill, I wouldn't know they were there. But then, the hill would block their vision, just as it blocks my ability. Line of sight in both cases."

"My sense has never failed me before," Jenkins admitted in a puzzled tone.

"So our sergeant of the royal guards has a magical talent too," Kren joked.

I was intrigued. "Could that be a magical talent, Murdock?"

The wizard took a gulp of water from his waterskin. "A sixth sense of being watched? Why not? Many forms of mental power have not been explored, and such talents may be more common than we think. Why is one man able to mesmerize audiences, while another puts them to sleep? Why can one man charm all whom he meets, and another leaves them cold? What mental projection accomplishes all that? Some of my peers feel that we cast too wide a net when we include the variations of human personality. Yet I think the same power that gives me advantage in negotiation and persuasion is merely a stronger version of the same talent marking any good speech-maker."

"I have my doubts about it being magic," Jenkins stated. "But whatever it is, mine isn't working worth a damn. We have an hour till dusk. Should we make a few more miles?"

Our travel was a bit slower now, for Murdock and Lorich did twice detect the presence of others ahead, and we had to avoid them by swinging north or south as seemed best before coming back to the road. We also saw sizable herds of shaggy bison grazing upon the short grass. It probably shouldn't have surprised us when one late afternoon we came around the side of a hill to discover a large village of the plains tribes. The village consisted of cone-shaped lodges—teepees—by the dozen, and surprising numbers of men, women, and children strolled about, while a good herd of horses was watched carefully by mounted warriors.

We quickly retreated, making sure we were out of sight of the village and that no other tribesmen had spotted us, or were near. We found a hollow well off the road where we could hunker down for the night. Late as it was, we decided to camp where we were rather than detouring around the village in the dark. There were adequate long-dried bison droppings to sustain a fire, but we did without in the proximity of the village, and ate a cold meal. At dawn we awakened and prepared to go around the village, but found that the lodges, people, and horses were gone, the village slipping away before dawn. They had gone northward, Murdock reported, probably to follow the buffalo.

We traveled another two days, and the next event of significance occurred as we stopped for a noon meal under a warm sun that belied the stiff, cool breeze blowing from the north. We sat in the grass with only Lorich still mounted, doing his turn as sentinel while the party relaxed. The last of the boiled eggs were portioned out to go along with the chewy waybread. The bread would last perhaps another week, and after that we'd have to bake our own from the sacks of flour we'd brought. Jason was about to bring out his map for a further look when Jenkins swore. "There it is again. That feeling. Wizard Lorich, isn't there anyone around?"

The lad concentrated. "No, Sergeant Jenkins. No one."

"Wizard Murdock?"

"Sorry, my friend," said Murdock. "There's no one out there."

Kren stood up. "Ahem. I don't mean to contradict

our illustrious magicians, but perhaps they might look at yonder rise?''

He pointed to the north.

That got us to our feet. We stared. Perhaps a half mile off, upon the crest of a low hill, a tiny figure upon horseback waited.

"So I wasn't wrong," Jenkins said. "That's a relief."

Murdock scratched his chin. "Incredible. Either that's a beastman, or a powerful wizard who can hide himself from other magicians. No one else could avoid detection."

"You young people have the good eyes," said Jason. "Can you make out any details?"

Heads shook. "Can't make out a thing at this distance. He's just too far away."

Lorich squinted in the sunlight as he strained to see. "So you were right, Sergeant Jenkins. There *was* someone there each time you thought we were being watched. But why did he show himself now? Did he make a mistake? He never showed himself before. Does he know we can see him?"

"Oh, no mistake," Kendall answered. "This one is a skilled tracker. He decided to let us know he was there. Though *why* he did is not so easily determined."

"But who is he?" Kren asked. That was my concern too.

"So many good questions," observed Murdock, "and so few answers."

"Well, whoever he is, and whatever his motives, we can't leave him there," said Jenkins firmly. "I recommend we prepare a little surprise for our distant friend."

And so we did.

The figure in the distance disappeared behind the rise. As soon as he did, the party mounted and continued on. Jenkins gave the lead of his packhorse to Lorich and split off from the party, staying low in hollows and behind rises so that he might sneak up on the tracker as he followed us.

An hour later the little sergeant rejoined us, his frus-

tration showing in the bright shade of red on his face.
"I thought I had him. Circled behind and came up on
him—and he wasn't there. Couldn't find any tracks, either."

"Perhaps if we tried it again," ventured Kren. This
time, the beastman accompanied the sergeant as they
split off. Eventually they rejoined us. With no better
luck.

"We'll need to form more than one ambush party,"
Jenkins reported tersely. "Wizard Murdock, you'll come
with me, please. And Mr. Lorich will go with Major
Kren. One more time, if you please."

The four split off, Jenkins and Murdock heading in
one direction, Kren and Lorich in another. They would
each swing out, take position where they could see the
tracker when he followed, and close in upon him. He
would have nowhere to go, and would be taken. Except
it didn't work out that way. The two ambush parties
returned hot and dusty and looking tired. "He's good,"
Kren admitted. "Very good."

"So what do we do?" I asked.

"Do?" responded Murdock. "We do nothing. We
tried three times without success. We have to admit we
have a follower—"

"A Tracker," said Kren.

"Yes, a Tracker," agreed Murdock. "We have a
Tracker, and can do nothing about him. We don't have
time to fool around. We'll continue westward as we have
so far. If our Tracker leaves us an opportunity, we'll see
what we can do about taking him. If not, we'll ignore
him. What other choice do we have?"

What other choice, indeed? But it wasn't a good feeling knowing this skilled hunter was following us.

Not a good feeling at all.

We'd passed the highest of the hills and the land did
indeed begin to level out, as Jason had indicated. From
one of the foothills we had a clear view in two directions. The arid plain stretched away to the west, flat and

brown and uninviting, a faint blue line marking the horizon far away. But whether the faint line was the Rockies, Kendall and Jason could not agree. Kendall thought it might be, while Jason said the mountains were still too far, and it was just a trick of the atmosphere.

To the south, running in almost a straight line from northeast to southwest, the cones of three volcanoes thrust upwards out of the plain, the nearest at least forty miles from us. Their peaks towered above our own elevation, wisps of smoke drifting skyward from their mouths.

"Those are the Three Lights," Jason said. "If I remember correctly, that is."

"You remember correctly," Kendall affirmed.

"Why do you call them the Three Lights?" asked Lorich.

"From the north, one or another would often be lit at night. On rare occasions, all three. We'll see what we can see tonight."

We set up camp that night in a lovely river valley, the watercourse no more than a dozen feet wide and a foot deep as it meandered in loops through the flat bottom of the valley. Rushes lined the banks, and trees and bushes were scattered around the lush meadows bordering the gently flowing ribbon of water. There were geese and ducks on the banks, and Kren had no trouble taking two geese with his bow for our evening meal.

It was dark by the time we finished the last morsel, and the campfire offered a cheery refuge against the night.

Lorich licked the grease from his fingers. "That was very good, Major Kren."

"Why are you thanking him?" Jenkins stated, standing over the seated party and keeping a dutiful first watch even while he talked. "All he did was kill the birds. You cooked them, and a fine job you did—"

"What's this?" objected Kren. "*All* I did was kill them? Who do you think *chose* the two juiciest, most succulent fowl in the valley? My expertise is just not fully appreciated.''

Jenkins ignored Kren. "Wizard Murdock, not only is your apprentice becoming a quite decent rider, he's also qualifying himself as a most respectable cook.''

Murdock settled back on an elbow against his saddle, which he'd laid at the top of his blanket as a pillow. "Well, it's always good to have an alternate career ready.''

"Indeed.'' said Jason. "And in that case, what would be Prince Arn's new career?''

Murdock frowned. "Don't ask.''

From far off there was a rumble like thunder. To the south, a faint red spot glowed high in the darkness, marking where one of the three volcanoes reminded us of its presence.

The Three Lights. A good name.

Lorich stood for a clearer view. "Are we in any danger?''

"I shouldn't think so,'' Kendall reassured him. "We must be thirty miles from the nearest cone. The whole side would have to blow off to threaten us, and that would be more bad luck than one could expect. It would make quite a bad day for all of us.''

I didn't tell him that I'd had such days.

"And do the volcanoes date back to the Cataclysm?'' the young wizard asked.

Jason answered. "Yes, they do, from what records say. Almost all the new volcanoes on the continent were formed in the months following the Cataclysm, a direct result of the geologic activity. In fact, the presence of these may be why Pacifica survived. Pacifica is located amongst old volcanic mountains, and it might have been thought that all would be destroyed in the quakes. But the Cataclysm was so great it must have shifted or tilted the continental plates, which accounts for the changes in coastline. The lava surging upward in the earth was diverted and vented elsewhere. We really can't explain why, just that it happened.''

Kren waxed philosophical. "To think that earthquakes could have brought the Ancient World to its end. Think how powerful the tremors must have been to destroy the cities. Look at the broken bridges and fallen overpasses. Steel, crete, nothing was strong enough to withstand its force."

Jason took out his pipe. "The quakes were powerful—more powerful than any seen in the history of Man. Even if such quakes occur only once every million years, the threat of that catastrophe is always present, no matter how small the chance it might occur in any particular year. And eventually, it will come. But as severe as the quakes were, it was not just the quakes that brought civilization so low and killed most of mankind."

"If it wasn't just the quakes," noted Kren, "then what else caused it?"

Kendall grinned at the beastman. "Want to guess?"

"No, I don't want to guess. I have no idea."

"Anyone else?" Kendall offered.

Murdock was smirking. "I know."

"You do, do you? All right, what was it?"

"Specialization."

"You have it," Jason confirmed.

"Specialization?" Lorich repeated. "What do you mean by that, Mr. Kendall?"

Kendall considered his words. "Umm, explaining it is the hard part."

"It's like this," Jason said, coming to his son's rescue. "In a small village, there might be a blacksmith to handle metalwork for the farmers, but the housewives all bake their own bread, and many weave their own cloth, and so on, the families self-sufficient in many ways. There is little specialization, except for the black-smith. One family is able to do most of what any other family in the village is able to do.

"In a large village there would still be a blacksmith, or even two or three. As well, there is often a baker to bake bread, a miller to grind grain, a weaver to make cloth, and so on. The families turn over duties to these others to accomplish so that they have more time to do their own tasks. Many of the families become specialized as bakers or millers or weavers. And each is dependent upon the other to supply him with bread or flour or cloth or whatever. The families are specializing, each becoming more knowledgeable and skillful in one specialty, while losing the practical knowledge of other basic tasks.

"Now apply this concept to the ancients, who carried specialization to extremes that were dangerous to contemplate. People did not know how to grow their own food. They didn't know how to keep their engines going, they did not know how the devices they used worked. Instead, each depended upon other individuals, other specialists, to accomplish some tiny part of the overall economy, and thus keep the society going. In this way they grew in population, but their society grew in complexity. Everyone depended upon everyone else. And everyone also depended upon the machines—the transportation vehicles, the communication devices, the continuous flow of oil and coal and electricity to the society."

Jason paused to get a drink from his waterskin, and Kendall picked up the explanation. "Even the poorest, least-developed portions of the globe depended on the sophisticated technology of civilization to sustain them, sometimes by the transfer of food from richer areas. As an example of their achievement, entire cities were built in deserts, totally dependent on a fragile water supply from canals and dams, and products shipped in from far away by train and truck.

"Their society was *complex*. And it was this specialization—this complexity—that brought them so low. When the fragile web of communication and transportation and production was broken, the fragments shattered completely. The simpler knowledge and skills and products of earlier times that might have filled the gap were unavailable, or had to be learned anew. Amidst the confusion following the giant quakes, the survivors had all they could do to find food to get them through the winters. The complexity of technology that had taken man to such astounding heights resulted in mankind dropping back into barbarism, with extinction a looming possibility.''

"So their technology doomed them," Lorich noted.

"Not the technology itself," Jason clarified. "Technology is neutral, neither good nor bad. It simply is. How it is used determines its purpose, its rightness or wrongness. As long as the web was maintained, it served them well. But once the web was broken, it unraveled completely. Nothing could restore it. The ancients had not built in any safeguards, any cutoffs, any redundancy to allow their society to recover from catastrophe. Their specialization was total, and their downfall was total. The survivors had no chance to restore anything. And that is why we endured four dark centuries before the Codes were instituted to rescue our societies and create a stable situation in which nations could once again contribute to the betterment of mankind.''

I knew he would find a way to bring up the Codes. Even Jason was not above extolling their virtues when the opportunity offered.

"And the moral of this story?" I asked, my temper made short by fatigue.

"Why, that should be clear," Kren stated before the Pacificans could answer. "Always live in very small villages.''

Beasts of the Prairie

"Murdock, we need to swing north to avoid the upper end of the rift," said Kendall the next morning, pointing out on the map the feature to which he referred. Even longer than the rift that formed part of the border between Kenesee and Virginia, this gash in the land apparently stretched southward in an irregular zigzag for hundreds of miles, and measured over a hundred meters at its widest point. From a rise, we saw the northernmost end of the rift ahead as a dark, narrow slash cutting through the brown grasses. As the Pacificans assured us, the rift grew wider as it ran beyond sight to the south and passed far west of the Three Lights.

Kren had an idea. "The Tracker will have to go around the rift too. Why don't we try to surprise him when he comes around? We'll never have a better chance, short of the mountains."

Murdock considered it. "We'll take an hour or two, then. But that's all. We can't keep wasting time worrying about him. It's already September 20th, according to my calendar. We need to make the mountains before October."

As we reached its northern end, the rift shrank to a modest gully that could be traversed at several points where the sides had collapsed into it. We crossed carefully and took position where we could peep back over a rise with a view of several miles of rift and prairie. Kren and Jenkins watched expectantly, their gaze taking in the vista in slow sweeps as they sat in the grass.

After a time, Jason snorted. "Well, I guess we can be going now."

"Has it been an hour already?" Kren asked, still watching with steadfast duty.

"The time doesn't matter," Jason answered. "Take a look over there."

On a distant rise to the west, a single mounted figure waited impassively, unperturbed. The Tracker had gotten ahead of us.

Jenkins and Kren looked at each other and shrugged.

Murdock gave orders to mount. "If there is no objection, we won't waste any more time on our distant companion. As long as he leaves us alone, we'll leave him alone. It's getting cooler each night, and we have a long ways to go."

We started forward, and the Tracker disappeared from view behind the rise. The old highway was even easier to follow now, for the short grasses made clear the evenness of the surface and allowed us to bypass any breaks in the crete without difficulty. The old roads had been essential to the good progress that we had enjoyed, and I wondered what it must have been like to travel in one of the ancient automobiles and cover hundreds of miles comfortably in a single day. Supposedly, it had been possible to cross the continent in a matter of days. Unbelievable.

We came across another herd of bison, this one several hundred strong. Surprisingly, the bison seemed to be following beasts of an entirely different sort. Amidst the bison, over a score of great, hairy mammoths—tusks curving into formidable points—encircled a half dozen of their young and grazed without concern. Downwind from our party, the big bull of the mammoths noted us and calmly strode forward, bison moving quickly out of his way. He took position between us and his herd.

Jenkins lifted his cap in salute to the beast. "Just passing by, good sir."

"The plains tribes hunt the buffalo, but not usually

the mammoth. They consider it bad luck," Kendall observed.

Kren laughed. "Bad luck for sure to go up against those tusks."

"What?" exclaimed Murdock. "Don't you want to try riding one of the mammoths? The big bull, perhaps?"

Kren's brow furrowed in memory. "Not today."

We kept going.

Murdock drew our attention to a hillside overlooking the scene. Lounging in the grass was a pride of sabertooths, their long fangs only half-visible until they yawned in the warmth of the afternoon, their huge sides glistening in the sun.

The predators must have recently fed well, for they were content to watch the mammoths and bison and horses and humans without the motive of hunger to alter their peaceful demeanor.

"Lord, but they're big," Kren exclaimed.

"Yes, they are magnificent," Jason agreed. "But best admired from afar."

Lorich studied the scene. "I wonder if that's why the bison stay with the mammoths. For protection."

We gave the big cats a wide berth, and noted that perhaps it would be better to pile the campfire a bit higher than usual tonight.

When we were well past the beasts the party relaxed a bit, riding in pairs and chatting about what we had seen and what we might see further on. I noted that Kendall had again sought out Lorich and was discussing some bit of history about the Old World. Kendall talked with the young wizard more than I would have liked. I paid attention when I could, but it wasn't possible to listen to every word they said, and often whoever rode beside me would be talking away, and I had to listen to what he might be saying as well. Jason was beside me today, and in the manner of old men was rambling on about various wounds he had treated, and making me thankful I had avoided such horrendous damage.

Still, it made me wonder. Did the Pacificans realize my one wizardly talent? Was Jason keeping me occupied while Kendall worked his way with Lorich? Were the two plotting to turn the lad against me? Or was I merely becoming paranoid?

I asked Murdock about it when I had the chance. "Murdock, the Pacificans know about Lorich's talents. All of them."

"I know," said the wizard. "Kendall talked to me about it one day."

"I'm worried about them." I'd already told Murdock about my suspicions regarding the Pacificans, and the dangers Robert faced—and I faced. "I think Kendall may be trying to sway Lorich. Confuse him, perhaps, about his loyalties, and use him as a tool. A weapon."

Murdock was silent for a long moment. "I like to think better than that of Kendall. In spite of what he's done in defense of the Codes, I think he has a good heart. But Lorich would be a temptation to any man with political motives. Our young wizard has killed a half dozen men with his power. He comes within twenty or thirty yards, reaches out mentally to the victim's heart or brain, squeezes, and the man falls dead. He'd be the perfect assassin, wouldn't you say? But I know Lorich is full of goodwill too. He wouldn't use his power for selfish purposes."

"Yes," I agreed. "Then again, every man has his weakness. And he could be misled. He wouldn't be the first of goodwill to be seduced by heart's desire or led astray by idealism."

Murdock stretched. "Didn't we have this conversation months ago when we first discovered his talent? Only we each took the other's side in this argument. I wouldn't worry about Lorich—but I will watch him for you."

I felt better just knowing that the wizard was aware and thinking about the problem. "Do you think there are others with Lorich's power?" I asked.

"It's possible, of course. But I don't think there is

anyone else like Lorich. Such abilities are unheard-of. Lorich's power has never been seen before. And I think that is a good thing. Though he is the first with such power, let us hope he is also the last.''

I had enough reason to be frightened upon this long journey. Our adventure should have been a challenge, the world against our united party, with each of us secure in the knowledge that our comrades were at hand. Instead, I had to worry about plots, and poisons, and betrayal. It took all my control to keep my resentment of the Pacificans from fanning into active hatred. They had taken away the joy of friendship and replaced it with the acid of suspicion, and this sickened me to my heart. For friendship was all I had left.

That evening my duty watch overlapped Kendall's, and so while our companions snored away around the fire, we paced together on the rise of ground surrounding the campsite, which was established in another hollow. The moon was only two days past full and shone brightly, so that it would have been hard for any creature to approach without coming to our notice.

I buttoned my coat, and watched Kendall as much as I did the landscape.

"Cold, Arn?" he asked in a low voice.

"It's getting cooler at night," I answered.

"That it is. And it'll be colder yet when we get into the mountains. We should be there in a week. We've made good time. But we have to cross the mountains before October is out, or we'll be in trouble."

We stopped and listened to the night sounds for a while before continuing on about the state of the horses, how well Jason was holding up, and the terrain ahead. At some point Lorich's name was mentioned.

"He's an interesting young man," the Pacifican commented. "He used to be so enthusiastic and cheerful about everything. And now, he's so much quieter. There seems to be a seriousness about him. A sadness."

"You know what happened in Arkan?"

"When the party was a traveling theater? He didn't mention it, but I've heard."

"He became enamored with a woman, a baker's wife named Regina, and helped her run away from her husband," I explained. "But she was only using Lorich as a means of escape. She had no interest in the lad."

"And so Lorich learned the ways of the world," Kendall stated wistfully. "Love is a precious gift, and sometimes not easily found."

"Yes, he learned that. And also, that the world is full of deceit."

"Poor lad."

I watched the Pacifican. "It would be terrible if others deceived him as well. Companions he trusted."

Kendall stood still. "That would be terrible. Is there someone you suspect?"

I turned the question upon him. "Who might give me cause?"

There was a moment of silence before he spoke. "I see."

I tried to keep my voice calm, my tone neutral. "You've found a goodly number of things to talk about with the young wizard. And shared much with him. I'm sure Lorich is quite gratified that a famous Pacifican has befriended him. Perhaps he has not asked himself why. But I have."

"I stated the why to you back in Texan," said Kendall. "Lorich is important. He has potential. He must understand the value of the Codes and the six nations. Only by understanding them can he embrace and stay loyal to the ideals of the Codes."

"And if loyalty to the Codes conflicts with loyalty to Kenesee?"

"Arn, loyalty to the Codes *is* loyalty to Kenesee."

"Some might debate that."

"Arn, have I lost your trust?"

My shoulders slumped. "Yes, Mr. Kendall, I'm afraid so."

"I'm sorry about that," said the Pacifican. "We've

been friends for so long. I value that friendship highly. That's why I'm here. I would like you to trust me, but I guess each man must follow his ideals, whatever the price.''

Whatever the price. And who would pay that price?

I was pondering a response when I swayed, and Kendall grabbed my arm for balance. No, I wasn't becoming dizzy. It was a slight tremor in the earth. At the same time, there was a pulse of light from the top of one volcano to the south.

"An eruption?" I asked the Pacifican.

"Possibly," he admitted, staring off to the south. "In any case, we're many miles from the cones, and in no danger."

We watched and listened, but there were no further tremors, no more pulses of light. However, we did hear a faint noise from the south, a gentle rumble, though we could not tell what it was. A horse snorted. Another whinnied. All had their ears back.

Suddenly, from out of the darkness came a wail fit to wake the dead. It certainly woke the sleepers in our party.

"Where? Where? What is it?" asked Kren, fumbling for his sword.

Jenkins kicked free of his blanket and leaped up. "Arn! Kendall! Are you all right?"

We waved and hurried into the firelight. "We're both fine," said the Pacifican.

Murdock cast out an open hand. "Shhh! Everyone be quiet." The far-off rumbling could still be heard, clearer now, but still distant. He and Jason exchanged a knowing glance. Jason dropped quickly to his knees and put an ear to the ground.

"You can feel the vibration in the earth. It's a stampede, all right."

Murdock nodded. "That's what I thought. And the noise is getting louder. Everyone saddle your horse. We have to leave. We have only minutes. Quickly now!"

The command was not questioned.

In a second we were racing around the campsite. Actually, there was more to do than just saddle the horses. Boots went on, and clothing, all in record time. The horses were skittish from our nervous activity, and even more so from the ominous signs of the approaching threat. I held Kren's horse by its halter, and he did the same for mine. Saddles were slung up and cinched tight. Bridles went on, and fingers flew over the straps. By this time, the rumble of noise was clearly audible, like approaching thunder, and the vibration in the earth could be felt through our boots.

We cinched on the pack frames for the horses, threw whatever we could gather onto the frames, and lashed the items down with a quick twist of rope. Kren finished his tasks and helped Kendall, whose one arm was inadequate for the task. I helped Lorich, while Murdock assisted Jason. Actually, the old healer was doing quite well all on his own, but he had to be careful packing his healer's bags, since they contained vials of powders and potions.

The rumble was very loud now.

Our blankets were still on the ground. "Forget them," advised Jason. "We're out of time. We have to go!"

And then we were mounting, half of us holding reins and leads to the packhorses while the others tried to swing into the saddles of their nervous mounts. Lorich, Jason, and Kendall first, who then took the leads for the packhorses. Jenkins, Murdock, and Kren made sure the others were safely saddled before they put foot to stirrup. I was the last, not through any brave gesture, but because my horse continued to dance away from me as I tried to mount.

"Sir, would you stop fooling around and get into the saddle?" Jenkins suggested with his usual subtlety.

I finally grabbed the mane in a tight fistful with one hand, got the merest toehold in the stirrup, and clambered into the saddle with all the grace of a pregnant cow. Not exactly the way Sergeant Major Nakasone had taught me, perhaps, but under the circumstances it would do.

The rumble was like a continuous roll of thunder now, and we could feel the very air resonating to the vibrations in the earth.

"Which way?" Murdock asked the healer.

Jason pointed to the northeast. "That way. Follow me. Ride!" He touched heels to his horse and the animal broke into a gallop, his packhorse trailing behind. Our horses needed little encouragement to follow. As we emerged from the hollow I looked back. On the southern rim, where Kendall and I had talked only minutes ago, a dark shadow, a roiling black stain, poured up and over the rise, descending into our campsite in a tide that stretched east and west for hundreds of yards.

Bison. Thousands of bison. Tens of thousands. And all of them stampeding directly toward us.

I realized now why Jason had chosen this direction. Northeast really was the only logical choice. East, because we'd covered some of this trail earlier in the day and, with the benefit of the full moon, should be able to retrace our steps without undue surprises wrecking our flight from danger. And north, because fleeing directly east would have taken us into the advancing herd.

Still, our escape was not assured. We charged forward, keeping ahead of the bison, then gradually lengthening the distance between our party and the forward edge of the herd. We galloped for almost a half mile before noting that the dark shadow of the herd was passing us by, and that we had at last removed ourselves from the path of the animals.

Jason slowed his mount, and we followed his example until the party came to a halt, horses shivering with fear, their eyes wide and nostrils flared, blowing hard from the desperate race. And upon them, their riders wheezed in the dust of ten thousand buffalo. The animals were still pounding their way northward, though it seemed as though their speed might have slowed a bit. Even the great beasts of the plains could not run forever.

My estimation of Jason had just gone up several notches. Not bad for an old healer.

"That," said Murdock dryly, "was very close."

"What was it, Master?" Lorich asked. "Why did those buffalo stampede?"

"An earth tremor," Kendall offered. "Probably associated with volcanic activity. It spooked the herd, and they fled north."

"Once they get moving, all you can do is get out of their way," Jason added. "Two minutes' delay, and we'd have been finished."

Lorich wiped his brow. "Then we owe our lives to Prince Arn and Mr. Kendall. They woke us just in time."

"It wasn't us," Kendall stated. "We didn't know what to make of the noise. But there was a yell, a wail, from out there, somewhere. That's what woke you."

"But—who was it who yelled?" the young wizard asked.

We looked at each other. "Our Tracker?" ventured Kren.

"That would be my guess," Murdock answered. "Obviously, he's familiar with the threat we faced, and knew we had to be roused."

I was puzzled. "Why should the Tracker help us? Who *is* he?"

"That does seem to be the question," Murdock replied. "But unless his trodden remains lie back near the campsite—which I thoroughly doubt is the case—we'll have to wait for him to reveal himself. At least, having us trampled to death does not seem to be his goal. Come, the herd has passed. Let's head back for the hollow and see if there's anything left of our blankets."

10

The Outpost

After recovering a grand total of three shredded and torn blankets from our campsite, we waited for the dawn before heading west once more. I was a bit tired after the night, but as Kren expressed it, "Better that than being churned to butter under the hooves of the bison."

The land was getting arid, and except for the river valleys, grass-covered earth gave way to clumps of brown weed and sagebrush. The horses seemed to get along on the weeds, though it took longer for them to forage a decent bellyful each night. The sagebrush provided our campfires. We would chop down the gnarly bushes each evening, and burn the twigs and small branches in a pit until we had a good bed of coals for cooking. Stones arranged around the pit heated nicely and served as foot warmers when we turned in for the night.

Before us were the Rockies, growing from a blue smudge upon the horizon to a distinct line to a looming wall of peaks and summits, rising out of the plain without benefit of foothills. Here, the plain. There, the mountains, thrusting up in sharp-edged defiance of the flatness that lay beneath. As the peaks grew larger, I saw that they were greater than the Smokies and other mountains of Kenesee, making those familiar heights seem mere hills in comparison. While our mountains were green and inviting with even the summits covered with trees and grass, these towered above us with their peaks showing barren gray flanks. We were awed at their height and majesty. I was also appalled. We had to get *through* these mountains, and all the rest that lay behind.

Five days after the stampede, and only a few miles from the forbidding slopes, we left the old highway and circled north to avoid the ruins of a great city. We found another old road, this one heading north, and made camp next to it in a dry streambed just before the sun went down behind the mountains.

"That used to be called Denver, one of the great cities of the ancients," Jason noted, gesturing at the ruins to the south and pointing out the location on his map. "As the map shows, an old road continues through the mountains just west of the .ruins. But we're not going that way. Lorich, why not?"

Lorich looked from the ruins to the map. He'd been tutored in the last few days. "Because, uh . . . the passes on the Denver road are more difficult to negotiate. Further north, near the ruins of Cheyenne, the terrain is less difficult and the passes through the mountains should be easier to travel—though the likelihood of meeting mountain clansmen is greater, for more live along the northern route."

"Exactly," Jason confirmed. "Very good, Wizard Lorich."

"And my Master will keep us out of the clansmen's way."

"Such lighthearted confidence from the young is to be expected, no matter how ill placed," Kren whispered, loud enough for all to hear, including our venerable elder wizard.

Jason ignored Kren and answered the young wizard. "You are more astute than certain other hairy members of our party, Wizard Lorich. As much as I hate to pay him a compliment, Murdock will do it, if anyone can."

Our beastman sat upright. "Confidence from the old, as well. Remarkable."

Murdock exchanged a glance with Jason. "Do you prefer to hold him while I hit, or shall I hold and you "

* * *

Two days later we arrived just a few miles from the ruins of the ancient city of Cheyenne, and came in sight of a plains tribe town. That's right, not a village, not a mobile collection of hide tents, but a permanent town. Only a mile from the mountains, the community was located on high ground surrounded by a narrow flood-plain. There were only a few teepees on the fringes of the settlement. Most structures were permanent wood and sod huts on both banks of a narrow river with a wooden bridge spanning its waters. Some of the huts were large, two-story structures that looked like they could have held most of the population, if needed. And perhaps that was their purpose. Garden patches were placed beside every hut. Fenced corrals were laid out for horses and cattle, and surrounding all were small culti-vated fields that had already been harvested.

Murdock had warned there were people ahead, and we had carefully chosen an elevated fold of ground where we could spy ahead. Only part of the town was visible, for much was blocked by the structures in the foreground.

Jason scrutinized the community. "Paul, it must be mountain clansmen."

Kendall hesitated. "I don't think so. This is where the plains tribes had a village last time I came through. And look at those teepees. The mountain clans don't use them."

From far away, we heard the distant clang of a black-smith's hammer on metal.

Kendall continued. "Jason, I think we're seeing the first full-fledged town of the plains tribes."

Lorich was quicker than I to see what that meant. "You mean this is their first permanent community?" he asked. "So the tribesmen will be part of an estab-lished nation. Their nation will develop weapons unhin-dered by the Codes, and put them in the hands of their fierce warriors. Isn't that a cause for fear?"

Kendall continued to stare at the town. "I don't think

so. There are four major plains tribes, and getting them to cooperate on anything is almost impossible. This settlement belongs to the Braska tribe. It's grown greatly in the last few years, and the Braska, at least, may indeed be taking the first steps to becoming a society of farmers and land dwellers. But I don't know whether any other permanent communities like this exist, and it would be a long time before the tribe could raise its population to the numbers needed to be a real threat."

"There's another thing," Kren added. "The hard warrior qualities that dominate the plains tribes' culture will change as they take up permanent settlements. Generation by generation, they'll adapt as their lives change and become easier. Their fierce attitude will dissipate amidst the trappings and comforts of established society. Likewise, their fanatic commitment to the tribe and its success will be replaced by individual self-interest. There will be a willingness—perhaps a flaming desire— to let *someone else* see to the well being of their people. And maybe that is both the benefit and curse of civilization and its comforts."

"I think that our beastman has stated the case," Kendall concluded.

Lorich had yet another question. "But why should the Braska tribe establish their first settlement here, so close to the mountains? Doesn't that put them at risk from attacks by the mountain clans?"

Our young wizard did ask good questions. I should have thought of it too.

"There is some risk," Kendall admitted. "But not as much as you might expect. You see, just beyond the town is the Outpost, and everything within five miles of the Outpost is under Pacifican truce. It's neutral territory. No fighting allowed."

Murdock shifted in his saddle, trying to find a more comfortable seat "So we've finally reached the Pacifican Outpost. The halfway point on our journey from Arkan."

Kren shook his head, bemused. "To come so far, and still be only halfway."

"Everything in the area is under truce, Mr. Kendall?" Lorich asked, still pursuing the subject. "How do you enforce that?"

Jason removed his hat and wiped sweat from his brow as he answered for his son. "Trade. If any of the plains tribes or mountain clans violate the truce, the Outpost restricts trade with them. Pacifica offers metals, pharmaceuticals, improved planting seed, books, medical knowledge, and a few finished products such as surgical instruments. It's a strong inducement, and usually works quite well."

Lorich nodded with understanding. "So with the truce in effect, we can just go down through the town to get to the Outpost."

Kendall studied the village. "Uhh, not quite."

It was Murdock's turn to ask a question. "Not quite?"

"Every ten years or so, the truce breaks down. The last major incident occurred because the chief of the Braska tribe needed a scapegoat after a very hungry winter. They burned down the Outpost and killed four Pacificans. But it was just a temporary dissatisfaction, and the Outpost was rebuilt the same summer with the help of the tribe."

"Ten years between incidents," Kren stated. "And just how long ago was the last incident?"

Kendall looked at the sky, his face innocent. "About ten years."

Why did I know he was going to say that?

Murdock adjusted his reins. "Shall we keep chatting, or go on and actually arrive in time to get a hot meal?"

We went on, skirting the settlement by a goodly distance and circling around to the north, where we made for a lone structure set a good mile from the settlement. The structure resembled nothing else than a blockhouse. But as we came closer I realized that it was a good deal larger in dimension than any blockhouse I had seen, though only two or three stories high. It was made of good-sized logs, had a heavy door, and window shutters with arrow slits. A puzzling decoration to the structure were two ten-foot wooden poles sticking out vertically from the roof, between which several metal wires had been strung. Maybe they used it for hanging laundry.

A small stream flowed into a pond near the front of the building before continuing on to join with the river that flowed through the town. In the water of the pond merrily splashed a duck with a twisted wing. Except for a willow tree and rushes growing near the pond, the ground was open, so that none could approach without notice. Certainly, our arrival had been observed. A rugged, square-featured man of middle age came out the front door, pulled it firmly shut behind him, and stepped forward to await us with arms folded across his chest and a patient smile. A dog with a mangled paw and one eye sat in the shade of the building, watching us approach.

We reined up before the man. The Kendalls stayed mounted, and the rest of us followed their example. I glanced beyond the man at the front of the Outpost. It was even more formidable close up. The door was metal-banded, and the shutters closed. Yet, hadn't I thought they were open only minutes before? And of more concern, was that a movement I saw in the dimness behind a shutter's arrow slit? Was a crossbow or other weapon being brought to bear? The man was conveniently not in the line of fire from any of the openings.

I decided not to make any sudden moves.

He spoke. "Greetings, friends. May I help you?"

Kendall responded. "Mr. Brusov?"

"Heinrich Brusov. And you are . . . ?"

The Pacifican allowed his Pacifican accent—normally only a hint of lilt—full expression. "I'm Paul Kendall. And this is my father, Jason Kendall. Did our message get through?"

Brusov studied Kendall's face. "Well, the beards don't help, but I recognize you, Mr. Kendall. We met during your visits to Pacifica. It was five or six years ago, I believe. Welcome. And it's an honor to meet the renowned Jason Kendall. Yes, your message was received, though we almost missed it. And it was passed on."

"That's a relief to know," said Jason.

"And these are your companions?"

Kendall introduced us each in turn. Brusov came forward and reached up to shake hands, looking us over closely as if gaining the measure of each man. He studied the beastman with scientific curiosity, and lifted an eyebrow when he came to me. "Prince Scar. It is my privilege." He stepped back when finished. "So these are the famous names we've heard about in dispatches and reports." He raised his voice, as if wishing to make sure others heard. "Well, I feel comfortable with such distinguished guests. Gentlemen, feel free to dismount. You must meet my wife. Ellen, come out and greet our visitors."

As we put heel to earth, the door opened. A woman with a ruggedly healthy look came out. Just short of middle age, she was pretty in her own way, and despite her long, loose dress appeared to have a very respectable figure, though putting on a few extra pounds at the waist in front. She put an arm around Brusov, who returned the favor. Doubtless we were seeing the hidden marksman who had watched us so carefully. She was a most tempting sight for men who had been on the trail for weeks. Yet the looks that passed between her and her husband left little doubt about our chances with the woman. Nor did we doubt that she'd have cheerily killed the whole lot of us had we threatened her husband. Brusov introduced us. "This is my wife, Ellen," he said, squeezing the woman and giving her another look.

Ah, well. If abstinence was good for the soul, we were becoming very good men, indeed.

Brusov waved a hand, as if to someone behind us, and we turned to look in unison. A mounted figure came forward, bow in hand and arrow nocked. Where had this one come from? Could it be our Tracker?

We looked at Murdock accusingly. "Harrumpf. We were so close to the Outpost, I didn't bother checking for anyone following."

"Nor did I," Lorich added.

I glanced at Jenkins.

"I was depending on our wizards," the little sergeant admitted.

Brusov made this introduction too. "That's Dakota. She's a Pacifican scout, and usually leads the supply trains back and forth. She's been ordered to guide you through the mountains."

Dakota was a *she*?

I wasn't the only one to give the scout Dakota a second look—and to recognize that it was most certainly a she who was dismounting and coming forward. She was two or three years older than I was. If Dakota was not a pretty woman, neither was she unattractive. Her cowhide jacket could not conceal a definite swelling of her shirt, nor her leggings hide the waist and hips of a woman. Yet beneath a floppy hat her hair was cropped close, and she had a wiry hardness about her in both face and limbs. When she held her head in a particular way, her features looked almost mannish, and her mannerisms lacked the femininity that might be expected of her sex.

The scout put the arrow back in its quiver, and spoke in a blunt voice, high but hard, that made no attempt to hide an element of scorn. "I've been following you for two miles. You should have realized."

Only two miles? Then she wasn't the Tracker.

With all the clues, I did wonder whether Dakota was one of those who preferred the companionship of her own sex. Normally, it wouldn't have bothered me, since I have little concern about anyone's orientation or activities as long as the participants are adults, are willing, and know how to avoid the pox and pregnancy. In this case, however, there was a definite paucity of women, and a preference for her own sex left no eligible females for my companions to dabble with. And, if truth be told,

for me to dabble with, as well. For I found I *was* ready
to dabble again—physically, if not in any other way.

It was quite encouraging, actually, and I felt the be-
ginnings of a smile forming upon my face.

Heinrich Brusov made introductions to the two
women, his language and grace such that I suspected he
could have functioned as comfortably in a throne room
as at an isolated outpost. His wife Ellen was gracious
and warm as she nodded and spoke a word of welcome
to each of us. Dakota's acquaintance was made with
only an arrogant and disinterested "hello" from her as
she met each of us. Kren, still covered, generated the
same disinterest. Murdock earned a snide comment.
"*Wizard* Murdock? Just what we need, another shaman
to prey on the superstitions of the tribes and clans."

Lorich retorted angrily. "Wizard Murdock is the
greatest magician in the world."

"Of course," she scoffed, turning to Lorich, and it
was only then that we saw a spark of interest in her
manner. She eyed him up and down, studying his awk-
ward form.

An emotion flickered across his face. Anger?

She reached out and touched the hump on Lorich's
shoulder.

Kren almost spoke out in objection, but stopped at a
gesture from Mr. Brusov.

The young wizard winced at the unexpected touch,
and finally met her eyes. His own were full of suspicion.
"I did not give you permission to touch me."

She ignored his words. "This is from birth?"

Lorich blinked. "Yes."

"Does it hurt?"

"No."

"Good." Her face broke into a smile. "What's your
first name?"

He hesitated, his eyes fixed upon her smile. "I don't
have any. I'm just Lorich."

"And I'm just Dakota. Welcome, Lorich. It's good to

meet you.'' And with that, she strode off around the side of the outpost.

Kren wore a frown. "Not too much on tact, is she?"

Mr. Brusov shrugged. "Dakota can be a bit abrupt at times, but she means well. She's an excellent scout, and you'll be glad she's guiding you. Come, take your horses around to the stable entrance, and then we'll see if we can't put together a hot meal for our illustrious emissaries."

Fully half the Outpost was actually a barn, with a score of narrow stalls on the ground level entered through a reinforced wooden door. The second floor was a loft piled high with rolled bales of hay, though a precise, narrow path to each shuttered firing slit was kept clear. The other half of the Outpost was living quarters, with a common area and kitchen entered from the front door, two back rooms used by the Brusovs, and a stair giving access to a dozen small rooms on the upper floor. A half dozen were used for storage of trade goods, another was used by Dakota, and yet another—the first room on the right at the top of the stairs—boasted a lock. It was the only lock in the Outpost. The other rooms were empty and provided our sleeping quarters. Well, even if there were no soft beds, a roof over our heads was a welcome change.

We saw to the horses for the rest of the afternoon, washed clothes, and bathed in the cold waters downstream of the pond. As the sun went below the mountains to the west we came inside, and Mr. Brusov shut and barred the Outpost doors. It was quite comforting to have stout doors between us and the dangers of the world, even if it did get a bit warm in the common room. The fireplace and an oven built into the bricks were responsible for the heat.

The aroma of fresh bread and cooking food filled the room. We pulled two long tables and their benches from against the walls. The tables were placed end to end, and set with plates, bowls, and cutlery. An oil lamp near the table center complemented the glow from the fireplace. Soon Mrs. Brusov led her husband, Murdock, and Kren in procession from the fireplace, each carrying serving plate, pot, or dish. Dinner was a thick soup of meat and vegetables served with corn bread, boiled eggs, and boiled corn still on the cob.

Besides the pitchers of cool water, Mr. Brusov opened a jug of wine with a flourish. "It's not every day that we get visitors, and never that we've had such distinguished figures as honor us tonight. I regret that we could not lay out a feast, but such as we have, you are welcome to. I know you're all hungry and tired after your travels, but please join me in saying grace."

Kren had just stuffed a hunk of corn bread into his mouth. He stopped, considered his best course, and swallowed with a gulp, nodding. "Grace. Yes, a good idea."

We bowed our heads.

"Father, for this meal we give thanks, and for the safe delivery of our guests to the Outpost. May your protection be with them until they return to their homes."

With a sincere "Amen" from all in the party, we dug in with knives, forks, spoons, and fingers, gobbling soup, bread, eggs, and corn with hearty gluttony. The food was good and in quantity, washed down with cold water or savory wine. Tired travelers could ask no more.

The Brusovs allowed my party to shovel in the food without interruption, while each in turn shared information about the status of the Outpost and the plains tribes and the mountain clans. There weren't as many tribesmen about as might usually be expected at this time of year. Many chiefs and subchiefs had taken their tribes and villages east to try raiding against the nations, encouraged by the belief that Arkan and Texan were weakened against their incursions, information we already knew. Mr. Brusov had tried to convince the chiefs that such an assumption about the nations could be a mistake, but the chiefs ignored him. No use letting common sense interfere with their desire for glory and goods.

When the bottom of the soup pot had been scraped

dry, the platters left barren of bread and eggs, and our plates heaped with corn husks, even I had to admit that I was, for the moment, satisfied. All was cleared away except for cups and the wine jug. Elbows and forearms were plopped on the tables in relaxed informality, and even a discreet burp or two was allowed. Pipes were lit, and the sweet smell of tobacco mingled with the lingering aroma of food.

"And now," Ellen Brusov stated with a smile that included us all, "it's your turn. Might you share your tale with us?" The words were accompanied by a telling glance at Jason and Kendall, as if she were asking a special question only they would understand.

Kendall smiled back. "Yes, Ellen. Everyone in the party knows our purpose and our destination." He recounted a brief version of the War Against the Alliance, mentioning which leaders and Pacifican advisors had precipitated it, and continued with our subsequent campaigns against Governor Rodes and General Murphy, and finally, Robert's plans for a Confederation of the six nations.

"And that's about it. Our communications with Pacifica were uncertain, and we couldn't be sure messages were getting through. King Robert's proposal was so significant that we thought a meeting with the Board of Administrators might be the best way of dealing with the issues. So here we are. It was a quiet, uneventful trip—" (Jenkins choked on his wine)—"except for the Tracker."

Dakota lifted her head. "The Tracker?"

Major Kren told the tale of the mysterious figure who stalked us so effectively.

Heinrich Brusov considered the information. "So you think he's no immediate threat?"

Murdock shrugged. "Who's to know? Certainly, he's done us no harm so far, and he did save us from the buffalo stampede."

"Still, we'll have to do something about him," Dakota declared with finality.

Ellen Brusov had listened carefully, eyeing each of us in turn as our roles in the events had been narrated. Now she cast a glance across the table at our beastman. "And Major Kren is going along as an observer in all this?" From her tone, she might have been asking if he wanted more coffee.

The beastman met her glance. "An observer. And an emissary, participating with the discretionary authority granted me by General Sokol, ambassador to Kenesee. The Beastwood is not subject to the Codes, and yet we recognized their value, and have followed them since their inception two hundred years ago. Voluntarily. So it is in our interest to know what the great nation of Pacifica is planning, and what it can mean for the Beastwood."

Ellen Brusov nodded. "And would the Beastwood join this Confederation, if it were invited?"

Kren considered his words. "King Robert declared his intention to invite the Beastwood to join. I do not know the minds of our High Council. Perhaps they would not respond to the invitation immediately, for the Council is cautious. But limited trade has already begun between the six nations and the Beastwood. It is proving very lucrative to our country. I suspect that the advantages of belonging to the Confederation will make themselves clear, and sooner rather than later."

"I see," the woman mused. "You're saying the Confederation is an idea whose time has come."

The beastman was silent, but Murdock responded for him. "Perhaps it is. But without the support of Pacifica, implementing the idea will be difficult."

"Or impossible," Dakota added in challenge.

Murdock shook his head. "Not impossible. Just at great cost, and with limited success. A mediocre plan supported by all factions is better than an excellent plan encountering resistance."

Dakota seemed about to argue further, but Ellen Brusov spoke up quickly. "Given the climactic events of the last two years, I think Jason and Kendall were right in bringing Prince Arn to Pacifica—not that anyone has asked my opinion. This is a matter for the Board of Administrators, though their decision will not be an easy one, I fear.''

Her husband had been listening quietly, puffing away at a corncob pipe stuffed with Kenesee tobacco from my hoard. Now he shifted on the bench and removed the pipe stem from his mouth. ''Perhaps our discussion would be most beneficial if focused upon *getting* the emissaries to Pacifica. After all, the merits of confederation will mean little if you don't make it through the passes alive.''

Kren nodded. ''Excellent point. I've always felt survival took precedence over philosophic considerations.''

A mischievous smile appeared on Lorich's face. Finally, the boy was smiling again. ''Major Kren, should we tell them the tale of our dinosaur hunt?''

Kren frowned. ''I'm sure they'd be bored.''

''True,'' said Murdock. ''Any story involving our hairy companion must by its nature be boring.''

''You see what I've had to put up with for the last month?'' Jason asked the three Pacificans. ''The first week wasn't bad. But after that . . .''

''Come now, Jason,'' Murdock admonished. ''You've enjoyed the banter no end, so admit it.''

''What shape is your party in?'' Ellen Brusov inquired.

Murdock looked at our faces for agreement. ''Pretty good, actually. The horses aren't in the condition they were when we started, but most are holding up well. One is getting a bit worn, and another is developing a bad leg, so we could use replacements for those, if that would be possible. We need more rations, of course, and we lost our blankets. For ourselves, I think we're all a bit tired of the long days in the saddle, but everyone is holding out well, even Jason.''

The healer cocked an eyebrow. ''Thought I couldn't get out of my rocking chair, is that it, Wizard?''

Kren leaped in. ''If we had as much padding in the

backside as Murdock, none of us would mind the saddle at all.''

"We can give you two fresh mounts," Heinrich Brusov stated. "And you're welcome to whatever supplies you need."

"Our thanks," said Murdock.

"But your timing is certainly fortunate. Another week or two, and I'd have to say you were starting too late. You wouldn't make it across the mountains before the snows hit the passes."

Dakota sipped wine from her cup. "Unless we run into trouble, we should make Pacifica before the snows. So I think it might be good if we let your party rest tomorrow, and leave the day after."

Both the Brusovs seemed surprised. "I thought you were anxious to get going as soon as possible," Heinrich stated.

Dakota looked at her cup a moment before responding. "I'd thought so. But now that I see how old some of them are, I think a day out of the saddle might be valuable. Certainly the horses could use a day of rest."

How old some of them were? Murdock pointed at Kren. "She must be talking about you."

Kren gestured at the scout. "Miss Dakota—"

She interrupted brusquely. "Not *Miss*. Just Dakota."

"Yes, ma'am."

"And don't call me *ma'am* either."

Kren paused, and somehow I got the distinct impression he was counting to ten. Finally, he went on. "Yes, Dakota. It was mentioned that you are a guide, a scout for supply trains from Pacifica."

She nodded. "A train leaves Pacifica every six months, spring and fall. I bring out the fall train, and remain here till the spring. The other scout takes the train back to Pacifica. Then he brings out the spring train, and stays here while I take the train back. Half a year here, half a year in Pacifica for each of us."

"The trains consist of a half dozen guards with a score or more of pack animals," Heinrich Brusov elaborated. "They deliver trade goods and supplies to the Outpost, stay a few days, then head back with rare hides and other furs that the tribes have sold. Of course, Pacifica doesn't really need the hides, but it does preserve the fiction that the trade is even-sided. And we accomplish our purpose of helping the tribes while maintaining the Outpost."

Murdock listened carefully. "So travel through the mountains is quite established, and the mountain clans are not a threat."

Young Dakota squinted at the venerable wizard as if she were an impatient teacher instructing a slow learner. Her tone was insultingly didactic. "For the supply trains, yes. The trains pass through the lands of several different clans. With a goodly donation in goods to each tribe—and the threat of military action if they break their word—the clans agreed to let the trains go through. Just the two trains each year, mind you. Stragglers, explorers, travelers are all fair game, as far as the clans are concerned. Don't forget that."

Lorich seemed about to say something, saw Murdock shake his head no, and refrained. Dakota noted Lorich's hesitation, and her squint smoothed out into open-eyed acceptance. "Yes, Lorich. You wanted to ask me something?"

Lorich took a deep breath. "The supply train has already left?"

"Naturally," she confirmed. "The train left over a week ago."

"Why didn't the train wait till we arrived, and we could have all gone together for safety?"

Heinrich Brusov tried to answer for Dakota, but he wasn't fast enough to cut off the scout's answer. "Orders only came after it left. Besides, you wouldn't be considered part of the train and would jeopardize its safety."

Murdock studied Dakota and Heinrich Brusov.

Kendall and Jason exchanged glances.

Something was going on, but I hadn't caught what it was.

Kren had. "Orders? What orders?"

"That I should guide you to Pacifica," Dakota offered, unaware of her mistake. And she *had* made a mistake. Kren's question had revealed it to the slower members of the party such as me.

"Who brought the orders?" Murdock asked, peering at the Pacificans. "Where is the courier? Or," he added after a pause, "was the message delivered in some other way?"

Dakota realized her error. She sat silent.

Brusov looked to Kendall and Jason for help, but Jason only shook his head. "My companions are not stupid, you know. They would have started asking questions sooner or later. I suspect Murdock already has some idea of the answer."

Brusov gave up the pretense. "What do you think is the answer, Wizard Murdock?"

Our magician contemplated his mug. "Given the wires strung upon the roof, and the speed with which you've received messages about us, I suspect Pacifica has use of a valuable Old World invention."

I thought of the museum in Kingsport, and the old wonders preserved there.

"Radio?" asked Kren in an awed voice.

"Radio," confirmed Jason.

The room fell silent. The Pacifican faces showed resignation. Their secret was out. The rest of us contemplated the idea. Radio. A bit of the Old World became reality. Not just cannons or muskets, not just mechanical things, but a wondrous communication device that seemed more akin to magic than any mere weapon.

Kren's eyes sparkled. "You have one here?"

Brusov nodded. "We have one here."

Lorich's eyes sparkled too. "May we see it?"

Brusov hesitated, and his wife put a hand over his. "What does it matter now? Come, gentlemen, and I'll show you."

With the scrape of benches we rose and followed her to the first room at the top of the stairs. The one with the lock upon the door. Murdock held a lamp for her as she inserted the key, removed the lock and allowed the door to swing open. She stepped in and gestured Murdock to follow. He entered, and the illumination showed us what we sought.

A table and chair were set against one wall, a cabinet of drawers against another, and what might have been a wood box sat on the floor next to the table. On the table was an oil lamp, and also what had the general appearance of a large bread box, but clearly wasn't. Two metal switches protruded from the front of the box, and a wire ran from the box up the wall and into a crack in the roofing. Two wires ran down from the bread box to an upright, very narrow box on the floor beneath the table, and from the narrow box protruded two pedals. Two more wires ran to a small device in front of the bread box.

Murdock peered at the table, his finger pointing to each element of the thing in turn while his lips moved silently, either knowing or guessing at their names.

Ellen Brusov provided definite answers. She pointed to the bread box. "Transmitter/receiver." The box on the floor. "Electrical generator." The small device. "Morse key." And finally, "The antenna is on the roof, as you know."

"A Morse key." Murdock repeated, studying the small instrument in front of the box. He pushed down several times on the key with a finger so that that it made a dull clicking noise with each push. "Amazing. No voice signals, I presume?"

"Just Morse," said the woman.

"Well!" was all Kren could say. "Well, well, well."

The next day was spent in work and leisure, sleeping late into the morning, eating a large breakfast, seeing to the horses and gear, and taking naps. Then, we met the challenge of lunch. After that it was another cold bath in the stream, weapons practice, walks about the Outpost grounds, relaxed smokes, and more naps. I was sitting on a wooden bench in the shade of the Outpost having another pipeful. The one-eyed dog was flopped on the ground beneath my bench, his head lying on my foot as he napped, man's faithful companion.

I watched Kren and Jenkins washing in the pond and fending off the duck with the twisted wing. The bird was attacking them with great persistence, apparently expecting them to provide something to eat. Heinrich Brusov wandered out, perhaps making sure all was well with his guests. "Coriolanus is rather insistent," he stated with a laugh when he noticed the beastman and sergeant trying to shoo away the duck.

"Coriolanus?" I repeated.

"That's what Dakota calls him. She found the thing injured near the pond. I think it escaped a fox. I wanted to have it for dinner, but she insisted on nursing it back to health and keeping it here. She couldn't fix the wing, but she did keep it alive. Same thing with old Hungry here." He reached down and scratched the dog's head. The animal immediately rolled over onto its back in anticipation of more. "Hungry limped his way to the Outpost as a pup. He must have come off second best in a fight with another mutt. I wouldn't let her name the dog Agrippa. Coriolanus was quite enough for one Outpost. To tell the truth, I didn't think Hungry was going to make it, but Dakota pulled him through, and he became another of her pets. She's like that. Finds a stray that's hurting, and just wants to make it better."

"I wouldn't have thought it of her," I said.

"I can understand that," he admitted. "But Dakota has her soft side. She just tries to hide it."

And she hides it so well, I thought to myself.

We chatted a bit more, then Heinrich went inside, Hungry put his head back upon my boot, and I switched my attention from the two bathing beauties to Kendall and Dakota as they wandered off together. The two were never out of view as they ambled slowly about the fields, deep in some weighty discussion; but they were out of range of my hearing. Now what were *they* talking about? What could Kendall be telling her? What plans might they be making? I could only watch and wait.

That evening brought an excellent meal of bread and salted pork that finished off the Brusovs' wine jug, Murdock and Kendall sharing tales of the six nations for the Brusovs, and an eventual retreat to our blankets. The day of rest had certainly been nice, and the amount of sleep Jason and Murdock took showed that the time off was not totally unwarranted.

And yet, it really hadn't been necessary to lose a whole day. The horses were in good shape, it only took an hour to secure the extra supplies we needed from the Brusov's stocks, and even Jason, our oldest member, was holding out quite well and could have gone on. I didn't worry about it. Dakota was the expert in the mountains, and we would have to trust to her expertise.

However, I found that perhaps it would be well not to trust her too much.

It was the middle of the night when I awoke, my throat dry, probably because of the second or third generous helping of salt pork. While each room had a chamber pot, there was no fresh water. But two pitchers of water were on the shelf in the common room, and I slipped out quietly so as not to disturb Murdock.

Padding barefoot down the hallway, I noticed a light coming from beneath the door of the "radio room," and heard a faint clicking noise. So that's what it sounded like when in use, a solid *click* rather than the dull *clack* when Murdock had tried it. Could someone be receiving a message—or "signal," as the Pacificans had called it?

I tried to make out the message from the sound alone, but found it an impossible task. Years before I had learned Morse for use with smoke, flags, and mirrors for military signals, but these *clicks* took getting used to, they blended into each other far too quickly for me to pick out more than an occasional letter.

Admitting defeat, I ignored the activity in the radio

room and went down the stairs with what seemed like a creak in the middle of every step. An oil lamp had been left burning low in the common room for the benefit of guests, and there was little problem finding the water pitchers and quenching my thirst. On the way back up the stairs I stepped along the edge of each step in order to avoid the noisy creaks that had accompanied my descent.

I had barely gained the top step when the door of the radio room opened and Dakota stepped out with a small oil lamp in hand. She almost ran into me, and let out a whispered oath in surprise. "Damn fool. You startled me."

"Sorry," I said. "Just getting a bit of water."

She swallowed, regained her composure, and then raised the lamp to peer at me more closely—the first time she'd given me more than a passing glance. "Are *you* Prince Arn, the one they call Prince Scar? Or is it the short one?"

Well, I had certainly made an impression upon this young woman, hadn't I? "No, it's not the short one," I stated irritably.

"So it's you." She studied my face for a long moment, and her own was set in—what? Consternation? Worry? Or was it determination? And did I see the flicker of what might have been . . . pity? Or was it all my imagination?

"Now I know. Good night, Prince Arn. Best we get some sleep."

And so I did, or at least I tried. But as I wrapped my blanket around me and lay upon the floorboards, my mind puzzled over the encounter. What message had Dakota sent—or received? And why the sudden concern with determining which of the party was Prince Arn? And why that flicker of pity?

My fear was that I would find out the answers to those questions.

PART • TWO

ACROSS THE MOUNTAINS

1

Into the Mountains

On the day of departure we were up and about at first light, saddling our mounts, arranging gear and supplies on the packhorses, and triple-checking our list to make sure that nothing was forgotten. Afterwards, Ellen Brusov called us to the table and we enjoyed a morning meal of hot biscuits with honey and jam, bacon, and coffee.

She laughed when we emptied the first biscuit plate before she could bring the second. "Well, it's a good thing you're leaving. Another few days, and there wouldn't be anything left for the winter."

Kendall held out his mug as the coffeepot came around. "The Kenesee folk are known to eat more than anyone else in the six nations."

"Like locusts, they are," Kren added.

Jenkins swallowed a mouthful of biscuit and honey. "Do I hear Major Kren—who needs his own supply train to sustain him—criticizing *others* for how much they eat?"

"A supply train is an exaggeration," Kren retorted. "A wagon or two will do nicely for my needs."

"We men of Kenesee aren't that bad," said Murdock. "Most of us just have healthy appetites. Then again, Prince Arn has been known to eat enough for three men, surpassing even my efforts at the supper table."

"It's time we were going." Dakota stood up, totally unimpressed with our attempts at humor, and went to the door. She looked at us. We were all still seated at the table.

Murdock smiled tolerantly. "Perhaps it is time we were on our way."

We brought the horses from their stalls, tightened cinches, and made one last equipment check before departure. Ellen Brusov waited for us to complete our preparations, ready to be helpful. Heinrich Brusov drifted about, exchanging lighthearted comments with party members.

Hungry came around for petting, and rolled over when Kren gave him some attention. "Good dog," the beast-man said, rubbing the animal's stomach. "Not like that duck. I'm surprised that thing hasn't attacked us yet today."

Lorich and Kren were arguing about whether it was Friday or Saturday. It was easy to lose track when traveling.

"It's Saturday, September 30th," Heinrich offered. "You have a month to get to Pacifica. Don't waste any of it."

When he reached our guide, he lowered his voice to a whisper. "Is everything all right, Dakota?"

She hesitated the briefest moment, then completed checking her horse's bit. "Everything's fine. Why do you ask?"

"You seem troubled this morning. Any reason?"

Dakota forced a smile. "No reason. Just concern about the trip. That's all."

He considered, then accepted the response. "If you say so. Take care of yourself. And listen to Jason and Kendall and Wizard Murdock. Their wisdom is not to be ignored."

"Oh, I'll *listen*," Dakota stated. "Don't worry about me."

"Time to go," Murdock announced before Dakota could say it, and so we mounted and set out, wishes of "Godspeed" following us from the Brusovs.

I gave a glance back, and saw two tiny figures giving

a final wave. There was a sinking feeling in the pit of my stomach. Kren noted my look. "Yes, I feel it too. Hard to leave a place of welcome and comfort and safety, no matter how great the lure of adventure."

I grimaced. "Lure of adventure? I don't feel any lure of adventure."

Kren laughed. "And they say you don't have a sense of humor."

The party headed north, reached the old road, and turned west. We rode in a column of twos, Dakota and Murdock in front, then Jason and Kendall, followed by Kren and me, and in the rear were Lorich and Jenkins. Each of us led a packhorse on a long lead, so that even as a column of twos, the party stretched out to a length of eight horses. A bit large for a party trying to sneak through the territories of the various mountain clans, but there was no helping it. We had to depend on the skills of Dakota and Murdock.

It was time for them to put those skills to use as the ancient highway entered the mountains. But one matter of importance was still to be resolved.

Dakota handed the lead line of her packhorse to Murdock as we marched. "Here. I'll go ahead to scout. Around noon I'll wait for you to catch up, and we'll eat."

I eavesdropped, of course. Might as well use my one magical talent and keep in practice.

"How far ahead will you be?" Murdock asked.

"A half mile. Maybe a mile. Depends."

"All right," the wizard said. And then he added something. "You have my permission."

Aha. I knew a challenge when I heard one.

Dakota looked at him. "I don't need your permission."

The wizard pushed up the brim of his hat. "I'm sorry, Dakota, I assumed you understood the command arrangements of our party. Prince Arn is the prime emissary, and he has the right to order us as he will. However, he's asked me to lead the party in the more mundane tasks of daily survival, and to get us safely to Pacifica. So in that sense, I am in command.''

"The scout is in command of our supply trains," Dakota said, her voice cold.

"I'm sure that works quite well for the supply trains. It would not work so well here.''

Dakota glanced at Jason and Kendall, who pretended not to hear the discussion going on in front of them. Or maybe they really couldn't hear anything. Murdock had lowered his voice when explaining the situation to our guide.

"What if I don't like that arrangement?" Dakota asked.

Murdock pointed to the rear. "Then you may return to the Outpost. We'll miss your guidance, but muddle on somehow without it.''

We rode on a few more steps, Dakota looking forward. She made up her mind. "With your permission, I'll ride ahead to scout.''

"Granted.''

She rode off at a proud canter, and one more issue was resolved. I was surprised. From everything I'd seen of the woman, her pride was paramount. I had expected her to leave us as soon as the wizard had put out his challenge. But something had tempered her response. Could it be an interest in Lorich?

Murdock looked back at us. "All right, we're back on the trail. Standard security. Be alert back there, Wizard Lorich, Sergeant Jenkins. Watch for the Tracker too.''

"Yes, Master.''

"Aye, sir. We're watching.''

And so we rode into the Rockies, and started the second half of our trek across the continent. Again, I could only look at the mountains with wonder. They rose out of the flat plain in stark beauty and challenge. The Smokies and other mountains of Kenesee were nothing like these giants. Only Kelly's Inferno and other volcanoes could match their size. Yet the mountains were not as they were for the Ancients, for the great earthquakes of long ago had shaken loose not just boulder or cliff, but whole mountainsides.

About noon on the first day we came upon Dakota resting beside the road, already taking her meal. We joined her. I had watch this time, and so remained mounted, scanning all directions for any sign of trouble. Far behind us, where the road we'd traveled rounded a prominence jutting out from a slope, a tiny mounted figure appeared.

I pointed. "Looks like our friend is still with us."

The others gave a glance, and then went back to their meal. Sight of the Tracker was no longer a cause for alarm, or even great interest.

Dakota was not so inclined. She stood and stared, studying our follower. Then she put away what remained of her meal and mounted. "When you finish, go on about a mile and stop."

"Going to arrange a little surprise for our Tracker?" asked Kren.

"If I may have your permission, Wizard Murdock." Her smile was almost a sneer.

Murdock ignored the tone of her voice. "You can try. But the Tracker is good. We haven't been able to bring him in yet. Want any help?"

"You'd just get in my way." With that, she set off.

Jenkins shook his head as she disappeared around a curve in the old road. "Why do you take that from her, sir? It's all I can do to keep from giving her a good shaking every time she opens her mouth."

Murdock chuckled. "She's young. The Wizard Speros once had a young apprentice long ago who thought he knew everything, too. Speros never had to say anything. The apprentice soon learned how little he knew. Give Dakota time. She'll come around."

We finished the meal and went another mile before halting, as Dakota had requested. The party waited a good hour, and then another, before our scout finally caught up with us. She was red-faced and empty-handed, her features set in frustration. "He's good," admitted Dakota. "Very good."

"Better luck next time," Murdock stated evenly. "Come, let's be on our way."

Over the days we followed the old road along slopes, into valleys, and through passes. Where the old bridges used to stand, we went down to the watercourses and used the fords that Dakota marked for us. They weren't that hard to find, actually. Rough trails left by the mountain clans led down to the fords, and once or twice we even found an ill-maintained wooden bridge built upon the foundation of ancient crete pillars that once supported a great bridge of the Old World. As we passed over, we could look down and see the remains of those bridges, each a jumble of rusted metal and broken crete resting at the bottom of a watercourse. Twice we had to swim the horses across. The rivers were still placid. Though we'd had showers, the heavier fall rains had not started yet.

Discoloration in the rock cliffs and mounds of rubble showed where great hunks of mountainside had separated and crashed into the lowlands during the Cataclysm six hundred years before. Where that happened the old road disappeared totally, and we had to detour into forest to avoid the hills of rocky debris that blocked the way. One time, we came to a great tunnel that was blocked with boulders, and had to make one of the widest and longest detours of the trip. Eventually we picked up the old road far on the other side of the tunnel. And so we continued our steady progress westward. Again, the sheer obstacle of these great mountains struck me, and I pondered how anyone could have traversed them before the Ancients built their great highways.

One thing I did notice was how much cooler it was as we progressed. Even the valleys were high above sea level, and always the general elevation rose, so that while days might be warm, nights became very brisk, and a good fire was needed to keep off the cold. Fortunately, the valley meadows were dotted by many stands of flourishing leafed trees, watered by the brooks and streams wending their way down the lowlands between peaks. The slopes were more often covered with coniferous evergreens such as pine and spruce, so that firewood was little problem.

Evenings were a welcome respite from the hours in the saddle. The packhorses were unburdened of supplies and pack frames, while the mounts were unsaddled. Four of us would ensure that all the animals were rubbed down and their hooves inspected and cleaned. Bridles were replaced with halters, and after being watered in the nearby stream the horses would be hobbled and allowed to graze before being tethered safe for the night. While the horses were taken care of, two of us would arrange the equipment about the campsite, start a fire, and get the evening meal prepared. The remaining two would search for firewood and ensure that there was a night's worth of fuel stacked nearby before it darkened.

In spite of the work to be done, everyone enjoyed the opportunity to stand and move about and shake out the stiffness. Certainly Jason would often dismount with a grimace, stretch, and put a hand to his aching back. But then, most of us had to stretch our own backs too, for we ached as well. I had to hand it to Jason. If my back felt so sore, then his aged ligaments must be screaming with pain. Yet he would not touch the powders and painkillers he carried in his healer's bag.

We asked him what he had there, and what he could spare to ease our discomfort.

"I've taken as much as I could for our use—and for trade, if need be," he responded "My powders include morphine and atropine and penicillin and two or three other medicines that might prove useful. But it's a long journey, and a lot can happen. So no asking for powders just to ease aches and pains. We'll need them for serious injuries."

* * *

Typically, Murdock would lead us forward through the morning, and about noon we would find Dakota waiting next to the road to join us for a meal, report any findings such as the tracks of clansmen, and inform us of what terrain or obstacles lay ahead. Then she would set off again, and we wouldn't see her until dusk, when we'd find her arranging a suitably discreet site near the road that she had selected for our camp that evening.

"Is this site satisfactory, Wizard Murdock?" she would ask, ill concealing the sarcasm in her voice. Usually Murdock would nod agreement with a tolerant—if weary—look.

One evening Kren started taking bets on how long it would take our patient wizard finally to confront the proud upstart.

Lorich listened without betting. "My Master shouldn't have to put up with such disrespect. It's my duty to talk to her."

Our beastman paused. "What? And prevent the confrontation we're all looking forward to? This should be better than when Murdock chewed you out for spiriting village wives away from their husbands."

Lorich turned red, and the beastman turned serious. "Don't worry, lad. It was a noble effort, if misplaced. You'll be able to laugh about it someday."

The young wizard chewed his lip. "I know, Major Kren. But I still have to talk to Dakota. I have to try."

Kren nodded. "You do that, lad. Sergeant Jenkins! How much did you say you wanted to bet?"

Later, as the evening chilled and the fire crackled and the sky darkened, Lorich did approach our scout. I considered whether I should refrain from listening this time, but decided to be dishonorable once again.

"Dakota, may I talk to you?" The young wizard spoke formally, but softly. Dakota gave him one of her rare smiles, nodded, and fell into step beside him as he limped off. I was not the only one in the party watching the pair as they made their way down the road. A hundred paces away he stopped and faced Dakota—just at the outer range of my wizardly talent, unfortunately, and I could not make out what they said.

It was another noble effort on the part of our Wizard Lorich. We wondered if there would be an explosion, an expletive, a stomping return on her part from the confrontation. But to our surprise, there was none. And if one looked carefully, even from this distance, the answer might have been found. Dakota stood fully as tall as Lorich, with her hands clasped behind her back, and to all indications staring at him intently, with a perky—and quite feminine—tilt of the head. The two of them stood in conversation for a long time. Dusk slid into night, and now they were only vague shadows on the road, still talking, for we heard Dakota's laugh even from the distance.

Given the experience of the one and the magical talent of the other, they were as safe as anyone could be in the wilderness, and when the hopes for an explosive exchange died away, we went about our own business of enjoying leisure time. I took out my pipe, cleaned the inside of the bowl with my knife, and tapped the loosened debris into the fire.

Jason joined me, holding a new, long-stemmed pipe instead of his usual one. "Decided it was time to break this one in. Maybe the longer stem will give me a cooler smoke." He looked at my own. "Same pipe as always, the one John Black gave you? They're like old friends after a while."

His words called up a scene from long ago of a lean, hard-featured man in the black uniform of the royal guards, standing in my chamber in the castle with his hand extended to me, offering the pipe and tobacco pouch I now carried. John Black, perhaps the greatest military commander of the century, offering me a gift.

I blinked, swallowed the lump in my throat, and nodded. Time to change the subject. "You want to borrow some tobacco again, right? When are you going to share yours, Jason?"

"Saving mine for an emergency. Besides, I saw the

size of that sack of good Kenesee tobacco you brought with you. You've enough for a company of smokers."

From beyond the firelight, Murdock called. "Arn, Jason, come see the sky."

We lit our pipes with a twig from the fire, which had burned down a good bit already, and took a few dozen steps outside the light and warmth to join the wizard towards the center of the meadow. With him were Kren, Kendall, and Jenkins, their heads tilted back, their eyes set upon the sky.

Jason and I followed their gaze, and I let out a gasp of surprise. Beside me, even Jason gave a grunt of appreciation. On the plains the party had enjoyed the days' endless horizons and beautiful skies in blues that caressed the eyes. When it was dark, the vast panorama of starlit night was impressive in its vast arc. Here, the mountains limited the sky to a narrower spectacle. Yet what we had was enough to match the grand expanse of the flatlands' panorama. The night was crisp and fresh and clear, with a clarity and sharpness that is unique, perhaps, to the elevations found in the high valleys on a cold night. Above us in a moonless sky, the stars shone with a beauty to take the breath away and a brilliance that I had never seen before. Even their number seemed greater than I had ever observed. Constellations leaped out of the clusters, as if ready to take on independent life and step down from their perch above. And beyond, the universe stretched out into the endless depths of space, and we shrank to insignificance in the wonder of creation.

"Isn't it glorious?" said Murdock.

The swish of feet through the meadow grass. Lorich and Dakota had finished their discussion at last and joined us. "Yes, Master," Lorich agreed. "It is beautiful."

And then we just stared, hardly noticing the crick in our necks.

Kendall's voice broke the awed silence.

Though the clouded dark of night
obscures the path and weighs the heart
and makes Man question How and Why,
the clouds must thin, and fade at last.
And lo, the distant stars shine out
in splendid spectacle of sight
to light the path and stay the night.
For merciful God, to guide our steps
has left His lanterns in the sky.

"Very nice," said Murdock. "I've never heard that before. Does it have a title?"

Still watching the sky, I sensed, rather than saw, Jason's nod. "It's called 'The Lanterns of God.' An old verse by an unknown poet."

Jenkins spoke. "I think he must have seen the sky as we're seeing it."

"The Lanterns of God. That could have a second meaning," said Murdock.

"And what meaning is that?" Jason asked, his normally grouchy voice almost placid.

"The lanterns of God are those good men and women who light the way for the rest of mankind," said the wizard. "God has given them to the world."

"That's you, Master," said Lorich. "You're one of God's lanterns."

Murdock laughed as if he had just heard the most ridiculous thing in the world. "Oh, no, Lorich. *Good* men and women. Not me."

At the words, I could just make out Kren shaking his head in disbelief. If not Murdock, who?

At last, with necks turning stiff and ears chilled, we returned to the fire and our blankets. Only the wizard Murdock remained in the darkness, his hands clasped behind his back, his eyes drinking in the stars.

Jenkins, who had first watch, noted the wizard's dark figure. "He never gets tired of the night sky, does he?"

"It's a hard thing to have the heart's desire within view, and yet never be able to touch," said Jason. "Our wizard wants the stars. He's not the first man to do so."

To our surprise, Lorich's talk with Dakota seemed to get results over the next few days. Her tone softened, and she hid—for the most part—her scorn of Murdock. And then one late afternoon she was given proof of the wizard's ability just as we were preparing to set up camp. "There are two travelers ahead, coming this way, probably mounted," Murdock informed the party. He moved us farther off the road to a hidden site and prohibited any fire or loud noises.

Dakota was duly impressed when, a few minutes later, two warriors of a mountain clan passed upon their horses, totally unaware of us watching them from amongst the trees.

"You knew they were coming," Dakota admitted. "Two of them, just like you said."

Murdock watched the warriors pass out of sight down the road. "A small talent, I admit. But useful at times, wouldn't you say?"

And with that the look of disdain disappeared, the sarcasm stopped, and she followed orders as readily as any of us did. For though we might lighten our journey with banter and jokes at poor Murdock's expense, the wizard's wise directives were followed quickly and completely. We had not gotten this far across the continent by doubting his wisdom or arguing with his judgment.

2

The Colorado Clan

We were a week into the mountains when Dakota gave us warning during breakfast. "There's a village ahead, a large one. It's the home of Chief Jones, the leader of the Colorado Clan."

"Jones? Chief *Jones*?" Murdock asked, dismayed. "What of the colorful names for tribal chiefs like Running Bear and Long Eyes and Swift Eagle and Great Heart?"

"Glad they don't name them like that at sea," Jenkins mumbled. "I can't see addressing Captain Grayson as Chief Flying Fish."

Dakota ignored the sergeant. "Those are names used by the American Indians of ancient times. These are mountain clans. His name is Jones. Peter Jones."

"Ah, well. Is it difficult going around the village?" Murdock asked.

"We can't go around it," she answered. "It sits at the bottom of a pass where the valley narrows. A choke point. They have lookouts."

Murdock looked at the scout. "I presume you have a way of overcoming that difficulty."

"Naturally," said Dakota. "We ride into the village and visit the chief."

Kren stopped stuffing his saddlebag and spoke curtly. "I thought you said only the supply trains could get through the clan territories, and that everyone else was fair game."

Dakota gave him a look. "That's what I said. The

171

only chief who is reasonable is Chief Jones of the Colorado Clan. He can be persuaded to let us through.''

Murdock saw her meaning. ''By reasonable, you mean we have to bribe him.''

''A small payment from Outpost resources,'' she stated. ''But he does care for his people, and would rather not lose warriors needlessly. Also, he likes to receive a nice gift when negotiations are over. Think about what you have to offer.''

And then Dakota rode off, leaving us to contemplate what we could spare.

On the prairie we'd regularly made forty miles or more each day without exhausting our mounts. The flatness of the terrain and the long, continuous stretches of old road made easy passage for both horses and riders. The mountains were a different matter. Inclines slowed progress both uphill *and* downhill. The days were growing shorter too. Dawn came later and dusk earlier, cutting the hours of daylight noticeably. Thirty miles was about the maximum we could hope to achieve on a good day, with a steady twenty-five miles or so daily being closer to the average.

It was proving to be a long, long journey.

Shortly after noon we found Dakota waiting for us in a hollow next to the road. Beyond the hollow, in the upper end of the valley, lay the village she had spoken of, a settlement of log cabins and lodges with steep, wood-shingled roofs, the front of each dwelling boasting one or more rich and soft furs as decoration and identification. It *was* a large settlement, for there must have been at least a hundred dwellings, including a dozen big lodges, and each of the lodges could have housed a score of unmarried warriors or maidens, at least. Fenced corrals and scattered pastures held horses, cattle, and sheep.

Kren sidled up next to Murdock just before we headed for the village. ''You comfortable with this, Murdock?'' he said, almost whispering.

''Not really,'' the wizard admitted. ''But she is our

guide, and she knows the way. If Jason and Kendall trust
her, then we will too."

"If you say so, great old one," the beastman said,
lowering and buttoning the flap of his heavy winter cap
across mouth and chin so that his hairy status was covered. "Hope they're in a good mood today."

Village security was tight. Some lookout must have
spotted us even as we left the hollow. At least three
dozen armed warriors stood in a silent clump upon the
road, a delegation waiting to receive us. Another score
had taken to horse, and waited on either side of the road.
Still more men could be seen loping off to take position
in other parts of the village, guarding against surprise
from flanks and rear. Behind the delegation crowded curious women and children anxious to see what the ex-
citement was all about.

Most of the people seemed to be dressed in practical
wool and cowhide, but one man in front who towered
almost a head over the rest had more interesting apparel.
He wore a long coat made of the furred skins of fox and
wolf and raccoon and two or three other animals that I
could not identify. The furs were crudely sewn into a
voluminous garment that extended down to his ankles,
and included a copious hood furred inside and out that
he had pulled up over his head against the day's chill,
so that his features were as hidden as our beastman's in
his cap.

He stepped forward, flanked on either side by a sub-
chieftain.

We drew to a halt in front of them and watched as
the mounted warriors trotted out to take position behind
us. We were nicely boxed in.

Dakota smiled at the crowd of women and children
and nodded at the warriors before bowing her head
deeply to the leader with formal ceremony. "Greetings,
Chief Jones."

The chief raised his arms and threw back his hood,
revealing a long, thin face, his black hair grown long
and pulled back into a bun. His warriors wore their hair

in the same manner, and most were bearded. He scanned our party carefully, then gave a nod back at Dakota and spoke in a deep, clear voice. "So it is you, Dakota. You come again so soon to the village of the Colorado Clan. Why?"

His words were in English, though the accent was strange and the pronunciation different for several words. Still, he could be understood.

"I come with friends," Dakota answered. "We wish to cross the land of the Colorado. But none may cross without the permission of Chief Jones."

"We will discuss it in my lodge," the chief responded, and turned away, followed by his subchieftains. The warriors parted, as did the crowd of women and children, and he strode through his people in regal assurance. We followed his path, the warriors ringing us in while the rest of the village came behind chattering with delight.

For all its size, the village was amazingly clean, matching any town or village in Kenesee, certainly. There were the usual smells of horse manure and wood fires and baking bread, as well as the sour smell of a leather tanner. Here and there, two- and four-wheeled carts stood empty, ready to be hitched up. The clansmen had a thriving community, apparently.

The mountain clans were certainly not nomadic. Houses and lodges were well-built structures with roofs designed to handle the heavy snows, and caulked tight to keep out the cold. Quantities of firewood were stacked next to each building, and to my surprise coal was mounded waist high in wooden enclosures next to the lodges. The main paths between buildings were even paved with rough bricks.

Arriving at one of the big lodges in the middle of the village, Chief Jones pushed open a stout wooden door and ducked his head to enter. His two subchieftains, one rotund and the other husky and each wearing a dark blue hat with a badge of rank, followed him in. We dismounted. Murdock studied the situation, and noted the eager clan members eyeing the horses greedily. "I presume we should leave guards with the horses?"

"It would be a good idea," Dakota agreed.

Jenkins, Kren, Kendall, and Lorich were delegated to watch the horses. Kren shook his head. "I'm sorry, Murdock. On our last adventure, I was just along as a companion. I played my role, and obeyed orders and was a good boy. This time I'm an emissary from the Beastwood. I should go too. If you order otherwise, I will obey for the good of the party. But you will be wrong to do so."

Murdock considered the request. "All right, oh hairy one. Sometimes I forget your status. You're right, for a change. Jason, would you mind—"

The healer cut him off. "All my seniority for naught. Ah, well. I'll take Kren's place out here. Go on in, but don't give away all the horses."

"Thank you, Jason. We'll be sure to keep a nag or two. Jenkins, try not to kill any of the villagers until we come out."

"The Chief is waiting," Dakota reminded us.

Kren and I followed Murdock and Dakota into the lodge, the beastman's status as emissary not too elevated to keep him from carrying a sack of carefully culled items from our supplies. It was quite warm inside. Fully half the structure was a single room, open to the roof in the center. Ladders climbed to a narrow loft with wooden railings and benches running around the edge of the room so members of the tribe could look onto the open center of the main floor and observe the activities. All the benches were empty. Wooden shutters on both the upper- and main-floor windows remained closed, and a dozen oil lamps provided illumination.

On the main floor, Chief Jones had assumed his place in a large wooden chair centered behind a long table. A smaller chair on either side of him held his two subchieftains, their caps off and lying in prominent display on the table before them. Behind the table was a great stone fireplace with a steaming cauldron upon the hearth.

The mud-caulked log walls boasted various spears, swords, and colorful shields arranged in symmetric displays.

Amidst all this, we sat on rough benches at a second table facing the chief and his men, first Dakota, then Murdock, me, and Kren. Dakota remained silent, and we took our cue from her.

The chief undid his coat, withdrew his arms, and let it lie on the back of his great chair. He wore a wool shirt and trousers, and was as lanky as he was tall. Yet when he pushed up the arms of his shirt because of the warmth, the muscles and sinew on his forearms were lean, hard cords.

"Well," said the chief to our scout, "now we can talk. What are you doing here, Emily?"

"Emily?" Kren blurted out with wicked glee. "Dakota's name is *Emily*?"

Chief Jones eyed the beastman. "When she made her first trip through the mountains and visited our clan, I named her Dakota because she reminded me of the women we've bought from the Dakota tribe—skinny, but fierce and proud. She liked the name more than her own, and took it. But in the lodge here where I named her, I can still call her Emily." He stared at Kren. "As namegiver, no one else but I have the right to call her by her old name."

Kren forced the smile off his face. "Dakota is a good name."

The chief grunted. "Wise of you to think so. I am Peter Jones, Head Chief of the Colorado Clan. These are my most trusted followers. This one is Faraday, the Clan Shaman. His wisdom is known throughout the clan, and all shamans hold him in respect. And here is Fierce Owl, the greatest warrior in all the clan." The shaman was the rotund clansman. The husky man, the warrior.

"Did you hear that, Arn?" Murdock whispered. "Fierce Owl. What a wonderful name."

"What's a shaman?" I was forced to ask.

"Wizard. Witch doctor. High priest. Medicine man. Take your pick."

Oblivious, Dakota made our introductions. "Traveling with me are famous men from Pacifica and from the nations of the east—"

Famous men? How good of her to finally recognize it.

"Seated here are Prince Arn of Kenesee, the actual Prince Scar of the stories you have heard, the one who defeated the Alliance." Eyebrows went up. "Next to him is Wizard Murdock of Kenesee, a great shaman known throughout his own land. And last is Major Kren, emissary from the Beastwood, north of Kenesee."

Fierce Owl's eyes widened and seemed to bulge, so I could guess at least one reason that he was named Owl. "From the Beastwood?"

There were grunts from the clansmen when Kren loosened his chin flap and pulled off the cap.

"Take off your coat and shirt too, Kren," said Dakota.

"You mean it?" Kren asked, fearing it was a joke. "I should take off my shirt?"

"Yes, do it," she ordered. And added softly, "It'll help."

Kren did as indicated, the dark hair on his chest and shoulders bringing muttered comments from the chief's men. The shaman and Fierce Owl actually came over and started running their hands over the beastman's shoulders and chest, feeling the hair to make sure it was real—to Kren's distress.

The chief noted the beastman's discomfort and grinned. "Enjoying yourself, Major Kren?"

Kren watched the warriors studying him. "I wouldn't mind so much if they were village maidens."

The clansmen all laughed, and the two touching Kren patted him on the shoulder in comradely fashion and came over to me. I could anticipate what they wanted, and spread the now ample whiskers of my beard aside so that they could see the scar across my cheek.

"You are young," Faraday the Shaman commented before the two returned to their seats.

"And who is left waiting outside?" the chief asked.

"Two Pacificans returning to their homeland after long years away. A sergeant of the Kenesee royal guards. And . . . an apprentice to Wizard Murdock."

"The hunchback," the shaman deduced.

Dakota was silent a moment. "Yes. The hunchback."

"Poor boy," said the chief. "How cruel of his parents. He should never have been allowed to live." He pondered. "We could put him out of his misery for you, if you want."

Murdock spoke up quickly. "We still find him useful at times. Cooking, cleaning, polishing boots. That sort of thing."

"Well, as you wish. But I did not think you so cold-hearted." Chief Jones pounded a carved elkhorn club on the table, and two middle-aged and matronly servers entered with a tray full of cups. The two women stared at Kren and giggled, though he had already put his shirt back on. A sharp word from Chief Jones reminded the women of their place. They set down the cups at the fireplace and began ladling from the cauldron into the cups, in danger of spilling the liquid because of their frequent glances at the beastman.

"Come now, gentlemen," said the chief. "Take off your caps and coats and make yourselves comfortable. We'll have a drink of cider and light a smoke before talking."

I tried the cider. It wasn't bad at all. An urn filled with tobacco also made its way around, and I filled my pipe. The tobacco was horrible, strong and acrid and with an unpleasant bite—more like prairie grass spiced with buffalo droppings than true tobacco. I coughed, but continued smoking out of politeness. The chief and both of his followers lit their own pipes.

The servers giggled anew at Kren, so the chief pointed at the door and they left quickly. Fierce Owl shook his head in wonder. "A grown beastman. So this is what the babies would have looked like."

"Babies?" Murdock inquired.

"Such children are still born to our women on occasion, covered with hair. Fewer now, for some reason. As with all the malformed, the infants are killed. To do anything else would be cruelty."

"That is most kind of you," Kren stated with a fixed smile.

"What do you do with yours?" the chief asked Murdock.

Our wizard hung his head. "We did the same. It was the law, made in a time when survival was more uncertain, when ignorance and fear were common. Recently we changed that law. We realized the beastmen were not evil, but simply men like ourselves. And so they have proven to be."

"So they may be," the chief agreed. "But the Beastwood is far away, and there is business to discuss. Why do you wish to cross the land of the Colorado Clan?"

Dakota did not mince her words. "These great men from the eastern nations wish to reach Pacifica. It's a diplomatic mission."

Chief Jones swirled the cider in his cup. "It sounds important. Perhaps that's why there are so many of you. Eight travelers and sixteen horses to pass through our lands." He leered. It was a pleasant change to see greed expressed so openly.

Dakota held out a piece of paper. "This is a letter to the Brusovs at the Outpost. They will give you whatever I list as payment. Now, what shall that payment be?"

What followed was an extended bout of haggling between Dakota and Chief Jones. They argued over everything, the chief asking for horses, medicinal powders, and anything else he could come up with, pointing out that Dakota was a cheap-hearted roamer who had no idea of the responsibilities of a great chief worn down by responsibility for the well-being of his people. Dakota countered with expressions of woe and disbelief at the chief's outright thievery and desire to put the Outpost out of business through his greed.

Murdock, Kren, and I were silent with appreciation. The bargaining would have put hardened Kenesee horse traders to shame. We were watching a match between two masters of the art, and paid them due homage with our attention.

Ultimately, the chief threw up his hands. "Emily, you have outdone me again. I must accept what you offer. Two good horses, and five pounds of healing powders and medicinals."

Dakota bowed her head. "If you accept my offer so soon, I admit my failure. You have gotten exactly what you wanted in the first place."

He shrugged. "I was willing to accept four pounds of powders. But you're getting better. One day you'll have the best of me, and I'll know it's time to hang up my coat and retire as chief."

"May that be long in the future," Dakota said politely.

"Let us hope so. And now, on to subjects more pleasant."

Dakota gave Kren a signal, and the beastman reached under his seat for the sack. In it were the gifts we were to give the chief for the privilege of being extorted. We had put together several items that Dakota thought would serve the purpose. A few of Jason's surgical instruments. A pair of winter boots. A sextant. And so on. Unfortunately, we had need of those items, as we had need of every item we had brought along.

I put a hand on Kren's arm, halting him. "Chief Jones," I said, "I am ready for another smoke. Allow me to offer you a pipeful of my tobacco." The three clansmen all readily accepted. I passed around my pouch, and soon we four were all puffing away.

They had expectant looks upon their faces, which soon turned to beaming smiles. "This is good," said Fierce Owl. "Very good."

"It even smells good," said the shaman.

"Good Kenesee leaf," I explained. "Dipped in Kenesee brandy for aroma and flavor." I stood, held up
my hands in a request for patience, and went outside.
Our four companions were still in the saddle and carefully guarding our other horses to keep the clanspeople
away from the supplies. Men, women, and children were
all clustered around and watching for an opportunity to
go exploring amidst the saddlebags and sacks on our
mounts. Lorich too was generating much interest, and
he had the attention of many children who had decided
taunts and jokes were quite the thing to complete their
day's entertainment.

"They're worse than Kenesee gutter rats," Jenkins
told me as I went to my packhorse. "I've a mind to
have Lorich take care of a few. For instructional purposes."

"We'll be done soon. Then we can leave." I found
the cloth bag I was looking for, emptied half its contents
into an empty sack we still carried, and took it back into
the lodge. The sack must have contained a good two
pounds of tobacco.

I sat down and handed it over to Dakota, who took it
to the chief. "Chief Jones, I present this gift to you from
my companions. May it bring you much enjoyment."

Trusting soul that he was, the chief opened the top
and examined the contents. Content that it was indeed
tobacco, he stuck in his nose and took a deep breath,
drinking in the aroma before passing it to his followers,
who stuck their noses in as well.

"A good gift. A good gift. And now business is finished," said the chief. "I'm in a good mood, Dakota. I
think we'll have a game this afternoon for our guests to
play."

Dakota grimaced. "Oh, no, Chief Jones. I don't think
that's a good idea. We really must be on our way."

"Nonsense," the chief insisted. "To leave now would
be an insult. Your party wouldn't want to insult the Colorado Clan, now would they?"

Dakota shook her head. "No, Chief. We have the greatest respect for your clan."

"Good. Fierce Owl. Let the people know that we will have games right now in the village circle."

"Yes, Chief." Fierce Owl left with much too much enthusiasm. I looked at Kren and Murdock, and then we all three stared at Dakota, the wizard speaking for us. "May we ask what kind of games these are?"

She shrugged. "The games are not to the death—"

This gave me some comfort.

"—Though some players do get killed, and maiming is common."

And that gave me no comfort at all.

We followed the chief and his shaman out of the lodge, grabbed the reins and leads of our horses, and threaded our way between cabins to a wide, open meadow just south of the village. Around the edge of the meadow, tree trunks had been laid every ten yards or so. Perhaps 150 yards from each other, a thick pole had been sunk into the ground at either end of the meadow, the top of each pole a good ten feet above the ground.

When we arrived, Chief Jones explained the game to us. "We call it 'Ball and Sticks.' One team wears shirts, the other team does not. Each man has a stick. One team starts at this pole and carries the ball. They have to reach the other pole with the ball. The other team tries to stop them. No player can leave the meadow unless injured."

"Simple enough idea," said Jenkins. "What are the rules?"

Chief Jones took a seat on a tree trunk. "Those *are* the rules."

Healthy men with sticks. And no rules.

Around us, villagers streamed by and took seats upon the tree trunks ringing the meadow, chattering happily and obviously thinking this was the greatest event of the month. Who knows, perhaps it was.

Fierce Owl stripped down to trousers and shoes.

"How many of your people wish to play? It's more fun with many players."

Apparently, we would get to wear our shirts. The party conferred as much as we could while still guarding our horses and supplies. Jason was too old, of course, as was Murdock. Lorich limped. Kendall had only one arm. As Dakota was a woman, the clan would not allow her to play. That admission she forced out through clenched teeth, humiliated by her ineligibility. That left only Jenkins, Kren, and their precious Prince Scar. Dakota dutifully informed the chief of our choices.

He shook his head emphatically. "Not enough. So few would be insulting to the Colorado Clan. Six players. Each team must have six players."

Well, that made it easier. Dakota couldn't play. And while Jason indicated his readiness, Murdock and the rest would not hear of it. "My dear friend," said Murdock. "All joking aside, you're the oldest. And perhaps more important, you're the healer. We need you to be healthy so that you can treat us, if necessary." The Pacifican was not happy about those facts, but he accepted the logic of our choice.

At least in the open, Jason and Dakota would have an easier time moving the horses about and keeping the villagers away from the supplies. It would be a challenge, but as long as they didn't stop to watch the game . . .

I saw Fierce Owl choosing his teammates. He pointed at different men, who whooped with pleasure and prepared for play. They were fit and well muscled, and most were only a few years older than I, probably the best in the village on battlefield or game field. Jenkins, Kren, and I could probably hold our own against such opponents. Possibly Murdock, who was still a formidable presence in battle. But Kendall? Lorich? How would they fare against healthy and eager opponents?

The ball and sticks were brought. The ball was a soft cowhide sphere about a foot in diameter, probably stuffed with cloth or leather scraps or such. The sticks—

a good two score of them dumped out of a sack—were two to four feet long. Some were like short staves, straight and only an inch in diameter, while others were cudgels, thick headed with a knot or bole at one end, and tapering to convenient handle size at the other end. Each was wrapped in leather, and seemed to be padded beneath the leather. The intent then was to hurt rather than maim.

I hefted several of the sticks, and finally decided upon a medium-length cudgel. My companions made their choices, and at last we had to strip down for the game. Jackets and hats came off, weapon belts were dropped, and everything was handed up to Jason and Dakota for safekeeping.

Jason gave his advice. "Stretch. Muscles and tendons all. It will help. No use getting unnecessary sprains when you don't have to. Looks like you'll have enough to worry about without that."

The six of us started stretching.

Shaman Faraday edged closer to Murdock. "Wizard, I want to ask you something before you play. Just in case."

Murdock was doing knee bends. "You may ask now. Just in case."

The shaman looked around furtively, and leaned close to the wizard. "Have you seen the Witch Woman?"

Murdock stopped. "Witch Woman? I've never heard of her before, and I've certainly never seen her. Who is she?"

"She is a witch, and a powerful shaman. Be careful if you meet her. She is quick to anger and dangerous."

"I see. Is she here?"

Shaman Faraday shook his head. "She has been away for a long time. A long time. But I dream of her. She is near. And she is coming."

"Time to start the game," Chief Jones announced impatiently, and so we took to the field.

Our six opponents were to have the ball first. Fierce Owl walked to the nearest post, the ball cradled against his chest in the crook of one arm, the other hand holding a long stick. His teammates spread out on either side of him.

"What's our strategy?" Kren asked Murdock.

"How should I know?" the wizard answered. "Jenkins, any ideas?"

"Let's form a line and go straight for the man with the ball and overwhelm him before the others can close."

It was as good a plan as any, I guess. We spread out and started running towards Fierce Owl, who touched the pole and trotted out to meet us. As we closed with him he brought his arm back, and sent the ball sailing through the air over our heads. One of his teammates knocked it down, picked it up, and began running full out for the post at the far end of the field. The crowd roared. There was no way any of us could catch him.

I caught a glimpse as a hawk-faced clansman ran past, a stick swung, and then a sharp pain in my side staggered me, and I dropped to one knee. Twirling his stick in victory, the hawk-faced clansman looked back and yipped derisively.

The crowd roared again.

Well, they'd been honest with us about what the game was. We just weren't being imaginative enough.

Fierce Owl trotted past with a cheery grin and a helpful attitude, his stick tucked under his arm. "Your turn. Start at the other post."

Jenkins came up. "Are you all right, sir?"

"Nothing serious. Just a few ribs cracked."

"That's a relief. Mr. Lorich, perhaps you could drop one or two of them when we start the next round?"

Murdock shook his head. "Sergeant Jenkins, I don't think killing his men is really the best way to impress Chief Jones. Now, how do we score a point for our team?"

We discussed strategy as we slowly strolled across the field. Concentrating our strength didn't work on defense, but it might on offense. We finished the strategy session as we reached the other post. A clan player tossed the ball to us good-naturedly. Apparently many clansmen administered damage to each other with enthusiasm, but without rancor. I did not share their attitude.

The clansmen formed up checkerboard fashion in two lines, some shallow, some deep. A flexible defense.

Lorich took the ball and tucked it against his chest as we had seen Fierce Owl do, then touched the post with his stick. We formed a tight wedge, with barely room to swing a stick between us. Kren was in front. I was on his left, and Jenkins on his right. Murdock was behind me, and Kendall was behind Jenkins. In the center of the wedge was Lorich.

"Ready?" asked Kren. "All right, let's go NOW." With that, we set off in unison at a gentle run, almost a shuffle, so that Lorich could keep his position. The clansmen gave whoops and closed on front and flanks. Two were before the beastman, and without missing a stride he swung his long cudgel, cracking it against the sticks of the clansmen. They didn't give way. Kren opened his arms, crashed into them, and all three went down. We swung to the left and kept going, Jenkins and I in front, Murdock and Kren behind in a box formation. We didn't plan it like that, but necessity had its way.

Two opponents closed with us from the front, and then we were flailing away with our sticks. It was like swordplay, and yet it wasn't. No shields, no single finishing blow. Nor was it staff fighting. The sticks were too short for that. It was two-handed club work, the pairs of us flailing away at each other.

I had the good-natured clansman against me, and the air rang with the crack of wood on wood as we tried to smash through each other's defense. One of his blows slid along my cudgel and crunched into my fingers. Another hit me in the shoulder, and a third on my hip. In return, I gave him one on the shoulder, and another in the side. Then I sidestepped his overhand stroke and rammed the end of my stick into his stomach. With an *oof* he sat down.

There was a disappointed chorus of moans from the spectators, along with a few cheers. A dozen paces away, Jenkins and Fierce Owl still danced around each other, parrying blows, while behind us Kren and his two clansmen were getting up, blood flowing from the forehead of one. Downfield, Murdock and Kendall had each kept a clansman busy so that Lorich was able to lope up to the post alone and score a point for our team.

My opponent got his breath and his smile back. "That was a fine move. I got carried away and forgot to watch for a thrust."

Well, if he could be gracious about it, so could Prince Scar—though Prince Arn wanted to beat him over the head with the cudgel. I *hurt*, and the game wasn't even over.

Which reminded me. "Uh, when does the game end?"

"End? Oh, probably after a few hours, though when clansmen from other villages come the game lasts all day, or until all the players are injured."

I was not encouraged.

He took my extended hand, and I pulled him up, the scene quite the essence of good sportsmanship. We walked back downfield together. I still wanted to beat him over the head, but it was hard not to like the man.

"You know, you must have impressed the Chief. We don't play the game with strangers, usually. Not unless we intend to finish them off."

"Oh?"

"And then we play with swords and spears. The clan always wins."

"I'm glad he likes us."

He grinned. "I knew you had to be a warrior. You're too good with the stick."

My companions had not escaped without damage. Except for Lorich, all of us had at least a scrape or bruise. A promising welt was rising on Kendall's forehead. "Times like this are when I really miss the arm," he winced, touching his face. "Still, it wasn't all one way."

Indeed, one of the clansmen seemed to have developed a limp, and another was moving a bit stiffly. Yes, we were certainly teaching them a thing or two. Unfortunately, they were teaching us a thing or six. Or seven.

Against their offense we decided to try the checkerboard defense the clan had used. Kendall and Lorich were to close with the ball carrier while the rest of us held back and guarded the other players.

The friendly clansman had the ball at the post this time, ran toward Lorich and Kendall, and then threw the ball beyond them to Fierce Owl. Two clansmen closed with Jenkins and Kren, and the *thunk* of stick on stick was heard across the field. Fierce Owl ran to the side, drawing Murdock and Kendall after him, then threw the ball back to Mr. Friendly Clansman. Unfortunately, there was no one watching him. He ran through the gap between Jenkins and Kren, who were too occupied to stop him. I was free and took off after Friendly, but stopped after a few steps. He was very fast, and had a dozen paces on me. No chance of catching him.

The spectators roared with approval, and his teammates ran to join Friendly. There was a swish, and a sharp pain in my side. The hawk-faced clansman looked back as he trotted off, chortling. He'd gotten me again.

We planned our strategy. The attempt we'd made last time was good, but would be expected. So we changed our tactics. Lorich was the ball carrier again, and Kren in front of him, but Jenkins and Kendall took position a dozen paces to the right while Murdock and I were a dozen paces to the left.

Our opponents had gone back to their checkerboard strategy, waiting for us to charge across the field. And we did.

The first line of three clansmen closed on Kren and Lorich, the two flank men coming in from the sides. "Now!" yelled Jenkins in his best parade voice. Murdock and I raced toward Kren and Lorich, while Jenkins and Kendall did the same. The three clansmen suddenly found themselves surrounded and set upon by all six of us for the few precious seconds before their teammates reacted. We took advantage of the time. The first three were pounded and dazed by the time the second line—which included Fierce Owl and Hawk-Face—came to their aid. For a good half minute, the clan roared from the sidelines as the two teams exchanged blows.

We'd decided the only way to have a chance was simply to beat the other team down. No running, no throwing the ball, no fancy strategy. Just depend upon surprise and the physical prowess Jenkins, Kren, and I could bring to the equation. Not that the others were any slouches. Murdock held his own against men half his age, while Kendall wielded his stick with enough strength to make his opponents need both hands to counter the blows. Most surprising of all was Lorich, who set the ball down and swung his long stick two-handed. In the end, three of the clansmen were on the ground, and we moved forward across the field at a walk, fending off the other three with little difficulty.

Score tied.

The clansmen got to their feet, some shakily. Hawk-Face was very slow getting up. Jenkins had made him a priority for attention, and I'd managed to give the clansman a few cudgel thumps myself. Even got in a kick or two.

Chief Jones stood up. "Next score decides the game."

Just when his team was to have the ball, of course.

Murdock bent with his hands upon his knees, trying to get his breath. "Thank goodness."

Kendall, breathing hard, nodded. "Agreed. Remember, everyone. Give your best—but we want them to win."

Jenkins was aghast. "What? Throw the game?"

Murdock nodded. "Mr. Kendall is right. We want a happy Chief Jones. Beating his clan will not make him happy."

Actually, we did do our best. But Kendall and Murdock and Lorich were tired, and the rest of us were starting to feel winded too—not to mention feeling bruised all over. We were lucky we hadn't suffered broken bones. The clansmen ran a play down one side of the field, and fooled us. Kren and Lorich were trampled in the rush, though neither suffered more than another blow or two in the process since the clansmen kept going, reaching the post as a team without interference.

The clan stood and clapped their hands above their heads while yipping for their unconquered heroes. Our team slowly limped over to Dakota and Jason, moving in as fine an imitation of old men as has ever been seen.

Dakota was still on horseback, while Jason had dismounted and had his medical kit open, examining each of us in turn. Dakota eyed Lorich, then shook her head at the rest of us. "Had enough fun yet?"

Jason continued his examinations "They did well. No one killed, no one permanently maimed. Our companions won't be sleeping very well for a few days, I suspect, but the bruises will fade. It could have been much worse."

"What was the name of this game?" Kren asked.

"Ball and Sticks," I offered, collapsing onto the grass.

"Not a game we need in Kenesee," Murdock added.

Chief Jones strode up in his fur coat. "Good game. Good game. My warriors were impressed."

Dakota bowed from the saddle. "Your clansmen were too much for my companions. And so we'll be leaving in the morning."

"What?" he asked, disappointed. "You don't want to try again tomorrow?"

Lorich covered his ears.

3

The Tunnel

When we left at dawn, a small crowd of villagers had nothing better to do than see us off. We took with us the cudgels and short staffs we had used in the "Ball and Sticks" game. Since we were such distinguished visitors to their clan and had played such a good game, we were given the sticks as mementos. We also took with us an abundant collection of scrapes, bumps, bruises, aches, and pains.

I brooded on the sack of tobacco we'd gifted to Chief Jones. I'd made my dissatisfaction known to my companions. "What I have left is not going to last through the winter."

Kren, who didn't smoke, found a bright side to the matter. "Wouldn't worry too much about it, Arn. After all, you might not last through the winter, either."

Though Chief Jones would warn his people to let our party pass unmolested, we still avoided any of the Colorado Clan. We discreetly bypassed villages and left the road to hide when clansmen passed.

On the fourth day after leaving Chief Jones and his wonderful games, Dakota pointed ahead. The land had opened up, and flatlands lay between the mountain chains. "Well, we don't have to worry about running into any of the Colorado Clan from this point on. We're entering the land of the Utah."

"The Utah Clan. Delightful," said Kren. "What game do they like to play?"

191

"You'd like it, beastman," Dakota shot back. "They call it 'Burning at the Stake.' "

"Such quaint customs," Kren replied. "Just like the plains tribes."

Of the mysterious Tracker, we saw no sign. Whether we had lost him, or he was just being more careful, none could say. We continued to assume he was out there, somewhere, biding his time.

The days had become brisk, and the evenings cold. The good weather passed, and the sky was overcast, and sometimes the lowering clouds dropped a steady drizzle that chilled us to the bone as we made our way westward, forcing us to find shelter each night in ruins or overhangs or under the pines. It took longer to start the fire each evening, for in the unremitting rain finding dry fuel became a challenge.

Huddled around the fire on such nights, we each found our own pursuits to pass the time. My companions talked about our progress so far, and listed what they missed most during our travels. Women went as an unspoken topic, for Dakota's presence tempered our comments about the fair sex. We all exercised—a necessity after so many hours in the saddle—or practiced with weapons. Sometimes we sang, or told stories, or just smoked and enjoyed being on solid ground instead of on horseback. Jenkins took up wood carving. I kept a journal. Kren learned magic tricks that Murdock showed him. Kendall practiced on a mouth organ. Dakota showed a real interest in the healing arts, and spent time with Jason, who showed her everything in his kit, explained the purpose of each, and then started giving her a basic course in the practice of medicine. He mentioned that she seemed to be an apt pupil.

This did not eat up all the time Dakota had in the evenings, though. Often, she and Lorich would wander off together. Never far, from what I could tell, and yet far enough to be out of sight of our curious glances. I saw them returning once holding hands, though they let each other go as they neared the camp, not realizing that they had already been seen.

It was on the third night inside the land of the Utah, when sleep was just stealing upon us, that the horses began to whinny and tug at their tethers, and we felt a distinct tremble in the earth. An earthquake. Nothing to be alarmed about. After all, there were no gigantic herds of bison in the mountains. We would not be trampled to death in our sleep.

However we all came awake and sat up as a gigantic cracking sound echoed down from ahead. The cracking was followed by an immense rumble, as if tons of rock were in motion. It was close, within a few hundred yards, but not on top of us. Still, the darkness meant that we really couldn't tell where the sound originated, and one never knew where bouncing boulders might go. The horses reacted with crazed fear, and we had to calm them. The rumbling faded away, and the horses quieted.

Dakota slapped her hat against a leg in frustration. "We'll have to be careful tomorrow. There's a large Utah village up a side valley to the south. They probably heard the noise, and will send scouts out."

In the shrouded silence of the night, those not on guard duty went back to sleep, waiting for the dawn to show us if the quake and rockslide would affect our journey in any way.

The next morning was clear, the clouds having passed during the night. The sun was shining upon us for the first time in days. We took morning meal, saddled up while Dakota rode ahead, then followed after her. Around the first bend we found her halted upon the old road, contemplating the mountainside before her. We had our answer about the rockslide of the night before. Thousands of tons of rock—a goodly slice of the cliff face that must have towered over the road—had cracked off and crumbled as it rolled down to the bottom of the valley. The old road was blocked. We would have to pick our way down and around the jumble of boulders.

An irksome detour, but I could imagine what might

have occurred had we ridden another ten minutes the night before and taken camp below that cliff. It did make one think. What domino game of decision carries each of us through life? Each tiny choice, each small decision seems totally innocuous and unimportant, until some larger force swoops down and strikes those unfortunates who happen to end up in the particular place at the particular time, and then the entire string of decisions is seen as leading to that result. In the end, some walk away, and others are crushed. Is it Providence, or Luck, or blind Chance? Does God have a Divine Plan over which he watches, or has he set the great clockwork of the universe running and withdrawn, letting us do what we might within the gears and springs? Or is there just the physicality of the universe, and Chance the only god to laugh at our fate?

I might have thought the last if I had been blind, if I had not seen the sky full of stars, nor beheld an entire universe glowing in the smile of a woman as I held her. Either sight would have convinced me of His existence. Together, the proof was irrefutable.

"Arn! Ready to join the living again?" It was Kren.

"Sorry. I was thinking."

"I warned you about that," the beastman quipped.

Except for Jenkins and Kren, the rest of the party had moved ahead a dozen paces, and were deep in conversation. "Aren't we going down the mountainside?" I asked.

"Take a look up there," Kren pointed.

I looked, and for the first time noticed an oddity in the cliff face. A hundred feet above, the cliff jutted out in a large overhang that seemed ready to crack off and thunder down upon us. The granite just below it had given way and caused the landslide. However, the thing of interest was that below the overhang was a strange cut in the wall of the cliff. Revealed was a tunnel exposed lengthwise for thirty feet or so, and perhaps ten feet high.

Kendall and Jason were proclaiming that it was necessary to explore the tunnel, while Dakota reminded them of the proximity of the Utah Clan.

"This is foolish," she stated conclusively. "We have to keep going. The Utahs will be here sooner or later. We've a good chance of getting clear of the fall area before they arrive."

Kendall continued to stare at the slice of exposed tunnel. "You're right, Dakota. But looking at that cut—I just think we should take a few minutes and make sure what's in there. What do you think, Murdock? It's your decision."

"It would be wonderful to explore the cave," Lorich piped up. Seeing the look on Dakota's face, he added, "But Dakota does have a good point. Do you sense anyone near right now, Master?"

Murdock considered the question. "No, no one right now. But that mountainside to the south blocks my ability. What is that, perhaps an hour away by horseback? Let's take a half hour to explore, then we'll be on our way. That should get us out of here before anyone comes."

I had considered tossing in my own opinion, which might have altered Murdock's decision. I might even have countermanded his order. It was my right, after all. But in the end, I said nothing. I was frightened by Dakota's concern, and yet understood the motivations behind Murdock's decision. The possibility of exploring a new ruin—perhaps even a well-preserved, sealed chamber from the Old World—gnawed at his curiosity. So little was left of the Ancients that had not been plundered or consumed. So little had not worn out or rusted away or become unusable. It was so rare to find anything unspoiled that the opportunity of discovery was like water to a man wandering in the desert.

Yet, this would not have been enough to keep us lingering while danger approached. More important and decisive was the possibility that something deadly might be found which could fall into the hands of the ignorant. Something to give petty tyrants the ability to inflict pain and death upon their enemies. That was the worry that motivated Kendall and Jason, and made Murdock choose as he did.

Dakota clenched her teeth, but made no objection to the decision.

Murdock described what we would do. Kendall and Jason would go, as well as Murdock himself. All three had more knowledge of the Old World, and could evaluate the significance, if any, of the find. Kren and I would also go, simply because we were curious and we wanted to and there was no reason not to. Lorich, Dakota, and Jenkins would wait hidden nearby with the horses and warn if anyone were coming.

Murdock took his oil lamp. We also took two sticks, wrapped cloth around one end of each, and soaked the cloth with oil for torches. The climb up the mounded rubble was not difficult, though care had to be taken not to turn an ankle on the odd chunks of rock that lay against each other. At the tunnel we paused, glancing in carefully without touching anything. The floor of the tunnel was flat and littered with rocks. Dust covered the floor and walls. Close to where we stood, the slice of exposed tunnel seemed to curve back into the earth, darkness waiting for us just a few yards within.

Kren lit his torch and led the way to the right, the rest of us following two abreast.

The tunnel was perhaps twelve feet wide at the bottom with convex walls of crete that curved up to a round ceiling twelve feet above the floor. Faint stripes in faded paint ran along the length of the floor. Every ten yards there was an old electric light set into the ceiling, each darkened bulb incased by a protective metal cage. Within twenty-five yards of the opening, we found the tunnel totally blocked with boulders and earth. There was an old shovel lying on the ground, a bit of rust around the edges. A small indentation had been made into the wall of rock and dirt, a pile marking the laughable progress of whoever had wielded the spade.

Kendall studied the obstacle, looked at the shovel, and

shook his head. "I'd say this dates from the Cataclysm, not last night's landslide. The tunnel is probably blocked with yards of rock in this direction. We might as well turn around."

The other way proved more promising. We passed the opening, bright with the day so that we had to shield our eyes, and continued on into the darkness, walking forward without hindrance. There were cracks here and there in the crete walls and ceiling, and several in the floor, including one that was a good six inches wide. Near the cracks, small chunks of masonry and rock littered the floor. Yet for all that, the tunnel was in remarkably good shape.

Jason noted its condition. "See how dry the air is? Water hasn't penetrated the tunnel. It's still intact, in spite of the cracks. Quite amazing."

We walked on for perhaps a hundred yards before the tunnel made a gradual ninety-degree turn to the right, deeper into the mountain. Fifty yards beyond the turn, the tunnel opened into a wider area, and in this were a dozen of the horseless vehicles of the ancients, some larger, some smaller. They were covered in dust, but unlike the vehicles I'd seen in the underground "garage" in the ruins of the plains city, these had little rust on them, though the rubber on the wheels was flat and crumbling. One large vehicle had a rear storage area that was covered with canvas, or what appeared to be canvas. As we walked between the vehicles I put out a hand and pressed my fingers against the material. It tore like paper. My hand went through the canvas, and a tiny cloud of dust wafted out and made me sneeze.

"They're in remarkably good condition," Jason noted as he peered at each vehicle in turn. "I suspect the exit to this complex must have been completely sealed in the rockfall we found blocking the other end of the tunnel, and very little moisture has made its way in since the Cataclysm. I bet ahead we'll find—yes, here it is."

The open area had ended at a wall that held the entrance to a smaller tunnel. Kren stopped and peered at what I can only imagine were the open leaves of a door to the smaller tunnel—but such a door. Metal six inches thick, set into huge metal hinges. Kren put a hand upon it. It wouldn't move. I wasn't surprised. He leaned against it and with a creak of protest the door swung out from the wall. He stopped the door and pushed it back against the wall, creaking all the way.

"Six hundred years, and the outer doors still work," said Jason. "This is an incredible find."

"A frightening find," Kendall echoed.

We went through the door and a dozen feet inside found an open portal with a second metal door, this one much thinner and with a piece of glass in the center. The door was a type that slid along a metal track set into the floor. Words had been printed below the glass. Jason wiped away the film of dust as Kren held the torch close.

CONTROLLED ENVIRONMENT
Keep Hatch Sealed

Kren led the way through the hatchway into a squared hallway a good eight feet wide. The walls and ceiling were constructed of some material I could not recognize, and the entire floor was covered with what appeared to be an immense rug. Jason called it carpeting. We walked straight along the hall, noting but passing by several open doors leading into rooms and into other, narrower hallways. One open metal door was sturdily made and bore a warning.

ARMORY
Restricted Area
Authorized Admittance Only

Jason and Kendall looked at each other. "We'll have to investigate this one," said Kendall. "But let's go on for now."

Further on, after we had gone perhaps thirty yards from the first hatchway, the hallway was blocked by another massive rockfall, the face of a great slab of rock making any further progress impossible. How much lay beyond this wall of granite, no one could know. We had gone as far as we could on the main hallway. We turned back to explore areas we had passed. Any one room was a find that would have sent Professor Wagner and the other scholars in Kingsport into rapture. The discovery of them all was numbing—too much, really, to absorb. We wandered back through the halls with a sense of unreality, accepting everything we saw with hardly an exclamation of wonder.

We found two barrackslike rooms with metal-framed bunks, as well as individual sleeping quarters. In all, they might have bedded a hundred people in the areas we saw. Other rooms were filled with equipment I had seen in pictures and museums, such as computers and picture screens and telephones. Still others held various machines, tables, desks, cabinets, and odd items I could only guess at.

There were books and papers, though most seemed so brittle and dry that to touch them would cause their dissolution. The value of their content, in some cases, might also be questioned. On a desk in one room was a small volume with a paper cover showing a scantily dressed woman. It was entitled *Willing Wives*. Kren tried to take it, but the book began to crumble, and he put it back on the desk with a sigh of regret.

In one room—a "command center," as Jason called it—we found a body. It was a male lying on his back, dressed in what might have been a uniform. His remains were mummified, the skin dried and stretched over his face, his mouth a gaping hole. The skin of his head was cut. A dark stain lay beneath him, as well as on the corner of a crete step. Jason examined the remains, mumbled to himself, but said nothing.

The party assembled, came back to the armory last of all, and looked inside. Seated on the floor, its back resting against crates, was another body. It was most likely a woman because she wore a skirt. Like the other body the remains were mummified, the skin stretched taut and dry over her skull, hair hanging just short of her neck. In her hand she held one of the Old World weapons. A pistol. The crates behind her were spattered with some dark stain similar to that under the other body. It was not hard to figure out the source of the stain, for the back of her skull lay on the floor beside her.

I considered her fate, and that of the other body we had found. "What happened here, Jason?"

He examined the corpse for a moment, stood, and wiped his hands on his pants. "This is my guess. The woman and the other man were in the command center. The rest of the staff of this place were assembled in the other part of the facility, beyond the wall of stone we found blocking the hallway. They were either at a meal, or a meeting, or possibly even a social event. The only ones left in this part were these two. The man was probably standing, and thrown to the ground by the force of the quake. His head hit the sharp edge of the crete step, and caused a concussion. Maybe killed him outright. I don't know.

"The woman survived, and tried to find help. That thing on the floor next to her is, I suspect, an electrical torch, or 'flashlight.' So the lighting must have failed and she was forced to use her torch, the only illumination in the darkness, as she searched for others and exit. But when the quake hit, the ceiling collapsed in the hallway and in the tunnel exit, sealing the two of them alone in this section of the facility. I suspect she panicked when she saw how isolated she was, and how far beyond help. She tried to dig herself out at the exit using a shovel, then realized the futility of that effort. After minutes, hours, perhaps days, she despaired. The poor creature opened the armory door, found a hand weapon, and killed herself with a bullet to the head."

Kren had been looking about the room as the healer talked, torch held aloft. There were racks mounted on the walls, and in the racks were weapons. Not primitive powder weapons such as the muskets that had proved so fearsome at the Battle of Tyler. Rather, these were rifles and machine guns—weapons of awesome power used at the height of the golden age of the Ancients.

Jason shook his head. "More guns."

"Are they usable?" I asked.

Kendall looked about, and nodded. "I think they might be, if there was fresh ammunition." He gestured at the wooden boxes and crates of various sizes and shapes stacked along the walls and in the center of the room. "But the ammunition—the old bullets—won't work. Most of the rounds went inert long ago. They won't fire. And without ammunition, the weapons are useless."

"Have the explosives gone inert too?" Kren asked, then peering at a crate, read from the stenciled letters on its side.

CAUTION: EXPLOSIVE
C-6
40 lbs.
Lot 344559-DFA-042035

"There's a good dozen crates of this, at least," the beastman added. He extended a hand to the metal ties securing the lid of the crate.

"I wouldn't touch that more than I had to," Jason cautioned. "To answer your question, explosives of the Old World become inert—or unstable. You never know which."

"What's C-6?" I asked. "Is it like gunpowder?"

"Much more powerful," Kendall advised. "Like the difference between a candle and a bonfire."

"So the woman who was trapped here, she could have escaped," said Kren. "She could have just blasted her way out."

"Possibly," said Kendall. "Maybe she didn't know anything about explosives, and was afraid to try. Or she panicked. Or just gave up. Who knows."

Jason studied the crates, then looked at his son. "If

the explosives aren't inert, there's enough here to bury this place."

"That is so," Kendall agreed. He was silent a moment, pondering his father's hint. "Wizard Murdock, we need to destroy this site, to seal it off, to make sure the clans don't get here. I don't want these people hauling crates of explosive into their homes. Dozens of people could be killed."

"You could set it off?" Murdock asked doubtfully.

Kendall nodded. "There'll be a box of fuses and detonators around here somewhere, most likely in a locked cabinet or such. A good percentage of those will work, based on past discoveries of such things. We could open a few crates of C-6, insert several fuses into each box, and light them all at the same time. Odds are that one or more will work, and one or another of the crates should hold some explosive that is not inert."

Kren was appalled. "A find like this, and you want to destroy it?"

"What's to be gained if we leave it?" Jason responded. "In Pacifica, we have access to much of the knowledge of the Old World, though most is theoretical, and more than we could ever use. I doubt that there are any surprises for our scholars. This was a military facility. If anything is left in here, it's the knowledge of death. Nothing that would help the advancement of our peoples. Best to leave it here, buried, where it can do no harm."

Kren took in the stacks of crates. "So many weapons, and in such good shape. Who knows, Jason, maybe the ammunition would work after all."

"I doubt that," said Kendall. "But it is for Murdock to decide in any case."

The wizard pondered the matter for a long minute, then made up his mind. "If there's nothing here of value, and the things in this room pose a threat to life and limb of innocents, there can be only one answer. We'll destroy this facility, if we're able. How long will it take?"

"Just a few minutes," Kendall replied. "Find the fuses, open the crates, insert the fuse caps between the bricks of explosive, and we're ready."

"Then let's do it," ordered Murdock. "We've more than used up our half hour."

Kren opened the crates while Jason found a cabinet at the back. Jason pried it open with an axe conveniently located in a small, glass-fronted box with a warning that read FOR USE IN FIRE ONLY. Gingerly he carried back a dozen fuses, each one six feet in length with a metal cap on one end. He cut off a six-inch length of one fuse and lit the small portion, counting as it burned about an inch. "A six-foot fuse should give us about twenty minutes," said Kendall. He helped Jason wedge the caps between the hard bricks of explosive and arranged it so that the ends of the fuses came together near one spot hanging off the edge of a crate.

"All ready," said the Pacifican. "Let's go out and make sure the rest of the party is ready to move. I'll come back in, light the fuses, and then we'll be on our way."

I followed Murdock out into the hall, and bumped into him as he came to an abrupt halt. Jason, following, bumped into me as I came to a halt. Ahead, the hall was filled with dozens of clansmen, the one in front with his arm wrapped around Lorich's neck and a knife at the young wizard's throat.

The clansman grinned wickedly. "Welcome to the land of the Utah."

4

The Witch Woman

Hopelessly outnumbered, surprised, and with no way to escape, there was little we could do. The clansmen in the tunnel threatened to cut Lorich's throat if we did not give up. Surrender did seem the logical choice. Murdock ordered us to drop our weapons. The man who had held Lorich grunted an order, and we soon had knives at our throats while other clansmen brought rope to tie us.

"Very good," said the man who issued orders. "Very smart, allowing us to take you prisoner instead of fighting honorably." He and a goodly number of his men laughed at that. I couldn't quite see the humor. All of the clansmen wore plain leather vests over their coats, although some of the vests were adorned with one or more bear claws hanging from thongs. The equivalent of the plains warriors' feathers, perhaps? The vest of the man giving orders had no bear claws, but medals, feathers, and various other tokens hung from his vest in profusion. The chief? Or perhaps their shaman? Or some other senior warrior?

The clansmen made quite a fuss over the beastman Kren and subjected him to the usual indignities. He remained tight-lipped while they looked under his shirt and tugged at his hair, and in the end they decided to treat him like the rest of the party—not that we were doing very well. They tied our wrists with enthusiastic roughness and shoved us into a corner to sit while they went through the underground facility.

An alert clansman with a torch and spear guarded us

with a smug look. We ignored him and stared at Lorich questioningly.

"What happened?" Murdock whispered.

The young wizard hung his head. "I'm sorry, Master," he whispered. "I made a check, and detected no one. They must have been behind the mountain. And then, a little while later, they appeared."

"A little while later," Murdock repeated the words slowly. "And by any chance were you a bit distracted during all this?"

"Yes, Master," Lorich admitted reluctantly. "I was, uhh, talking. To Dakota."

"What a surprise. And our scout was equally distracted, I take it?"

"Yes, Master, she was. But even Sergeant Jenkins was surprised, and he'd been watching. He didn't see them either. The clansmen appeared suddenly, and they came straight for us, even though we were hidden in the trees. Dakota said their village chief wasn't with them, but recognized the leader as the village shaman, a man named Preston. Master, he must have wizardly powers, for he detected us. That's why they approached so stealthily, and why they found us so easily. I can feel him, though he's trying to mask himself. He's not powerful."

Murdock nodded. "I see. Yes, I think you're right. Well, let's look for opportunities and see if we can get out of this mess."

It was hard to be severe with the young wizard. His remorse was obvious, and the responsibility had to be shared with Jenkins and Dakota. If two such able adventurers were surprised, the clansmen certainly knew their trade.

Our captors plundered the facility with delight, despoiling rooms while taking useless items such as chairs, phones, and even rulers, according to the whim of each clansman. A more ridiculous collection of ancient arcana could not be imagined, especially since plastic items were brittle with age. Many cracked, broke, even crumbled as they were handled.

More ominously, the chief and his minions searched the Armory with greater purpose. In spite of Kendall's frantic warning to their leader, Shaman Preston, they took two boxes of the explosive from the stack. They also looked into and took two long crates before prodding us out of the tunnel and into the light of day. We cringed each time a clansman bumped a crate against wall or floor as they waddled out with the heavy containers. Then they got the bright idea that maybe they should let their prisoners do the work.

Unbinding our hands but linking us to each other by a rope strung around our necks, my companions and I were forced to team up to carry the boxes and crates. The younger and healthier of us made sure we took ends of the larger, heavier crates, and left the two boxes of explosive for the others. Thus encumbered, we struggled to keep pace along the path to the Utah village, a score of warriors on horseback before us, and as many behind. Gloomy as our situation was, it did provide the opportunity for a few discreet words to be exchanged.

"What happened?" Kren asked Dakota in a less-than-civil tone. "Lorich said you were distracted."

For the first time, I saw Dakota flush. "And where were all of you brave explorers, beastman? You were gone for an hour, at least. I warned Murdock. You thought I was fooling?"

Murdock's voice was calm. "Dakota, how bad is it for us?"

She eyed the leader of the warriors. "Shaman Preston isn't the shaman of all the Utah, just of this village, this region. Still, he's dangerous. Chief Gilbert, the village chief, might be reasonable if he's in a good mood. We'll probably have to offer him one of us for—"

A warrior prodded Dakota in the back with a spear. She fell silent, and we concentrated on placing our feet so as not to stumble We came to the clan village about noon, Jason wheezing badly. Part of the way had been uphill through a narrowing valley, and they had kept us walking without respite. I was feeling tired myself, my arms aching, and I could only imagine what a man in his sixties would be suffering.

The Utah settlement was less than half the size of the Colorado town of Chief Jones, and lacked touches such as the bricked walkways. But otherwise there was little to tell the two apart. Pastures holding flocks of sheep and small herds of cattle, plowed fields, and an orchard surrounded a low wooden stockade set in valley lowland. The stockade enclosed a few dozen log cabins, two or three wooden lodges with bark roofs, sheds for horses, and an open circle of ground on the side nearest the stream that flowed by.

The shaman gave an order, and the two long crates were put down in a field a hundred yards from the stockade. Another order, and we proceeded through the gates to the open circle of ground, the two boxes of explosive were taken from us, and our wrists and ankles were tied again. The inevitable crowd of women and children and dogs gathered and watched, and they descended upon Kren with wonder and delight. He only roared when an old crone tried to see how far the hair went below his waist.

The shaman barked at several of his warriors, who trotted around the side of a lodge and came back bearing a pair of ten-foot-tall poles that were at least six inches thick. They went out to the center of the open circle and began removing rocks that filled two narrow holes in the ground. Each hole was in the middle of a blackened piece of earth. For some reason, their activity made me very uneasy.

Murdock tried his best, speaking sweet reasonableness and oozing goodwill and friendship and likability. "We have heard of the great Shaman Preston of the Utah. We know he will wish to speak with us. We have much to offer, and together—"

The shaman crashed a fist into Murdock's jaw.

This was not going well at all.

Dakota spoke up. "Shaman Preston, where is Chief Gilbert?"

"Chief Gilbert is dead," said the shaman.

I did not like the look on Dakota's face when she heard the news.

The shaman was speaking loudly now, as if addressing the crowd rather than just my party. As I suppose he was. "The sickness took him. Many have been sick, and many have died. God is punishing us because we have not honored Him properly. We've been tolerant of the sinners in the other clans, and not punished them as God wants. We have not made war, we have not taken prisoners, we have not offered sacrifice. But now, God is giving us the opportunity to offer Him sacrifice and make war for his glory."

Offer sacrifice? I didn't like the sound of that. He said it so . . . so eagerly.

"God is good," concluded the shaman.

"God is good," echoed many from the crowd, and stared at us with anticipation. The warriors working on the holes were now inserting the end of a pole into each hole, and wedging the poles erect with a few of the rocks they had just removed. And I realized I shouldn't call them poles. More properly, they were *stakes*. And I knew what happened when someone was tied to a stake.

So these were the Utahs. Suddenly, Chief Jones and his Colorado Clan were looking very civilized indeed.

"Tonight, we offer a sacrifice. God will be pleased!"

"God will be pleased!" the clan repeated.

"I will choose now. Line the captives up." The shaman went past each of us, looking into our faces. He studied Jenkins, then passed him by. Dakota, he passed. Jason, he passed. Murdock, he stopped at and studied closely.

"You. You're a shaman, aren't you?" He gave a signal, and two warriors hauled Murdock out of line.

"Master!" Lorich shouted.

"Do nothing," warned Murdock, as a spearpoint menaced the young wizard.

It was Kren's turn. The shaman shook his head in wonder, and then passed the beastman by.

I was the next, then Kendall, and Lorich last of all. The shaman stopped in front of me, and for a long minute pondered, tilting his head deep in thought. At last he said, "Are you a shaman?"

Dakota spoke up for me. "Yes, he's a shaman all right."

My throat was dry, my voice a croak. "Why?"

He glanced at Dakota, then back at me. "Shamans are very important. They must be taken care of."

So. If I admitted I was a shaman, I'd be safe from selection like Murdock and one of my companions would have to be chosen for death instead. And Kendall was the next one in line. I remembered Megan's words to me in faraway Tyler, and the thought of her holding a baby. I took a deep breath, and silently cursed myself for a fool before answering. "No, I'm not a shaman."

Shaman Preston grunted. "I don't believe you."

A signal, and they pulled me out of line to join Murdock. I felt more surprise than relief, but was swept with pity for my comrades. They were all eligible for sacrifice, while Murdock and I were safe, saved by our abilities. And Lorich, of course. I waited for the shaman to continue down the line to Kendall, but he didn't even bother. Instead, he spread his arms wide to his people and swept them towards Murdock and me.

"I have chosen. These two burn tonight."

The clan roared with pleasure.

They dragged us over to the stakes, stripped off all but trousers and shirts, put our backs to the wood and secured us at knee, waist, and neck with ropes. The rest of the party they hustled into an open-sided shed, tied them securely to the hay crib, and posted two guards. I tried to figure out a scenario in which we could fight our way out. I still had my knife in its shoulder sheath. They hadn't found that. Lorich could take out five or six of the clan, including the shaman. That left only forty or fifty warriors for the rest of us to deal with.

"Steady, Arn," Murdock encouraged. "Don't give up hope."

Give up hope? Just because we were prisoners a thousand miles from home in the power of a clan that intended to roast us for its religious rituals? Just because there was no chance of rescue or escape? Now why should I give up hope?

With only a single shirt on, the chill in the mountain air began to penetrate all too quickly. It was getting colder. Yet I didn't mind the cold, for I knew things would be heating up soon.

In a fine display of community spirit, the clan members all brought firewood for the festivities, piling it liberally around Murdock and me until we were almost waist high in fuel. The Utah clan certainly did know how to build a good fire. There was a generous pile of tinder right in front of me, covered with a fine kindling of twigs and small branches, then a medium kindling of larger branches placed all around me, and finally stout, dry branches that would burn hot and quick stacked on top. They did the same for Murdock. Apparently, they'd had practice at this sort of thing.

Their work complete, the villagers went away and left us in peace. Murdock and I looked at each other. There wasn't a lot to say.

But at least we weren't bereft of all entertainment. The fields outside the town were on higher ground, and over the low stockade we could just see two clansmen attempting to put a tubelike thing atop a metal tripod. They had made sure the women and children stayed away, and the two men worked in confident isolation, open crates stacked next to them.

"What are they doing, Arn?" Murdock asked. "I can't quite make it out from this distance." The wizard was getting to the age where he needed spectacles—assuming he would survive the day.

I told him what I could see. "Looks like they're putting one of the larger weapons together. A light artillery piece. Or maybe a rocket launcher, which is sort of the same thing. I can't quite be sure which it is. There were many different weapons, and I've only seen the one in the museum in Kingsport, and pictures of a few others. They're loading something in. Either a projectile or a rocket.''

Murdock squinted. "Good, it's pointed out at the mountainside. At least they aren't aiming at us. Do they seem to know what they're doing?''

"No, but then again, those things were—''

"—Designed to be used by idiots. I know. I read the same manuals. Well, tell me when they start to play with the control pad.''

One of the men huddled over the side of the tube.

"They're playing with it.''

"Now we'll see whether the chemicals in those weapons are inert or—''

There was a blinding flash and a giant hand pressed against me. I could feel things flying through the air above my head. The briefest moment later, a thunderous, deafening blast assailed my ears.

"Murdock! Murdock, are you all right?''

The wizard coughed. "Well, we know the chemicals aren't inert. Jason and Kendall were right. Such things are more dangerous to the user than to his enemy.''

Every man, woman, and child in the community poured from their habitations, and headed for the gates of the stockade. A cloud of smoke over the field slowly cleared. Where the two clansmen had been working was now a gaping hole a dozen feet across and three feet deep. Weapon, crates, and men were all gone.

"I think the initial explosion set off the other projectiles,'' Murdock speculated.

It sounded reasonable to me.

"What happened?'' Kren shouted from the shed, desperately working at the ropes holding his wrists to the hayrack while Jenkins resorted to using his teeth. The two guards had run off with the rest to investigate the noise. Kren and Jenkins were not having much success, nor were the others with their bonds. But they quickly got one idea.

"All together now," said Kren. "One, two, *three*!" As one, our companions pulled together against the hay-rack, and with a crack it came apart and they tumbled to the ground. However, the tightly secured ropes around their wrists and ankles remained, and we had only a minute or two to take advantage of the situation. Now in the fairy stories I've read, a minute or two would be all we needed for Kren and Jenkins to slip their ropes, free the others, come and untie us, and together make a quick escape across the stream and into the woods on the farside.

It was not quite that easy. Two minutes is not a lot of time to work apart sturdy half-inch ropes carefully secured around one's limbs. The clansmen flowed out of the town, inspected the site of the disaster, and flowed right back into town, making their way directly toward us in a crowd. Their intention was quite clear. We were to blame, somehow, and retribution would be swift.

Shaman Preston would have none of it. He put himself between us and the front of the crowd. "STOP!"

And stop they did. A few explanations of why this would spoil the proper sacrifice and not make God happy, a few arguments from the more perturbed of the clansmen, a few threats from the shaman, and a compromise was reached. They would not bludgeon us all to death at once. But they would move up the sacrifice a bit. From later to . . . now.

Several warriors went to our comrades, gave them a good assortment of kicks and blows as they lay upon the ground, and dragged them over to what remained of the hayrack and secured them to the thick endposts that were still intact. So much for rescue from that quarter.

Above the stockade, I saw four warriors very carefully carrying the two boxes of explosive out of the village and far off into the fields, where they gingerly lowered them to the ground and then backed off quickly. The clansmen had learned one lesson, at least.

Maybe we could play upon their superstitions. "Murdock, tell them it's not dark yet. God will be angry if they sacrifice us during daylight."

Shaman Preston heard and gave me a look of contempt. "Next you'll be warning us that you'll darken the sky if we don't let you go."

"Well, I had been thinking of that," Murdock admitted.

"We poor, ignorant clansmen won't know anything about orbits and eclipses, will we?"

A clansman brought a pot of hot, liquid tallow and dribbled it over the wood around Murdock's and my stakes, while others fetched burning brands and waited expectantly. My heart leaped into my throat, and I couldn't breathe. How long does it take to burn to death?

Shaman Preston held up his hands, and the clansmen bowed their heads. "Let us pray."

And then a rough woman's voice spoke out from the back of the crowd. "And what are you praying for, Shaman?"

His head darted forward like a bird's, eyes piercing the crowd in search of the speaker, and then he found her. The shaman spoke with surprise and displeasure. "Witch Woman!"

The crowd muttered in confusion, and a lane opened between the shaman and a figure at the back. Slowly, resolutely, the short, stout woman waddled forward. I had not believed my ears when I'd heard her voice, and now I did not believe my eyes. The sight was familiar. She wore a long, loose skirt of wool and a hip-length coat, open now, revealing a colorful shirt held in place at her ample waist by a wide belt with a large metal buckle. Upon her head was a wide-brimmed felt hat, fairly new, with three eagle feathers tucked into the band. From beneath it, black hair streaked with gray hung straight down to her shoulders, and framed the round, red face and squinting eyes that peeped out in sullen stolidity.

She was thought to have perished at the Battle of Lex-

ington over a year before. We had found her faded old
hat covered with blood in the fountain of the town
square, and assumed she was killed by the rampaging
soldiers of the Alliance. And yet she was not dead. She
lived.

Crazy Mary lived.

And Crazy Mary was the Witch Woman.

Perhaps there was hope after all.

Crazy Mary stopped before the shaman, ignoring
Murdock and me. She gestured at the men with the
brands. "Put them down."

A few of the younger clansmen in the crowd started
to object, but older warriors quickly hushed them. The
burning brands dropped to the earth. I managed to get
my heart back into my chest and found opportunity to
breathe again. I swallowed, thought of croaking out a
greeting to our rescuer, and decided better of it. No use
distracting her and interrupting negotiations.

The shaman seemed to regain his composure—or
most of it, at least. With some reluctance, he nodded to
Crazy Mary. "Welcome, Witch Woman. The years have
passed. But you come again to the land of the Utah."

She grunted. "Why are my friends held prisoner?"

The shaman's eyes widened. "Your friends? These
are your friends?"

"Yes."

"They are crossing our land. They have no permission."

"Neither do I. Do *I* need permission?"

He seemed about to give an answer, but thought better
of it. "The Witch Woman comes and goes as she will.
She does not need the permission of any clan."

Crazy Mary didn't move an inch. She was like a stone
before the clan leader. "Humph. That's true. You know
who I am. You know what my powers are."

"We remember. Those old enough to remember."

"And you know I will not be put off."

Shaman Preston kept his temper. "What do you want?"

"I want the prisoners. All of them. And their horses. And their equipment. They have a task to complete. An important task for the Utah. For the Colorado. For the Wyoming and the Mexique. For all the clans, for all the plains tribes, for all men. I have foreseen it."

"We must sacrifice," the shaman objected. "God has put a sickness upon our clan. We must sacrifice to remove the curse."

"And I say the sickness is not God's curse. But I can give you *my* curse. Or, I can give you my blessing. I think the Utah need every blessing they can get. Let your people decide."

He sighed. "All right. Ask my people."

She turned to the crowd, presenting her back to the shaman. If he wished, a single blow would have finished her, there and then. But he didn't dare.

"Are there any here who would deny me what I want?" she asked loudly. "Are there any here who would challenge me?"

Several young warriors were again about to voice their indignation, but stern-faced men of experience grabbed arms and whispered words, and the youths held their tongues.

What in the world had Mary done to earn such respect, such fear?

She turned back to the shaman. "We will camp in your town tonight, and you will show us welcome."

He realized it was time to submit. "Yes, Witch Woman. It will be done."

Another order from the shaman, and clansmen cut the ropes binding us to the stakes, while others freed our comrades from the shed. When they cut the last of the ropes I took a step and folded to my knees, my limbs as weak as jelly.

Murdock stepped next to me, wobbly himself, and helped me up. "My legs are numb too, Arn. The ropes were tight."

He was being kind. My weakness was not due to tight ropes.

We set up camp right there in the town circle, building a campfire out of the fuel that was to have been used to roast Murdock and me. Our horses were brought back to us, as well as our gear—or most of it. We never did get some things back, though Crazy Mary objected and the shaman spouted orders and warriors ran around looking into lodges and cabins. A warm coat, an extra pair of boots, a goodly portion of our flour, and other assorted items had all vanished. The Utah were good at making things disappear.

So we settled into the night camping within the Utah town. We had two on guard duty at all times, and the rest of us clustered close to the fire as we ate. Jason was the only one not at the fire. Tired as he was, he had still declared to the shaman that he was a healer, and offered his services to the clan. The shaman didn't think much of the offer until Jason mentioned that, "I have healing powders that might help." The village was out of powders.

As the rest of us ate, I noted that Lorich and Dakota were seated next to each other, and when she thought no one was looking she stared at his face and slid fingers through his hair with a gentle hand. Incredible as it might seem, I realized that Dakota might actually be fond of Lorich. Whether it was love, I couldn't say for sure. But it had all the looks of true affection. After a time Lorich's arm went around Dakota's shoulder, and she leaned into his side in the classic pose of man and woman across the ages.

I exchanged glances with Murdock and Kren, but nothing was said. What was there to say? In matters of the heart, there is a point where outsiders can do no more, and the lovers must take responsibility for their relationship. We could only hope Lorich wouldn't be hurt again, and trust that the look on Dakota's face meant he wouldn't be.

But we did take the opportunity to ask Mary questions.

"Shouldn't we have left this place? Why didn't we go while there was still light?" Jenkins asked, watching the occasional clansman walking through the town in the darkness. "What if they change their minds?"

Crazy Mary stirred her bowl of Utah meat and rice with a spoon. "Leaving would be a sign of weakness. Shaman Preston might decide to come after us. Here, all can see I fear nothing. They will not risk making me angry."

"What did you do to put such respect into them?" Murdock asked nonchalantly, but listening carefully.

"You really want to know?" she warned.

He nodded. "We are curious, I must admit."

A buzzing wave of pain, a white light of nauseating agony that blurred out vision and hearing and sense and thought seared my mind, worse than any headache I'd ever had or ever imagined. As quickly as it came, it passed, and I could see by the stunned faces of my companions that they had experienced the same. Kendall had dropped his bowl, and Jenkins's hands shook as he held onto his.

Kren blinked, dazed. "So much for curiosity,"

"Good Lord," I said.

"Master, that's almost like what I feel after I—" Lorich caught himself, and fell silent. If that's what poor Lorich endured for days after using his talent, he certainly did pay the price for his power.

Dakota swallowed and shook her head in denial. "Psychic talents aren't that strong. We've done studies in Pacifica."

Crazy Mary looked at Dakota. "Humph. If you've done studies and know better, then there is no need for me to say more."

And on the topic of magic, Mary would not say another word.

"Are you the Tracker?" Kren asked.

The Tracker! I hadn't even thought of that.

"The Tracker?" Mary asked, chewing. "Who is the Tracker?"

"Someone has been following us across the plains," Jenkins said. "We could never catch him—or her. Was that you?"

She grunted. "You have been very good at avoiding humans. And very stupid at avoiding trouble."

Dakota leaned forward within Lorich's embrace. "So. It *was* you."

Mary shrugged.

"And you warned us of the buffalo stampede on the plains by shouting," Lorich added.

She didn't even bother responding this time.

"How were you able to follow us and avoid us too?" Kren asked. "I would have said it couldn't be done, but you did it."

Mary took the compliment as her due. "I was born of a plains tribe, the Kansas, and sold to the Colorado Clan when I was twelve, and captured with my village by the Utah when I was fifteen. When I grew into my power, I went where I would. I know the plains, and the mountains, and how to survive. I know the clan chiefs and the tribal chiefs. And just as Murdock knew when tribesmen or clansmen were near, so I knew where you were. Following a beacon such as Murdock or Lorich is no great trick."

"But why?" Dakota asked. "Why have you followed these people so far?"

"He knows," Mary said, looking at me.

I nodded glumly. "Mary is my seer. My soothsayer. My oracle. My prophet. I've known her since childhood, when I was a gutter rat. She goes off for years, and then pops up to bring me warnings of doom. Never good news. Just doom. Until now. She must have seen I would have need of her. And here she is."

Mary nodded. "I had a vision of you at the stake. And other visions."

"Why didn't you just join the party instead of staying

alone out there?'' Lorich asked. ''We would have welcomed you into our company.''

Mary snorted. ''So the young wizard is content with one basket for all his eggs.''

''Oh,'' said Lorich.

''What happened to you?'' asked Murdock. ''We thought you had died at Lexington.''

Mary finished her bowl. ''I did not die.''

''What a revelation!'' stated Jenkins, standing behind me on guard duty but listening to the conversation.

Mary seemed to consider turning him into a frog, then perhaps decided it was not worth the trouble.

''I thought it was my last day, my last moments. I went out into the town square. The soldiers were everywhere, getting drunk. I sat down next to the fountain and waited. A soldier came up to me. I expected him to kill me, but he wanted something else. He attacked me. I used my knife.''

She took off her new hat and ran a finger down one of the eagle feathers in the brim. ''And now I wear three feathers in my hat.''

''We found your old hat in the fountain,'' I added.

''It was bloodied by him, and of no use anymore. I tossed it into the fountain. And I realized my vision had lied. No, not lied. I saw my hat in the water. But I thought it meant I was to die. Visions are dangerous. Their meaning can be hard to fathom.''

''Then what did you do?'' I asked.

''When the burning started, I walked out the gate.''

''That's it?'' Jenkins asked. ''You just walked out without being accosted?''

''The soldiers were very drunk. There was great confusion. I didn't even have to use my powers.''

There were more questions, but Mary was not inclined to answer further. ''That's enough. No more now. I'll go with you to Pacifica.''

''Mary, there is one more thing,'' Kendall said. He told her about the tunnel, the fused explosives within the armory, and the need to seal the ancient facility up again. Mary saw the wisdom of this action, but doubted that the party could escape the tribe after destroying the tunnel.

"You ride west. Ride hard. I'll light the fuses and seal the tunnel and wait for Shaman Preston and his warriors."

"Wait for them?" Lorich asked. "They'll be angry. They'll kill you."

Mary shook her head. "If they catch us after many miles and days, they will not be easy to reason with. But I'll stay near the tunnel and meet them. I'll tell them that it is my doing, not yours. I'll say it is God's Will that the tunnel be sealed. Preston will not like it, but he'll be able to do nothing."

"Except to you," Murdock added.

"He won't harm me. The danger is to you. I'll hold him to his word. You are under my protection and will be permitted to cross his land. I'll join you later."

It made sense, in a way. She knew the trails. It would give us a better chance of escape than anything else we tried. "Now I'm going to sleep," she stated, and there was little for us to do but follow her example.

Jason returned while I was on guard duty, the healer having spent hours with the villagers. "I'm not quite sure what it is that's afflicted the village. It's taken about half the old and sick, and a few of the children. It seems to have run its course, and most have recovered, but I did what I could for those who were still at risk. I'll leave some powders with Shaman Preston. I know there had been sickness at Chief Jones's town as well, but few there had died. The Colorado Clan had powders, and that made the difference."

The healer had a bite to eat, and then lay down with a groan, closed his eyes, and was fast asleep within a minute. When my guard duty was over, I was profoundly happy to sleep too, for my eyes had been closing on me even as I'd stood. Being burned at the stake is emotionally exhausting.

Tomorrow morning would come soon enough. Crazy Mary would destroy the tunnel, and we would see if we could get away with our lives.

5

Loyalties

The party rose in darkness. Quietly rolling up our bedding, preparing the horses, and mounting, we threaded our way at the walk through the Utah Clan town to the gates in the stockade just as dawn was breaking. There was no one about except the two sentries on duty who eyed us, exchanged a few words, then opened the gates for our passage. They knew we were scheduled to leave this morning, and Shaman Preston had agreed to it. There was no need to rouse the village or the shaman.

We maintained our pace for a hundred yards or so outside the stockade before urging our mounts to a trot. They shouldn't follow us, but a bit of distance couldn't hurt. The full light of day was just filling the valley when we came around the mountain and saw the landslide ahead of us, the tunnel a short, black string against the sheet of gray rock that was the cliff side.

We stopped below the rockfall. Mary would have to edge around the eastern side of the slide to reach the tunnel, while we had to head west. Kendall spoke. "Remember, Mary, you have twenty minutes or so to get clear. That's all. I'm not sure how much more of the cliff will come down when the explosives go off. A good chunk, I should think. So when you come out, head east back along the old road a half mile or so, and take shelter behind rocks or trees."

Mary grunted. "So far?"

"Yes. There may be debris flying through the air. No

221

use taking chances. I've never seen this much explosive ignited before''

"I will do as you say.'

"We'll continue west along the road. Join us as soon as you can."

With that, the party started off as she watched us depart. I hesitated and reined to a halt beside her. "Thank you, Mary."

Her face was expressionless. "Go on, boy."

And so I did.

It was more than an hour later that we heard a muted *foompf* behind us. The valley had curved, and we could no longer see the cliff. But a haze of dust slowly rolled out across the width of the valley.

Kendall smiled. "She's done it."

"Is the Tracker all right?" Kren asked the wizards.

"There's a mountainside between us. We won't know until she rejoins us—or doesn't," Murdock answered.

We pushed hard that day, and camped late in the afternoon in a spot that left a long, uninterrupted view behind without any mountainside to shield followers from view by eye or by magical talent. We waited expectantly, but no Mary came. The party bedded down with speculation about her fate, but hopeful that she would take advantage of the ample moonlight to catch up with us. Yet the next morning there was no sign of her, nor did she appear that day, or the next. Our hopes faded and we no longer talked of her, but faced the fact that Crazy Mary would not be joining us.

Three days later we came out of the mountains, greeted immediately by the ruins of an ancient city set into a dry, flat lowland. There was little vegetation, and the mounds of rubble stood out against the dry earth. Yet at the center of the circle of ruins, surviving girders and cornices of brick or crete thrust up three, four, or even five stories into the air, providing an outline of the great dwellings of the past, and bringing home just how great the cities of the golden age really were.

We didn't linger to appreciate or explore, but followed the old road down into the lowlands, leaving it to circle to the north around the ruins and picking another old road up on the other side. Here, we were able again to gauge the true size of the old highways, for though much was covered by the dusty earth, there were parts where the highway had been blown clear by the wind. Two ribbons of crete paralleled each other, and the full width of each could be realized. These were not great mysteries to us, certainly. One could visualize what the whole must have been from the pieces that were not overgrown by vegetation. Yet seeing these stretches of the old road gave one pause, for though the crete was frequently cracked and broken by the great cataclysmic quakes, from a distance these stretches must have appeared quite the same to the Ancients.

The road followed the bend of what Jason said had once been a great lake, but was now merely a floodplain into which flowed a slow, murky river. "We should make good time in the next day or two. This desert is a clan boundary, sort of a no-man's-land, and not many bother to cross it." It was cool for man and horse, and the flat, clear terrain allowed us to see (and be seen, of course) for many miles. Our only need was to stop at a watercourse each evening, not only to provide drinking water, but also to find forage along the banks for our horses to eat. Again, Dakota knew where to go and when to stop, and we had little problem putting forty miles behind us on that day near the dried lake.

But the days had grown chillier, the nights colder, the sky more often gray. Dakota watched the weather carefully, sniffing the wind. "There'll be snow coming soon. We'll have to hope it's not heavy."

That same day, Lorich told Jason he had a sore throat. There was nothing immediate to worry about, and so we continued on and finished a good day of travel. The next morning the young wizard woke up flushed and feverish, complaining of stomach queasiness and weakness. Kren admitted that he too had awakened with a sore throat.

Jason looked them over, declared it was probably just the flu, but added that he would watch it to be sure.

Getting Murdock and a concerned Dakota aside, he was more blunt. "It might be the flu. Or it might be the disease ravaging the Utah Clan. So far it's only the two of them. We'll have to wait to see."

Murdock nodded. "I agree. But best you know—I have a sore throat too."

By noon Lorich was weaving in the saddle, and while we ate he went behind a rock and was sick. Jason examined the lad again, and reported to Murdock. "The boy's fever is worse. I don't think he'll be able to go on much longer. I recommend we find a spot to rest for a few days."

"Couldn't we make a carrier for the horse to drag behind?" Jenkins asked.

Jason considered it. "No, that won't do. I suspect we'll have more down with it soon, not just Lorich. And this is nothing to take lightly. The sick will need rest, and a carrier is bumpy and exhausting. I don't intend to lose anyone in this party if I can help it."

Dakota looked at the sky, frowned, and bit her lip. "There's some ruins a few miles ahead in a valley. They might do."

The wind was picking up, and snowflakes were already falling as we reached the site that Dakota had picked out as our refuge. The ruins were off the old road a bit. Several cracked crete walls still stood, backing into a hillside and actually forming two small rooms with a connecting doorway and low crete ceilings. We weren't quite sure of their original purpose, but it was clear that the rooms had been used as a bear's den repeatedly over the years. Other walls just outside stood open to the elements. The area around was mostly forested, but nearby was a wide meadow, and on the other side of the meadow a stream.

Dakota and Kren helped Lorich into one of the rooms and began clearing out the rubbish. Dakota left no doubts as to our immediate needs. "Murdock, I don't like this wind. It could be a blizzard coming. Better gather enough firewood for three days.''

The horses were tethered in the meadow so they could forage as long as possible under the watchful eyes of Jason and Kendall, while the rest of us set to work, bringing armload after armload of wood to the ruins and stacking it against the outside walls. We continued to collect wood while Kren and Jenkins took the small bow saw and ax the party carried, going after pine branches to spread across the crete floor of the rooms and use as insulation for our bedding.

By the time we were nearly done, the wind was blowing hard, and everything beyond a hundred yards was gray. The snow increased, stinging our eyes as we hurried to finish our preparations. At last, with visibility down to a hundred feet, we brought the horses to just outside our shelter and tethered them in a narrow space between a wall and a thick stand of pines where they could cluster together for warmth. We had purposely left those trees intact. They formed a shelter that was open to the sky, but blocked out the fierce wind. The horses would have to endure the storm.

As would we.

Leaving only Kendall outside to keep first watch, we stuffed a cut pine tree into the entrance to serve as insulation and settled in quickly, putting saddles and supplies against the walls, forming pine boughs into beds, and getting a fire going in the middle of one of the rooms. Then, it was merely a matter of waiting, eight people stuffed into two small rooms with little to do. We prepared food for the evening meal, examined all our equipment, and took up our usual campsite activities, a combination of conversation and individual pursuits to pass the time. Clothes were mended, the ax and saw sharpened, bridles and saddles examined, and repairs made.

Outside, the wind had started to howl, and visibility must have been down to a few feet. Kendall and all of us had warning from Dakota never to lose contact with the crete walls of the shelter, for one could get lost in this storm only a dozen steps from safety and shelter. After an hour, Kendall came in and I went out, to be greeted by a blast of icy air in my face.

I was happy to have the deep hood of my coat pulled far over my head, and tried to keep my back to the wind as much as possible. The side where the horses were sheltered was better, and I went along the tether line, giving each a reassuring pat and examining their halters and leads to make sure all was secure. And then I paced up and down in the cold, waiting for my hour to end. And so it went. We slept through the night, awakened only occasionally by Lorich's coughing, the changing of the watch, and the urgency of nature as one or another of us stumbled outside for relief.

By the faint light of the sky, we could tell that morning had come. Lorich was worse, his fever higher than before, the lad lying on his bedding quite weak and miserable. Joining Lorich on the sick list this morning were Murdock and Kren, suffering the stomach upset, fever, and weakness that characterized the illness. Jason made rounds of his patients, and then shared his findings with all. "Well, whether this is what plagued the Utah or not really doesn't matter. It seems to be severe enough, whatever it is. We're all healthy adults, and that's important. It was the old and the sick that were fatal victims for the Utah, not the healthy. I think this is Lorich's worst day. We'll watch him closely and try to keep him comfortable until the fever breaks. I'll administer a powder if I see any real danger."

We made sure all the ill ones drank as much water and soup broth as they could hold, were kept comfortably warm or cool as necessary, and were helped outside to be sick or relieve themselves.

It was a long, dull day, the sick put into one of the rooms, and the rest of us going into the other. A second fire was lit, so that each room had its own source of heat, and we grumbled that our flour had been stolen by the Utah so we couldn't bake any fresh bread. By the end of the day the blizzard had blown itself out, the wind lessened to a normal whistle, and the snow stopped, though the temperature remained well below freezing. Although drifts of several feet were piled up against the windward walls, other areas in the open were almost free of snow. It was, as Dakota said, just a minor storm, a light snowfall made worse by high winds. Yet if this was minor, I really didn't want to see anything major.

Lorich's fever broke in the middle of the night, and he rested quietly at last. But the next morning found Murdock and Kren worse, and Jenkins was added to the sick list. Four of our party were sick. Only I and the three Pacificans—Kendall, Jason, and Dakota—were still on our feet.

Though Jenkins tried to be. "I'm all right," he protested, attempting to sit up in his bedding. "A royal guard is never sick."

Jason pushed him back down with one gentle hand. "And a royal guard never disobeys an order. Unless you need to go outside, you lie down."

In the next three days we saw Murdock, Kren, and Jenkins each go through the worst of the fever and begin their recovery. By the third day Lorich was able to stand, though too still too weak to do much more. Despite a bit of shakiness, he was able to help care for his comrades. He gave particular attention to Murdock, fussing over the wizard like a mother hen. For once, the ill Murdock did not object.

On that same afternoon as the ill rested quietly, I grew bored and put on my greatcoat. "Where's the bow saw? I'm going out to get some more firewood." We had already gone through the original supply, and each day had foraged for more. It was my turn again.

From his bed, Kren grinned weakly and offered an old joke. "You can never have enough firewood."

I grinned back at the beastman, but inside, I felt my heart twist. Firewood. That's what Angela and I had used as an excuse to get away from the party and go into the woods to be alone.

Murdock spoke softly to the beastman. "It might be a bit soon to joke about such things. Too many memories."

"Bah," said Kren. "He's had enough time to mope around. It's time to move on."

I swallowed the lump in my throat and ignored the rest of their conversation.

Dakota put down the rope she was examining and put on her coat. "I'll go with you, Arn."

Now, that was a change. She had never wanted to help me before. Yet the firewood joke had triggered a line of thought. I let my fantasies wander. Perhaps with Lorich sick, Dakota was feeling a bit randy and she was attracted by my good looks? Not that I would do anything to our scout, even if she offered. Not after I'd seen how Lorich cared for her. But if she were to be in an amorous mood, I'd certainly let him know of her infidelity. If one warning didn't work, perhaps another would.

Then reality came back to me. Dakota wanting me? Hah! Fat chance of that. What I had to worry about was not my seduction, but my safety. This was the woman who looked at me strangely. This was the Pacifican who had long conversations with Mr. Kendall. This was a time when Jenkins, my protector, lay sweating in a feverish sleep under his blankets. Still, what could a woman do to me?

"Why don't I come with you," Kendall volunteered.

So Kendall wanted to come too. Now I had to worry about two Pacificans. I felt like shouting at Jenkins to stop pretending to be sick, but refrained. Nonchalantly, I buckled on my sword belt.

Dakota stared at the other Pacifican for a moment, gave me a quick look, and followed us out. After that, I made sure to keep both of them in front of me as we tromped through the trees. And in the end, all we did was actually collect firewood.

When we had finished our task and returned to the comfortable warmth of the rooms, I noted to Jason the fact that none of the Pacificans had been struck by the sickness, and asked if it might be some type of natural immunity of his country. He shook his head. "Natural immunity, hardly. We've had vaccinations. Mine were long ago, but they're still effective, apparently. At least against this virus."

"What about me? How come I'm still healthy?" I asked the healer.

"Wait a day or two."

Jason was right. Just as the last of the ill regained their strength and we thought we might be able to move on, I came down with the sickness—worse than any of them.

Jason announced the obvious to the party. "Well, Arn has it now, maybe mixed in with a case of pneumonia. Hear that rumbling cough? His lungs are congested. His fever is quite high too, given it's only his first day sick. We'll have to watch him."

Dakota's frown deepened. "How long will it be before he can travel?"

"Four days to a week," Jason stated.

"That's too long," Dakota objected. "I smell more snow coming. We've got to get through the passes soon. Otherwise, we may not get through them at all."

"Can he travel sick?" asked the beastman.

Jason thought about that. "I'd say the risk was too great. He's in enough danger right here. Out there in the cold all day—I wouldn't like his chances."

Dakota threw back her shoulders and looked at the others. "It's either him—or all of us."

Murdock, sitting on his bedding, looked up at her. "What do you mean by that?"

"Just what I said. You say we can't take him. Then either we leave him, or we die with him. Don't you see? The passes could be snowed shut at any time. We'd be stuck down here in this valley. For the winter. The whole winter. Six months. How are we going to survive? On horsemeat?"

"If need be," Jenkins replied firmly.

Lorich spoke more gently. "Dakota, we can't leave Prince Arn. We just can't."

"You don't know what it's like to be isolated in these mountains. The snow gets to be five or ten feet high, even down here in the valley. You'd be stuck inside these rooms for months even if we do find enough food to keep us alive."

"We will not leave Arn. Or anyone," Murdock stated with finality.

I had been listening from my bed, though with my temple throbbing it was hard to pay attention. I have to credit my next words to the delirium of the fever, or from a deep knowledge that whatever I might say, they would be ignored. "Murdock, take the others. Go."

"I knew he was going to say that," said Jenkins.

"Listen to me," I croaked.

"Did you hear something?" Kren asked the wizard. "Sounded like a voice on the wind. Must have been the cackle of a fox."

"I'm giving an order."

Murdock listened. "You're right. Sounds like a fox. Never could abide their yapping."

Well, so much for heroics. I'd tried. I had a firm talk with my subconscious about the stupidity and danger of such heroic ploys. One day, others might take me up on my suggestions.

My comrades continued to ignore me as they began to discuss how best to survive if we were stuck here for the winter. Dakota threw up her hands and gave in. I listened for a while, and then drifted off into a sweaty, fever-wracked sleep. It was to last two full days.

Dimly I became aware of my breathing, my smell, my thirst. I swallowed with difficulty and opened my eyes a crack. The lids were crusted, and I had to blink several times before the room came into focus. A fire burned with only an occasional pop or crackle of a log. I was in the inner room, all alone. A waterskin lay near my bedding. I tried to reach for it, but lacked the strength, and my skull seemed to explode when I turned my head. But my skin was cool. The fever had broken. Unfortunately, I still had the cough; but it didn't sound as bad as it had.

So. I was still alive. A pleasant discovery.

Dakota pushed aside the blanket we had hung across the doorway between the two rooms, let it fall back into place behind her, and stared down at me with a surprised expression.

"Prince Arn. I . . . didn't think you'd be awake."

"Thirsty," I tried to say, but my effort ended in a cough that sent another flash of pain through my head.

She shook her head, as if shaking off uncertainty. "I must be quick." She leaned over and pulled my blanket down to the waist, so that I lay in only my damp shirt. Then, she took something out of her pocket. Her dart gun.

She slid back a part at the rear of the gun and took two small, pointy metal tubes from her pocket, inserting them into the chambers. Her hands shook the tiniest bit, but did not interfere with her efficient handling of the weapon. No wasted motion

She closed the rear, pulled back a small metal rod, and there was a click. Again, and another click. The firing springs had been set. Somehow, I didn't think the darts were loaded with nonlethal chemicals.

"Dakota," I gasped. "Don't do this."

She raised the gun. "I'm sorry."

The curtain lifted and Lorich, unsuspecting, stepped in. "Dakota," he whispered, "is anything wro—" He stopped with a gasp.

A startled Dakota swung the dart gun to point at him. "Lorich!" she groaned. "What are you doing here?"

"I—I was coming back, and I felt your distress."

"Arn's distress," Dakota stated.

"No, it wasn't," said Lorich. "It was you."

She took a breath and clenched her teeth. "I have a job to do. Step over there." She gestured with the gun to the opposite corner of the room.

Lorich hesitated, then moved slowly to the spot she'd indicated. "Dakota, we have to talk this over. You can't do this. Prince Arn is my friend."

"I have my orders," said Dakota. She looked at me. "From the Board of Administrators in Pacifica. The orders came the night you saw me coming out of the radio room at the Outpost."

Lorich moaned. "Dakota, I can't let you do this."

"You can't stop me," Dakota said, ignorant of Lorich's powers. And that was reassuring. He'd surely strike her down with his talent before she could harm me.

Wouldn't he?

I wondered whether I still had my shoulder knife in place, or if they had removed it during my illness. No, it was gone. They'd taken it off to make me more comfortable.

"I'll try to stop you," said the young wizard.

"Lorich, what can you do? I have the gun. Listen to me." Dakota stared at him. "I have to do this. And then I'm running, heading through the passes to Pacifica. Come with me. I want you to. We haven't had much time together. Just a little. But now we'll have all the time we want."

The young wizard stood unmoving, staring at her face.

"Hurry, Lorich. We have to leave quickly. Decide."

I had to say something. I had to counter the effects of her words. "She's using you, Lorich. She doesn't love you."

Her eyes flashed at me. "How would you know, you sullen clod?" She looked back to Lorich. "Lorich. You can come with me. We can be happy. You and I. Don't throw all that away. Come with me."

Lorich stood unmoving, his mouth working silently, agony upon his face.

The blanket at the doorway stirred again, and Kendall stepped in. "How is—Good Lord!"

Dakota cursed and swung her gun to point at him now.

Kendall looked at me, at Lorich, at Dakota. He took it all in, and without further thought lunged at the woman, his one arm extended to grab her weapon hand.

So he wasn't conspiring with Dakota. Kendall didn't want me dead.

Dakota didn't hesitate. There was a sharp *snick*, the gun firing just before Kendall was upon her. Dakota did not miss with her dart. The end was visible in Kendall's forearm, metallic against the gray of his shirt. Apparently the poison or nerve agent took time to spread its effect from a distant limb, for Kendall was able to continue struggling, if only briefly. Kendall held Dakota's wrist in his one hand while her free hand sought to tear free of his grasp. Whether Kendall's one arm would have been enough to match Dakota's two would never be answered, for in a moment his grip loosened and he went to his knees. Kendall sagged against a wall, helpless, staring at Dakota and gasping for air while the drama went on above him.

One dart left.

Dakota attempted to take aim at me, but Lorich had placed himself between us. She swore. "Get out of the way." He reached for her, ignoring the fact that the gun was aimed right at his chest. I expected the poor lad soon to have a dart in him. But Dakota hesitated, her face torn with inner conflict, and he grabbed her gun hand with both of his, trying to twist the weapon free, pleading with her through clenched teeth. "No, Dakota. Please, no."

What was he waiting for? Why didn't he just use his power?

They struggled for a moment, only a short moment, the space of a heartbeat or two, and yet to me it was a long, epic battle that I cannot erase from memory. They swayed, grunting with effort, and suddenly there was that cold, deadly *snick* once again.

The two combatants held each other in the following silence, horror upon the features of each. The dart had pierced Dakota in the chest, just below her collarbone, and close to vital organs and nerves. And it was that much quicker in its effect. She grimaced and sank to the ground, Lorich still holding on to her, his eyes wide and desperate. Dakota looked around in confusion, and then focused upon the man cradling her in his arms. "Oh, Lorich. Finally I was happy." And then the spasms went through her, one, two, three. And after she stopped trembling, she did not draw another breath.

The boy sat on the floor shocked, holding the body of the woman to him and staring at me in disbelief. "She can't be dead."

What could I say?

There were more voices outside, the blanket was thrust aside, and exclamation followed as Jason and Murdock rushed in. The healer looked to Dakota, saw the open, staring eyes, saw the dart in her chest, and knew it was too late to help her. He knelt next to the gasping Kendall, looked him over quickly, and saw the dart in his arm.

The healer let out a groan. "Oh, my son."

Kendall opened his eyes. "Something . . . isn't right. Why did Dakota . . . want to kill Arn? Why not wait . . . till we arrive?"

Jason forced out words. "I'll find out, Paul. I'll find out."

"Tell Megan . . ." Kendall fell silent as the spasms hit, and in the end he too was left with eyes staring lifelessly at the little room where he had drawn his last breath. Whatever he had wanted to say was lost. That is one of the many untidy things about death. Last words don't usually get said.

Kendall was gone. Another friend, gone. And he *was* a friend. In spite of my suspicions, in spite of what he had done to protect the Codes, he had been my protector and friend, even to the last. Even at the cost of his life. My grief was tempered by the realization that friendship might indeed be true, and that I had seen such loyalty displayed in all its glory. No greater love hath man . . .

But what would I tell Megan?
I felt weary unto death.

They buried Kendall and Dakota in the meadow, digging shallow graves next to each other and covering the earth with rocks so that wolves couldn't dig up the bodies. Two days later I was able to ride, and we could continue our journey through the passes because the snows had mercifully held off, in spite of Dakota's warnings. Perhaps she had told us that just to serve her purpose. Or perhaps we were just lucky. In any case, as we finished our preparations for travel, Lorich and Jason went out to the meadow to visit the graves for one last time.

Murdock gestured to me. "You haven't seen the graves. Go with them."

"I don't need to."

"Go. That's an order."

So I went. Jason and Lorich stood next to each other, looking at the freshly turned earth and the stones.

Jason, his eyes red behind his spectacles, took a deep breath. "It's hard when a child must bury a parent. The only thing worse is when a parent must bury a child."

I nodded, silent.

"He was a good son." The quaver in his voice was noticeable. "And I guess that's all I have to say. I'm glad I had this chance to say good-bye." He reached down and stroked a stone on the grave. "Good-bye, Paul." With bent shoulders, his years now heavy upon him, Jason turned away and went back to where our companions waited.

"Good-bye, Paul," I echoed Jason, the words spoken in my head only, perhaps, but still spoken. And so I had said my farewell, and maybe now Murdock would be happy. For a moment I considered going with Jason and leaving Lorich alone, but something stopped me.

The young wizard held his hat, turning it in his hands while he stared down at the grave. "Prince Arn?"

I wished Murdock was with us. I was not good at this. "Yes, Lorich?"

"You warned me. You were right."

"No, Lorich. I was wrong."

"She was just using me."

"She wasn't using you. She didn't need you to accomplish her task."

He mulled this over. "Do you—do you think she loved me?"

I answered honestly. "Yes, Lorich, I think she did. She could have killed you with the dart gun, and she didn't. Just as you could have killed her with your power, and you didn't."

He was silent a long moment. "I have a confession to make, Prince Arn."

"Oh?"

"I'm unworthy to be your friend. I am a disgrace to my calling. I am dishonored."

What was this all about? "Hardly," I objected.

"It's true. When Dakota—when she wanted me to go with her and let her kill you—" He struggled for breath. "I—I hesitated. I was tempted, Prince Arn. I considered it!"

His words evoked only a shrug from me. This I already knew. "Lorich, you were tempted. That's natural. But you resisted, and that's the difference."

Who could blame the lad for feeling temptation? The only dishonor would have been to succumb to the temptation, selfishly to purchase his life with Dakota by ending someone else's. He wouldn't pay that price. The purchase wasn't worth it.

"You understand."

"Yes, Lorich, I understand."

"I haven't lost your friendship?"

"No, Lorich, I'm still your friend."

There were tears streaming down his cheeks now. "I feel my heart will break. I loved her so. I miss her so much."

"I know," I said hoarsely, swallowing the lump in my throat and putting an arm around his shoulder as he sobbed. "I know."

6

Arrival

We were fortunate in our travels. The snow held off, and a week of fair weather allowed us to clear the high passes. The horses were tired and worn, and we were too. We looked like vagabonds. The only accomplishment of the miles had been to lighten the load of the horses in the last few weeks; supplies were low, and we were almost out of food. So it was with relief when, a good twenty miles beyond the passes, the old road took us to the banks of a very respectable river.

"This is it," said Jason, unable to hide the fatigue in his voice. "The western border of Pacifica. If I remember correctly, there should be a way—yes, there it is." He pointed to a narrow dirt path that ran near our bank of the river. "We should follow the path north a few miles to where the river narrows. We'll find a bridge there we can cross by."

Murdock scanned the woods on the far side of the river. "There are people over there. Two, no, three."

Jason nodded and pushed his spectacles higher on his nose. "Watchers. They have a lookout position near the river."

"Really?" said Kren. "They hide themselves well. There's no sign of them."

"As I said, Major Kren, they're Watchers. I wouldn't have told you they were there if Murdock hadn't detected them."

We followed the path along the river, and eventually came to the bridge Jason had spoken of. It was a sturdy affair of wooden logs and planking, the far end blocked by a stone keep with a wooden gate set into it. The gate was closed.

Jason and Murdock led us onto the bridge, halting a dozen paces from the gate and waiting patiently. The face of a man appeared in an opening above. "Good day. I am required to ask your business." The voice carried a strong Pacifican accent.

Jason responded clearly, allowing his own accent to echo that of the other Pacifican. "I am Jason Kendall, former representative of Pacifica to Kenesee of the six nations. I am returning home. These are emissaries of the six nations come to talk to the Board of Administrators."

"I see. Well, Mr. Kendall, you may enter through the postern. Your companions will have to wait a bit."

Jason dismounted as a small door set within the gate was opened. Bending over, he went through and the door was closed behind him.

We waited for perhaps ten minutes, still mounted, before Lorich grew impatient. "Perhaps they've forgotten about us."

Jenkins shook his head. "Oh, no, they haven't forgotten. They're watching right now." He raised his voice. "But I don't think they'll mind if we dismount and stretch while we wait."

"That will be acceptable," came a voice from above.

Murdock gave a nod, and soon we were all standing next to our horses. It was good to be on our feet again. The better part of an hour went by before we heard a rasping sound, and the gates swung open, revealing a short passageway that led off the bridge. Jason stepped out from the shadows within, and we all mounted and were on our way. At the other end of the passageway waited a horseman dressed in a brown uniform, our new guide, who turned without a word and led the way along a curving dirt road until it intersected another old road, which we followed to the west. On both sides were only forested hills.

Jenkins had been eyeing the guide. The man carried what appeared to be a short sword at his waist, as well as some type of rifle holstered beside his saddle. At last Jenkins could restrain himself no longer. "Jason, our guide is carrying a rifle. Does Pacifica use muskets, or is that a more advanced powder weapon?"

Jason puffed on his pipe. "No powder weapons— though we could produce them quickly enough, in need. Last time I was in Pacifica, the basic fire weapon was the air rifle. Let's ask our guide for comment."

The guide stiffened at Jason's words, perturbed no doubt by his countryman's casual willingness to share secrets with the outlanders. But he kept his peace and answered simply. "Yes, sir. We still use air rifles."

"What is an air rifle?" Lorich asked, beating me to it.

"It fires a metal slug propelled by compressed air," Jason explained. "The rifle needs to be pumped up between shots to attain pressure."

Kren looked doubtful. "Air compression? Can that be effective?"

Jason held up a hand and brought our small column to a halt. "Let me assure you that it creates just as much work for a physician as any ball from a powder musket. Perhaps our guide will demonstrate."

Dutifully the guide pulled the short-barreled rifle from its holster, placed a formed slug into the rifle's chamber, and then pulled a pump lever once, twice, thrice. The fourth pull was made against great resistance.

"The weapon can be loaded and pumped up while lying prone on the ground," the guide offered, unable to prevent a note of pride in his voice. "A great advantage over archers."

An archer had to be standing or kneeling. Which made a much better target for someone who could fire from a prone position.

"Please pick a target for me," the guide asked. It was apparent he was not averse to showing the outlanders his skills.

I pointed to a black lump hanging from a tree perhaps forty yards away. "Try that wasp's nest."

The guide grinned. "Wouldn't want to try this last summer, when the wasps were in it." He brought the rifle to his shoulder, sighted, and there was a faint *pffft*. The nest separated from the tree and bounced upon the ground. The guide reloaded and fired again. *Pffft*. The nest jumped, a large chunk flying off. Another round, *pffft*, and the nest disintegrated.

Powder weapons, and now air weapons. Mankind was so clever.

Kren grunted. "Seems effective."

"In my time, lethal range was fifty yards," said Jason, "and at forty it would penetrate leather armor as well. Perhaps they've improved them since then."

"A bit," said the guide, cautiously. "Just a bit."

We continued on our way.

"So, Jason, will we be seeing other wonders of the Pacificans?" asked Kren.

"You won't be seeing any. At least, not for a while. Our border is kept as a primitive 'frontier,' a protective belt of wilderness, something like the beastmen do on the edges of the Beastwood."

"We have none of the wonders of Pacifica," cautioned the beastman. "No radios, certainly. But what else will we see? Horseless wagons? Railroad trains? Airplanes?"

I laughed at a thought—and was pleasantly surprised that I had indeed laughed, without effort. "Professor Wagner thought airplanes were only a fantasy of the Ancients, and that manned flight was impossible. Or at least, that's what he told us. I wonder now if he wasn't having his little joke."

"I can understand his feelings," said Murdock. "To believe that the giant metal planes of the Ancients actually flew is difficult. And yet, they did."

"You might want to rein in your imagination," Jason cautioned. "The wonders of Pacifica may be less than you thought, and yet wonders nonetheless. Be patient."

We continued on the road through the afternoon, and came at last to a large clearing in which was set a fort of earthworks and wooden palisades and towers. Above the open gate was a sign: BORDER FORT SEVEN. Inside were log buildings and stables and a small parade ground. The fort was a permanent establishment, with brick walks connecting the buildings and rounded natural stones lining grassed areas. Pacifican cavalry, sixty or seventy men and their horses, were housed in the fort, though I suspected the place could hold three times as many without difficulty. Mounted, each cavalryman carried a saber in a scabbard on one side of the saddle, and a holstered rifle on the other.

There was some interest in our arrival, and a squad of men came out and lined up at attention with short-barreled air rifles upon their shoulders, serving both as guard of honor and security against the ragged, barbaric outlanders who came to their encampment. For we were decrepit and barbaric-looking after a thousand miles on the trail. Our hair had grown long and unkempt, our beards were full, our clothes had become dirty and worn, and we had all lost weight—which, in Murdock's case, pleased him no end. Our horses—once fat and healthy—had become bony, worn-out nags. Topping it off, the party had run out of soap two weeks before, and we all smelled horrible. Much longer and we'd certainly come down with lice and fleas as well. The soldiers watched with interest and speculated between themselves, but otherwise went about their duties without interruption.

Our guide halted us in front of a building that bore a sign above its porch:

HEADQUARTERS
Border Fort Seven

Using my deductive abilities, I took it to be the headquarters. Major Miller would have been quite proud of me.

On the porch was the commander of the Pacifican

cavalry company, a Captain Ahmed. He was a short, efficient-looking man who relieved the guide of his charges and greeted us each with a friendly handshake.

"Weren't there supposed to be two more members in your party?" the captain asked.

"They've been delayed," Jason said, and left it at that.

Our horses were taken to the stables, and the captain escorted us into one of the log buildings, a well-built, two-story barracks that was not in use. Each room had at least one glassed window. Not a wonder, perhaps, but significant to me was that the panes of glass were larger than any I had seen in the six nations, and clearer.

Our party was housed in one long room with a score of bunks along each wall, tables and benches in the center. We were allowed to step onto the front porch of the building, but not off it. And except for escorted visits to the outhouse and bathhouse, the room and porch was where we stayed for two days, our meals brought to us by Pacifican soldiers. Jason was the only member of our party who was allowed to roam the fort at will, but he ended up spending most of his time with us. We did have a chance in the bathhouse to wash our clothes, cut our hair, and shave off the beards that had grown during the miles on horseback. And each of us in turn had a good session in the showers—once we had heated water and hauled it up to the shower reservoir.

The Pacificans had very good soap.

Soon after arriving, Jason explained what was happening. "We'll be here until the Board of Administrators arrives to meet with us. It should be two or three days, at most."

"Reminds me of our stay in the Beastwood, when we waited to see the Senior Council," I commented.

"I remember," said Jason. "Major Kren, now you know what it's like. Boredom. Uncertainty. Fear."

"Ahh, I see," said Kren. "It's like marriage."

Jason took the opportunity to remind us of the seriousness of our mission. "Say nothing of Dakota and

Paul, and what has happened. They know now that they're not with us. I'll raise the matter with the Board of Administrators at the proper moment."

Thus washed and content, I was sitting on the porch with Murdock and Jason on the afternoon of the second day, smoking my pipe and enjoying the bright sunshine and the relative warmth as the temperature rose above freezing. There was a flurry of activity, and a Pacifican company of infantry marched into the fort, about one hundred and twenty men or so. They wore the same brown uniform and cap as the cavalry, but the shoulder patches were different, of course, and each carried a pack on his back. All were armed with a rifle slung over the shoulder. Their infantry rifles had longer barrels than those of the cavalry, and at the side of each man hung what looked to be a short sword.

"It's a bayonet," said Jason. "Fits over the muzzle end of the rifle, and makes a very effective stabbing weapon against sword or short spear."

Captain Ahmed greeted the infantry commander, and I took the opportunity to listen from my place on the porch. "Captain Lawrence. Good to see you again."

"And you, Captain Ahmed."

"We were notified of your coming, but I'm still surprised they sent you. Does the Board really think more troops are needed? The Watchers report all quiet on the border."

Captain Lawrence glanced our way, regarding us calmly. He was a sturdily built figure with a piercing glance. Not a man to cross, from all appearances. He looked back at Captain Ahmed and smiled. "You know our leaders. Always cautious, always safe, always comfortable."

Ahmed grinned. "That's so. Well, let's get your men settled and we'll talk later. You can take Barracks C and D. And we'll have a hot meal ready for them tonight."

"Couldn't ask for more," said Lawrence, and passed an order to his waiting subordinate, Lieutenant Quang, who got the men moving. "Tell me," Lawrence continued, casting another glance our way, "is one of those three men Arn Brant?"

"Yes, indeed," said Ahmed. "The one on the left, the young one, is Prince Arn. The other is Wizard Murdock, his advisor, and Jason Kendall.

"You're sure it's Brant? He looks pretty young."

"He's got the scar, and the birthmark. And former representative Kendall affirms his identity."

"I've heard of Jason Kendall. I wouldn't put too much stock into what he says. He's been in the East too long, and gave up his position twenty years ago. What kind of man does that? I don't think he can be trusted."

Captain Ahmed was thoughtful. "Maybe not. But he has friends on the Board, I understand, and still retains the respect of many. Who can know for sure?"

Lawrence grinned. "Perhaps you're right. Well, I guess it doesn't matter.. It's Arn Brant who is the concern. He doesn't look very impressive."

"Yes, but from what his companions say, he's lucky. That's all it takes, you know."

At one time I might have scoffed, "Yes, I was so lucky." But as the words sprang into my head, there also came the realization that it was true. I was lucky. Lucky to have men such as Murdock and Jason as my companions, lucky to have known men such as John Black and Paul Kendall, lucky to have loved a woman that loved me too, and lucky to be alive. In spite of everything, in spite of all the loss and all the pain, I was lucky. I hardly knew what to make of it. Such self-revelation was quite startling to me. Could the fever have addled my brain?

It stormed that night, and the wind whistled around the eaves and drove sleet against the shutters. It was good to be in a soft bunk under warm blankets and listen to the wind, the embers of the fire providing a dim but pleasant glow to the room. We slept more soundly than we had in months, warm and fed and comfortable. The next morning was uneventful, the wind abating but a light sleet continuing. At noon while we ate thick chicken soup and rich, dark bread, Jenkins looked out the window and pointed.

"Wizard Murdock, people arriving."

There was a rush to the window. Jason did not bother rising, and I left the table reluctantly. The Pacifican cooks certainly knew their chicken soup.

I joined my comrades, who were clustered about the panes. An open coach pulled by a team of draft horses came to a halt in front of the neighboring building. The coach was little more than a wagon, though provided with four benches and a tarp stretched upon hoops to provide overhead cover. Huddled together on the benches were over a dozen passengers well bundled in various colored coats and cloaks and hoods and hats. Citizens, not military. Behind, another seven or eight citizens had chosen to ride on horseback. Riders and passengers dismounted—some clumsily—and went into the building.

Jenkins stroked his chin. "They look pretty clean for having ridden all morning in messy weather, wouldn't you say?"

"I'd noticed that," said Kren

Murdock was thoughtful. "Jason, I never asked. How many members does your Board of Administrators have?"

Jason took a sip of coffee. "About two dozen. There's a Chair, a Secretary, and general members. It's an unwieldy body, but the system seems to work—more or less."

"And by any chance," Jenkins asked, appalled, "are some of the Board members women?"

"This isn't Kenesee," Jason said bluntly.

An hour later we were summoned to the building into which the administrators had gone, and found ourselves in a large room set up for a conference. The walls were chinked logs, of course, with a wooden floor just like our barracks. A metal stove sat in one corner, making the room quite comfortable.

Wooden armchairs in a semicircle were carefully arranged for the board members, in the center of which was a narrow table with two chairs behind it. There were twenty-one board members present, about equally divided between men and women. Most were middle-aged, a few were grayheads, and two sported white hair and must have been in their seventies. None was young. The hair on all, men and women, was not long, and there were only one or two beards on the men, though several males did sport mustaches. Their clothing was a wide array, ranging from robes and wrapped heads to coats and trousers. The women tended toward long woolen skirts of various hues.

Two women stood behind the table. One was gray-haired, tall, thin, and severe, with hard lines and a prominent nose. A dignified woman, but she could not have been a beauty even in her youth. The other was brown-haired and short. Though certainly in her forties, she was very pleasant to look at, with fine features, an inviting smile and, from what I could see before she sat, a good figure.

I was glad we'd had a chance to wash and shave, or our barbaric look would have served us ill in the presence of the finely coifed and tailored members of the board. As it was, we had done all we could, and would have to depend on words rather than appearance. There were five chairs in a row facing the board. I took the center chair. Murdock and Kren next to me left and right, with Lorich and Jenkins in the outer chairs. Jason sat on a bench against the wall, for although he was our companion, he was a Pacifican and not one of the delegation. The only other people in the room were a dozen soldiers from Captain Lawrence's infantry company spaced along the walls as guards, Captains Ahmed and Lawrence seated on a bench at the back, and two scribes at a table to the side, ready to record.

The board members studied all of us, but Kren received a disproportionate share of glances, and there were several muttered conversations about him. At least no one tried to examine how far down his hair went.

The thin, hard-faced woman tapped a small gavel on the table. "This special meeting of the Board of Administrators will now begin. Although it is unprecedented, we have been visited by a delegation from the nation of Kenesee. We are here to evaluate a proposal they are bringing us.

"I wish to express welcome to the Kenesee delegation, and make at least minimal introductions. While there are too many of us to introduce every Board member right now, I am Anita Freiburg, Chair of the Board. Seated next to me is Louise Dacolla, Secretary. For the knowledge of the Kenesee delegation, Secretary Dacolla and I will run the meeting, but any decisions made or measures taken are by the majority vote of the full Board. Now, you may begin."

In response, Jason rose and stepped forward. "Members of the Board, I am Jason Kendall, former Pacifican representative to the Kingdom of Kenesee. My son, Paul Kendall, filled that position after me. On behalf of the Kenesee delegation and myself, may I express our appreciation for your coming to this meeting place and your prompt response to our arrival." Jason then introduced each of us in turn, starting with me and ending with Sergeant Jenkins. When he was finished, he returned to his bench.

There were a great many appraising looks when I stood up.

Chair Freiburg put up a hand. "If I may say something before you begin. Prince Arn, on behalf of the Board and all Pacifica, I do need to extend our regrets to the six nations. We are fully aware that several Pacifican representatives—sworn to uphold the tenets of the Codes in letter and spirit—fomented rebellion and violation of the Codes. Their treachery caused the War Against the Alliance—as you have come to call it—and the thousands of deaths that resulted. We are sorry that

Pacificans brought this about, and can only restate that we would have prevented their actions, had we been able. The information we received was contradictory at best, and we refrained from acting for fear of worsening the situation rather than rectifying it. And now, you may begin your presentation.''

There was much at stake, and I needed to play my small part well. I took a deep breath. "Your apology is unnecessary," I stated, speaking only those words extemporaneously. I then swung into my prepared speech. "On behalf of Kenesee, our greetings to the Board of Administrators of Pacifica. While I represent my brother, King Robert Brant of Kenesee, and am tasked with making any decisions necessary for our delegation, I present to you my trusted advisor, Desjardins Murdock, who will act as our spokesman and negotiator." And then I quickly sat down, quite proud of myself.

My words generated some lifted eyebrows and an exchange of questioning glances, but Murdock rose with dignity, nodded at me respectfully, and stepped forward until he was just in front of the chair and secretary's table, and right at the center of the semicircle of chairs. He scanned their faces, a warm smile on his, allowing his "magic" to work at full effect. I felt friendship, common sense, trustworthiness, and goodwill radiate from the wizard like warmth from a stove.

"Members of the Board of Administrators of the great nation of Pacifica, I thank you for this opportunity to speak. As Prince Arn stated, I am Wizard Murdock of Kenesee."

There were a few smiles at Murdock's title. "A Kenesee *wizard*," snickered one bald and fat board member to his neighbor, resisting Murdock's early charm. "The six nations are as backward as the clans."

Murdock continued, totally unperturbed, weaving his spell. "On behalf of all the nations, may I thank Pacifica for all she has done throughout the last two centuries. While we may not know every aspect of the role played by Pacifica, we know enough to understand that the prosperity and peace we enjoy has been due to the benevolent efforts and sacrifices made by you on our behalf over the long years.''

Benevolent? Well, I might not have used that word.

Our wizard went on. ''However, the climactic events of the last two years have resulted in unprecedented changes. Before I present any proposal for your consideration, I would like to review those events in detail for the benefit of all Board members. May I do so, Chair Freiburg?''

''You may,'' she said, and Murdock began his narration. Without benefit of notes or prompts, our wizard spoke for over an hour, detailing first the previous relations of each of the six nations to each other, the success of the Codes of Progress, and the level of technology that existed throughout the east. He also mentioned the presence of the Beastwood, and the role they were to play in events. Murdock went into the scheming and maneuvering of the Pacifican representatives such as Gregor Pi-Ling and national leaders such as Governor Rodes of Virginia, and what they did trying to coerce Kenesee and the other nations to go along with their schemes. Kenesee resistance under King Reuel had precipitated the War Against the Alliance, in which five nations had attacked Kenesee.

Murdock continued the story, telling of the military maneuvers, the difficult odds, and the threat a victory of the Alliance would have posed to the Codes. The story of our eventual victory was punctuated with his list of the names and titles of the good and great men we had lost in the struggle, including King Reuel and General John Black.

The story then passed to the events of the past year, when my party had traveled to Texan and helped instigate a rebellion to overthrow the evil President of Texan, General Jack Murphy, while Robert turned back the Virginian Army on Kenesee soil and overthrew Governor Rodes. The powder muskets used by the Texans and the cannons being cast by the Virginians were described in all their horror.

The Pacificans—and my party as well—were hanging on Murdock's narrative, mesmerized by the story he was telling. Well, perhaps it wasn't the story alone that held our attention. Even without his charming manner, Murdock was an orator of rare ability, and could ensnare an audience like few others. Combined with the power of his tale and his warm demeanor, he had quite an effect upon the Board. In fact, several of the women and one of the men were looking at him with stares of appreciation that went well beyond the diplomatic.

Murdock paused and asked if a break might not be appreciated by all. Certainly, he himself could use a few minutes to refresh before continuing. The Chair granted the request.

Lorich brought Murdock a cup of water. "Master, you were excellent. I never understood so clearly what happened."

Murdock gave the young wizard a smile. "That was the easy part. We've informed them of the situation. Now we need to present our proposal, the arguments for change, and the benefits of agreement."

Kren put a hand on Murdock's shoulder. "Well, you've certainly impressed the women. If they get to be more than you can handle—"

"I know. You'll be glad to take one or two off my hands. A true friend in need."

"Always willing to do his share," piped in Sergeant Jenkins.

"Master, would you really—"

"No, I wouldn't. And you should know better than to ask."

After a quarter hour, the meeting resumed.

Invited to continue his presentation, Murdock stood in the middle of the semicircle and waited until, in the absolute silence, all eyes were upon him. And then he spoke. The Pacificans had enforced the Codes for almost two hundred years and they had, on the whole, served the nations of the east well. Horrors had been avoided through the Codes.

Still, there were other things to consider both for long-standing problems and for new developments wrought by the recent struggles.

Weapons were only tools. The men who wielded them determined history. Wars had beset them over the generations with a depressing regularity, but nothing in the last two hundred years had compared to the human devastation resulting from the actions of the renegade Pacifican advisors. Their treachery had ignited a war that brought about the deaths of half the Pacifican advisors, not to mention the tens of thousands of dead from the six nations.

Most importantly, the cat was out of the bag. Powder weapons had made their appearance on the battlefield again. To expect the nations to ignore their existence and potential was unrealistic. The production of such weapons might be controlled—under a strong, centralized government—but could not be totally prevented.

Almost as important, though not as dramatic, the board had to consider the very successes of the Codes and of Pacifican beneficence. Encouraged by health measures proposed by the Pacificans, aided by pharmaceuticals rediscovered by the Pacificans, the populations of the six nations were increasing rapidly. Yet access to simple technology, which could benefit and feed these increasing numbers, was stymied by the Codes.

Times had changed. Realities had to be considered as Pacifica strove to do good for all the nations and peoples of the continent.

Murdock smiled. "And that, esteemed Members of the Board, brings us to the reason we have spent long weeks crossing the continent. We bring you the proposal of King Robert of Kenesee. We ask that you approve the formation of a Confederation that would unite the six nations. We ask that Pacifica recognize the need for change, and allow progress to go forward under the watchful eye of the new Confederation, which will control and minimize new weaponry while maximizing the development of peaceful technology. We ask you to revise the Codes of Progress, or at least allow the de facto revision taking place even as we speak. We ask that Pacifica support this new direction for the six nations, and guide it to a successful future rather than bringing forces to bear that would end in more bloody wars and the enforcement of rules that no longer apply.''

With that, Murdock sat down, and I tried to count the number of mouths that hung open. So there it was. We had completed our task. We had delivered the proposal from King Robert.

And in response, the board sat in numbed silence.

At last, a studious-looking man with spectacles stood. ''Madam Chair.''

''The Chair recognizes Administrator Tanaka.''

Tanaka raised his hands in a gesture of confusion. ''Madam Chair, while many of us are sympathetic to the difficulties faced by the six nations, I must express shock at the proposal offered, and ask the delegation from Kenesee if they are serious about this matter.'' He sat down.

Murdock rose. ''I must assure the Board of our deadly seriousness. We have seen friends die, we have shed our own blood, for the ideals embodied in the Codes. And because we have given so much for the Codes, we feel we may ask for change with good heart.''

The fat man who liked to snicker rose as Murdock sat. ''Madam Chair?''

''The Chair recognizes Administrator Hodges.''

''Thank you, Madam Chair. I consider it an act of arrogance and disrespect, an act of dishonor and treachery, for this delegation from Kenesee blatantly to propose we change the system by which they have prospered for the last two centuries. I move that we go to private session and determine how best to deal with the imperious King Robert and his delegation.''

That set the members chattering amongst themselves.

Once again, things were not going well. I could imagine what would happen if they went into closed session feeling that our proposal was treacherous and dishonorable. We would not be happy with the result.

Murdock was about to rise and present an argument, but Jason came forward to center, gesturing the wizard to stay in his seat. Gradually, the noise abated, and Jason spoke. "Madame Chair, I have relevant matters to discuss. May I address the Board?"

Before the chair could speak, Secretary Dacolla placed a hand on her arm. "Madame Chair, it should be remembered that a motion has been made. A vote should be taken on that motion."

Freiburg hesitated, then began to nod her head in agreement with Secretary Dacolla.

Administrator Tanaka raised his hand quickly. "Ahem. Madame Chair, may I remind you that relevant discussion may be allowed before voting on a motion. Jason Kendall is one of the most respected representatives to the outlands we've ever had. He is also an old friend of several of us on this Board. To take action on this matter without hearing him would be an act of disrespect, and put us into a closed session without adequate information. We must hear him out."

There was a chorus of agreement from perhaps half the administrators, and after noting it, Freiburg tapped her gavel lightly against the table. "If the information is relevant, Jason Kendall may speak before a vote is taken."

The room fell silent, and Jason studied the administrators with a critical eye. "I must warn the Board members. What I have to say will not be pleasant. There has been treachery, but it is not by Kenesee. The treachery has occurred here.

"In Pacifica."

7

Debate and Decision

If our revelations had brought shocked silence or muttered comment, Jason's statement brought a torrent of denunciations, denials, and exclamations of disbelief.

"Impossible."

"An insult to our nation."

"Is he a traitor?"

"No more discussion."

Chairman Freiburg pounded her gavel for order.

Never missing a chance, the fat man, Hodges, stood. "Madam Chair, I again move that we retire to closed session. I think we need hear no more from Jason Kendall."

Administrator Tanaka stood in turn. "Madam Chair, we need to hear what Jason has to say. Now, more than ever."

Freiburg hesitated, gavel in hand, clearly uncertain what to do. She looked about at the other members, gauging their feelings.

Secretary Dacolla spoke firmly to the chair. "Anita, enough of this. We need to go to closed session."

Jason, still standing in the middle of the semicircle of administrators, took a step forward, placing him almost at the table. He looked at Chair Freiburg and smiled. "Do you fear my words so much? I have but one question to ask. Are you not willing to listen?"

And there it hung, all on a thread.

The woman's eyes met Jason's. And after a long moment, she sighed. "Ask your question."

Jason continued to hold the chair with his eyes. "A Pacifican guide met us at the Colorado Outpost under orders from the Board to guide us through the mountains. A young woman nicknamed Dakota."

He paused expectantly, and the chair did not disappoint him. "That is correct. I remember the decision taken by the Board, and the order that was sent. And I believe Dakota was indeed the name of the guide at the Outpost."

Jason's glance did not waver. "Then that part is confirmed, and brings us to my question, which is addressed to you, Madam Chair. It is a very important question. Did you order our guide to murder Prince Arn?"

The room was silent again, but the puzzled frowns on many faces of the board members indicated the impact of Jason's question.

Chair Freiburg's face expressed amazement. "*What*? Did I order your guide to murder Prince Arn? The answer to that ridiculous question is NO. I never gave any such order. Why would you ask such a thing?"

Jason had the opening he needed. "I ask, Madam Chair, because at the Outpost Dakota received a radio message from Pacifica—from the Board of Administrators—ordering her to kill Prince Arn before he could reach Pacifica."

"God have mercy," said one of the administrators.

"I gave no such order. Such a decision would have required a two-thirds vote of the Board. And only the Secretary and I have access to the verification codes for such a message."

Jason nodded. "And you didn't send that message. So that leaves . . ."

Chair Freiburg shook her head. "That cannot be. But I'll let her tell you herself. Secretary Dacolla, I apologize in advance, but I must ask you. Did you send any message to this guide, Dakota, at the Outpost?"

Dacolla shook her head. "No, I did not. You may check the records."

"That's what I assumed." The chair turned back to

Jason. "I think we need to talk to Dakota. Is she here?"

Jason bit his lip for control, took a deep breath, and went on. There was not another sound in the room. "Dakota is dead, Madam Chair. She was killed in the attempt to assassinate Prince Arn."

There were gasps from the board members.

"Also killed was my son, Paul Kendall—"

More gasps.

"—Who was trying to prevent the assassination. Before she died, Dakota revealed she was acting under orders. She assumed those orders were valid, representing the will of the Board of Administrators, and not the will of any one administrator or cabal of administrators. She was attempting to do her duty, as she believed it to be. I understand duty. I did it long enough. I have—with difficulty, I must admit—forgiven her for causing the death of my son.

"But I will not forgive the persons who gave that order, who took the power of life and death into their own hands and acted without the approval of the Board. I will spend the rest of my life finding them out. They can depend on that."

Administrator Hodges lifted his bulk up again. At least he was getting his exercise this evening. "Madam Chair, why should we believe any of this? What proof do we have that any of this occurred? What evidence?"

Jason stared at Hodges as if he were a patient with a strange disease. "Proof? My dead son is proof. Evidence? Dakota's death is evidence. They lie next to each other in the frozen earth."

"We don't know that," said Hodges.

"No, you don't, Administrator. Perhaps my grief and Lorich's grief are not enough to prove our story. But you must ask yourselves a question. Why should we lie? What is there to gain? The truth would come out. Why would the delegation from Kenesee come all this way, why would Paul attempt to come all this way, just to fabricate a story? It defies all logic."

And it did. Most of the administrators recognized that.

There was much discussion following Jason's speech, with members shouting questions at the chair and the secretary about how such a thing could have happened. Foolish questions. It isn't difficult to circumvent procedures, to falsify or destroy records, and accomplish the illegal. Deniability is easily achieved, especially if more than one individual is involved, and they can provide alibis for each other.

And then the board got over the shock of the revelation, and Tanaka recommended that they question each of us in turn about the tragedy in order to ensure an accurate account of events. While Jason was questioned, I and my companions were put into another room under guard to sit in separate corners without communicating. Jason was with the board a long time, but at last they called me, and I went in.

The questions came unrelentingly, asked by one of the scribes from a list that had been made, with questions for clarification coming from administrators. I related the whole incident, and everything that I could think of in as truthful a manner as possible. After an hour they sent me back to wait while Lorich went in. They took a long time with him, too. The story was the same, I knew, and there was no lie to be found between our versions of events. Murdock and Kren and Jenkins were each called in turn, and provided yet more testimony on events. The board finished with them and called me back for more questions.

There was some curiosity about my life, as they had heard reports of the unlikely victory at Lexington and my role in the events of the last two years. Even tales of the inviolability of my promise had reached the board, thanks to some of Kendall's reports through the years. They asked about King Robert, his knowledge of Pacifica, and his intentions, and stated that they knew I had destroyed the muskets in Texan. I spoke as truthfully as I could. But I took a deep breath, and warned them that while I agreed with the Codes and respected their efforts, I would stand by my brother in this matter.

Eventually, all the questions were answered, and my companions came back in. Hours had passed, but Jason had remained seated on his bench listening while the board questioned us. Now he came to the center just as my companions sat.

"With your permission, Madam Chair? Thank you. I will conclude shortly. Only a few things remain to be said. I believe that most of you know my history. I was a loyal and devoted follower of the ideals our nation has followed: to prevent mankind from going extinct on this continent, to bring enlightenment and peace to the other nations that we helped create, and to foster a better world. In order to achieve these worthy ends, I thought that some regrettable and unfortunate realities had to be faced. I accepted the idea that the end justifies the means. I felt the purchase was worth the price.

"To that end, I trained for, and accepted, the position of Pacifican representative, and served in that capacity for almost twenty years in Kenesee. It was a thrilling adventure, true, but it involved sacrifices too. I left my home and friends behind, and I returned to Pacifica only twice in those twenty years. When my wife traveled to Kenesee with our young son to be with me, she died in an accident during the journey. Only my son was left to me.

"I instilled in Paul the same devotion I had felt for our purposes, for the great experiment that Pacifica was attempting as she guided the six nations to prosperity. But over the years the deeds I had to perform weighed upon me, and at last I gave it up. I reverted to my original profession, medicine, and served as a healer—an unlicensed physician—in Kenesee and the Beastwood. And my efforts there helped dull the guilt I felt over what I had done as a representative. I still follow the ideals of Pacifica, but I have not been able to stem my doubts about our methods. And that is my story.

"I have only this observation to make about the proposal that the Kenesee delegation brings to you. *Someone* ordered Dakota to kill the Prince of Kenesee. So even here in Pacifica, divisiveness and factional politics have affected the efforts to enforce the Codes. How can we impose order on others when we have no order ourselves? We must look inside ourselves. We can no longer rule by poison and dagger.

"The great experiment is ending, or at least, evolving into something beyond our control. Times have indeed changed. It is time for the secrecy, the intrigue, the manipulation, to end. It is time to cease endorsing an ignoble means to a noble end. The ideal may remain, but the methods must be tempered by the changes that have come about, some by the very success and progress achieved by the Codes of Progress.

"If we persist in clinging just to the words of the Codes without seeing the underlying spirit of those words, we lose all moral authority in dealing with the nations of the continent. The six nations are far away. Do not let our isolation here in Pacifica—our ignorance of what is really happening—strangle the dynamic of growth and change that has been set loose. To do so would fly in the face of everything we've worked for in the larger sense of the greater good of mankind, if not in the smaller concern of weapons control. Further attempts to guide progress must be by persuasion and example, not intimidation and assassination.

"Let Pacifica show its greatness now in your decision. Consider the Kenesee proposal for Confederation carefully, and strive to see the greater ideal embodied in the words that we have followed so long. The greater good for all mankind."

The healer went back to his bench, and sat with a hand over his face. Too many memories, perhaps, for a man who had sacrificed too much for too long.

A discussion—to put it politely—began between various administrators, and almost everyone had something to say. It became clear that the Board was divided into factions. Hodges led one faction that was not friendly to any changes in the Codes or their enforcement. For him, the Codes were inviolate. The other faction was dominated by Tanaka, who despite his astonishment at our initial proposal, recognized that adaptability was necessary to the health of the great experiment. The rest of the Board members were undecided, and listened to both viewpoints with troubled expressions.

The discussion should have been tabled early on. A strong Chair would have accomplished that. But it was clear that Chair Freiburg was weak. She did not exhibit the strength or character that might have been expected from the leader of the vaunted Pacifica. My respect for the nation had taken a sharp turn downward. These squabbling administrators were the farsighted leaders guiding the development of the continent?

Secretary Dacolla was gritting her teeth, attempting to control her impatience, Well, I would have been exasperated too. Having constantly to guide the indecisive Madam Freiburg must have been frustrating

The secretary spoke, and could not hide the exasperation in her voice. ''I think it's time we vote on the motion to go to a closed session.''

''Yes,'' said the chair, noting the secretary's unhappiness. But then, out of politeness, added a last question that she immediately regretted. ''I assume that we have heard all relevant testimony from the delegation?''

Rather than the affirmation she'd expected from my party, Major Kren popped up and strode forward. ''I'd like to say something.''

''Oh,'' said Freiburg, surprised. But she couldn't have Kren sit back down now. ''Well, if it's relevant.''

The beastman grinned and folded his arms across his chest. ''I have been sent by the leaders of the Beastwood to act as an observer, but also as an emissary to represent the interests of the Beastwood in dealing with the great nation of Pacifica. You have no representative in the Beastwood, nor have you been able to infiltrate our country with your agents. We have built a society that has remained independent for hundreds of years, and served us well. We have not had the Codes enforced upon us, and yet we have adopted them, recognizing the advantages to be gained. We have limited our weapons and technological process voluntarily.

"However, if the six nations remain independent, the chance of more powder weapons being built is too great. The Beastwood will have to start developing powder weapons too, in anticipation of other nations' violating the Codes. The only way to prevent this is to provide a guarantee that the other nations will not do so. The Beastwood has been invited to join the Confederation that King Robert is organizing, and that would provide the security needed, the centralized control that would prevent renegades and hotheads from building powder weapons.

"Therefore, the Beastwood urges you to accept the proposal of King Robert."

Kren sat down.

"Does the Beastwood really feel that way about it?" Jenkins whispered.

Kren casually smoothed the hair on his head before whispering back. "Well, they should."

Our beastman had gotten carried away once again.

"Thank you, Major Kren," said the chair. "And now we will vote on the motion to go to a closed session. All in favor?" A forest of hands went up. "The motion is passed. All but Board members will now leave the room."

My party returned to the barracks. It was late in the day, and the table was already laden with a plate of bread, a pot of bean soup, and a large, square pan of apple cobbler that filled the room with a delicious smell of sugar and spice. We brought out our plates and mugs and cutlery, and set to with great appetite. Through the window we could see soldiers bring pots and plates over to the building in which the board was located. They would be eating soon too.

Over the meal we discussed our meeting with the board, and each gave his opinion on the success of our proposal. Jason spoke last. "Well, we've done all we can. But as our beastman said, I think we 'shook them up.' Perhaps in all the tragedy, some good might come out of the assassination attempt, some value might be found in the deaths of Paul and Dakota. Even those most dogmatically supportive of the Codes seemed stunned and grieved by what has happened. They'll break to eat soon, though I suspect they'll be debating this issue late into the night. When they break, I'll wander over and see what I can find out. We'll just have to be patient until then.''

A half hour later, Jason sauntered over to the porch of the other building, sat on the steps, and lit his pipe in the twilight, puffing away at the long-stemmed instrument with pleasure. The Pacificans had tobacco— though how they obtained it, I had no idea—and Jason had supplemented our diminishing stock with a pound purchased at the fort's tiny store. I wondered if they had somehow gotten the tobacco in trade from one of the six nations, for it certainly reminded me of good Kenesee leaf.

Their meal concluded, a number of the administrators came out on the porch, each with a mug of coffee. Several of the men lit up their pipes. Jason greeted them, and several joined him on the steps, while others broke up into twos and threes, each forming a little pocket of discussion. I took advantage of my ''hearing'' talent and listened in, picking up one conversation after another, searching for something of value.

''Goodness, I'd forgotten how beautiful it can be out here.''

''Isaac, you've got to agree that it's too soon for the children to get married. My son just isn't ready to settle down yet.''

''Can I borrow some tobacco?''

''You know, maybe this Kenesee problem was a good thing. It brings us back to realities.''

''No, James, I don't think you're going to get lucky tonight, so stop leering at me.''

Nothing of interest. Amazingly, they were not mentioning our proposal. Or perhaps not so amazing. They had probably been ordered not to discuss it outside the closed session. Jason had risen from the porch and was strolling around the fort with Administrator Tanaka and a woman board member whose name I could not remember.

Eventually the members were called back in, and Jason returned to us, slipping onto a bench beside us with a groan of age and refilling his mug with coffee. He sipped at it unconcernedly until Kren could take no more.

"Aaannnnddd?" the beastman asked. "What did you find out."

Satisfied at having tried Kren's patience, the healer lowered his mug .

"Nothing," said Jason. "The debate on the proposal is just starting, and everyone has something to say. It seems our statements this afternoon made an impression. I think they're actually giving the proposal serious consideration. And that's an achievement. But for now, we'll just have to be patient."

And so we were. Or tried to be. Under lamps hung from the ceiling, Jenkins played Murdock at chess, while the rest of us sat down to a game of four queens down, and followed it with several hours of poker. Midway through the evening Kren owed me the wealth of the Beastwood, but by the end I owed Kren the treasury of Kenesee. We didn't worry about it. It was doubtful either Robert or the Beastwood Senior Council would honor our game.

It was late night before Murdock glanced up from the chessboard to the barracks window. "Jason, there's some activity out there. The meeting may be over."

Jason tamped some tobacco into his pipe, lit up, and set out for the other building. The rest of us put away the cards and sat around speculating to no purpose. At last, the old healer returned, still nursing a stream of smoke from the single pipeful.

He approached the table and stopped, looking down at us. "No decision has been reached tonight. The Board is going to let everyone sleep on it until tomorrow morning. A vote will be taken then.''

Murdock tapped a finger on the table. ''And do we have any chance?''

Slowly, a smile creased the healer's face. ''From what I've been told, we have an excellent chance. Those in the moderate center are reluctantly convinced that the Codes must be changed. Even several of Hodges's faction—the dedicated supporters of the Codes—feel that enough has happened among the six nations that some change is necessary. The tragedy with Paul and Dakota was the critical thing. The Board was stunned that there was duplicity within its ranks, and realized the fallibility of the great experiment. So, unless there is a drastic turn of heart by tomorrow morning, the Board will vote to allow the Confederation to exist, and to use limited numbers of powder weapons to enforce a ban on any further development of weapons.''

We went to bed that night feeling secure and gratified. We might not have identified the renegade administrator who'd given the fatal order to Dakota, but otherwise our long journey had been successful. All the weeks in the saddle were worthwhile, the senseless deaths of Paul Kendall and Dakota given meaning and purpose. Prince Scar and his party had done their part, and could relax amidst the security of Pacifica and await the coming of spring and the journey back east. All was well.

Or so we thought, until we were awakened in the middle of the night and found that everything had changed.

8

Means and Ends

It is not pleasant to be awakened by the muzzle of a rifle pressed against one's chest. And yet there it was, a duty-minded Pacifican soldier holding the weapon firmly against me. "Don't move," he ordered.

I had no intention of disobeying him.

"What is the meaning of this?" growled Jason from his bunk. There was a soldier threatening the healer and each of my companions in like manner, except for Murdock, who had been on watch. He was standing against the wall with two rifles on him, while another half dozen soldiers waited with rifles at the ready. There was little he could have done. The soldiers making night rounds normally stuck their heads into the barracks to make sure all were present. When that happened this time, the other soldiers had probably slid in behind, and Murdock had no chance to raise the alarm. Or maybe in wisdom he had recognized the odds and kept silent to prevent us from resisting and being shot.

Watching attentively over the work was Captain Lawrence. "Good job, Lieutenant Quang. Get them tied up."

Lieutenant Quang, a nondescript man with a thick mustache, gave the order. The waiting soldiers leaned their weapons on the wall and came forward with ropes. Within minutes we were bound at the wrist and ankle, each of us lying on his stomach in his bunk with hands tied behind his back. I couldn't see my man, but I was able to watch the man tying Lorich. The Pacificans knew their knots.

I was developing a distinct dislike for being tied up.

"Now, search them and collect their weapons," Lieutenant Quang ordered, nervously smoothing out his mustache with a practiced finger.

With my party tied and helpless, all of the solders were able to participate in the search. They patted us down, then went through our bags and kits. Swords and knives, bows and arrows, sticks and cudgels were all collected, including the little spring dart gun of Jason's. I was wearing a thick cotton shirt in bed, and underneath was the knife sheath between my shoulder blades. After weeks on the trail, I was used to sleeping with it on, and that night had been too lazy to take it off. For all their thoroughness, the soldiers did not find it. What use the one small blade might be was another matter entirely. As far as I was concerned, they might as well have taken it too.

Captain Ahmed entered with Secretary Dacolla. Ahmed looked troubled, but assumed a posture of attention before his fellow officer before speaking. "Captain Lawrence, the Secretary has informed me of the plot against the Board, and the suspicion that some of my men may be involved. As the Secretary ordered, my men are restricted to barracks, and their rifles and sabers placed under lock in the armory. Here are the keys."

Lawrence took the ring of keys. "Very good, Captain Ahmed."

"According to the Secretary's instructions, I now place myself under your command."

"Very good. Please surrender your sword to Lieutenant Quang."

"My sword?" The expression on Ahmed's face went from puzzlement to grim doubt.

Captain Lawrence nodded. "That is the order."

"But why?"

"Everything will be straightened out later. Right now, this is for your own protection. You wouldn't want to be implicated with the guilty plotters, would you?"

Reluctantly, Ahmed removed his sword belt and handed it over to the lieutenant.

"Likewise, we'll have to tie you," Lawrence said matter of factly.

"That is too much," Ahmed declared. "I protest."

Captain Lawrence shook his head. "Lieutenant Quang!"

Quang gave an order, and two rifles were aimed at Captain Ahmed.

Too late to resist, the cavalry commander was soon lying on a bunk, as securely bound as the rest of us. "And that," said Lawrence to Secretary Dacolla with satisfaction, "takes care of that. All those who might offer resistance are confined, except for the Board members. We merely have to wake them and get them over here."

"Over here?" Secretary Dacolla asked sharply, as if demanding an answer of a subordinate, and then caught herself. She placed a hand on the arm of Captain Lawrence, and her voice softened. "Why here?"

"The second floor has a large storeroom without windows. We can lock the administrators in. And then we'll only have to guard two buildings. This one and the cavalry barracks."

"Of course," said Secretary Dacolla, with real or feigned admiration.

Lawrence smiled at the woman, and the look that passed between them indicated that their relationship went beyond just that of leader and subordinate. Well, they did make a handsome couple, though Dacolla must have been at least ten years older than Captain Lawrence.

Jason snorted. "Secretary Dacolla, are you actually trying to manage a political coup? Just you and one company of infantry?"

The secretary looked at Lawrence, eyed his listening men, and looked at him again with a question written clearly on her face.

Lawrence grinned. "You can speak freely, Louise. These men are my action squad, loyal and committed to our cause. They know what we're doing, and why."

Well, that was a valuable scrap of information. Not all the men of Lawrence's company were committed to the plot, just misinformed about what was happening. We'd have to remember that.

Dacolla smiled sweetly at Jason and answered his question. "Not just me. There are five of us, out of the twenty-one members of the Board, who feel we cannot allow the great experiment to be subverted. Those who would do so are betraying the ideals we've served for two hundred years. We've worked too hard for too long. And then you come, preaching treason. And those fools fell for it. I would have preferred the Board to have rejected your proposal, and make all these actions unnecessary. But I can count votes. Your ridiculous Kenesee proposal would have passed. And that cannot be allowed."

Jason's face grew hard. "It was you who ordered Dakota to kill Prince Arn, wasn't it?"

"Who ordered it does not matter. You can see what's happened since he arrived. Without him, there might have been no vote on the proposal. To give such an order was merely doing what we've done all along. No more, no less."

Jason shook his head in disbelief. "Unauthorized, you took it upon yourself to order assassination."

"Oh, come now, Kendall," she answered. "What do our representatives to the six nations do every day? We train them and send them out, and give them the discretion to do what is necessary. They judge those who violate the Codes, and decide who should be stopped. We have granted them a license to terminate. They don't stop to ask permission."

"Yes," said Jason, "but their license comes from the Board, which votes to grant it. It doesn't come from one individual, one member of that Board."

"When the Board loses its good sense, then someone has to act."

"And *you* are that someone, I take it."

"I think that's enough conversation for now. Captain Lawrence, let's waken the Board members."

They and the soldiers left, taking along our weapons but leaving two men to guard us. A short time later, the awakened administrators were hustled through our door, many of them wearing only their bedclothes and a coat hurriedly thrown on. They were uttering oaths and protests, and when they saw us a new wave of objections was raised. But these quickly became muted as the members realized the seriousness of the situation. Five soldiers took the captive board members up the stairs, a door slammed and locked, and the five soldiers tromped back down the steps and out into the night. The same two men continued to guard us, and they now took seats by the fire, putting their backs to the hearth and watching us alertly.

What to do now? What *could* we do now? Over a hundred infantry armed with rifles controlled the fort. The board and Captain Ahmed's cavalry company—all those who might be sympathetic to our plight—were sharing that plight. Little hope of rescue from any of them. And so we were on our own. What might Secretary Dacolla and her cohorts be planning for us on the morrow? Of course, they might have just slain us as we lay sleeping in our bunks, but perhaps they saw some use for us yet. Or maybe they felt we had more information to offer. Or maybe they lacked the sheer ruthlessness to eliminate such a large number of people with a single, bloody stroke.

But did we want to depend on the belief that they would not take our lives? I turned my head and glanced over the faces of my fellow captives. They had been doing some thinking too. I caught Lorich's eye, looked at the guards, came back to Lorich and lifted an eyebrow in question. The young wizard glanced at Murdock, who gave a slight nod. Both looked at me. Kren and Jenkins and Jason and Ahmed all silently watched the exchange, waiting. There was, indeed, nothing else to do.

I nodded to Lorich.

He picked out one of the two guards, squinted, and tensed. The guard stiffened with a grunt, and rolled onto the floor with only a faint bump. Startled, his companion reached over to help. "What's wrong, Mack? What's—" And then he too stiffened before slumping over his comrade.

Lorich took a deep breath and closed his eyes.

"Well-done," I whispered. Young as he was, Lorich was racking up a larger body count than any of us. Except for me, perhaps. I still excelled in ordering men to their deaths. It seemed to be a talent of the royal family.

Ahmed's eyes had grown wide as he watched the guards drop. "How did you do that?" he said, turning over and sitting up. Jenkins had tried to get his arms over his buttocks and to the front, but failed. He hopped over to Ahmed's bunk, sat down, and put his back to Ahmed's. "Just leave your hands still, sir. I'll work at your ropes."

I twisted onto my back, lifted my legs, folded my trunk, and stretched my arms downward. The ropes bit into my wrists and I felt something in my back go *crick*, but I slipped my hands further down, past my hips and over my buttocks and then down around my ankles and feet. My hands were in front of me. Ten more pounds, and I couldn't have done it. Ten more years, and I might not have been able to do it. I wondered if I'd ruined my back.

And now, what to do?

A weapon is also a tool.

I passed my tied wrists back up over and behind my head, reached, and came back with the knife in my hand, the blade gleaming in the firelight. What a wonderful gift it had turned out to be. How long I had carried it, wondering when it would be of use. And finally, the time had come. I offered a silent prayer. *Thank you, John.*

Kren grinned and turned his back to me so I could get at his wrists. "Well done, Arn. Now hurry."

I started cutting, and the sharp blade made quick work. Kren shook off the ropes, flexed his fingers to regain circulation, and took the knife to attack Jenkins's bonds.

"What about me?" I asked, extending my hands.

"We'll get to you, sir," Jenkins said. "Just don't want you getting free and trying to win this one all by yourself again."

"I wouldn't do that," I assured him.

"Ha!" was all Jenkins said, whether from the ropes coming off his wrists or at my words, I was not sure.

Kren went to Murdock and Captain Ahmed and then the rest of the party, leaving me for last. "So nice to be remembered," I told him as he cut away at the rope.

"Usually we save the best for last," the beastman stated. "But in this case . . ."

Most of the others were at work on the ropes binding their ankles, but Kren saved me the trouble and started to hack away at mine. The knife was losing its edge, but still did the job. Jenkins and Murdock had taken the bayonets of the guards, and were also cutting away the leg bonds. In a few moments we were all free, Captain Ahmed showing Kren and Jenkins how to use the guards' rifles. Ahmed and Murdock took the bayonets, while I took my knife back.

"Two of you should put on the guards' uniforms," said Captain Ahmed. "I'll go upstairs and see if I can't free the Board members. There's a lock on their door. For God's sake, don't make much noise. There's probably more guards on the porch."

Recognizing a good suggestion, Jenkins and I undressed the dead soldiers and slipped on their coats and caps. Jenkins's clothes were a size too large, and mine a size too small, but they'd do.

Ahmed came back down the stairs. Behind him came Chair Freiburg, leading a wary line of administrators. She reached the bottom of the stairs, and the others clus-

tered about her, many gasping or making hurriedly muf-
fled exclamations as they saw the two bodies lying in
front of the fireplace, eyes wide-open in the death stare.

Freiburg looked to Ahmed and me, and spoke softly.
"We did not expect such duplicity and treachery in our
ranks. It has never happened in Pacifica before. But decisive action is needed. Military action. And that is your
specialty. What do you wish us to do?"

Tanaka was next to her. "Four or five of us have
served in the Pacifican Army. We'll do whatever we can
to help."

Well, what did we want them to do? What did any of
us need to do? In other words, we needed . . .

"A plan," said Kren. "We need a plan."

Murdock and Ahmed and I studied the floor, each of
us waiting for one of the others to show his genius—
which meant that Murdock and Ahmed would be waiting for a long time unless one of them came up with a
good idea.

"What's the situation outside?" asked Jenkins.

We didn't know. The window shutters were all closed
in the building, and we didn't dare go out into the hall
or on the porch in case more guards waited.

"Let's find out," suggested Ahmed. "Sergeant Jenkins, Major Kren, take a look out the different windows
in this barracks. But don't open the shutters. I'd bet Captain Lawrence has men watching with orders to fire if
the shutters are opened. Just extinguish lamps and peep
out the cracks."

In three or four minutes they came back. "We looked
around," said Jenkins, not at all intimidated by Ahmed's
rank and speaking up before anyone else. "It looks like
there are two guards on the porch, so keep your voices
down. About a third of the infantry company is on duty,
say forty men or so. There's a score stationed in the
towers and outer walls of the fort, and another score are
keeping warm around two large fires in the square. The
rest have probably gone back to their barracks."

"Lanterns have been hung on the corners of our

building and the other barracks housing my cavalry-men," said Ahmed. "There are clear lines of sight from the towers, so sneaking out through the windows or back door will be difficult. It looks like Secretary Dacolla and Captain Lawrence have taken over the headquarters building. It's ablaze with lamps. And that's all we know."

"Very smoothly done," said Jason, who had been silent up to this point. "Decisive action, and efficient. They disarmed and confined the cavalry company, neu-tralized our party, and then imprisoned the Board of Ad-ministrators. In less than an hour Secretary Dacolla has successfully pulled off her coup. And when she returns to the capital, who will dispute her story—whatever it might be? It seems most of the infantry are just obeying orders. They don't really know what is going on, and will interpret events according to whatever story they're told—unless witnesses such as the imprisoned admin-istrators or we are left to tell the truth."

Captain Ahmed did not look happy. "That still doesn't answer the question of what we should do."

"It offers a clue," said Murdock. "We need to get Secretary Dacolla and Captain Lawrence in here. If we can take them—eliminate them, if necessary—it's pos-sible the plot will fall apart. The troops can be reasoned with."

And so, with me in my nice Pacifican uniform, Cap-tain Ahmed and I had the privilege of strolling out onto the porch and confronting the two guards who stood together chatting. We stayed near the door, in the shad-ows. "The outlanders want to see Captain Lawrence and Secretary Dacolla," said Ahmed. "They say they have information that is valuable."

"What kind of information?" asked the taller of the guards.

"Don't know. But they seemed sincere. Maybe it *is* something important. The Captain should be told."

"I see," said the taller guard. He was silent a mo-ment, hesitating. "I'll go tell the Captain."

He strode off toward the headquarters building while Ahmed and I went back inside. "It seems to be working," I told them. "Everyone take your places, and follow the plan."

I felt my heart pounding in my chest, and my hands had gone cold. Nothing new, just the usual terror I experienced when my life was in jeopardy.

Within a few minutes we heard voices outside, and a loud call. "Captain Ahmed! Prince Arn! You can come out now." Jenkins beat me to the window, and we both peeped out through a crack in the shutter. The outside was lit with torches and lanterns. Around the building ran a solid line of infantry, rifles at the ready.

Jenkins swore. "The guards must have recognized one of you. The game is up."

The voice came again. "This is Lieutenant Quang speaking. Prince Arn, Captain Ahmed, come out with your party. Resistance is futile."

We discussed it, Kren and Jenkins both arguing against surrender. But what was there to do, really? Two rifles against a hundred? Not quite a fair fight. Far better to hope for mercy.

"Prince Arn, we're waiting. We'll torch the barracks, if it comes to that."

Such a serious young man.

We put aside our weapons, yelled up to the administrators that they should remain in their room for safety, and Murdock led us out onto the porch.

The front of the barracks was ablaze with dozens of torches and lanterns held by the rear rank of infantry, while the front rank kept their rifles trained our way. With all the light, we could not see beyond the ring of men. The world was dark to us. Lieutenant Quang stood directly before us where a gap opened in the line of soldiers. "Kneel and raise your hands," he ordered.

We did so. Ahmed, Kren, Lorich, Jason, Murdock, Jenkins, and I. And there we were, all in a row. Lorich didn't look well. The rifles were still aimed at us, but the tension went out of the ranks of soldiers. They could relax a bit, for there was nothing we could do in such a position. We were, to all appearances, helpless.

The scene was quiet except for the crackle of the two fires in the square. The smell of oil from the lamps was in the air, mixing with the smell of burning wood.

Two soldiers edged past us carefully and entered the barracks. A minute later they came out. "The administrators are upstairs, though the lock is broken on their door. Burt and LaRose are dead. Not a mark on them, but they're dead."

Mutters ran through the ranks. They were not happy to hear their fellows had been slain.

A door opened in the headquarters building. Six figures came out and crossed the square to our building. Secretary Dacolla, Captain Lawrence, Administrator Hodges, and three other members of the board who backed the coup. They stopped next to Quang and looked at us with satisfaction.

Captain Lawrence smiled. "Good job, Lieutenant. Did they give you any trouble?"

"No trouble, sir. But they killed Burt and LaRose."

Lawrence frowned. "They were good men. Someone will have to face the noose for that. Perhaps all of them."

Now the plotters had their excuse for killing us, and their men would hardly object.

Jenkins gave me a look. Well, maybe surrender hadn't been such a good idea after all.

"Would you really kill us?" Lorich asked in a tremulous voice.

Dacolla and Lawrence exchanged a brief glance, and I knew we were doomed. They had already decided what would happen to us. The two dead soldiers had nothing to do with their decision.

"Lieutenant Quang," said Lawrence, "take the— uhh."

He got no further. Captain Lawrence stiffened and his eyes seemed to bulge. With a shiver, he went down like a tree falling, face first.

There had been no sound, no movement, nothing to account for his sudden fall. Yet there he lay, the eyes of every person glued to the body and trying to comprehend what had happened.

Secretary Dacolla stared at him with puzzlement and disbelief. "Captain Lawrence? What's wrong, Johnnie? What—"

Dacolla in turn stiffened, eyes wide, and twisted into collapse, landing on her back with eyes staring, unseeing, into the blackness of the sky.

The administrators drew back in a tight cluster. The men in the ranks crouched and brought their rifles up, ready to fire at those of us kneeling on the porch. It was our total stillness and silence that saved us. A word, a twitch, might have earned us a volley. But kneeling with arms up in surrender, unmoving, it was clear that we were not the assailants. The soldiers swiveled their heads left and right, looking for enemies, and coming back to us at last when they found none.

Lieutenant Quang drew his sword and went into a crouch. "Every second man, watch the rear. Do you see anything?"

"Nothing sir. Our men are on the walls. There's no one else within the fort in position to fire."

Quang reached out tentatively to touch the body of the secretary, placed his fingers on her neck, then pulled back his hand. "She's dead. And so is the Captain. What's going on here?"

Murdock recovered first, as usual. He took the chance and ventured to speak. "Quang. Lieutenant Quang."

"It's their fault," said a sergeant standing behind the rank of soldiers and pointing with his rifle. I think he was one of Lawrence's action squad. He darted forward to the step of the porch. "Well, now it's their turn."

He placed his foot on the stoop, but never took another step. Stiffening, he plummeted to the ground in a heap.

Quang looked on in disbelief.

Down the line of my companions, I noticed a movement. Lorich was trembling, his uplifted arms wavering.

"He's dead, Lieutenant Quang," said Murdock calmly. "They're all dead. We have that power. And you'll be next if you don't listen. Do you understand that? Will you listen?"

Quang swallowed, trying to hide his fear. "I'm listening. What is happening? What have you done?"

"We know you're just a loyal subordinate doing as he's ordered," Murdock soothed in a clear voice that carried to all.

Hah. Quang was a trusted conspirator of Dacolla and Lawrence, without a doubt. He was no innocent follower led astray. But I saw where clever Murdock was taking him.

"This revolt was perpetrated by Secretary Dacolla and Captain Lawrence and those four administrators standing behind you. They seized power illegally and immorally, and arrested the other members of the Board in order to do it. But the leaders of this revolt, of this coup, are dead. Dacolla and Lawrence are dead. Without them, the coup cannot succeed. Free the Board and arrest those four administrators. You'll be a hero to Pacifica."

The administrators spoke up, led by the fat Hodges who so liked to hear himself talk. They had no illusions that they could pretend they were innocent. Hodges was addressing the infantrymen, and not us. "Don't listen to outlanders. The Board was going to betray Pacifica and all it stands for. We prevented that betrayal. We're going to establish a new Board, a new government without the corruption of the old."

A woman's voice came from the door behind me. "And what will this new government offer our people, Administrator Hodges?" Chair Freiburg asked. She stepped forward to the edge of the porch. "Will you hold elections? Will you provide a more benevolent leadership than the nation already has? Hardly likely."

"You're the one who allowed this to happen," shouted Hodges. "You're weak. If you had led the Board properly, they would have voted correctly. None of this would have happened. You don't deserve to lead this country."

Freiburg glared at the administrator. "You're probably right. I am weak. This shouldn't have happened. But my weakness was trust. I trusted Secretary Dacolla. I trusted her when she explained why she had ordered the infantry here. I trusted her advice. I trusted her loyalty. That is a weakness of mine. One of many, I must admit. And I do. I will resign and allow another administrator to become Chair. But first, I will deal with you.

"Weakness can be strength, and strength can be weakness. Our strength lies in our people. And to our people, I will appeal. I say to those of you assembled in the ranks, the loyal defenders of Pacifica, that Secretary Dacolla and Captain Lawrence deceived you. The Board has not betrayed the ideals and goals of Pacifica. The Administrative Rules give us the power to change things as we might for the good of the land. And that, we planned to do. But Dacolla and Lawrence would have none of it. They thought to impose a dictatorship—their dictatorship—upon the nation. That cannot be allowed to happen."

She certainly had their attention now.

Freiburg swept the ranks with her eyes. "The outlander Murdock has stated that you are loyal followers who have been misled, and indeed you have been. You are guilty of nothing but believing your commander and following orders." Now, she focused completely on Lieutenant Quang. "And for that, I swear that I will give complete pardon to every officer and soldier here. No punishment, no reassignment, no penalty of any sort. Simply give your support to the duly elected Board, and all will be well.

"So decide. Decide now."

Lieutenant Quang's mouth was open as he struggled to get enough air to serve him. He glanced at the men in the ranks, who watched him with silent eyes. He looked at the bodies sprawled before him. He looked back at the four administrators, just as frightened as he was.

If he gave the word, there could still be a bloodbath. And my companions and I would be the first to die.

Lieutenant Quang shook his head as if to clear it, looked up at Chair Freiburg, and nodded. "Yes, ma'am." He turned to his men and his voice rang out. "Company, shoulder arms. Sergeant Vanucci, put these four administrators under arrest and detain them in the headquarters building. Madam Chair, I await your orders."

There was a collective sigh of relief from my companions, except for one. Lorich lowered his head to the floor of the porch, his hands pressed to his skull, and emitted a loud groan of pain. Murdock and my companions immediately crawled over, clustering around him.

"How are you, Lorich?" asked Murdock.

Lorich's eyes were almost closed. "Master? Did I—did I . . . do right?"

Murdock stroked the boy's brow and brushed back the corn-silk hair with gentle fingers. "Don't call me Master. I'm not your Master anymore, Lorich. Tonight, you've graduated. You're a wizard, and a great one, at that. Yes, you did right. And you did well. Very well, indeed. I'm proud of you, Lorich."

The lad tried to smile, but pressed his lips together as another wave of pain struck him. It was all Lorich's doing, of course. Without prompting, without having a chance to confer with his master, he had seen opportunity and taken it, dropping the two leaders of the coup while they were still in our presence and while there was a chance to appeal to their followers' good sense. And it had worked. And now he was paying the price.

The lad was formidable.

Jason grunted as he tried to get up, his legs stiff. I extended an arm to help him, and gave a groan too as I stood. My knees hurt.

The rest of the administrators flooded out onto the porch, milling about like a barnyard of hens cackling to each other about the weather. Their most frequent question was "How did you *do* that?"

Murdock handled their questions. "Once in century, a person is blessed—or cursed—with psychic powers greater than the norm. And the result is a wizard of greatness . . ." He said more, but without identifying Lorich. The administrators looked at the suffering young wizard and managed to put two and two together.

Tanaka shook his head. "And here we've been ignoring extra-sensory powers. We felt they were inconsequential, and that reports of such powers were exaggerated. Another mistake we've made."

Chair Freiburg paid them little note. She gave orders, and they were obeyed. Captain Ahmed went to the headquarters building to get the keys to the armory, then headed for the barracks of his cavalry company. Releasing his men, they followed him over to the armory and were soon standing in ranks, armed and ready. One squad escorted the four culpable administrators over to headquarters, while the other squads peeled off, some heading for the walls, others taking position in key locations about the fort.

When this was done, Lieutenant Quang assembled the infantry company, stacked arms, and marched his men over to the two barracks that housed them. They broke ranks and went in. Captain Ahmed collected their weapons and had them safely stored in the armory. The men were pardoned, but no use taking chances.

And with that, the great Pacifican coup was finished.

But I was not.

"Madam Chair!"

She was startled by my call. "Yes, Prince Arn?"

I took a breath. If Lorich could do it, then so could I. "Madame Chair, I ask the Board of Administrators to meet in open session and allow me to speak to them."

"You want us to meet *now*, Prince Arn? Couldn't it wait till morning?"

Murdock squeezed my elbow and whispered. "Arn, what are you doing?"

"No, Madam Chair. Things need to be said tonight."

He squeezed my elbow again. Harder. "Arn. Wait till you've cooled off."

But I didn't want to cool off. It was important to speak to the board while the members were still shaken by the events of the night. Now was the moment for action. I had to seize it just as Lorich had seized his moment on the porch.

I waited for Freiburg to make her decision. What could she do? We had just given Pacifica back to the board. Was she to refuse my request?

Her thoughts seemed to follow the same line as mine. "All right, Prince Arn. Members! The Board will be meeting in five minutes within the headquarters building."

The meeting seemed eerily like the first, and yet oddly different. So much had changed in just a few hours. The strangers around us suddenly seemed like old comrades. Captain Ahmed waited to one side, a chastened and wary Lieutenant Quang seated next to him. But the guards along the walls were all cavalrymen, not Quang's infantry.

Jason had resumed his seat on the bench along the other wall, and at their table sat the two scribes. My companions and I took the same seats before the board. The only one missing was Lorich, who had been led to his bunk and left there to endure the days of agony that were the price for his wizardly achievement.

Just sixteen members of the board were left, and they looked at the five empty seats in their semicircle with sadness and regret.

Chair Freiburg called the meeting to order. One administrator stated they should take the opportunity to elect a new Secretary. Freiburg countered the idea. "Tomorrow you can elect a new Secretary *and* a new Chair." There was a protest from the administrators, and a motion made to hold elections immediately. The motion was carried. Freiburg received the only nomination for chair. She looked down at the desk, dabbed at the corner of each eye, and looked up. "This honor is undeserved. I will try to be a better Chair. A stronger Chair. I thank you for the opportunity to do so. And now, nominations for the position of Secretary will be accepted." The nominations were secured, and a ballot vote completed. After that, Secretary Tanaka took his seat at the table next to Freiburg.

With these preliminaries—for me they were preliminaries, if not for the Pacificans—out of the way, Freiburg turned to me. "Prince Arn has requested this meeting of the Board so that he may address the members. Though I'm still not quite sure how they accomplished it, they have eliminated the leaders of the revolt and given Pacifica back to its rightful leaders. Because of the critical role he and his friends played in this, we look forward to his address. And before that, we must also extend the heartfelt thanks of all."

There was a round of applause from the members, and every Pacifican in the room joined in. Kren and Jenkins enjoyed it with satisfied smirks, while Murdock's smile was tempered. He was eyeing me carefully, worried about what I would say. And with good cause.

"And now, we will hear from Prince Arn."

I rose and walked forward, favoring one leg. It had taken a lot of punishment in the last two years, and kneeling on the hard planks of the porch hadn't helped.

In no mood for niceties, I leaped right into it.

"As you know, under King Robert's guidance the six nations and the Beastwood are forming a Confederation to prevent future conflicts between our countries. The Confederation will also allow us to control the development of powder weapons or other improper forms of destruction, while determining appropriate forms of technological development to meet the needs of our expanding populations. These changes are already going on.

"We came here to Pacifica with a proposal from King Robert for your consideration. We requested that you not oppose our course. We asked you to consider adjusting the Codes to reflect the realities under which the six nations labor. We did this out of respect and fear, for we looked on you as the patriarch of nations, as the distant, legendary land across the continent that had led us to the prosperity we enjoyed. We saw you as better, wiser, higher than us, providing the guidelines and gifts for us to achieve economic stability, to relieve the fears of starvation and plague, and to give thoughts to peace and freedom.

"Yet, whatever technological wonders you still have in the interior of Pacifica, your hearts are no better than ours, your passions no more in control, your intellect no greater. You bicker and connive and maneuver for personal advantage, just as we do. You muddle through, just as we do. You are just one more nation on the American continent. No more, no less."

The room was absolutely silent and still, all hanging upon my words. And every word was extemporaneous. Quite a heady feeling, to be an orator for once instead of reciting from a memorized text. It was amazing that I was actually able to pull this off—assuming I was pulling it off. I plunged on.

"And so, I'm withdrawing the proposal we offered to Pacifica. I'm not asking you to accept what we do. We'll do it anyway, whether you approve or not, whether you send out assassination teams or not, whether you undermine our efforts or not. And we'll rewrite the Codes to please ourselves, because you're not omnipotent, you're not any better informed than we are, you're not any wiser than we are. You're too far away, too distant, too removed to know what we need. It's time for us to do it ourselves.

"But I will offer this new proposal. We still have much to learn from Pacifica, and much to admire about you. So we offer you membership in the Confederation. Not as ruler, not as dominator, but as a fellow nation bound to others for the common good. You may be the first among equals, but it will be as equals that we deal with each other. Gradually, as we advance and progress and grow, we'll fill in the geographic void that lies between us, and welcome the plains tribes and the mountain clans into our ranks as well. And we'll unite the continent once again.''

"That is my proposal. Accept it or not, it is the future.''

I limped back to my chair, earning strange stares from my companions.

Jenkins chuckled. "He does have a flair for the dramatic, don't you think?''

Kren shook his head. "I didn't think so. But I'll have to revise my opinion.''

I sat down. Murdock appraised me closely and leaned close. "Arn, that was impressive. Foolhardy, perhaps, but impressive. Why did you do it?''

The deed done, I grew sheepish before the great wizard. "Sorry. I was mad. I came all this way, and then they tie me up. I'm tired of being tied up.''

"Well, you've either succeeded beyond Robert's wildest dreams—or you've gotten us all killed.''

The administrators were studying me, and their stares were as intense as those of my companions. What would they decide? Had I signed our death warrants through my petulant defiance? It was all Lorich's fault. He had inspired me to be decisive.

But it was too late now. We could only wait and see.

My stomach began to churn, and I wondered if I could make it outside before I was sick.

9

Home Again

Though the warmth of spring made itself felt in April, we waited until May before starting our long trek back across the continent. The first part was the easiest, traveling from the capital of Pacifica back to Border Fort Seven where we had arrived the previous fall. At the fort, we checked out our mounts and equipment one last time and said good-bye to Jason Kendall.

Jason had insisted on accompanying us back to the fort, perhaps just to have something to do. His winter of grief had been hard, and the old healer had aged during the cold months. His shoulders were stooped now, his spectacles serving eyes that always seemed tired. He put out his arm to shake hands, but Murdock brushed it aside and enclosed him in a hug.

"Good-bye, my old friend," said the wizard. "You won't have to worry about keeping me alive anymore."

Released at last, Jason coughed in embarrassment. "You know, I didn't think saying good-bye would be so difficult. I've become used to you all—yes, even the ridiculous banter you and Kren indulge in. I'm going to miss you. I'm going to miss Kenesee, and the Beastwood too. But I know they'll be well served by your return. God be with you." And he stood in the warmth of the sun, silently watching as we mounted and waved good-bye and started on our journey.

And so there were only Murdock and Kren and Lorich and Jenkins to accompany me—though we were escorted by a full regiment of Pacifican cavalry, over seven hundred troopers complete with a supply train of mules and two-wheel carts. The Board of Administrators was making sure we arrived back safely.

Likewise, two of the younger and more adventurous administrators also came along to negotiate new agreements with the mountain clans. Pacifica was reaching out, extending her hand and beginning the improvements to travel that would be necessary for the future. The clan chiefs might not be happy about this new attitude of their western neighbor, but there was little they could do about it. Seven hundred cavalry had their effect.

Also joining the Pacifican force was a company of engineers. They made maps and charts as we went, noting locations for bridges or parts of the old road that could be easily cleared to prevent the need for lengthy detour, and helped in various ways to ease the passage of the supply train. Lastly, there were two radio teams. One had Arkan for its destination, while the other would accompany us back to Kenesee. Communication had been too uncertain since the relay stations in the east were destroyed by Pacifican Representative Pi-Ling and his conspirators during the War Against the Alliance. It was time to restore them.

With all these people in tow, we still made good time through the mountains, enjoying the spring green and delayed only by the many watercourses that ran fast and full, fed by the melting snow that still tipped the higher mountains. At these obstacles, the engineers proved their worth.

Our appearance had to be an unpleasant surprise for the clans. When we came to Shaman Preston's village, the gates were closed and the warriors lined the wall, ready to defend their homes. We'd brought only two squadrons with us to the village, leaving the rest of the regiment on the old road. But the Utah knew how large a force was coming down upon them. Certainly, we were greeted with more respect from Shaman Preston, and he decided God didn't require our being burnt at the stake.

Murdock and I were quick to ask him about Crazy Mary. What had happened to her?

Shaman Preston grunted. "The Witch Woman? She stayed with us for a time. I was very angry with her for destroying the tunnel and told her she should stay through the winter to bring us luck. Otherwise, I would pursue you. She agreed. But she left a month ago, heading south. She said to say hello. She will see you again. Someday. And that's all she said."

I felt good that Mary had not been killed. I don't know why, given the amount of bad news she'd repeatedly passed on to me over the years. I was becoming softhearted.

We left a squadron of cavalry with one of the administrators, who was going to meet with the Chief of the Utah and negotiate a new agreement on travel and trade. Change was coming, we warned Shaman Preston. He only grunted.

Less than a month after leaving Pacifica we cleared the last of the mountains and spread before us were the vast plains. And there, outside the plains tribe settlement, was the Outpost where we had stopped and met Dakota. Only this time, the Outpost was surrounded by neat rows of tents of a regiment of Arkan cavalry, while the horsemen themselves waited in the open fields, mounted and ready in battle order in case the approaching regiment that accompanied my party had hostile intentions. But the Arkan leader that came out to greet us as we exited from the mountains was our old acquaintance Major Miller, accompanied by his loyal Sergeant Nordstrom. Only now Major Miller was Colonel Miller, and commander of the regiment. A well-deserved promotion, in my view, though it prompted a comment from our beastman.

"Everyone gets promoted but me," said Kren gloomily.

"But think of the compensation," Jenkins retorted. "You get to listen to Murdock's insults."

Miller greeted us with relief. "Prince Scar! So it is

you, at last. I was afraid we might be facing a major engagement when scouts reported a force of cavalry approaching. It's a relief to know we can avoid that unfortunate event."

"So you survived the tribe's raid last fall," I stated, surprised to see him. "But what are you doing here?"

"Waiting for you, naturally. King Robert knew you couldn't return until the spring—assuming you returned at all. He asked King Herrick to assist your passage back to the Confederation. King Herrick sent out two regiments. The other is at Denver, and will join us for the journey back. It was quite an adventure moving a force this size across the plains, but we've set up supply points every hundred miles guarded by strong detachments. The tribes haven't been too happy with us. We've had some skirmishes and a battle or two. But the tribes can never agree on united action, and we've been able to beat off their efforts. And now that you're here, we can complete our mission and escort you back to Arkan."

Everyone was so interested in my safe return. It was quite comforting.

"And what's happening in Arkan?" I asked.

Colonel Miller summarized some of the changes that were planned for the nations. Not much had actually been done yet, but that was understandable. Such things couldn't be rushed. "It will be a time of new ways and uncertainty," he said, "but it won't be for the worse. As always, good men must do what they can to make things work."

We greeted the Brusovs at the Outpost, who expressed their happiness at seeing us again, and their regret at the tragedy that had befallen Dakota and Kendall. They notified Pacifica that we had arrived safely, and passed on a radio message that the Board of Administrators wished us a safe journey. The Brusovs had been warned that the Pacifican regiment would be staying for a month to convince the clans and tribes that Pacifica was serious about opening the old road and making it safe for traffic. The plains tribes and mountain clans must have been quite put out. Suddenly, there were regiments from the civilized nations everywhere.

They would have to get used to it.

We stayed with the Brusovs for a day and found they had a new addition to the family, a three-month-old baby girl they had named Dakota. I wondered how the original, unsentimental Dakota would have felt about such foolishness. The evening was a good one, for we enjoyed another wonderful meal and a night of songs and dancing. Ellen Brusov probably never danced so much in her life.

The night was also a revelation for the Arkan and Pacifican soldiers. The Pacificans set up tents next to the Arkans, and a great deal of fraternization took place, including a goodly dose of gambling and trade, not to mention night-long conversations. The men of Pacifica viewed the common men from one of the six nations (now the Confederation) with a growing awareness. The Arkans were not as primitive as they had thought. The Arkans, for their part, realized the legendary Pacificans might enjoy more education, but otherwise their soldiers were just as uncouth as any good Arkan from the ranks.

We left the Outpost and the Pacificans with regret, headed south to Denver where we picked up the other Arkan regiment, and then started back east along the old road. We saw herds of bison and mammoths, but other animals avoided us. The size of our main body and the noise we made gave early warning to all creatures so that saber-tooths, wolves, foxes, and other creatures made themselves scarce, which was fine with me.

Our little army made it back to Arkan without major incident. The two Arkan cavalry regiments were called down and dispersed to their homes, except for two squadrons that Colonel Miller kept on duty to escort us through Arkan. We visited King Herrick in the walled town of Tulsa and found out what was happening in the new Confederation. All of the six nations had joined, though the Beastwood Council was dragging its feet and only considering the offer. King Herrick greeted the Pacifican radio team with wonder—and with grave doubt. The renegade Pacificans' influence in the War Against the Alliance was too recent to forget. My reassurances seemed to mollify him, and he agreed to allow it to set up operation in Tulsa, though certainly not in his castle.

I had made it clear to Murdock that I was not traveling by water if I could avoid it, and so we still had a long overland journey to finish. But letters could get back to Kingsport much faster going by courier to the Arkan coast and then aboard one of the fast schooners plying the route between Arkan and Kenesee. I took the opportunity at King Herrick's castle to write letters to Robert and Megan.

My letter to Robert was a brief overview of what had occurred, including Mr. Kendall's death and our success, as well as including a short announcement for all the newspapers in the six nations. The announcement from the Pacifican Board of Administrators instructed the Pacifican enforcement teams—or "Pacifican Mission Units," as the announcement addressed them—to cease their activities, go to Kingsport, and register their presence with the King's Castle. The announcement included the board's "confirmation code" of letters and numbers that verified to the enforcement teams that it was an official instruction from the board, and not some trick of the Confederation.

My letter assumed, of course, that Robert had avoided assassination by the Pacificans during the months I'd been gone, and was alive and well.

I also included in my letter to Robert a request that he, as an act of kindness, personally deliver my letter to Megan for me so she could know the tragic events. In Megan's letter I informed her as gently as possible of her husband's demise, and gave a more detailed account of his death. Some might criticize me for not delivering this information in person. And they would be right to do so. But right or not, I did it this way.

We continued on our journey home by following the old road from Tulsa northeast past the walled town of

Springfield to the Sippi River. There we crossed the Sippi by ferry and followed the old road where it traversed the land north of the Great Swamp. When we arrived at the Ohio River and reached that river's ferry landing, we took our leave of Colonel Miller and Sergeant Nordstrom.

"I don't imagine we'll be seeing you again soon," said Murdock.

Miller surprised us. "Don't be too sure of that. King Robert is organizing a law enforcement academy for the Confederation. It will be in Kingsport, and I've been asked to represent Arkan and be on the faculty. I'll be arriving in a few months, so don't go committing any more crimes."

"None that you'll care about," Murdock said.

When the ferry landed I was recognized at the little village on the bank by a veteran of the war. He was not quiet about who had just crossed the river. My return to Kenesee soil was thus greeted with cheers and waves and handshaking, and we took the opportunity to have a meal and buy good Kenesee tobacco. Further south we approached Curtis and stopped at the site of the Battle of the Crossroads. It was hard to tell a battle had ever been fought here, for it was high summer and crops were growing lush, while pastures were tall with grass. Murdock and Jenkins pointed out positions and recalled the events of that day for Kren. I hadn't been back here since the battle, and sat on my horse in silence while listening to them. It had been a desperate battle, won by General Black's audacity and genius. Memories of him flooded back, and I missed him all over again. I took out the pipe he had given me, filled it with fresh Kenesee leaf, and smoked a bowlful in his honor. The smoke swirled into my eyes and made me blink and sniffle.

Murdock noted it. "Need my kerchief again, Arn?"

"No, Murdock," I answered slowly. "My own will do. But thank you anyway."

And then it was time to move on.

We took the road to Nash. Feted and entertained for

a day by the nobility there, we continued on our journey
with a new escort of three companies from Nash's cavalry regiment. Thence it was on to Redbank, and finally
the last leg down to Kingsport itself.

By this time couriers had notified Kingsport that we'd
be arriving, and they were ready for us. The bells were
pealing even as we came within sight of the walls, which
were festooned for a holiday. The battlements were lined
with militia in full regalia, and the town's two cavalry
regiments lined the road leading into the north gate. Inside the walls, infantry lined the King's Way to the Castle, and it seemed as if every citizen of the town was
turned out in their Sunday best, cheering and waving as
we went by.

Kren was enjoying it no end, grinning broadly, waving and saluting left and right as if the crowds were for
him alone. "It may only be reflected glory," he laughed,
"but glory it is. And honestly earned. Why not enjoy
it?"

Jenkins grabbed Lorich's hand in delight and held it
up. The crowd responded with more cheers. "See, lad,
that's for you, too. You've helped it happen as much as
anybody."

Lorich nodded. "It seems impossible. Like a dream.
It's so nice to be home."

I smiled and waved dutifully, finding that I was actually pleased by it all. Even the uncertainty of seeing
Megan did not prevent me from enjoying the moment.

We came to the castle, and royal guards were at attention on the battlements and in the courtyard, lining
an open area in the center and keeping back the crowd
of court and staff who applauded as we came in through
the gates.

On the steps to the king's house Robert stood, beaming. Surrounding him were High Wizard O'Dowd and
Professor Wagner and Dr. Amani and Sergeant Major
Nakasone and Ambassador Sokol from the Beastwood
and a dozen other high officials and trusted advisors.

To one side, golden-haired Megan stood, a child in

her arms. Her father, Sir Meredith, had his arm around her shoulder. On her other side was Beth, who held the hand of little Sabrena. Together, Beth and Sabrena pranced down the steps and raced up to the party. With a bound, Jenkins leaped from his horse and swept Beth up in his arms, twirling her around him so that her black hair and skirt swirled about her. The courtyard roared its approval of the greeting.

"Oh, my love," Beth said, burying her head in his shoulder. "I worried so."

"I'm here, and I'm safe, and I've got you now," Jenkins answered, clutching her too him. "And I won't ever let you go."

With less notice, Murdock reached down, took Sabrena's hands, and lifted her up into his saddle. Sabrena had grown several inches, but was still small for her age. The girl's face was serious as she stared at the wizard, as if making sure it was indeed Murdock, and then a smile peeked through. "I know how to ride now," she said. "And I missed you."

I took it all in, and then returned my gaze to the porch. Sir Meredith waved to me in fond greeting. I waved back, but my eyes shifted to Megan. Tears rolled down her cheeks, but her eyes met mine and did not turn away. Perhaps Megan knew now what I had gone through when I lost Angela. Or perhaps motherhood simply brings out the forgiveness in a woman. Whatever the cause, through the tears she nodded to me.

And I nodded back.

"So it's really true, Arn?"

Robert's face was split by a broad smile. He was looking well, and he seemed hardly to need the cane, though his limp was still pronounced. But there was more gray in his hair than I had seen before I'd departed on the trip across the continent

We were alone in the large royal chambers, his rooms, seated in comfortable chairs at a table near the fireplace. Two oil lamps on the mantel cast a gentle light across the room. The hearth was cold during the hot summer months, and the shutters on the window were open to the night. Robert's rooms were as I remembered them, as was my own.

The only change had been the addition of a small iron stove in each chamber. I had grown used to the stoves of the Pacificans, and knew how much more efficient they were than fireplaces. Yet, I could not avoid the feeling that something would be lost. In winter, the crackle of the logs would be muted, the beauty of the flames hidden within the confines of the metal. I pondered the trade-off for a moment while Robert poured mugs of beer.

Robert removed his crown and placed it on the mantel, from which hung his cane. Both were discarded for the evening. The afternoon had been too busy to talk, and dinner had been a time of speeches and entertainment and eating. Only now, as the twilight faded, had the two of us found a moment to really converse. Brothers, who had not talked for many months.

I smiled in return and responded to his question. "Is what true?"

"The wonders of Pacifica, first of all. You actually saw a railroad?"

I nodded "The golden age might have thought it laughable, but they did have two small steam engines, and track that ran the length of Pacifica, with spurs to several key towns. A train runs every day. The children called it a choo-choo."

Robert laughed. "A choo-choo?"

"You had to hear it to understand."

"And they have flying machines? Airplanes?"

"Yes, a few small ones," I explained. "Just a motor and wooden frame covered by lacquered cloth, but they do fly."

He nodded with satisfaction. "And electricity, of course. Do they have many electric lights?"

"Yes, Robert. They do. They have generators powered by the river current. Which reminds me, I hardly mentioned their irrigation system. They've constructed small dams and canals to water their fields from the rivers. It's quite impressive to see. But that's not electricity, so let me get back to the subject. All their main buildings have electric lights, and some of their homes. And the electricity allows them to have radio, too. I brought along a radio team of Pacificans. You must see it! You can contact the Board of Administrators whenever you want to ask for advice or send them instructions.''

Robert sat back, contented. But my mention of the board had reminded him of other matters, and he put aside his delight in technology. "You know, it was a relief getting your letter and knowing you were alive. And that message from the Board to the Pacifican enforcement teams was so simple, and yet so effective. They were in Kingsport, Arn! They'd been here all winter, waiting for me to leave the castle. I was virtually a prisoner in my own castle, and that was hard. Often I wanted to go out, but then I'd remember Jason's plea, and the importance of what we were each doing. And so I kept myself safe, and waited. Your letter came just a week ago. We put the message out in the Kenesee paper the next day. And only three days ago, the enforcement team turned themselves in. And I was able to leave the castle at last!''

"I'm glad you kept yourself safe, Robert. That was wise.''

"Yes,'' he agreed. "Wise, indeed, as it turns out. We'll give the Pacificans their freedom and let them contact the Board by the radio you brought. But tell me of the administrators. You sketched out an explanation of the coup and why they agreed to belong to the Confederation. But tell me in detail.''

I explained the events that my party's arrival in Pacifica had caused the previous fall, and the outcome. "They were no wiser than we are, no better as people. They just have more technology, and several well-intentioned—if arrogant—ideals and traditions. At first when they started their 'great experiment,' they didn't want to see humankind go extinct. And they always wanted better conditions for their fellow men. But their efforts were not altogether altruistic. They thought that keeping the continent technologically limited would ensure their own safety.

"They needed to be convinced that times had changed. Our population in the east is growing, and we need technology. You were right about that, Robert. And firm words gave them pause. They realized their assassins might fail, or that the unification would go on without you and me because it was an idea whose time had come. So just eliminating us was no longer enough. We—or our successors—might actually unite the continent, and they would then be the mistrusted outsiders, with no control at all. Better to be a part of the Confederation and influence it from within as a member state, rather than watch the continent advance without their influence."

Robert reached across the table and put a hand on my arm. "And that was your doing, Arn. You accomplished all that."

"Hardly," I corrected him. "It was Murdock who convinced them to allow us to confederate and to change the Codes. After that, the coup left the Board shaken and unsure of their own moral superiority. I saw their weakness of the moment and pushed them. And even then, they debated through the night and late into the next morning before voting."

Robert squeezed my arm. "Still, it was a bold and dangerous thing to do, to push them so. You were very lucky—and perhaps you were depending on that."

I lit my pipe from a match and puffed contentedly. "I was angry. I get that way after being terrified. And yes, I was lucky. But it's the luck of having good men like Jason Kendall to speak his heart, and Murdock to convince the Board and Lorich to act without orders and Kren to boldly proclaim what he thinks is right. Each played their role."

"And Sergeant Jenkins?" Robert asked with a sly

grin. "Didn't he contribute to your success?"

I watched the smoke swirl up to the ceiling. "Without him, I doubt we would have made it to Pacifica in the first place. The great would not get very far without the sergeants of the world."

"Something we forget too often," Robert mused. "I saw him at dinner with his Beth. A happier man would be hard to find."

"Yes," I agreed. "I just wish the rest of us were as fortunate."

Robert set down his mug. "We've paid the price for our success, haven't we? Here, come to the window with me, Arn. Now, look there."

I stared out. Above, the stars were already filling the night sky. Below in the courtyard, a lamp glowed in each corner. But in one corner the lamp was unusually bright. No, not a lamp. It was too intense for any single flame. It reminded me of Pacifica, where—

"Robert, an electric light!"

His face lit with a glow of pleasure as bright as the electric bulb. "You didn't see it with all the activity of your arrival. It's barely noticeable during the day. Professor Wagner oversaw its development. Took our university six months to produce. The electricity comes from a wind-driven generator on the battlements. The bulbs only last about forty hours or so, but Wagner says that can be improved with time.

"We're working on small versions of steam engines, too. Electricity and steam power will start us off quite nicely. And if the Pacificans share their techniques, we can advance all the faster."

If I had not seen such wonders in Pacifica, I would have doubted my eyes. "This is a great achievement. Soon you'll have lights everywhere, and steam engines too."

Robert laughed. "I wish it were that easy. We're just starting to make the tools to make the tools to produce such items. We had the knowledge in books, but translating that into physical reality is quite a challenge. A dozen fields of science and engineering were studied to produce that glowing bulb. We learned much, but realized how difficult the simple things are. We'll make progress, but it will be slow, Arn, even with Pacifica's help. Our lives will be drawing to a close before we've harnessed the technology of the Ancients. And even then, our achievements will be but primitive versions of their most basic machines.''

· I thought about Robert's words. ''Murdock doesn't think we can ever achieve the golden age again. That Man has used up all the easy resources.''

Robert rubbed his chin. ''Murdock might be right. Or not. I've discussed this with the university faculty and engineers and the finest craftsmen in Kenesee, for hours and hours. You stated in your report that the Pacificans number almost four hundred thousand, a fairly dense population for the area they inhabit. Even counting them, there are less than two million people on this continent, Arn. They are too few, spread too thin, to achieve the specialized society that the ancients were able to achieve with their hundreds of millions. At our population level, we'll be doing well to match the Pacificans and produce steam engines and electrical generators in quantity during our lifetime.

''Yet, with the steam engines and hybrid grains from the Pacificans, we can plant more ground and enjoy higher yields. We can feed a larger population, and with new pharmaceuticals keep them alive and healthy. Then, in fifty or a hundred years, when the population is two, three, or ten times what it is now, perhaps we'll be able to support a more specialized society, and move ahead to more complex machines.

''That doesn't mean we'll reach a golden age, Arn. Murdock is right about the coal and oil and gas that the Ancients consumed. It would be hard to find them in quantity. Yet, there is wind power, and waterpower. Perhaps we can make better use of those than the Old World, and enjoy our own achievements, whatever they might be.''

He made it sound so attractive, so easy. And yet, there was a serpent in the garden.

"What about powder weapons, Robert? Will we produce those too?"

"We're already working on a musket that uses a percussion cap," Robert stated with satisfaction. "And the first cannon should be ready before the fall. Soon, we'll have the weapons we need to ensure the unity and control of the Confederation—without having to depend on Pacifica."

I hesitated for a long time. Yet, I couldn't keep myself from speaking.

"Robert, destroy the powder weapons."

He turned to stare at me. "What?"

"In spite of their deadliness—no, *because* of their deadliness—couldn't we leave this area of development alone? Can't we spare the world the existence of these weapons?"

"Arn, that was the whole idea of the Confederation, to prevent the making of powder weapons by every petty tyrant. Others will develop the weapons if we don't."

"Let them," I replied, surprised at my vehemence. "Robert, keep the ban on powder weapons. Perhaps someone will try to produce powder guns. But it doesn't have to be King Robert and Prince Arn who do it. It doesn't have to be Kenesee that starts the cycle of destruction again. Let history say that we resisted the temptation until the last extremity, forced to it once others had forged such devices. Let the history books record the names of villains who follow in the footsteps of Pi-Ling and General Murphy and Governor Rodes. Not our names."

Robert tilted his head as he studied me. "Arn, I didn't think you felt so strongly about any political matter. Even if I consider your request, dare we take such a risk?"

"Is it really such a risk?" I countered. "We would know if someone began producing such weapons, and could respond quickly. And who could stand against the might of the Confederation?''

"So you'd have me stop development into powder weapons.''

I shook my head. "Perhaps research would be all right. Find out the way to produce such weapons. But keep the knowledge and methods hidden, a last resort in case someone else begins production.''

Robert hesitated, but a cold resolve began to form in his features. I spoke before he could reply.

"And if that is not enough, there is one reason more.''

Robert's curiosity got the better of him. "And what reason is that?''

My answer was a simple one. "Because I ask it of you.''

Robert turned back to the window, leaned against the stone ledge, and stared out. Below there was light, but beyond the castle the lights of the town were dim, and beyond the walls of the town the hills were dark.

His voice was soft. "And you think that will make a difference to me? Because you ask it?''

"Yes, Robert. I do.''

After a long minute, he spoke. "Arn, Arn, Arn. You are quite remarkable. Did you know that?'' He put his arm around my shoulder. "It's against my better judgment, but I'll cancel production. We'll do without the terrible powder weapons. Prince Scar has won another victory.''

"Not my victory,'' I corrected him.

"No? All right, dear brother. If not yours, then whose?''

I gestured out the window.

And he understood.

Epilog

My companions and I wended our way out of Dallas through the north gate, all of us walking on foot casually and enjoying the day. Next to me strolled Murdock, and behind were Jenkins and Beth. Sabrena walked between the newlyweds, holding a hand of each. At a discreet distance back, twenty mounted royal guardsman followed watchfully. We walked several hundred yards in the cool morning sunshine before stopping where a cart path led off to the west. The path wended its way through a line of trees and brush towards a low rise beyond.

The town cemetery.

I could see tombstones. "Well. We're here at last."

Murdock listened to this brilliant observation with patience. "So we are. Our last day in Dallas. And your last chance to visit the graves."

There was nothing else to do. The diplomatic duties had just been an excuse. This was why I had come.

Still, I tarried. "Does anyone want to come with me?"

Jenkins, dressed in civilian clothes now, shook his head. "Beth and I came out yesterday. We've said our good-byes."

I hadn't realized that. But the two had done enough for me already. They had come with me to Texan just to keep me company. Jenkins had left the guards to marry, and was no longer under my command. But while I had lost a sergeant, I had gained a friend.

Beth smiled at me. "We'll wait here under the trees. I think this is something you have to do alone, Arn."

"Yes. You're probably right."

A gesture from me to Sergeant Phillips, and the waiting guards dismounted, broke ranks, and sat down in the grass next to the road. They knew my orders.

"Come, I'll go up with you to the rise," said Murdock, and led the way.

Murdock took the path through the line of trees, across a creek, and to a stone-and-crete archway that had been erected over the path. There was no fence or ditch bounding the graveyard. Just the arch. And beyond, scattered across the rise and down into a hollow were the markers. Hundreds of markers. Stone-and-crete tablets, wooden crosses, pillars, and even a statue or two identified the resting place of the dead.

My head throbbed, my throat was dry, and my hands were cold. "Where?" I asked.

He pointed. "Down there. Not far from the creek. I'll wait here. You go ahead."

It was a long, slow walk along the base of the rise, around the tombstones and crosses, past graves well tended or grassed over. And finally, ahead, I saw two graves with identical headstones. Perhaps President Chalmers had given orders that the graves be tended for my visit, or perhaps they had been cared for this way throughout the year. Whatever the case, the wild grass had been cropped short atop, the stones were erect and straight, the site clean and proper.

I took a deep breath and strode up to where I could read the inscriptions.

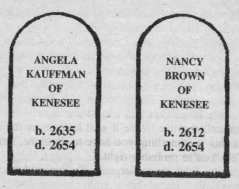

ANGELA
KAUFFMAN
OF
KENESEE

b. 2635
d. 2654

NANCY
BROWN
OF
KENESEE

b. 2612
d. 2654

I sank forward to my knees, then sat back upon my heels. I felt faint.

So, there they were. Down below, just a few feet away, Angela. My Angela. And Nancy, my mother. Just a few feet. I could uproot the grass, dig through the soil, and be able to touch Angela, to hold her in my arms for one last time.

I shook my head to clear the spots forming before my eyes, and found my vision slowly focusing, my heartbeat slowing, the pounding in my temples lessening. How silly. To imagine digging through the earth. Angela was gone, her spirit flown away, her soul gone to heaven. Nothing remained but the lifeless and broken remains of the woman I had known. All that was left was a husk, a rotting shell already turning back into the elements of which it was composed, so that perhaps only the bones were left, and even those would slowly give themselves back to the earth.

I sat unmoving, contemplating that reality.

At last, a huge sigh escaped from me. "I'm sorry, Angela." One part of me looked on, and thought how ridiculous—to be talking to silent headstones. And then more words poured out.

"I'm sorry I couldn't save you. I tried. They've made up songs about our attack on the castle. About all I did to get to you. And about you on the battlements, with

Bartholomew. But I don't listen to the songs. It hurts too much.

"We won the war, and Texan has a good leader. And I went to Pacifica, and now the nations are united in a Confederation. We're hoping that will bring us peace. And maybe, just maybe, Robert will have that better world he dreams of. But it cost us Mr. Kendall. Maybe you've seen him where you are. Megan is very sad. Now she knows what it's like to lose someone. And I think she's forgiven me a bit for that reason.

"Besides that, everyone is well, I guess. I'm all right too. I've been off the opiate for a year, and part of that is due to you. I knew you wouldn't approve of it. And I wanted to please you. The only problem is that you're not here.

"You know about Nancy Brown, I suppose. She's right there beside you. Mother died shortly after General Murphy captured us. They put her in a pauper's grave, but Murdock had her found, and she was put to rest here with you. That way, you can keep each other company."

I paused, and laughed. "Isn't this silly? You aren't here, nor is Mother. Yet, I'm talking to you. Can you both hear me? I can't hear you. There's only the breeze rustling through the leaves, and the birds, and the crickets. Sort of nice, actually. Peaceful, and green, and there's a creek running nearby. I think you'd like it."

I babbled on a bit more, perhaps to Angela, perhaps to Nancy Brown. About what, I don't remember. I wasn't quite right, I suspect. A touch of the sun. But eventually I found it time to go, and discovered my legs stiff and numb when I stood.

It was time to leave. To leave Angela behind. My chest tightened, and it was hard to breathe, and harder to talk.

"I came back to Texan to see you. There were other excuses for the journey, but it was to see you. So now I'm here, and I've visited the graves, and my visit with you is almost over. I don't think I'll be coming back this way. So, I won't be visiting you again. At least, not for a long, long while. But you and Nancy have each other for company. And maybe that really doesn't mean much to you, because you're not really here. But I find . . . it means much . . . to me."

I turned away then, and did not look back.

Murdock sat waiting in the shade of a small tree chewing on a stalk of grass. He stood up and tossed the stalk aside. "Hello, Arn."

"Hello, Murdock."

"Is everything all right?"

I thought about it. "Perhaps it is. I hope so."

Murdock nodded. "I hope so, too. Come, let's join the others and be on our way. It's almost noon. We should be moving along."

Noon? It had been early morning just a few minutes ago. I took a deep breath of air. It was warm and sweet. And the sky was blue. And the birds sang their joyous song.

"It's a beautiful day, isn't it, Murdock."

He studied me, then smiled.

"Yes, Arn. It is a beautiful day."

AVON · EOS

VISIT A NEW WORLD AT
www.AvonBooks.com/Eos

- Take our **SF IQ test.**

- Read about world-building and **participate** in the creation of a universe.

- Post a review or comment and get chosen as our **"Fan of the Month."**

- Subscribe to our monthly e-mail **newsletter** for all the buzz on upcoming science fiction and fantasy.

- Browse through our list of new and upcoming titles and read **chapter excerpts.**

EOS 0898